DOWN THESE STREETS

Alone

The Journey to Deliverance

RA-RA M. J.

Lone Blue Wolf Publishing Company, LLC:
PO Box 41298
Houston, TX 77241
Lonebluewolf@bluewolfpenman.com

ISBN: 978-0-9981754-0-9
ISBN: 978-0-9981754-1-6

Printed in the United States of America
Cover Design by Roland Ali Pantin
Creative Consultation by RA-RA M. J.

Unless otherwise noted, all Biblical Scriptures are taken from the New King James Version by Thomas Nelson (1982). Used by permission. All rights reserved.

CONTENTS

ACKNOWLEDGEMENTS

To my grandparents (may my grandmother rest
in peace) for their unwavering care of me;

To the Holy Spirit for guiding me in the composition of this book,

To T. W. for being an angel of light, giving
me counsel to return to the faith,

To Sister D. T. Smith Henderson for being an anointed
woman of God, you helped me to understand the Holy
Scriptures in ways I never believed possible;

Thank you, Reverend K. Flowers, and Sister A.
Guild for your anointed prayers and support;

To Dr. M. Stanley Butler and C. L. Fellows, thank you
for your unwavering friendships throughout the years.
Thank you for your anchors in Jesus Christ, which kept
me tethered to the light of the Most High God.

THOUGHTS FROM THE AUTHOR

THOUGHTS FROM THE AUTHOR

Dear Readers,

Globally, millions of people suffer from various types of mental illness. Organizations specializing in mental health compile the data based upon diagnosis and self-reporting. Assuming that such information is voluntary, it is speculated that there are still many individuals, who are mentally ill and have not sought treatment. I implore you that if you know of anyone, including yourself, who may be mentally ill, please seek professional and spiritual help.

You will find that the discourse within this book discusses psychological issues such as anxiety and depression, abuse, self-identity and personal growth, homosexuality, Christianity and the world through the lens of an African-American male. I wholeheartedly believe that my advanced education in psychology combined with personal experience qualifies me to embark upon the construction of the present narrative.

It should be noted, however, that for all intent and purposes, this book does not endeavor to romanticize homosexuality. Rather, the entire focus of this book encompasses personal growth and deliverance into the destiny God has ordained. In my opinion, there are numerous fiction novels narrating plots that revolve around homosexuality to stimulate the imagination and entertain. I am aware of very few books that address homosexuality from the perspective of deliverance.

While I am no pastor, minister or biblical scholar, my faith is rooted in Christianity. There are no other gods I serve other than God the Father, God the Son—Jesus Christ, and the Holy Spirit. In the infinite scope of God's governance, my grandparents were influential in my early acquisition of biblical knowledge. However, my walk along the path of light was inconsistent. Trial and error embedded in personal growth have made my relationship with God stronger today. Testimony is one the greatest tools for witnessing the awesome power of God. The vision which God has imbued me for the breadth of this book, I pray, is a blessing for all of you. Be delivered in Faith.

Grace and Peace,

Ra-Ra M. J.

READER'S ADVISORY

There are moments in this story where the point-of-view switches between third and first-person.

OASIS IN THE WASTELAND

Help is possible even in a place of seemingly perpetual desolation. If only we believed.

Time is a perpetual phenomenon. Oftentimes, we seldom take notice of its passage until something impactful or meaningful transpires in our lives and disrupts our reverie. The cycle of life and death, and changing seasons remind us of forces working around and through us, beyond the capacity of our consciousness and perception. Present time marked the third week in September. The brilliant green leaves had begun to turn. Soon, they would transition to shades of orange, red and gold, proclaiming the arrival of the fall season.

Time held significant meaning for Hakeem. Self-deprecation made him sensitive to the passage of time. Hakeem believed that life had yet to unveil all that he imagined. A thirty-fourth birthday would come in the early fall, which he accepted unenthusiastically. The idea of getting older worried him more than ever now, as few things had changed for the better since last year. Depression had sunken in from constantly thinking about not reaching his full potential. Certainly, Hakeem lived and breathed as some people might remind him of the obvious. But how grateful could anyone be when they didn't see value in the life they lived?

A clipboard lay across Hakeem's lap supporting the registration forms for first-time visitors at the mental-health clinic as he looked out the window. He disdained completing forms—paper-based and electronically. He deemed the practice tedious. All of the possible allergies, hereditary conditions, past medical treatment, insurance, and emergency contact information had to be provided. Long past were the days when as a child, his grandmother and mother had filled out medical forms for him. Back then, he had not considered the cumbersomeness of the task because someone else had done the work.

The clinic's waiting room was cozy and contemporary. A blend of navy and red microfiber, and suede upholstery outfitted chairs of smoothly polished oak frames. Mounted black flat-screen televisions occupied opposite eggshell-painted walls in the lobby, set to identical channels to reduce the chaos and competing sounds in the waiting-area. In the center, stationed in front of the sitting area was the receptionists' desk. Its' counter extended the length of the room.

Occasionally, Hakeem saw the head of a staff member pass behind the glass window. He sat in the corner farthest from the desk to observe the environment. He agreed to schedule the appointment for 1:45 P.M., not expecting the waiting room to be half-filled with patients. Only fifteen minutes until his therapy session and the forms secured by the clipboard were still incomplete.

Hakeem's attention roamed the waiting area again. A Caucasian woman hoisted an infant in front of her face. He assumed the baby to be male based upon the clothing. The powder blue onesie with a horse and cowboy pattern were the giveaway. The mother cooed softly as the baby yawned. The baby looked sleepily at his mother and brought a tiny fist to his mouth, signaling feeding time. She cuddled the infant to her breast, retrieving a bottle of milk from the baby bag close by. The baby suckled hungrily.

Hakeem envied children who had caring mothers.

A young Caucasian woman sat across from the mother and baby. Blonde hair hung forward, partially obscuring the face as she interacted busily with a pink rhinestoned phone. Hakeem appraised the woman's beauty until she suddenly looked up and their eyes met. Self-conscious, he redirected his eyes to the unattended clipboard, too nervous to see whether she was still looking. He filled in the two fields requesting contact information and flipped to the last page.

Looking up again, Hakeem saw a black woman and little boy exit the door on the far side of the lobby. They headed for the chairs along the opposite wall. The woman made eye contact with him briefly as she sat down. Red and black streaked, matted hairweave gone-days-without-combing made her overall appearance look unfinished. Hakeem remembered someone labeling the hairstyle, the "bed head" look. If weaves were more manageable than natural hair, shouldn't there be an improvement in the presentation? Kinky, jelled-down roots fading into straight, often tinted hair didn't make sense to him. Braids on the other hand were a different story. They projected ethnic appeal.

Daydreaming, Hakeem pictured running fingers through the woman's artificially-extended hair. His teenage crush, Kema, use to ask him to help grease her scalp. Her hair was soft. If she didn't rock natural hair, it was styled in braids. His thoughts shifted back to the woman sitting across the room. Her tracks could either be sewn or glued. Whatever the case, Hakeem knew his fingertips would contact one of the textures and be creeped out.

Suddenly, Hakeem became aware of eyes. The little boy's eyes were affixed to him. The woman dug into her black purse—a hobo, he thought it was called, refocusing on the boy. *What was he looking at?* For some unknown reason, his presence tended to draw attention from children. *Is it my expression again?* His expressions were constantly perceived as stern according to what some people said. He assumed the feedback probable, for he smiled only when the occasion necessitated it. But he wouldn't give a disarming smile lest the woman catch him in the act and think something weird was going on. He thought it strange for men to smile at other people's children anyway. The idea made him shudder, as he remembered instances from his past. The boy rested his head on the woman's arm and continued staring unblinkingly. *He will lose interest soon enough*, Hakeem thought.

He gave the forms a final review, hastily filling in any remaining empty fields and signed the Patient Information Consent sheet. He passed the clipboard through the glass window to the woman sitting on the other side and returned to his seat. The time on the smartphone displayed 1:40 P.M. Perhaps the therapist would not come at exactly 1:45 P.M. He had just completed the medical forms to enable the clerk to enter his information into their patient record-keeping system. As he waited, he imagined how the therapy session would flow. He was obsessed with trying to anticipate events and the habit lent to his worries.

"Lewis," announced a female voice.

Hakeem refocused, hearing his last name. He turned in the direction of the voice, seeing a middle-aged Black woman standing in the doorway on the left side of the lobby. She held a clipboard to her breasts as she surveyed the area. Hakeem stood to walk forward and his keys fell to the floor. He stooped and grabbed them quickly before continuing onward.

"Mr. Lewis?" She asked when he approached.

"Yes," he replied.

She extended her right arm and stepped aside, signaling him to walk through the door in the likeness of a flight-attendant motioning passengers to board a plane.

Hakeem whiffed pineapple and vanilla as she walked alongside. There was something intoxicating about the scent of a woman who maintained good hygiene. He avoided making eye contact with her, looking at the walls instead. The dimly lit hallway made the paint appear sickly green. Pear green—the true hue, shone where the ceiling lights secured twelve feet above, brightly illuminated. Hakeem wondered who chose the shade of paint.

In stride, they bypassed offices on each side of the hallway. The woman entered through a door on the right into an average sized office of roughly 11-feet by 10-feet. A dark and lacquered cherry-oak desk occupied the centermost area between the east and west walls, leaving space for passage on either side. Two matching black leather chairs were positioned in front of the desk. A burgundy micro-fibered chaise and ottoman rested along the north wall.

Hakeem supposed that if he stretched out on the chaise, he would fall fast asleep.

The woman strolled around the desk and stood behind it, watching as he closed the door.

Hakeem prepared to sit down in the right chair of the pair when she extended a hand for a handshake.

"My name is Gail White," she began. "I am a psychiatrist"—she gave a disarming smile—"Do you prefer that I address you by your first or last name?"

"First name," he replied. "I don't like being addressed by my last name. Makes me feel old." In the absence of being associated with a role of important repute, he didn't see the benefit of being addressed formally by last name.

Long braids were swept back from Gail's face and hung between her shoulder blades.

Ethnically regal! Hakeem wondered whether her natural hair was long.

Her even-toned, carob-brown skin was free of foundation, defying modern fashion trends. Gold eye-shadow lightly canvassed her eyelids and mascara darkened the lashes, enhancing dark brown irises. Burnished bronze lipstick tinted plump lips. Black-framed glasses added austerity to her otherwise apparent attractiveness. The short tan jacket worn atop a flower-printed blouse, black skirt, and tan pumps silently conveyed a proud intelligence shrouded in sophistication.

Gail smiled. "Thanks for the clarification. Is this your first time here? Or have you met with another therapist previously?"

"First visit," he answered in short.

"Wonderful! Tell me the reason for your visit and how I may be able to help you." She sat upright in her chair, resting forearms on the desk and clasped her hands.

"Someone recommended that I come here…to talk to somebody… about some things."

"Some things such as…?"

Hakeem perceived her silence as a cue to continue. "My emotional problems, I guess." He fidgeted with his hands. *Where do I begin? And for that matter, how can Gail help me?*

Recognizing the signs of stress and an apparent need for anger-management, Josefina Rodriguez referred him to the clinic. Josefina was a human capital management software developer at Kaleidoscope

Technologies where he was employed. She had brought her 30-year-old son, Angel to the clinic to be treated for similar psychological problems.

Josefina witnessed Hakeem's emotional breakdown and observed him unravel on a sales manager. When he calmed, she suggested that he was burning out and jeopardizing his job and health. Even though Hakeem knew Josephina meant well, he initially dismissed her assessment, believing in his own stress management efforts. As far as he was concerned, he didn't need counseling or medicine. He was fine and in control. Venting released pressure, eliminating the need to see a doctor. But not being the regular-doctor-visiting-patient type, it was impossible to know whether he needed treatment or medication anyway.

Hakeem remained self-reliant, confident that he was mentally healthy until the panic attacks and restless nights began. Dreading work one morning, as was his usual disposition, his chest constricted. He likened the pressure to being squeezed by an invisible force. He inhaled deeply, hoping to decrease the growing intensity of the pain. The constriction didn't abate, which caused him to pull onto the shoulder of Interstate-85. Reclining the driver's seat, he laid back and closed his eyes, praying for the pain to past. The pain gradually dissipated only to return every time he stressed whether awake or asleep.

If Hakeem slept uninterrupted in excess of four and a half hours, he was fortunate. Many nights he depended upon sleeping aids, whereas alcohol proved sufficient when sleeping pills were ineffective. The latter method was usually reserved for the weekends to avoid hangovers on workdays. Hakeem wanted full access to his faculties on the job.

Yet, for all Hakeem tried to maintain control, he was losing hold. It seemed that life was unwilling to give a much-desired long-term break from struggle. The situation was a tooth-grinder and fist-clincher. He wanted to inflict damage upon his problems—subtle and formless elements of rules and systems that were far beyond his scope of governance. Still, the desire to fight never subsided. He was a time bomb and the minutes were winding down to seconds. Life wasn't supposed to be as it was in his world and he didn't know how to deal with it. And sometimes, a part of him didn't want to.

How many African-American men took the initiative to see a

psychologist or psychiatrist, not to mention, knew what to say when they met one? The Black Man—the embodiment of strength and a pillar in the Black community was expected to be in full emotional control. For a man to confess to family and friends that he dealt with emotional issues signaled weakness or even worse, "softness".

Softness identified in Black males was a stigma associated with femininity and frowned upon within the African-American community. Moreover, people with mental disorders that were neurologically and physiologically impairing, were incorrectly classified as "slow", "retarded", or "crazy". They were often alienated from the rest of the household, isolated to a bedroom behind a closed door, or sitting alone in a corner as others looked on or actively ignored them. Only when the individual harmed themselves or another person, was a psychological disorder considered a possibility for their actions. It was too late then, as the damage had already been done.

Historically, many in the Black community considered mental disabilities the White Man's disease. It was this ignorance among African-Americans that allowed depression, anxiety, and other mental disorders to rage unchecked. Certainly, there was a basis for such lack of knowledge; as slavery, discrimination and segregation perpetuated the erection of barriers preventing African-Americans access to adequate education, impeding the evolution of intellect. It was not happenstance that uneducated Blacks were incapable of distinguishing between depression, anxiety, and other mental disorders.

African-Americans were systematically and subconsciously conditioned to endure various types of adversity from the removal of Black men from their homes and family to the rape of Black women and the selling of Black children during slavery. These events were not only emotionally disruptive, but also triggered the onset of psychological problems that were misunderstood, and thus, could not be treated adequately. Socioeconomic disadvantages in the guise of poverty, limited income, housing, and healthcare or lack thereof, only added to the dilemma.

From generation to generation, the African-American's approach to effective management of mental illness and the harsh realities of their environment was suppression and silence by virtue of their inescapable predicament, accompanied with an unspoken fear. Prior to the enactment of the Civil Rights Act of 1964, a Black person behaving abnormally in public could have been severely beaten or killed. Pervasive prejudice and discrimination did not extend mercy to Blacks under most circumstances. And why would anyone non-Black display sympathy when African-Americans were historically considered subhuman? Fast forward 52 years into the future and many of the African-Americans' misconceptions pertaining to mental illness still circulated. The socioeconomic status of African-Americans had not changed significantly and neither had the stigma. The African-American community needs transformation and growth, which can only come by way of education and acceptance. Until African-Americans shed fear, denial, and embraced transparent dialogue concerning mental illness, ignorance within their community will remain.

"How are you feeling now, Hakeem?"

"Umm…I'm not sure exactly." He began. *Was I silent long?* "When I think about it, it's not just one thing that I'm feeling." He paused, searching…trying to decide what he wanted to discuss first. The clock was ticking.

Gail organized white sheets of paper in a folder. "Please continue." She addressed him without looking up. "We can start wherever you feel most comfortable. Everything that we discuss in this room is and will remain confidential unless there's reason to believe that you intend to impose harm upon yourself or others."

Hakeem nodded. *Careful,* he warned himself, understanding the Hippocratic Oath. He didn't want to be locked up or detained for saying something crazy. A practitioner in the medical profession could alert the proper authorities when a patient posed a threat.

"Did you go to work today?" She asked, breaking the silence.

"I did."

"How was it?"

"I hate my job," he stated flatly.

"Why do you hate your job?"

"It's not what I want to do."

"What would you like to do?"

"Training. Counseling, maybe."

"What kind of work do you do now?"

"I'm a project manager at a human resources technology consulting firm."

"How long have you been in that position?"

"Just made five years two months ago. But I've been with the company for eight years."

"A long time, huh?"

"Yeah."

"Have you tried finding another job?"

"Yes. I've applied to eighty-one internal job postings in my tenure. Out of that number, I've landed ten interviews."

"Really? Why do you think that happened?"

"The hiring managers always select other candidates for the positions. I've learned over the years that the relationship between management and HR is extremely underhanded. They encourage employees to apply for jobs to avoid posting the positions externally. But the job is already set aside for pre-selected employees. As long as HR and management can show on paper that they interviewed a minimum number of qualified candidates, they put whoever they want into the position."

"I'm sorry to hear that. I can imagine your frustration working there." The concern was evident in Gail's expression, her brow furrowing slightly. "What is the name of the company you work for?"

"Kaleidoscope Technologies."

Gail sighed. "I've heard of that company. The son of a close friend of mine use to work there. She said that he complained constantly about management. Eventually, he landed an internship with a competitor and resigned."

Lucky him.

Gail had stopped writing while talking. Her shoulders were relaxed against the high-backed office chair.

"Because of your challenges with Kaleidoscope, have you considered finding a job elsewhere?"

"I have. Just haven't been consistent in my search."

"Are you looking for jobs in the fields that you mentioned?"

"Yes. I have two master's degrees—one in Human Resource Management and the other, Psychology," he blurted. He believed the degrees defined him.

Gail beamed. "That is wonderful! What accomplishments!" she raved. "Yeeesss! Your education gives you a range of career options."

Hakeem grinned. It felt good for someone to be excited about him. He had worked hard. "I'm also working on a third master's degree."

"Alright. What degree are you pursuing?"

"An MBA."

She was delighted. "You have a solid foundation of knowledge and experience to build on."

"I guess you could say that, although I haven't made any progress career-wise."

"What do you believe is the problem?"

"I've thought of several possible reasons." Hakeem paused to think before continuing. He found he was doing that more frequently. All of his thoughts were competing for first place. "I know that my inconsistency in job searching is part of the problem."

"Something that I hope you'll be improving within the near future," Gail interjected.

"Right. I've thought about my qualifications, whether I've been over- or under-qualified for some jobs."

"Are you applying for jobs in which you're qualified?"

"Oh, yeah. I don't see the point of applying for jobs in which I possess virtually no transferrable knowledge or skill. It's not uncommon for employers to expect incumbents to 'hit the ground running.' Unless it's a company that hires batches of employees at a time, not much is invested into new-hire training. But I do wonder sometimes if my education is intimidating."

"What types of jobs have you applied to?"

"Mostly those similar to the job I have. My thought is, if I can find a job similar to project management, then I can promote internally to the job I really want."

"So, you haven't applied for many jobs related to training or counseling?"

"Not outside the company. No."

"Hmm…" Gail began and then pursed her lips. "Do you want to stay in Corporate America? Is that where you want to round out your career?"

"Haven't given it much thought. I'm not particularly fond of Corporate America. I only do what I do for a paycheck. Most of the mid and upper-tier jobs pay a lot of money, which I've been trying to obtain. But one has to tread through politics and discrimination. I know without a doubt there is racism in the hiring practices of many companies here in Atlanta."

"What makes you think racism and discrimination are factors in employment decisions?"

"Behavioral signals and word choice convey much about a person. I've been in the presence of White interviewers, who act nervous in my presence or uninterested, not wanting to give direct eye-contact or walk at a distance in front or behind me. When it comes to my education, it's always an interrogation—asking me, 'Why do you have so much education?' Not wanting to shake my hand before and after the interview, pretending to be distracted by some object—a folder or pen to avoid close interaction with me, or their tight-lipped smiles and hardened eyes. When they share details about their company's work culture and job responsibilities, there is a lot of emphasis on the negative aspects and very little about the positives. It's almost like they don't want me working there. So, they try to discourage me."

Gail was silent. She observed him periodically between jotting notations into the folder in her lap.

Hakeem wondered if he sounded crazy. One thing for sure, he could read body language. He knew when someone disliked him. "Because this is the Historic South, racism remains prevalent. The unemployment rate for African-Americans according to national statistics is one and a half to double that of the overall average."

He took a course in employment law in pursuit of the Human Resource Management degree. He read the statistics reported by the

U.S. Bureau of Labor Statistics. The unemployment rate for both African-American men and women nearly doubled that of Caucasians, reflecting insignificant change over the past fifty years.

Earl, his father, had advised against moving to Atlanta. Earl believed that relocating to the city was a bad idea, knowing about racism in the South. Immovable in executing his plans, Hakeem dismissed Earl's advice. He dismissed the possibility that his resume or interview skills were deficient. The feedback he received pertaining to both at Kaleidoscope were often favorable. He continued to obtain degrees understanding that advanced education put him on par with White job-seekers. If endeavors for entrepreneurship were nonexistent, African-Americans had to accumulate as much education as possible to be competitive in a predominantly White workforce. Limited education made it easier for racist HR employees to discriminate against African-Americans seeking employment.

Hakeem saw Gail nod in agreement. He was inwardly relieved to meet another African-American who understood. At Kaleidoscope, few Black coworkers exhibited any overt awareness of the problem. Meanwhile, the people bouncing between executive and senior-level positions were for the majority, White employees. When Black employees promoted, they usually advanced to another service-oriented, frontline position. Even when the job was classified "management", it contained a service-oriented element. There were many Black supervisors on the frontline and fewer in director-level positions, or positions entitling executive authority. When courageous employees expressed their concerns, other coworkers feigned ignorance but continued whispering in secret.

The regional director once told the supervisors they were unqualified for director-level positions. It was a direct insult, given that most of those supervisors' tenure exceeded ten years, and some held various degrees. It was common knowledge that the regional director had not obtained a four-year degree. The irony was that the majority of the supervisors were Black.

Hakeem believed that part of the ignorance and cowardice to challenge workplace inequality lay in conditioned inferiority. They feared losing their jobs, blacklisting, or some other form of retaliation.

Atlanta is home to many intelligent, well-educated African-Americans. If only they woke up and stopped rushing to the trough with their heads bowed. Hakeem would submit to no man or woman. Let them think what they would. He would defy anyone.

The Historical Confederate South effectively and unequivocally subjugated many Blacks into submission. It is evident in socioeconomic disparities—inequality in employment, gentrification, and public education—systems that to this day, still maintain components of embedded racism and discrimination. The hope of defeating systematic oppression is to undermine it through active participation in legislation and working alongside those of the majority who are willing to eradicate the issues. Unfortunately, some Black people could be appeased by doggie-treats, which distracted them from the main course. Award the Black employee with something of inconsequential value, yet capable of pacification, and they lost sight of the ultimate goal—overcoming inequality. By then, they had invested significant time sowing into an organization without a prosperous return-on-investment—just working paycheck to paycheck.

"I am a Georgia native. I definitely know where you're coming from. Corporate America is…political…bureaucratic. There's a never-ending struggle in ascending the career-ladder and trying to win popularity contests. And I can't forget the glass-ceiling effect."

"That's exactly right!" Hakeem agreed. Discrimination in employment didn't just target race. Women of all demographics fought against barriers in underemployment and unemployment. Only in specific occupations and professions did women outnumber men. Statistical data didn't fabricate these occurrences. But in all of the chaos, African-Americans ranked low with regards to employment preferences.

"It might behoove you to search for jobs that are reflective of your educational background. Have you considered working in the public sector? There are careers in training and development."

"A little bit. But when I think of training and development in the public sector, teaching comes to mind. Teachers don't get paid enough though."

Long before Hakeem started working at Kaleidoscope, his

grandparents wanted him to be a teacher. And he thought teaching was a good idea until hearing that teachers did not get paid a lot of money. From that point onward, planning to pursue a career in teaching became undesirable.

"That's true in some school districts. However, I would like you to ask yourself this question, 'is money your only concern or do you want happiness?'"

"I do like money," he replied without hesitation, thinking about all the things he had acquired with it and everything he was unable to. "But I do want to be happy."

"Okay. So, what drives your interests in training and development, and counseling?"

"Helping people. I like to help others develop and grow. There's something about watching people evolve and understanding what drives them—what makes them who they are."

"Does your reasoning also apply to your interest in counseling?"

"Yeah. I love psychology…understanding how the mind works and influences behavior."

"I must say, counseling and therapy are equally rewarding."

Hakeem only nodded in agreement—self-conscious about his past. It made him feel unqualified to counsel others. What could he possibly teach people considering his checkered history?

"I believe your goals are very realistic, based on what you've told me. Training and development do involve some counseling. It manifests through teaching, encouraging, and influencing others to change or develop."

Gail smiled again. Hakeem figured she was trying to reassure him as much as possible.

"Is there anything else about your job you'd like to discuss?"

He did not want to sound negative, except all he had were complaints about Kaleidoscope Technologies and life.

"Like I said, I hate my job." Hakeem became bitter. "They constantly take, take, take and only give pennies back. My supervisor has a lot of expectations from me, yet he won't even give me a fair performance appraisal. Other companies out there will pay more for the same type of work that I do. I deserve more money than what I currently make!"

His heartbeat quickened. It happened mostly when he thought about Kaleidoscope. He hoped a panic attack didn't happen while in therapy.

Gail notated in the folder as he talked. It was going to take more than an hour to discuss every problem. He fell silent and tried to stabilize racing thoughts. *How many sessions was it going to take?*

Gail's gaze was steady. Her face betrayed nothing of her inner thoughts.

Hakeem shrugged his shoulders. "I'm unsatisfied with where I am in my life. I've been going at this career thing for a while, and the results are unsatisfactory. I just want to be rewarded adequately for the work I contribute. I've had a couple panic attacks in the past few months. I can't sleep more than four to five hours. I'm tired almost all the time."

"Are these panic attacks frequent?" she asked, adding entries in the folder.

What was she writing? "I've had several in a week."

"What brings the panic attacks on? Or do you know?"

"They usually occur when I'm thinking about Kaleidoscope, and how the place pisses me off."

"Okay. And you say that you're unable to sleep more than five hours? How long has that been happening?"

"For several months now."

"What do you think may be preventing you from sleeping?"

"I think a lot...so much that there isn't a time when I'm not thinking. My mind is always on that job, my career, finances. I can't stop worrying."

"That's not good." Gail observed him with concern. "How are your eating habits? Do you exercise?"

"I eat healthy I think—fruits and vegetables and what not. I do cardio at least three times per week."

"Good. Maintaining your physical health and having a healthy diet is important."

Hakeem feared every kind of illness. Once he turned thirty, his physical health became more important. Reading about heart disease, hypertension, and diabetes in African-Americans influenced him to modify eating habits and invest more time into exercising. He was already quick-tempered. Poor physical health would only intensify his psychological problems.

"Do you mind if I share some thoughts with you regarding your perspectives?"

"No, I don't mind." He accepted constructive criticism.

"First, I'd like to point out that you have a logical perspective with regards to hard work," she affirmed. "And it's in your perspective that I'd like to bring some clarity into your situation."

Please do. He was interested to see how she could help.

"Given what I've heard, your expectations of your job are very important to you. Your desire for increased compensation, career opportunities, and respect attributes to your frustration, correct?"

"Right."

"I wholeheartedly sympathize with you. But the reality is that when we base our decisions primarily on others or things, it is not uncommon to be disappointed when situations don't happen the way we expect."

Gail removed her glasses and placed the specs on the desk. Her eyes bored directly into his. "When situations don't turn out as we desire, we become vulnerable to bitterness, anger, depression, or any combination of unhealthy emotions in the absence of positive thinking."

"I can see that," Hakeem agreed. His close friend, Ian Mitchell had counseled much the same. During the conversation, he recanted to Ian how another friend was regularly unavailable when needed. Ian advised him to adjust his expectations.

Hakeem had not implemented Ian's advice consistently. Now here he was, sitting in therapy receiving similar counsel.

"Kaleidoscope has apparently taken a toll on you and it is one of several reasons why you cannot rest and are always on edge. How many hours do you spend at work?"

"Fifty hours per week. Sometimes more."

"In addition to school?"

"Yes."

"When was the last time you took a vacation?"

"Four years ago."

"Where did you go?"

"Orlando."

"Why have you gone so long without taking a break?"

"Because I dislike being off for extended periods of time. I'm inundated with work when I return. If something goes wrong while I'm gone, my supervisor expects me to fix all of it."

Hakeem believed that if he worked most of the time, he could be in front of everything as it happened—to control every situation.

"I see." Gail closed the folder. "What I'd like us to do during our next couple of sessions, is help you modify your thinking habits."

"Okay," he said while worrying the hangnail in the left index finger. He fidgeted with his hands when there were too many thoughts. Maybe he would mention his other problems in the next session.

Gail reached across the desk and grabbed a small blue square-shaped stack of paper. She began writing.

"One thing is for certain. If for any reason you aren't able to go to work, somebody else will be assigned to your job duties. It is critical that you manage your health first and foremost. I want you to get these prescriptions filled. One will help you to sleep and the second is for your anxiety."

Hakeem took the two pale blue sticky notes as Gail handed them over. The clinic's name, *Promise of Tomorrow* was printed on each.

"I'd like to know when we meet again whether your sleep has improved."

She accompanied him to the front desk in the lobby. The waiting area was still half full. She addressed the woman sitting behind the glass window. "Candace, please schedule Mr. Lewis for an appointment next week."

Gail turned to him. "Enjoy the rest of your week," she said and walked away.

"Mr. Lewis, what day next week is good for you?"

Candace's pretty round face was soft and pleasant. She had to be short the way her breast bunched on the desk without hunching over.

"Next Thursday." *Just a little over a week.*

"Morning or afternoon?"

"Afternoon," he confirmed. An afternoon appointment was the optimal choice because he could work the first half of the day, head to the clinic and get home before rush hour peaked.

"There's an opening for 1:30 P.M., 2:30 P.M., and 3:30 P.M."

"Make it 1:30 P.M." He wanted to avoid any delays that traffic might cause at 2:30 in the afternoon. Rush hour picked up at three o'clock. He also wanted to complete as much work as possible before leaving early. *Relax.* The schedule would just have to do. He had to stop trying to control everything.

PIGS IN LIPSTICK
PIGS IN LIPSTICK

*There's no amount of wealth or finery that can long disguise
a mess. Its stench and disorderly chaos eventually projects
from within to the outside.*

*H*akeem walked to the black two-door coupe. He loved sports
cars. They boosted his ego when he felt worn down like the
abraded soles of a pair of shoes. Hearing the coupe thrum
with power as it accelerated, ramping from 0 to 60 in 5.0 seconds was
exhilarating.

3:15 P.M displayed on his watch. He had to get back on the home
side of town before the traffic escalated. Tossing the prescriptions onto
the passenger seat, he pressed the push-start ignition and activated the
air-conditioner. The air inside stifled from the sunlight passing through
the closed windows. He propped an elbow on the leather armrest,
finding its surface clammy. The temperature had caused the material
to secrete its sticky leather treatment conditioner.

Hakeem felt drained although somewhat relieved. It was refreshing
talk to someone about his private thoughts. He lowered the sun visor
and looked at himself in the vanity mirror. He thought he resembled
his father more than mother. The lateral canthi turned downwards
instead of the reverse like Rosalyn. She had once stated they had the
same eyes. Hakeem concluded that she must have been referring to the
brightness within the irises. He had Earl's facial structure and features.
Black eyebrows, thicker along the inner brow, naturally thinned as they
extended outwards. A facial hair pattern nearly identical to Earl's was

now a shadow, covered his reddish-brown skin along the cheekbones and throat. With more gray hair growing in the beard, he shaved regularly, leaving behind a mustache and goatee that framed full lips. The sharp edge in his tapered-fade disappeared as the hair regrew. It was time for a fresh cut.

The temperature inside the coupe cooled. Hakeem flipped the sun visor and drove out of the parking lot. Overhead, the sun blaze in the clear blue sky. Hot as it was, he still found Atlanta's climate far preferable to Minneapolis. In relocating to the city nine years ago, he had not expected to experience the offerings of warmer temperatures in the late fall through early winter. In Atlanta, people could wear shorts much later in the year than in northern states. Hakeem made a habit of wearing summer clothes for as long as the weather permitted.

Hakeem had not foreseen long-term residency in the city or anywhere else for that matter. Three years later, approaching the age of 29, the reality could no longer be ignored. Each year passed with little thought given to plans for the future. Lack of achievement evidenced time taken for granted. A Bachelor of Arts in Psychology rested on the top shelf in the bedroom closet, buried under stacks of clothes.

Kaleidoscope's tuition reimbursement policy offered no provision for advanced degrees in general psychology. Hakeem owed Ian gratitude for insight regarding Industrial and Organizational Psychology specialization—an applied field of psychology, which Kaleidoscope covered in its tuition reimbursement program. Once confirmed, he immediately enrolled with the partnering university and obtained a master's degree within three years.

Positive and forward-looking friends are invaluable. Those who genuinely wish you success, impart the knowledge and wisdom necessary for you to grow.

Hakeem's thoughts re-centered on the traffic. Just a year ago, anyone could get a head start on rush-hour any time before 4 P.M. during the week. But each year, traffic worsened from the influx of thousands of transients. The result was a hodge-podge of drivers from all over the country—a combination that produced a constant problem for commuters traversing the city.

Traffic was in the early stages of forming its daily pileup on Interstate-285. Vehicles sped pass as Hakeem merged onto the ramp from I-75. A car raced by on the passenger side, riding the shoulder, and then cut over in front. After traveling a mile, a car cut across the 5-lane interstate from the express lane. Hakeem swore. The drivers were an interesting sort all around the metropolitan area. It seemed that everyone drove for themselves, oblivious to how their habits affected others. *But isn't that a common aspect of life in this world—people thinking only of themselves?*

The flow of traffic changed constantly as commuters merged and exited the interstate from nearby thruways. Hakeem looked out the driver's side window seeing the peaks of the Concourse at Landmark Center rising above the treetops on the westbound side of Interstate 285. Despite the official name of the twin towers, some ATLiens tended to refer to the buildings as King and Queen because of the distinguishable lattice design of each "crown" at the very top of the edifices. In November and December, the towers' nightlights illuminated red, white and green, coordinating with the annual holiday colors.

≈≈≈≈≈≈≈

Hakeem turned into the open parking space in front of the four-storey apartment building. The varied-level complex sprawled across a property of rolling land. Rather than grade the ground's surface completely, the architects built into the land, erecting four- and five-storey structures. Entrance to his apartment was possible from the north side by ascending three flights of stairs or two flights on the south end.

The leasing consultant had disclosed that the complex was five years old at the time. Two-toned brown and beige cobblestones covered the exterior walls of every building. Besides the overall upkeep of the property and relative newness of the apartments' interior, the architecture was the only external feature that Hakeem found appealing. His opinions changed after signing the lease. He began to notice the dingy concrete walkways that maintenance failed to power wash regularly. Cobwebs hung in the corners of the archways and ceilings. Fearful of a spider falling, Hakeem purchased insecticide and vigorously sprayed the door-jamb and windows inside the apartment, in addition to the rails of the staircase in the breezeway. He believed that where a web hung, a spider lurked, and the idea unnerved him. If one ever fell, it might be over for both of them. On numerous occasions, he nearly stepped in fresh dog excrement while crossing the lawn to his car. Some of the pet owners made no effort to clean up behind their furry animals or take advantage of the stations located throughout the property.

Returning home late one night, the scent of marijuana assaulted Hakeem in the breezeway. A Caucasian male and female stood partially hidden by the staircase leading to the second floor of the building. Both appeared to be in the late twenties judging from their presentation—graphic tees, tattered jeans, and poorly dyed hair in which golden-brown roots could benefit from touchups, suggesting their approximate ages.

The apartment complex was comprised of approximately 55 percent Caucasian. Some were friendly—smiling or speaking in passing while others said nothing. Hakeem emerged from his apartment one night and apparently startled the white lady living next door. She nearly ripped the door to her apartment from its hinge trying to enter and re-enable the locks. Not a second passed as the door met the jamb when he heard: *click, click.* His scruffy black beard, hoodie, blue jeans, and black boots must have been intimidating. Did she believe that he, living next door, was going to rob her? He didn't give a rat's butt about her apartment, and whatever was in there that smelled like an ancient woman. Whenever she opened the door, the air current carried with it a scent of decomposing flowers, musk, and dust. How the smell developed perplexed him. A woman or her possessions should not smell that pungent in his opinion.

Hakeem entered the 2-bedroom apartment, inhaling the vanilla and lavender aroma that persisted throughout the rooms. The hallway extended diagonally left and opened into a shorter hallway containing a bathroom, washer and dryer closet, and a spare undecorated bedroom at the end. Decoration was unnecessary, as he preferred living by himself. Instead of paying for additional storage space, the second bedroom fulfilled the purpose. Boxes and a set of 20-inch rims lined the wall along the upper-right corner while books and an ironing board occupied the lower right. Plastic tubs filled with sweaters and pullover shirts folded department-store presentation-style took up space along the third wall. Suits, dress shirts, and shoes hung in the walk-in closet. He saw logic in separating the casual, business, and formal wear.

The main hallway opened into an L-shaped space with the living room orienting to the left and the dining area near the adjacent wall. Directly across from the dining area was a shallow rectangular kitchen. The stove and refrigerator faced each other from opposite sides of the floor. The wall in the dining area partitioned the master bedroom, bathroom, and walk-in closet as customary of contemporary roommate-designed floorplans.

≈≈≈≈≈≈≈

Sitting on the bed, Hakeem removed his boots—harnessed black leather, tan sole, and one and three-quarter heel. He preferred boots— versatile footwear that could be coordinated with jeans or slacks. He draped the dark-washed blue jeans and plaid button-down shirt he had worn across the top of the laundry hamper. He loved clothing in general, and how to accessorize clothing was one thing he could do well. There was pride in the practice because he felt that in some way, his outer appearance distracted from the ugliness deep within. Sometimes compliments were comforting, that is, when they seemed genuine. He learned a long time ago to consider the basis of a person's verbalized thoughts. Some people were disingenuous.

Laying back across a cream and blue paisley comforter, Hakeem stared at the white-painted ceiling, its surface a pattern of dried overlapping daises. He reflected on Gail's counsel regarding his expectations. He tended to think in terms of what should be and how people should behave—becoming sometimes vexed by things beyond personal control. Learning how to respond healthily and effectively to life situations was critical to positive psychological development and social interaction. He understood that much.

The first one-hour therapy session did not allot enough time to unload every problem. Hakeem also thought about how Gail might respond if he eventually disclosed everything else. He worried again, remembering suddenly that the prescription had not been filled. Tomorrow, he would not forget to go to the grocery store.

Before Hakeem fell asleep with thoughts of the day's events still circulating, he looked at the alarm clock on the cherry wood nightstand. 5:30 P.M. A nap would give him a boost to tackle the homework assignment later. Something always needed to be done.

≈≈≈≈≈≈≈

The message indicator flashed on the desk phone. *Probably a client's voicemail*, Hakeem figured. Rarely were there days when clients missed the opportunity to leave voicemails when he left the office. Even with backup support, they distrusted working with anyone else. He exhibited a strong work ethic amongst his peers, setting a standard in which the clients had become accustomed. As he explained to Gail, the demands of the job were the main reason for not choosing to vacation regularly. When out of the office, the work collected and no one in the department invested the time to deliver the same quality of work on a consistent basis.

He looked at the message indicator once more. *Whoever it was would just have to wait.* Once he drank his coffee, he'd be better able to deal with them and the day ahead.

Sounds of footsteps and chatter drifted over the gray five and a half-foot wall of his cube as coworkers entered the office from the elevators. The cubicles formed quads such that the space of each area was perpendicularly proportioned. There was no sign of nosey coworker, Rowena in her cube. Rowena announced her arrival by the habitual morning arguments she had with her boyfriend over the phone. Everyone in the office knew the details of her relationship—how her boyfriend didn't come home until the next morning and the various females that called her house.

Hakeem preferred that Rowena kept her business private. He was devoid of sympathy for her, believing her characteristically deceitful.

She smiled and talked to everyone while watching everything, and then reported her observations to management. She monitored everything that he did too—having mentioned his extended lunch breaks in the company gym. For as much work that he contributed to Kaleidoscope, he deserved at least a two-hour lunch break. He restrained himself from confrontation because it would be a verbal exchange warranting HR intervention and celebrated the days when she was absent. On those days, thoughts of cussing her out were virtually nonexistent.

He rotated his chair towards the opening of the cubicle while sipping the coffee. Across the walkway, Tariq entered his cube, head bobbing to music in his earphones. Throughout the day, they carried on discussions about music, celebrities, socioeconomic issues, and relationships.

Hakeem admired Tariq for the relationship with his beautiful wife, Anaya who also worked at Kaleidoscope. He was open to the idea of finding someone to share his own life with on a long-term basis. As it was, the possibility looked grim.

Pivoting the chair clockwise, Hakeem glimpsed the backpack jutting out from underneath the desk and nudged it out of view with a foot. Work was far from his mind at the moment. It would remain as such, until he got around to doing it. *How much longer must I endure?*

"And how was your weekend?"

Despite the wryness, Hakeem knew Alex's voice.

"You're asking the wrong question," he responded, tensing.

Alex stood inside the cubicle wearing a white short-sleeve utility shirt and fitted blue jeans that slightly covered the top line of black dress shoes. Creases from excessive wear spanned the vamp. The shoes had seen better days but he kept a fresh cut. Shiny, neat brush waves covered his scalp. Except for a triangular-contoured goatee, very little facial hair concealed his light-brown complexion. Excitement animated brown eyes framed with short lashes.

"The wrong question?" Alex mocked laughingly, taking a seat in the vacant chair along the back wall of the cubicle.

"You didn't call me back. Did you forget we made plans?" Hakeem pressed, turning around to face him squarely. He had an idea of what happened but asked anyway. Alex went missing in action for a man

25

and would even stand friends up for one, which made him unreliable in context.

Hakeem remembered when Alex agreed to pick him up from the airport upon returning from a business trip. Unexpectedly, Robert, their mutual friend, came to the airport instead. Robert stated that Alex was on a date and unable to meet him as agreed. After failing to return calls, Alex called him several days later. The date, whoever he was, had moved on. Alex didn't provide any details about the man, and Hakeem did not bother to inquire. He suspected the usual considering Alex's track record. There was an instance where Alex entered into a short-term relationship and communicated only when the man left his presence. That time, Hakeem stopped speaking to Alex for four months. No one put him on rotation if he could do something about it. When the relationship dissolved, a despondent Alex stood in the doorway of his cubicle to make amends. They always made peace.

They had made plans to hang out for dinner and a movie during the past weekend. Alex claimed he needed to clear his mind. He was in a rocky situation with Rick—a man he met online several months ago. Based on the information Alex confided, Rick was bad news. He said that Rick had not called in a week since their last argument. Apparently, Rick was back on the scene like so many of Alex's former associates who he permitted to come and go without stipulations. When they returned, Alex shut down everything and everyone. The way he made adjustments for men, a person might think Jesus returned.

"Chiiillle……"—Alex drawled—"I apologize."

Hakeem closed his eyes and cringed covertly. He hated when Alex talked gay in public, as the behavior drew the attention of others to their conversation, hearing a Black man conversing in a feminine manner. When he spoke in the characteristic lingo, he exhibited the behavior in environments where those less inclined to approve were absent. He preferred to be discreet and private concerning his sexuality, whereas Alex was loud—boldly announcing his orientation to the world.

Hakeem imagined that some people made assumptions concerning his sexual orientation, but they lacked the courage to confront him directly. He was not the type of individual to press for personal information. He would sooner swear the inquirer to hell and back than answer their questions. Furthermore, as far as he was concerned, whatever took place in the bedroom between two consenting adults was none of the world's business.

"Uh-huh,"—he waved dismissively—"Had I known you'd stand me up, I would've made other plans."

"I'm sorry, chile. Rick and I had to meet to discuss some things."

"Oh. So did you meet in a public place or your bedroom?"

Alex skirted the insult. "Rick was back in town for the weekend and said that we needed to talk. He wants us to spend more time together." he said gleefully.

If it were at all possible for Alex's smile to latterly split his face, it would have.

Hakeem forced a smile. Sunshine or rain, day or night, seldom did a person ask for his phone number. He was unapproachable, so people claimed. He also lacked the confidence to initiate pursuit. The few times he expressed interest in someone, he experienced rejection. Club and bar-hopping ceased a year ago, leaving online dating a last resort, and those experiences were touch and go. The men who frequented the clubs and bars regularly also cruised the online dating sites. There was no doubt in Hakeem's mind how those conversations would progress. If the men were uninterested face-to-face, they would be just as apathetic online.

Luck in dating seemed to deplete without replenishment. The men Hakeem chatted with over the past few months were uninterested. A few continued to communicate but nothing substantial emerged from those conversations. He lacked what other gay men offered—spontaneity and sensuality, which eliminated him from the competition. The cycle of meeting new people and going through the process of self-disclosure only for the acquaintances to end within weeks was tiring. The gay life pained more than it comforted.

"And you're just speaking to me now? Our plans completely escaped your mind?"

"You should have reminded me," Alex retorted.

"That's strange. You don't need a reminder from me to do the things you want to do."

Alex's smile faded. "Like I said, Hakeem, I apologize."

The exchange exhausted Hakeem. "Just tell me what happened." Alex's loyalties changed on a whim. He decided that their friendship had reached a plateau.

"Are you sure you want to hear?" Alex ascertained.

"Yeah," Hakeem feigned excitement. He lacked in friendship from having a small social network. In part, he only had an ounce of tolerance for the gay community. His disposition limited his capacity to establish substantial social connections. It wasn't the first time Alex rotated him for a one-night stand. And as long they remained friends, he could expect to be dumped whenever it suited Alex.

As Alex began to reveal the details of his weekend excursion, the desk phone rang. Hakeem read the caller ID. Genevieve Kelly flashed on the display. She preferred to be called Genna. He guessed that she had left the voicemail. Genna habitually called the morning after leaving a voicemail the previous day. She seldom allowed him to initiate follow-up calls since she never let twenty-four hours pass without someone addressing her concerns.

"I have to take this," Hakeem told Alex, lifting the receiver from its cradle and covering the mouthpiece with a free hand. "We can do lunch."

"Alright. What time are you taking lunch?"

"Around noon," he whispered.

Genna created the distraction he needed. Deep down, he didn't want to hear about Alex's escapades. *The same stupid stories! Some people never change. Expectations...* Gail's advice came to mind before his feelings overrode sensibility. He must continue to remind himself to adjust his expectations. It was a major step in learning how to deal with life positively.

Hakeem had been there for Alex—his sounding board put away on a shelf, utilized only in times of need, especially when men cheated or walked out. The only credit that Alex earned was through the committal of an invaluable act of selflessness—providing emotional support when Evelyn passed away. Hakeem was grateful for the support and encouragement. But Alex remained true to character and he wanted him to change. If Alex could see their friendship as he saw it, their relationship might improve. *Wishful thinking*... Either he was losing his wits, or age was restructuring his needs, and Alex was incapable of accommodating both. *Expectations*....

ROTTEN STRAWBERRIES AND SOURED CREAM

ROTTEN STRAWBERRIES AND SOURED CREAM

*Forever will I believe that a child's experiences are to be filled
with joyous memories instead of dark recollections, which
will haunt them for a lifetime.*

"Hello, Genna."

"Hakeem!"—she began in an exasperated tone—"We
have a fire drill!"

No, you have a fire drill. His irritation surged.

"What happened?" he asked, trying to sound concerned. The
customers called even when their problem was not his issue. They
should have called the salesperson who sold the services. The customers
had their business cards.

"No one in payroll has been trained on the time-keeping software
you sold us. We have to start using it no later than tomorrow. Our pay
period closes on Friday and we have hundreds of entries!"

You sold? He repeated the accusation to himself, trying to get past
it. *It isn't my software, and I wasn't the one who sold it!* He kept quiet
nonetheless and continued listening to her vent.

"Ray and his team came out here and installed the software package,
then told us you would train us on how to use it."

*Where were those instructions in the plan? I'm the project manager, not
Ray!* Hakeem bit his bottom lip to keep from releasing a rush of outrage.
Ray was a squirrely man who talked fast and made promises he couldn't
fulfill independently. Meet your professional salesman!

Ray did nothing except sell and averaged two times Hakeem's salary.

At the end of every quarter, Ray received a sizeable commission check while he received a monetary conversion of hourly wages. Hakeem had no patience for Ray. The level of responsibility and accountability sharply differed between them, with the majority of it swimming in his lap.

Ray was also notorious for putting Hakeem in compromising situations. With another mutual client, he led a project call without inviting him. Systems, technical configurations, and backend processes weren't Ray's forte. After the meeting, he sent an email explaining the client's requirements along with an unrealistic deadline. No one consulted implementation or the I.T. department to determine whether it was possible to accommodate the customer's request. Ray tried to push the project through as he promised the customer a short turnaround. Hakeem confronted him for lacking oversight. In response, Ray contacted his supervisor, Bill Wilcox, claiming it was difficult to work with him. No. Ray made Hakeem's job strenuous.

Rather than broach the subject from a position of neutrality, Bill defended Ray automatically, claiming he was working under pressure. Truth be told, Hakeem worked under pressured every day. But somehow, Bill overlooked the reality directly under his nose.

Hakeem didn't waver in his perspective. He refused to acquiesce on the matter of principle—knowing the scope of the job. He told Bill that Ray knew the process for qualifying clients for customized services and that project management was not Ray's area of expertise. Even Bill didn't know the processes. However, Bill told Hakeem that he needed to build stronger internal partnerships. Nevertheless, Hakeem's difference of opinion remained unchanged and it cost higher ratings in performance evaluation. When he received the annual review, he contested immediately, involving senior-manager, Dale Klein.

Hakeem disliked Dale acutely. Dale interacted with few minorities—a behavior that was the exact opposite of his interaction with white employees in the company. Bill and Dale worked in tandem, delaying his performance review until the window closed for employee disputes. When the window closed, HR accepted the final performance appraisal that managers submitted. Hakeem wanted to slam punches into their faces when they denied his request for re-evaluation.

"I apologize for the inconvenience, Genna. When is your team available for a webinar?" Hakeem's fist clenched. He wanted to hit something—an action likely to result in termination. *Always filling the gap for someone else!*

"What about 1:00 P.M., today?"

"I'm available."

"Okay. Let me see who needs training and I will send you a conference bridge."

"Sounds great." He released a sigh of submission, tired of the fire drills.

"Thank you, Hakeem!"

As soon as the call ended, a shadow cast across the computer monitor. Turning around, he saw Bill looking at him. *What do you want?*

"Hakeem, hey! I got a call from Ray. Have you spoken to him?"

"Spoken with Ray about what?" he asked briskly. Bill's feigned ignorance annoyed him.

"He said something about a client…Horizons, I think. Something about them needing training."

It's People on the Horizons! Hakeem grimaced with disgust. Bill knew nothing when it came to the dynamics of the clients managed by his team. All he knew how to do sufficiently was to delegate. When upper-management issued a new directive, Bill agreed regardless of the wrongness in the direction. He was that 'yes-manager', who tried to convince the team that it was okay to go on a red traffic light. Many times, policies contained numerous red flags because senior management refused to listen to the employees who worked the front lines and understood firsthand operational needs. Bill simply agreed with his superiors despite the consumer complaints that escalated through the team.

Hakeem perceived Bill's objective. Bill sought promotion to an assistant director-level position. He was complicit in an effort to achieve that goal. Hakeem despised him, as he considered him weak and intentionally deceptive. He held anyone who willfully disguised the truth or set people up for failure to profit themselves in contempt.

"I just spoke with Genna. Ray did not train her team as planned."

"Why? Was he expecting you to do it?" Bill asked. His blue eyes were open wide.

What do you mean, was Ray expecting me to do it?! "I don't know what he expected!"—Hakeem clipped, bucking his eyes—"I scheduled a training session for this afternoon."

"Good, good. Thanks. I want to avoid an escalation."

Relief bloomed on Bill's face as he ran long bony fingers through a boxed haircut and exited the cubicle. Hakeem suspected that he was mainly concerned that Ray might contact the director. The wrong feedback could hurt his chances for advancement.

Hakeem's eyes narrowed. *We wouldn't want you to not get that promotion you're aiming for.*

≈≈≈≈≈≈≈

Three months ago, Hakeem applied for a supervisor position within the customer service department. Since the hiring manager, Sally Dunley was Bill's former boss, he thought that Bill would at least advocate on his behalf. He was a consistent top performer on Bill's team, not to mention qualified. Bill's involvement consisted of an elementary email to Sally, informing her of his interests in becoming a supervisor.

It was Sharon Black, another supervisor, who informed Hakeem that both Sally and the director were working in tandem to cherry-pick candidates for the multiple openings. Sharon knew about their antics since she participated in the staff meetings where management discussed the hiring plans openly. She hated office politics but like Bill, her inaction enabled inequitable practices to persist in the workplace.

Just before the first round of interviews took place, Hakeem and several coworkers received generic emails from HR stating they were unqualified. With two master's degrees and nine years of experience at Kaleidoscope, the communication was absurd. He challenged the decision by forwarding the email to the HR manager, advising her to reconsider on the merit of his experience. He waited two days to allow the HR manager time to respond before forwarding the email to Bill. The HR manager did not reply, and rather than leverage his influence as a supervisor, Bill asked Hakeem to keep him in the loop regarding the outcome. Bill had removed himself from active involvement as an assistant-director position opened. It was common knowledge at Kaleidoscope that the former assistant-director had resigned, and Bill aspired to occupy the vacancy.

Hakeem discerned Bill's motivations. The director, Bill's mentor, was the hiring manager for the assistant-director position! If Bill advocated aggressively for Hakeem, then he risked undermining his own chances for advancement in challenging Sally and the director. Whenever a conflict of interest existed, Bill aligned with whatever position that proved most self-beneficial. He would not risk stepping on anyone's toes, and thus, lessen his chances for promotion.

As in most work environments, blackballing was oftentimes difficult to prove because of its subtle execution. Yet, evidence of its concealed presence could be found in evaluating the career challenges of employees who fought against the status quo. Integrity and morality have costs that few people desire to pay. In the long run, Bill didn't get the job as anticipated. The same politics that impeded Hakeem from advancement also affected him. He should have stayed the course and championed Hakeem. Bill gained nothing through his defection but lost all of Hakeem's trust in him as a leader. Some managers fail to grasp that trust is an essential component of effective leadership. Managers are hard-pressed to gain trust, respect, and commitment when employees perceive them as deceptive, dishonest, incompetent, uncommunicative, and inconsistent.

In the midst of shifting alliances, Sally invited Hakeem to interview for the same position he was previously denied. Surprised, he told Sharon who was equally amazed that HR granted the opportunity. She divulged that an investigation transpired in the department and believed that the applicants originally denied, were given chances to interview as a consequence of the probe. Subsequently, Hakeem participated in two rounds of interviews with Sally and her peers. He received a rejection email a month later. Within the same week, he crossed paths with assistant-director Davinder, who helped facilitate the second interview. When they made eye contact, Davinder quickly looked away, turned around and walked in the opposite direction. Dust might have lifted from the carpet as he hurried away. Not a single "hello" or "good-bye." Hakeem interpreted the behavior as a sign of guilt. Expectations…

≈≈≈≈≈≈≈

Elbow resting on the sill of the driver side window, Hakeem gingerly gnawed on the knuckle of the left index finger. Traffic was bumper-to-bumper. Life when he started at Kaleidoscope to present cycled through his mind. Thinking interrupted the monotony of the daily commute. The smart sign suspended over the interstate displayed a traffic accident two miles ahead. No one was going anywhere for at least, the next forty-five minutes.

Quality of life improved in 2006 when Kaleidoscope extended Hakeem an offer of employment, elevating him above the poverty line. He quit working two part-time jobs and re-entered the office setting as a client support representative. Initially, the job demands were taxing. He lacked practical experience in the field of human resource management. Apprehensive about being fired for doing something wrong, he tirelessly availed himself of Kaleidoscope's knowledgebase to learn everything about the industry and the company's practices. He carried forth the memories of Evelyn, who instilled the value of self-teaching rather than waiting for someone else to undertake the task.

Hakeem developed proficiency in achieving customer satisfaction and resolution, positioning him as a top performer within the department. However, irate and disrespectful customers always tested his patience. He could not resist jamming up a customer when they denigrated him. It was one thing to insult the company but to refer to him in a derogatory manner was another matter. In many instances, the clients' reasons for displeasure were valid. They just needed to direct their frustration elsewhere in Hakeem's opinion. Pay at Kaleidoscope fell short of compensating for verbal abuse.

While instructing a customer to contact their company administrator for technical assistance with an HR feed, the customer told Hakeem that for $8 an hour, he knew the script well. Hakeem responded with an insult—telling the customer that he was lucky to have a job considering the company was on the verge of folding due to numerous lawsuits. The customer demanded to speak with a supervisor but Hakeem denied the request and disconnected the call. He wasn't going to allow anyone to be disrespectful if he could do something about it.

Employment at Kaleidoscope granted Hakeem luxuries that were previously limited. He shopped incessantly with a predilection for buying name brand sneakers, boots, cologne, and watches. Most of his material possessions remained stored away, price tags still intact. He gradually weaned from dependency upon grandparents—Joseph and Evelyn Lewis. They saw their grandson finally graduating into independence.

Hakeem's job performance and resourcefulness overshadowed the more aggressive traits, enabling advancement to the role of team lead within eighteen months. During that period, his on-the-job experience broadened to encompass a technical background. The professional growth positioned him to be recommended for an organization-wide project seven months later. The initial assignment was to function as an advisor for the customer service unit but given business needs, transitioned into a trainer role.

The same year—Hakeem's third year of tenure at Kaleidoscope, marked a major milestone. On the brink of turning 29, a smattering of plan-deficient ideas comprised an outlook of the future. He found passion in training and development, for it drew upon his creative talents, challenging him to pursue new pathways of thought. Ian advised pursuing a master's degree that could integrate his education in psychology and developmental opportunities at Kaleidoscope. From that advice, Hakeem enrolled in graduate school and gradually began to see the pieces of his life fitting together.

Hakeem's friendship with Ian represented one of two invaluable non-familial associations. Few qualified as wise in his close-knit circle of associations. Ian had gained a wealth of wisdom in the course of his academic and ministerial pursuits. Ian's advice was no small inducement. Looking back seven years later, Hakeem deemed Ian's advice as God-directed. God sent messages through others to get the attention of His sheep that strayed from the flock. In 2012, Hakeem completed the master's degree program. Evelyn did not live to witness the achievement.

With education building an intellectual framework in which to integrate work experience, Hakeem was certain of obtaining a satisfying career in training at Kaleidoscope. But just over the horizon the walls of opposition peaked. Kaleidoscope's management and employees alike, benefitted from his expertise. The training team specifically, leeched all they could—siphoning knowledge to develop their curriculums. Ironically, some of the trainers stated that he needed further development to become an official trainer. What else was there to prove when he successfully demonstrated the capabilities to facilitate, teach, design, develop and implement a training program?

The positive feedback Hakeem received from management and peers across other departments were testaments to his proficiency. When he expressed interest in training, the department manager, Damien Spraggs, casually dismissed his instrumental role by suggesting that certifications in training could strengthen his candidacy for a position. Damien constantly focused on Hakeem's limited practical experience in their one-on-one conversations. Education, experience and job performance should have been sufficient for an internal employee's consideration. Damien had been disengaged from the training sequence that Hakeem organized, and the latter's accomplishments shed light on the obvious. His ability to independently organize information foreshadowed raw talent that could potentially outshine Damien.

Damien's smokescreens vexed Hakeem. Why was he unmotivated to hire him? The question elicited Hakeem's recollection of a situation that occurred before their formal acquaintance. Around the time he became team-lead, an investigation ensued in the training department. A group of new hires filed a joint complaint concerning a trainer's inappropriate conduct, and HR removed the employee from the training class. A circumstance of limited staffing and Hakeem's role as a training assistant positioned him to assume the trainer's responsibilities for the duration of the new hires' training. Since the trainer was Damien's subordinate, upper-management placed accountability. Meanwhile, Hakeem's prowess drew the spotlight. The new hires raved how he brought real-world experiences into the learning environment, diminishing the training team's glory.

There was no tangible proof of Damien's bias. He subtly masked whatever resentments harbored. Hakeem interviewed for training positions as they posted on the internal job boards and each time, Damien selected another candidate. Hakeem attributed few situations to coincidence, especially when he understood that motivation drove individual behavior.

Accumulated student loan debt from undergrad made Hakeem desperate for money. He abandoned attempts to enter the training department and applied for a project manager position. Damien had continued to block his efforts. Landing a training job seemed impossible but other jobs could still provide for his ultimate goal—an increased salary. Hakeem made a positive impression on the hiring manager who offered him the position. The manager confided that his reputed competence in part, gave him an advantage over other candidates.

Seven months of acclimation in the role and Hakeem's performance climbed steadily into the ten percent category of top performers. Knowledge of the job's entailments reduced the learning curve. For a while, he coasted smoothly until the culture of Kaleidoscope converted into a profit-hankering entity. Decision-makers implemented new tactics to maximize profits, downsized work units, and consolidated job roles. The workload increased substantially without salary treatments for the retained employees. Senior- and mid-level managers continued receiving ample bonuses even when the company performed poorly. Where was the equitable justification in management receiving incentives when the employees who worked against a rising tidal wave, did not receive raises? It made sense when Hakeem finally saw Kaleidoscope's landscape for what it was—a modern-day cotton-picking field.

Hakeem had worked for different companies, oblivious to the impact of leadership and organizational culture on workplace dynamics. Until walking through Kaleidoscope's doors and resuming educational pursuits, he considered a paycheck to be the sole purpose for working. He underwent a cognitive restructuring in the industrial-organizational psychology coursework. Through new lenses, he began to dislike what he witnessed inside the company.

There were those who perceived Hakeem as a rising leader. He was a servant-leader in-progress endeavoring to help others succeed. However, management wanted to exploit his ability to achieve results and influence for two reasons: 1) to generate more revenue for the company and bonuses for senior management; and 2) to align employees with organizational objectives. Kaleidoscope's management did not have its employees' best interests at heart and for this reason, Hakeem resisted their attempts to utilize him for the sole benefit of the decision makers. His obstinacy cost him more opportunities than a few.

The slogan: "*Want a future with a company of good ol' backstabbers? Come on over and join Kaleidoscope's management team,*" should have been written on the company's front doors. When an employee filed a grievance with HR, the personnel sometimes, violated confidentiality and informed the employee's manager of the complaint. The manager retaliated against the grieving employee—trying to set them up for progressive disciplinary action. Kaleidoscope was a prime example of Corporate America in every sense of the concept.

Upper-management supposedly solicited "honest" feedback from low-level employees. Hakeem spoke candidly in company meetings about the oppressive work environment and shared ideas concerning what might potentially improve the climate. Consequently, his reputation suffered because members of management perceived him as a negative employee. Sharon had voiced the unspoken perception—that there were members of management who felt they had to tread carefully around him. Hakeem thought it a small price to pay compared to doing what he considered morally right.

Just because circumstances exists does not mean that a person has to yield to them. Hakeem would sooner quit before surrendering to the schemes of management. At one point, he considered repairing damage to his reputation but tossed the idea. Remaining true to himself meant more than constructing a new identity of someone he did not respect. Sharon said that some of her peers sold themselves to the devil to advance within the company. That is what management required for promotion. Anytime an individual deliberately engaged in wrongdoing to gain a personal advantage, it was downright corrupt in Hakeem's book. No amount of money was worth that much to lose his soul, integrity, or dignity.

Hakeem held many of management personnel in contempt for their duplicitous bearings. His former supervisor, George Paine, described him as a wolf that evaded conformity. In constructive criticism, George enjoined Hakeem, coaching that in order to succeed at Kaleidoscope, he must don sheep's clothing. Hakeem thought pretending to be a sheep was preposterous and laughed at George. He believed that those who absolved the corrupt were corruptible. People who revered integrity and honor fought to uphold those principles at all costs because the opposing side was not going to care at all.

George eventually resigned from Kaleidoscope for the same reasons Hakeem fought. The difference between them was that George patiently complied. Hakeem resisted office politics and brown-nosing was out of the question. Phoniness agitated him like old grease in the gut and he failed at the game. He would feel better if management displayed their impertinent natures overtly, leveling the playing field. Then every employee could express his or her feelings. There were several people in management he wanted to give a piece of his mind. All he needed was a permit. There were many days when he was ready to proceed without one.

Hakeem did not anticipate that his actions would negatively affect his career. For five years, he was complacent as a project manager while persevering in attaining the second master's degree. Thereupon, he resumed applying for jobs. Forever it seemed that a brick wall stood before him. In the stretch of nine years, he had applied to eighty-one internal jobs, promoting only once. He stopped denying the possibility that management had blackballed him from advancement, the damage irreversible.

≈≈≈≈≈≈≈

The distance between vehicles steadily widened as the rapid flow of traffic recommenced. The corners of Hakeem's eyes moistened from trying to envision an escape from his mire. Questions flooded his mind. Each racing thought supplanted the previous. *What if I never escaped? What if I was destined to live a long life replete with tribulations? Do I want to live through any of it? Wasn't I meant for something greater? If so, what was the greater something? All of the talents I possess, they are going to waste. Would old age be replete with pain and regret?*

A pain suddenly bloomed in Hakeem's chest. He was working up a panic attack from cogitating. He deeply inhaled gulps of air to alleviate the constricting feeling. The pains were worsening, causing him to fear an eventual stroke or heart attack. The prescription needed to be filled and it was best that the task be completed before going home. The grocery store down the street from the apartment had a pharmacy. Besides, chocolate-chip and pecan cookie dough needed to be picked up anyway. The cookies would provide some comfort.

PERMANENT STAINS

PERMANENT STAINS

No matter the hope or applied effort, some stains in our lives can never be removed.

*H*akeem sat on the merlot microfiber loveseat, regrouping by watching the sunlight shrink in contrast to the growing shadow of the evening's darkness.

The cellphone rang. He looked at the caller ID on the white and silver smartphone. Rosalyn Lewis flashed across the display. He hesitated. Whenever Rosalyn called, he was reluctant to answer because their conversations typically escalated when she said something offensive. Hakeem had less patience for Rosalyn when his feelings were churning and didn't accept her calls during those times.

Rosalyn, 56, lived in Philadelphia, in a four-bedroom apartment with one of her two daughters, Layla. Katrina had married and lived in Newark, New Jersey. Tyrell, the youngest of Rosalyn's four children, lived with his girlfriend three blocks away. Hakeem's disdain for the neighborhood was profound. He had witnessed on numerous occasions, robberies in broad daylight, fights, shootings, and vandalism. A sensible person thought twice about having a nice car without an alarm and club. Drug addicts and dealers shamelessly roamed the streets. The former searched for opportunities to steal and sell anything valuable to get money and flip it into drugs while the latter oversaw the exchange of illegal product and recruited those looking for a quick come-up.

Tall apartment buildings rested atop land lots, stretching to the sky. Their rust-red brick frames had faded to brown from constant exposure to pollution and the elements. Iron bars gated windows rather than screens. On the interiors, addicts and the homeless released their bodily wastes in the elevators and emergency exits. Used condoms lay discarded in the corners of the stairway where the concrete-painted walls peeled and were slick with grime. The exit lights, dimmed or broken altogether, shaded deviant activities.

Liberated from that environment, Hakeem reflected in amazement that he survived. He knew several people still living in the same projects twenty years later. A few associates had died in the same community of which they were products. He remembered Andre, 15, who lived on the fifth floor, gunned down on the basketball court one summer night following a drug-related dispute. Antoine, a schoolmate, was setup by a jealous ex-girlfriend. Her brother shot him in the street. Those years were dark and the more recent past grimmer still.

Memories of the last time Hakeem saw Rosalyn a year ago, came to mind. Before the drugs, he considered her very pretty. She might have made for a successful career as a model—5'8" tall, which a pair of stilettos could have easily made up the difference in height on the runway. An Afro of copper-tinted, 4-inch corkscrew curls replaced long wavy hair that once hung like liquefied ebony. Hazel eyes that once sparkled like glowing amber through thick lashes on a canvas of syrupy smooth skin were now hardened.

Hakeem looked at the phone again as it rang a fourth and final ring, realizing he owed his mother a call. He made contact at least once a week to make sure she was okay. Just one call per week was all that could be managed. Anything more was like trying to swallow a bottle of B-Complex pills without water.

Unlocking the phone, he tapped the phone symbol next to Rosalyn's name. She answered on the second ring. "Hello."

"It's Hakeem, Ma," he said with a bit of annoyance. She seldom caught onto his voice. She said it always sounded different. It was a pathetic excuse. The octaves in which he spoke should have been recognizable.

"Oh…Hi. How are you?" The usual somber tone was in her voice.

"I'm okay. I saw that you called."

"Yeah. I called to let you know that your grandfather made me upset."

"Okay," he said carefully, irritation stirring. "What happened?"

"I asked for some money to pay a bill, and he told me that he couldn't send any until the first of the month. Asking me what I needed the money for."

Seriously? Hakeem wrestled with himself to hold his tongue. *Anyone who loaned money possessed the right to ask how the money was going to be spent.*

"Do you have some money to send me?"

"No, I don't," he replied crisply. "I'm barely able to pay my bills." It was the truth. But he would have denied her the money even if he had it. Rosalyn loved money—her own and everyone else's she could access.

Hakeem would never forget what Evelyn divulged about Rosalyn receiving settlement money from a car accident 12 years ago. The story went that she was riding along with her boyfriend and someone hit them from behind, wrecking the vehicle. Rosalyn suffered a spinal injury and a ruptured disk. When the case settled, she cleared at least $75,000 from the insurance claim. Meanwhile, he was attending college with Joseph and Evelyn supplementing his income.

During a particular visit to Minneapolis, they learned he used public transportation to commute to school and work—a challenge during the frigid winters. Evelyn had asked Rosalyn whether she intended to provide financial assistance while he attended school and struggled to maintain employment. Rosalyn flatly stated that she had done enough. Whatever six and a half years' worth of monetary contributions totaled, paled in comparison to the financial support her parents provided her son from birth to present. Fortunately, Joseph and Evelyn continued to support their grandson. They bought Hakeem his first and second car at 22 and 24 when a driver caused him to run off the highway.

Evelyn withheld Rosalyn's response from Hakeem for several years. By then, Rosalyn was asking them for money. She had bought herself new furniture and clothes, and jewelry for her friends but sent no money to him. Evelyn revealed that someone stole several material items that Rosalyn purchased with the settlement money. Her drug-addict boyfriend filched her debit card and cleared the account, robbing the children of financial resources. Rosalyn eventually found herself back where she started—ground zero.

You won't be getting a dime from me!

"Oh, okay. I thought you were making the big bucks down there?"

"Who told you that?" *And what did it matter how ever much I made?*

"I thought you said you had some executive job."

"I don't know where you got that from. I told you I'm a project manager for a company. They don't pay me enough, considering all that I—," he went silent. This conversation wasn't about him or the job. It was about Rosalyn and her selfishness. He redirected the conversation to her main reason for calling.

"Daddy is on a fixed income just like you," Hakeem began. He addressed Joseph as "Daddy" because Joseph assumed the role that Earl should have fulfilled. "So, I don't understand how you can be mad. Money doesn't flow in abundance for him."

"Yeah, I know. I just don't like Dad talking to me like I'm a child."

Rosalyn had returned from Clinton City, North Carolina over a month ago. As was the norm, she took advantage of every opportunity to shop at Joseph's expense. Rosalyn claimed she needed items that were unavailable in Philadelphia. How was it more difficult to find anything in a larger city than a country town?

Hakeem knew that Rosalyn told lies to get what she wanted. She needed money to pay bills before. But when she spoke to Joseph and him during separate conversations, the amount of the bill changed. He wanted to tell Joseph that she lied and did so the second time around. With Joseph in his late seventies and Evelyn deceased 6 years, he was none the wiser. Joseph was grateful whenever any of his children came home. Only two of the three were alive.

Hakeem believed that Rosalyn used his grandfather. Her behavior irritated him. When the odds stacked, she seized the chance to refresh Joseph's memory that alongside Evelyn, they sacrificed everything for her brothers. Despite Rosalyn's accusations, Joseph responded positively. Feeling guilty for the years of neglect that she experienced, he obliged her.

Nonetheless, Hakeem believed that if Evelyn were alive, she would have shut down Rosalyn's antics. He listened to her complaints, void of sympathy. Adults who were habitually dependent upon their parents were sometimes, treated like children, as the parents were not confident in their ability to care for themselves. Hakeem was a living witness. Whenever he needed money, Joseph and Evelyn expressed concern and wanted insight into his quality of life.

"It's to be expected," Hakeem said. "You asked Daddy for money when he doesn't have it to give, and you got upset. Call the people back and make payment arrangements."

"I guess you're right. I didn't think about doing that."

Hakeem looked at the phone. Now was not the time to listen to Rosalyn's issues and he was uninterested in making time. He was trying to make sense of his own troubles and figure out how to resolve each problem. He wondered how much longer she was going to talk.

"How long do you think they will give me to pay?"

"It depends on when the bill is due. Be sure to ask when you call."

"Where's Layla?" he asked, steering the conversation onto another subject.

"She's somewhere…probably with her boyfriend. I don't know. But I know one thing….she needs to find her own place. Every time Layla comes in here, she has something new. She's working and her boyfriend gives her money."

Layla's boyfriend probably did give her money. So what?

"Okay." He wanted to refrain from commenting. Rosalyn was being her same ol' self.

"Layla should be paying me more to stay here," she persisted.

"How much is she paying?" Hakeem felt an explosion coming on and was not going to be able to remain silent too much longer.

"A hundred dollars."

"Is that what you two agreed upon?" he asked bluntly.

"Yeah….we did."

"Sooo…was there an increase in your rent?"

"No. It's still the same."

"Then what's the problem, if Layla is paying her share of the rent based upon the agreement you two have?" He asked the bold questions for Rosalyn to see her own selfish ignorance.

"If she can bring in new clothes and purses, she can get her own place!"

Same ol' Rosalyn. She hadn't changed. Every time I try to have a cordial conversation, her selfish character surfaces somehow.

"And you wonder why you have problems with your children?" He seldom initiated contact with Layla. They usually spoke on major holidays and birthdays. Though as the eldest, he felt the need to defend her from Rosalyn. He had no problems putting their mother in her place.

"This is my house! If ya'll don't like my rules, then get out!" Rosalyn flared.

"That's fine," he said, unfazed by her temper. He had dealt with it before. "But say what you mean and mean what you say. You told Layla that she only had to pay $100. Now you want her to pay more because she brings in a new purse or clothes?"

Hakeem smoldered. He paid rent too. The amount remained the same, month after month, regardless of the amount of merchandise brought home. Rosalyn was living in a four-bedroom apartment, subsidized by Philadelphia Public Housing. She was not even paying market rent! He thought it an impertinent act to request Layla to pay more than the initial agreement.

"Well…if Layla's doing it like that, she can find herself an apartment. I'm sure she'll be alright."

Damn! She is selfish as she ever was. It was time to wrap up the conversation, lest it continued going downhill. He was full of ammunition. "I have to get ready for work tomorrow. I will talk to you later."

"Okay. Have a good night." Rosalyn was unbothered.

Hakeem looked at the phone pissed. *Whatever.* It was time to take the medication. If he didn't, the anxiety was going to cause a panic attack.

≈≈≈≈≈≈≈

As far as Hakeem could remember, the mother-son relationship existing between Rosalyn and himself struggled. There were no memories worthy of being suspended in picture frames. Unlike other teenagers in the Projects, he was a late-bloomer—not athletic or interested in sports and did not exhibit the masculine traits of male peers, and sexually inactive with females. In the projects, it was a common occurrence for teenagers to lose their virginity before the age of sixteen. When you lived in those environments, life was unfiltered and raw.

Rosalyn perceived the delayed development as the onset of homosexuality. Rosalyn kept vigil because she grew up watching her gay brother, Daryle. According to Rosalyn, Hakeem exhibited similar patterns of behavior. She disliked Daryle's lifestyle choices and was adamant that it would not manifest in her son. There was no love lost between the two siblings. Their rivalry was as intense as the contention existing between mother and son.

Whether Rosalyn believed it or not, her parenting style played a role in Hakeem's development. She was also a hypocrite. In her bedroom, she kept pornographic magazines and VHS tapes of naked gay men. Hakeem had seen Rosalyn and her girlfriends watching the films as they smoked marijuana. He wasn't a stranger to pornography anyway since her boyfriend, Arnold maintained a collection of heterosexual-oriented adult movies.

Left alone in the apartment one day, washing and putting away everyone's laundry, a 12-year-old Hakeem located Rosalyn's stash hidden behind dresses hung in her closet. From the moment of discovery, every time he was left alone in the apartment for an extended period of time, he ventured into her room and skimmed the magazines and films. On other occasions, he switched to straight porn, reviewing the same scenes. Fascination took control to the extent that he could not stop looking at pornography. It was six years into the future when he masturbated for the first time. Definitively, the need to experience immediate sexual gratification did not fuel his viewing habits. Something from the past contributed to his inappropriate and immature behavior.

Hakeem never understood how Rosalyn knew of his tampering with the magazines. Perhaps he forgot to close a magazine after viewing it. Maybe Rosalyn had a photographic memory of how she left the magazines in the closet. Nevertheless, she summoned him into her bedroom on a Saturday morning and proceeded to interrogate. She wanted to know why he looked at the magazines to which he was void of a providing a satisfactory explanation. He had been curious about the books and she wanted to know the reason. Rosalyn asked whether someone showed him naked pictures before. She wanted to know if someone touched or did something inappropriate to him. If so, who was it? She was relentless, asking a series of questions. Hakeem answered as much as possible.

There was Cousin Byron who was in his late-twenties and had lived in the basement of Joseph and Evelyn's house for a year. Hakeem was around the age of seven when Byron began fondling him and on one occasion, exposed himself while babysitting. He then modeled Byron's behavior and began fondling a girl around the same age in school. To Hakeem's knowledge, the incidents went unreported. Had the girl told someone, the sexual abuse he experienced might have been exposed much sooner.

In contrast to Byron, Daryle's methods were subtle. He seized opportunities to whoop Hakeem undressed to touch him inappropriately. Daryle's perversions persisted until he moved out of state for employment.

There was no doubt in Rosalyn's mind concerning the truth of Hakeem's confession. She claimed to have witnessed Daryle molesting children when they were young, but no one reported the instances. As for Byron, family members had suspected his dual sexuality over the years. Enraged, Rosalyn phoned Joseph and Evelyn, armed with the knowledge of what happened to Hakeem in the eleven years of living in their custody. They were genuinely ignorant of the molestation he endured. Joseph worked late hours and Evelyn juggled various jobs.

It was not uncommon for Hakeem to be left in the care of different babysitters. Sometimes a relative assumed the duty and other times, a family friend. A female cousin, who married into the family tended to prod his buttocks with a flyswatter while he napped on her living room floor. Hakeem, however, only told Rosalyn about Byron and Daryle. Hakeem did not mention the female cousin because he wasn't sure if it really mattered what she had done. Notably, mistaking traumatic and inappropriate situations as ordinary events is common among the abused.

Hakeem was a problem child and everywhere he went, he misbehaved. Unfortunately, the abusers exploited his misconduct to perpetrate their unnatural appetites. This is how abusers operated and were able to persistently cause psychological and physiological damage. Thus, Hakeem withheld the information from Joseph and Evelyn because of guilt and shame. He knew that if he told what happened, they would also learn of his misbehavior while in the care of those they trusted. Like Rosalyn, Evelyn was too much of an authoritarian, which factored into Hakeem moving to Philadelphia. There had been strife between grandma and grandson too.

Rosalyn arranged for Hakeem to receive professional counseling. Both Byron and Daryle denied the accusations, as there was no tangible, physiological proof of their tampering. No one filed a police report because the process was not pursued. Moreover, Hakeem thought that following through would satisfy Rosalyn's resentment of Daryle, and that was not his objective. She was no more sympathetic after learning about the abuse than before. Thus, he fought back through obstinacy whenever possible. She could threaten and beat him all that she dared, but he would decide when compliance was necessary.

Although counseling was a step in the right direction, Rosalyn turned most sessions into disasters. She dominated the conversations and on more than one occasion, the therapist asked her to leave the room to focus more on Hakeem. During a particular session, the therapist asked him whether he liked boys or girls—a question that Hakeem failed to answer quickly. Rosalyn bombarded the conversation with her declarations. When Hakeem spoke finally, saying that he liked girls, her eyes narrowed and jaws tightened. She remained quiet until someone said something that did not align with her demands. Rosalyn was intransigent. No son of hers was going to be gay, and she voiced her stance on the subject in the therapist's presence. Concluding that counseling was not propelling Hakeem towards the path she hoped, Rosalyn canceled therapy altogether.

Rosalyn did not know the extent of Hakeem's fascination with girls. In fact, he kept her in the dark about his feelings. She was a bully and he disliked bullies. There was no shortage of intimidators. Hakeem felt that mentioning anything about his interests would be a demonstration of proving himself to Rosalyn. His defiant nature refused to oblige her.

She would never know that a female cousin, two years his senior, introduced him and two girls who were sisters, to a game of seven-eleven. The sisters, Yolanda and Lisa, were members of the religious congregation where Joseph and Evelyn worshipped. Yolanda and Hakeem were of the same age, and Lisa was their junior. The game seven-eleven, derived its' name from the enactment of "seven pumps and eleven humps". There in the basement of his grandparents' house, Hakeem, the cousin and two sisters secretly played the game. Subsequently, whenever Yolanda and Lisa visited, the three of them returned to the basement to play seven-eleven.

In the fifth-grade, during a class party, Hakeem kissed a girl after dancing to reggae music. By this time, he was living in Philadelphia. He might have pursued her further had she not lost interest. She said that he was weird in front of classmates. Embarrassed and shunned, Hakeem believed her opinion partially correct. He was insecure and introverted compared to peers.

Despite Rosalyn's efforts, Hakeem was for the majority, sexually inactive as a teenager. One day, she threatened to pay a drug addict living in the building to rape him. She continued to rage that none of her children were growing up to be "fa---ts." When she saw his defiance, she viciously taunted, "at least I have another son that I know won't be gay." She even suggested that he might molest his siblings. It was her ignorance and hatred for Daryle that motivated the verbal abuse. All gay people are not molesters, and all molesters are not gay.

Rosalyn was more concerned with protecting her pride than her children's welfare. She cared about preventing Hakeem from being gay, even if the desired outcome required the use of coercive force. Rosalyn was too ignorant to see that in many ways, she was no better than the molesters. Then she would have understood his dislike of her. Hakeem once confided in a female friend that he hated Rosalyn. When word circled back, she was furious, called him evil and ungrateful, and threatened to throw him onto the street.

There were many times when Rosalyn called Hakeem evil. She claimed that a female friend saw darkness in him and advised her to be wary. Rosalyn did not try to ascertain the true nature of the alleged darkness. Instead, she took her friend's warning and assumed the extreme. A concerned and selfless mother could make the connection between the negative experiences her child endured and the behavior they exhibited. Whatever connections Rosalyn made, her subsequent actions were more destructive than supportive.

≈≈≈≈≈≈≈

Child molestation is not limited to penetration or complete sexual gratification. Sexual petting or fondling of the private areas, exposure to nudity, or sexual activity (e.g., pornography), are also examples of molestation. Understanding this assertion is important, because in the context of consensual sex between adults, the activities aforementioned are usually purposed for sexual stimulation. Thus, sexually stimulating children is inappropriate.

Hakeem remembered the sensations that coursed through his body when touched inappropriately. Any part of the body that is struck with sufficient force feels pain. When the body is touched or caressed, senses are awakened and stimulated. Each instance describes auto-physiological responses that people exhibit minimal conscious control. Most notably, children experience greater difficulty controlling their emotions and physical reactions. They become proficient at demonstrating self-control through effective learning and reinforcement strategies, which produce healthy thoughts and behaviors. Without healthy relationships and proper instruction, they develop self-destructive habits.

A part of Hakeem knew that the attentions of his perpetrators were wrong. But limited intelligence prevented him from making the correct attributions. It was this internal confusion that he kept secret—a silence that would motivate him to make counterproductive decisions in adulthood. In hindsight, he realized it was his undoing. Perhaps if given quality emotional support, he could have managed his feelings effectively. Children are simply ill-equipped to manage the emotions that accompany intimacy and sexual activity. Presentation without adequate education and appropriate interventions can negatively affect a youth's development into adulthood.

Joseph and Evelyn exposed Hakeem to Biblical doctrine at an early age. It was the Biblical teachings that partly contributed to his shame. Consistent with Christian faith, their religion taught abstinence until marriage—an ideology proselytized by devoted followers, who in turn, passed the teachings onto their offspring. Advocacy for abstinence and marriage were sound advice because once experienced, opened were the gates of emotion and sensuality that accompanied sexual activity.

Hakeem remembered the play-girlfriends from daycare through fourth-grade. There was no doubt in his mind that at some point, he was interested in girls. Unfortunately, abuse derailed him in the natural course of development. Blame should not be assigned to a child for the confusion that moderates their feelings by virtue of abuse. He lacked understanding regarding what was happening to him as a child. It was a difficult enough task for some adults to sort through their thoughts and feelings. Rosalyn was not the type of parent who tried to understand situations from someone else's perspective. Terminating the counseling sessions was proof of her character. She was then and now, a person with tunnel vision.

≈≈≈≈≈≈≈

Hakeem found solace in comic-books, video-games, and anime—all favorite pastimes. These interests always interfered with his academic performance. Incomplete and missing homework reflected the amount of focus allocated to academia. At least one "F" or "D" appeared on the report cards. In response, Rosalyn methodically confiscated all leisure reading materials and games, supplementing the habitual practice with punishment for varying lengths of time. But her efforts failed to deter his deviance. He acquired more comics from a cousin and classmates.

When teachers caught him reading comics instead of completing class assignments, they confiscated the distractions. They returned the comics to Rosalyn during parent-teacher meetings. Hakeem's disruptive behavior motivated the teachers to send home daily progress-reports. Their commentary expressed his potential for success hindered by constant failure to demonstrate intellectual aptitude and focus.

Hakeem possessed a knack for art and design—a subject that he excelled. Teachers complimented his artistic talents. In third-grade, he replicated a paper doll from a book, drawing the female figure and its clothes. When he took the paper doll to school, a female classmate stole the work and denied committing the act. Hakeem strongly believed she was responsible for the doll's disappearance and confronted her. Angered, he trimmed a portion of her blonde hair, motivating her confession but not cooperation in returning the doll. Nonetheless, Joseph and Evelyn had to meet with the principal and the girl's parents for mediation. Hakeem narrowly missed expulsion for his behavior and despite the situation, remained unapologetic. The girl never should have stolen his paper doll as far as he was concerned.

Infatuation with dolls continued into the teenage years, much to Rosalyn's chagrin. Hakeem found the fashions most intriguing and consistently demonstrated a talent in the area of design. Much to his disappointment, little support was provided at home.

In the sixth grade, Hakeem risked expulsion again for igniting a fire behind the church next to the school. Earlier that morning, he found a lighter on the ground and tucked it in his pocket. Following dismissal, he led two classmates behind the church where they discovered a box of donated shoes. There in the ally, Hakeem ignited a sheet of notebook paper that a draft of wind quickly extinguished. Persistent, he relit the paper. Upon hearing the sound of a door opening around the corner, he tossed the paper into the shoebox, and the three fled onto the street. Unintentionally, the discarded sheet of paper continued to smolder and set the entire box ablaze. Less than a block away, he happened to turn around and saw smoke billowing into the sky as a priest tried to fan the flames. The flames could not be subdued and burned the priest's hand.

Hakeem was unsure how the school principal knew of his involvement with the fire. It was possible that one of his classmates reported the incident, even though he had coached them on what to say in preparation for questioning. Confession only came forth in the presence of Rosalyn, the school principal, and priest when his alibis were disproved. He was suspended for five days.

At fourteen, he envisioned going to high school for fashion design. However, this aspiration was not part of Rosalyn's career plans for him. She attempted to circumvent him from selecting high schools that he preferred. She wanted him to go to school for computers, which he steadfastly refused. He determined that his career choices were not hers to make. He thought computer programming was boring and this attitude persisted throughout maturity. He could not imagine sitting in front of a computer, entering codes for the rest of his life. Thus, he shortlisted the schools he preferred anyway—the majority being performing arts-based and presented the selections to Rosalyn as the deadline for enrollment loomed close. His strategy in conjunction with Rosalyn's personal struggles kept her distracted, and successfully enabled him to enroll in a school of his choosing. The school eventually proved disappointing. Its art-focused curriculum fell short of his expectations.

Rosalyn maintained a critical opinion regarding Hakeem's singing ability. As with most young males, vocal ranges can reach the soprano register. At the onset of puberty and occurring throughout the process of maturation, the larynx grows and the male's voice changes—usually deepening considerably in comparison to females. While neighborhood friends advised her to place him in a performing arts school, she was convinced that his voice would eventually change. She was certain he would lose vocal range—a belief that never materialized and exposed the source of her unwillingness to be supportive. Rosalyn once aspired to be a singer herself. The reason that she did not become a singer was apparent. Life choices and substance abuse hindered her from staying the course to achieving the goal.

If Rosalyn ever considered whether her demands were destructive, it would have been surprising. From the age of eleven to sixteen and a half, Hakeem missed many of the pleasures of growing up as a teenager. Outside of school, he was home fulfilling motherly household duties— cooking, cleaning, and babysitting his siblings. He was fifteen when he began to understand the severity of her drug problem, which started out as marijuana and transitioned to cocaine use. The addiction destabilized quality of life in the apartment as constant bickering between Arnold and Rosalyn became a characteristic of the environment. Hakeem sometimes awakened to late night arguments concerning her addiction. She was in denial about being dependent upon the drugs.

It seemed that every situation contained conflict. Summer jobs were discouraged because Rosalyn feared the additional income would interfere with her public assistance. A family friend advised her that Hakeem was approaching the age to start working at least a few hours after school. Rosalyn stated that he could not draw income without her having money. Joseph sporadically mailed him allowances, as he understood their living situation. Rosalyn tried hard to intercept the funds, claiming that she needed supplies for the household. Hakeem undermined those efforts constantly, spending the money on everything he could to prevent her from gaining access. His sidestepping infuriated her because she could not break him. She then resorted to threats of tossing him onto the streets.

Where Hakeem could not acquire objects through honest means, he pilfered. Twice, he impulsively stole $20 from Rosalyn's purse to buy trinkets and snacks. She initially thought Arnold took the money and accused him, triggering an intense argument. Rather than deliver a beating when she learned Hakeem was responsible, she filled the kitchen sink with cold water. She then plunged his face repeatedly to teach him a lesson, all the while insulting him with profanity.

Hakeem acknowledged his guilt and over time, something changed within. He stopped stealing—a behavior change that wasn't necessarily because of Rosalyn's chosen method of discipline. An important connection was made. He began to understand how his actions created ripple-effects. Rosalyn and Arnold were already feuding about other issues. Stealing only widened the rift in their unraveling relationship.

As Rosalyn mistreated Hakeem, Arnold victimized her. On two memorable occasions, Hakeem intervened. The first time he defended Rosalyn occurred when Arnold tried to force her head through iron grates that secured the kitchen windows. While playing video-games with cousins in his bedroom, he overheard Rosalyn telling Arnold that she was leaving him. She was upset because he had not been home in several days. Arnold disappeared frequently to entertain other women. Their angry voices made Hakeem tense and distracted him from playing the game. His stomach began to churn from anxiety. Having witnessed arguments between other family members as a child, he could sense when violence was imminent.

Victims of repeated abuse acquire sensitivity to impending trouble and danger. It is probable that the reaction develops from the victim's ability to recognize patterns in a perpetrator's behavior, in addition to changes in their social environment. The victim braced himself or herself if unable to escape as they feared the worst to occur.

When Hakeem heard Rosalyn cry out, he rushed into the living-room to see what happened. He saw her stepping back from the metal bars that secured the windows. Arnold had tried to force her head through the bars! Hakeem did not know if she was in pain, but shock was evident on her face, and he became instantly angry. No matter the rancor between Rosalyn and himself, no one was going to hurt his mother if he could stop the perpetrator.

Rosalyn and Arnold turned to see him enter the room. Arnold taunted, "what you gonna' do, punk?" he asked.

"Why don't you come and find out?" Hakeem had replied.

Confident that he could take Hakeem, Arnold accepted the challenge. There was a wall that partitioned the living-room from the kitchen area, allowing entrance from opposite ends. Hakeem walked around it to get a closer look at Rosalyn. Arnold entered the kitchen from the other side. A knife lay in the sink and he thought to use it just as Arnold rushed forward. In a flurry of fists, a soon-to-be fifteen Hakeem proved to be a match. Rosalyn called the police but forwent pressing charges against Arnold. Arnold, however, told her that Hakeem needed to go.

Two days later, Hakeem came home from school and Rosalyn told him that it was best to apologize to Arnold for being disrespectful. Knowing little concerning the dynamics of intimate relationships, Hakeem thought she was stupid for giving such advice. He expressed an apology in a letter to appease them, but genuineness was absent from the heart. It was then that he perceived Rosalyn as a weak woman. She was emotionally and financially dependent upon Arnold, who used her vulnerabilities to his advantage.

Perpetrators are most effective when their victims are impotent.

The second confrontation between Hakeem and Arnold ensued when Rosalyn and the children returned home late one night. They had visited family in a neighboring city. Motivated by the guilt of his own infidelity, Arnold believed that she was cheating on him. An argument erupted in her bedroom. Arnold proceeded to choke Rosalyn and she wrestled with him, trying to reach the phone to call the police. He snatched the phone from her, hitting her in the face in the process.

Again, Hakeem intervened in their squabble and slammed a glass ashtray into the nape of Arnold's neck. The blow stunned Arnold long enough for Rosalyn to escape his grasp. Hakeem fled from the apartment in confusion and Arnold labored after him. Arnold cornered him in the hallway and they fought. The brawl ended with Arnold breaking his hand. Hakeem had dodged a blow aimed for his face, causing Arnold to strike a brick wall instead. It was the last time he ever witnessed or heard about Arnold physically attacking Rosalyn. While he didn't love her as a son should a mother, he wasn't an advocate of the abuse she suffered. Hakeem didn't believe a man should assault a woman or the reverse. But who was he and what did his opinion matter in their relationship?

Hakeem continued attending to household duties as expected of him while growing increasingly resentful of his siblings, who did not share in the responsibilities. In many ways, he identified with the fairytale character, Cinderella—cleaning as siblings leisured. They were not forced to clean behind themselves. Rosalyn and Arnold excused their behavior as being the nature of children and did nothing to rectify the situation. The irony in Rosalyn's stance was that she learned how to do household chores as a child. How else do children learn to be functional, self-sufficient adults if parents do not teach them principles of responsibility during early stages of development? No. Rosalyn and Arnold displayed favoritism, which embittered Hakeem further.

One day, at wit's end, Hakeem chastised Layla when she unloaded all of the toys from the chest after he packed them moments earlier. He grabbed her by an arm and was about to force her to collect all the toys when Rosalyn intervened. She said that Layla didn't have to listen to him. Angry, Hakeem muttered under his breath and Rosalyn overheard. She advanced upon him with the intent to unleash a strike. A struggling match began and terminated when he caught her fist and pushed her away.

According to Rosalyn's later account, a dangerous glint appeared in his eyes motivated her to send him to live with Earl. Now sixteen, Hakeem was glad. An opportunity for escape had finally arrived. To hell with them all, he thought at the time.

Arnold drove the family to the Greyhound Bus Station. Hakeem remembered the day as if it had recently transpired. Gripped in his fist was Rosalyn's hard blue, 1970's styled suitcase to be loaded onto the undercarriage of the bus. He wore a long-sleeve orange and blue plaid shirt with navy blue chinos, and rust-colored square-toed cowboy boots. Overcast obscured the sun, allowing the dampness of the mid-morning air to linger. Despite the weather conditions, he was on the brink of bursting with the joy of freedom. Each step taken towards the bus distanced him farther from Rosalyn and the life he knew. As the bus departed the station, he vowed that if he ever moved back to Philly, it would be into his own residence. She could not live with him.

The bus exited the terminal. Hakeem looked not once out of the window at the family being left behind. Intent on putting the past behind, he affixed his eyes to the back of the driver's head, ready to start the new chapter.

≈≈≈≈≈≈≈

There seems to be a consensus among experts that sexual abuse is a learned behavior. This chapter illustrates this theory through the narrative of young Hakeem fondling a female classmate. Speculatively, it is unlikely that a child will display sexual behavior without prior visual and/or physical exposure. Sources of exposure may include any or all of the following events:

1) molestation or rape; 2) observation of others engaging in sexual activity within a home environment; and/or 3) viewership of sexual activity on the television and elsewhere.

If a child is exhibiting sexual behaviors, then they should be closely observed and evaluated. In certain cases it may also be necessary to involve child protective services. The main objective of these recommendations is to provide traumatized or victimized children with interventions to prevent harm to themselves and others. We should not want children imprinting sexually deviant behaviors onto others or develop psychological abnormalities.

SEESAWS AND MERRY-GO-ROUNDS

SEESAWS AND MERRY-GO-ROUNDS

Whether life takes a person up and down or round and round, it's going to be a dynamic ride.

Rosalyn's drug addiction weathered the relationship with her children. Addictions gratified the thoughts and emotions that funneled into the habit, creating a negative feedback loop. Substance abuse temporarily neutralized destructive thoughts and emotions through stimulation of the pleasure center in the brain.

Before Rosalyn succumbed to dependence, she had at the very least, established a motherly connection with the younger children. Hakeem perceived that Arnold living in the household attributed to some of her affections towards the children. She had even remarked during a verbal exchange that his siblings were 'planned.' It was an insensitive retort because Earl was a married man, who shirked his responsibility. Earl's absence adversely affected Hakeem. But what married man planned to sire kids with a woman other than his wife?

There are households where a mother or father extends preferential treatment towards certain offspring when biological co-parentage exists within the home. The child who is the product of a previous intimate relationship or marriage, is sometimes the outcast. Parents who underestimate their children's ability to perceive favoritism when it occurs, are responsible for the resentment the children later display.

Arnold denigrated Rosalyn and her addiction to cajole the affections of the children. He successfully distracted them from focusing on his abusive history, infidelity, drug dealings, and willful denial of being their biological father. Only when a court order settled a child support dispute between Rosalyn and him after their separation, he could no longer deny being the biological father of all three children. Layla, Katrina, nor Tyrell faulted him as Rosalyn was the perceived enemy. A combination of resentment and gratification hindered their ability to perceive the truth.

Hakeem believed that his siblings were unjustified in the way they treated Rosalyn. When the children were sick, it was Rosalyn who rushed them to the hospital in the middle of the night while their father shared someone else's pillow. And while it was true that she neglected them, there was no comparison to the pain and suffering she caused her eldest son. Even as young adults, they expected her to cater to their desires, whereas Hakeem disassociated and tried to sustain himself.

Hakeem also believed that Layla chose to live with Rosalyn because of a lack in quality alternatives. Questionable traffic through Arnold's house was constant, and Layla's boyfriend struggled with providing stable living arrangements. As a server, she could not afford an apartment independently. Thus, living with Rosalyn was the best option among the choices given.

Katrina was fortunate to realize her dreams fresh out of college. She obtained certification in culinary arts and opened a small bistro in Newark with her husband. She was accomplished indeed.

Hakeem noticed that Rosalyn treaded carefully whenever Katrina was the topic of conversation. Katrina had achieved more than the family ever dreamed and for all everyone knew, she was happy. Hakeem had heard she was pregnant with her first child but nothing further. Katrina rarely visited Rosalyn or Philly—a tendency she shared with him.

Of the siblings, Tyrell communicated with Arnold the most. As soon as Tyrell could, he moved into a one-bedroom apartment with his girlfriend. Rosalyn had visited the apartment months after he moved and found the place disorganized. Tyrell was the least responsible, and Arnold did not encourage him to go to college or obtain a decent job. He was uneducated himself. Tyrell was too superficial to see that his father meant him more harm than good. As long as Arnold unconditionally filled the gap between his dependence and independence without catapulting him into responsibility, Tyrell would mature at a slower pace.

As the eldest, Hakeem wanted to give Layla and Tyrell advice where their parents had failed. He always dismissed the idea because his communications were inconsistent. Who was he to provide long-distance counsel to any of the siblings? Getting involved also meant being caught up in the tug-of-war between Rosalyn and Arnold, as they fought for influential control over the children. Hakeem had no power over them and wanted to avoid reigniting conflict with Arnold. Their last argument pertained to Tyrell not wanting to go to school.

Rosalyn was visiting Joseph at the time, and Hakeem drove up from Atlanta. He heard her arguing with Arnold over the phone regarding Tyrell. Arnold told Rosalyn that there was nothing wrong with Tyrell, 16, going to parties. His opinion held despite knowing that Tyrell's academic performance steadily declined.

When Arnold became disrespectful towards Rosalyn, Hakeem interrupted the conversation. He did not give a rat's butt about Arnold, and no one was going to be uncivil on Joseph's telephone line. Arnold insulted him for entering the argument. Hakeem returned every gibe. This was one of his main grievances with particularly Layla and Tyrell—they never defended Rosalyn from Arnold whose character was just as invidious. They were habitually biased, and their attitude peeved him.

Tyrell moved into Arnold's house after the argument. Two months later, he was answering Rosalyn's house phone. He had moved back home. Chaos and filth eroded the desire to live with Arnold. Tyrell might never admit it, but deep down, he knew that pertaining to safety, Rosalyn's household was the better choice.

≈≈≈≈≈≈≈

Frequent were the moments when Hakeem's thoughts were overwhelming. Their incessant noise permeated the dark room in which he stood. He would rather be elsewhere. *Not now.* He scrolled through the contact list on his phone and located Ian's number. They had not spoken in two weeks. When Ian was available, he answered on the first ring. Real friends recognized patterns in each other's behavior.

"Hakeem! What's goin' on, brotha?" Ian asked.

"Not much. Family gettin' on my nerves." Exchanges of pleasantries were unnecessary. Neither of them exhibited a habit of making flowery speeches.

Ian chuckled. "Bruh, let's not even go there. I'm dealin' with Connie and her kids right now."

It sounded like it. Somewhere in Ian's apartment, a television blared at top volume. Hakeem heard occasional laughter.

"Wow!" He had met Ian's younger sister, Connie. She was the opposite of her older brother. Ian was a street-smart intellectual while Connie was flighty and boisterous. Some might have classified her as a loud-mouthed Black woman.

Ian was from the Newark, New Jersey and had moved to Minneapolis to attend Metropolitan State University to double-major in accounting and business. As a pastor's son, he was also active in ministry. It was in a physics course where friendship began. They both lacked proficiency in the subject and decided to team up as study partners. Ian's spiritual grounding shone forth and Hakeem developed a greater interest in church.

"Yeah, man. That's why we ain't talked in a minute. Been helpin' Connie since her baby-daddy bounced."

"Where are the kids?"

"Here until she gets off work. She's been comin' by to swoop them up after work later and later. Bet not be another dude, cause she can take em' with her. I love my nieces and nephews, but I'm not gonna help their momma layup."

Hakeem laughed. Ian was real talk. "How is Jessica?"

"Man, we just split up. She patched things up with her ex once he got out of prison."

"Sorry to hear that."

"Yeah, yeah, I'm alright. God showed me that the end was comin' a while back. I was the one who continued to hold on instead of letting go. Actually, I'm kinda glad though, cause I've gotten off track messin' around with her."

Ian's perspectives were refreshing. Sometimes, Hakeem almost felt compelled to express his sentiments. Ian was a confident heterosexual, who was unaffected by people's sexual preferences but no less observant.

It was how Hakeem referred to random men in his personal life that caught Ian's attention. Rather than lie and identify his male associations as female, Hakeem referred to them as "they". During a study session, Ian directly asked if "they" referred to a man. Hakeem admitted the truth, expecting their friendship to end. But Ian never changed.

"It's a learning lesson for sure."

"Definitely. So, what's dis about your family?"

"My mother and sister are trippin'. She's pissed because she wants my sister to pay more rent."

"Sounds like you and me in the same boat. Always somethin' ain't it?"

"Yes, sir."

"What are you gonna' do?"

"I don't know. I'm thinking about convincing my sister to find her own place."

"And which sister is this?"

"Layla."

"How old is she?"

"Twenty-three."

"Oh, yeah. It's time then. She's old enough to fly the coop. So why the uncertainty?"

"Cause I don't speak to any of them regularly."

"Okay, but you're still the oldest. You know your mother more than they do. It's not like you're giving your siblings ultimatums. You're giving them advice, which is to their benefit. Not yours."

"Right, right."

"You know what?"—Ian paused—"Sometimes when I look at my nieces and nephews, I wonder about how my children will be. Some of these younger generations grow up with a sense of entitlement and are irresponsible. My nieces and nephews are not exceptions. They are unappreciative no matter what their parents do for them."

"Your nieces' and nephews' behaviors are in part, products of how they're raised. I received few extras from my grandparents without having to earn them. So now, I rarely expect anything to be free. When responsibility is instilled in a child's development, I believe their sense of entitlement can be modified."

Layla, Katrina, and Tyrell weren't raised under the principal that they had to earn anything. Whatever they wanted, Rosalyn and Arnold unconditionally gratified them. Hakeem was uncertain whether their actions were reflective of inexperience as parents or beliefs that giving children what they wanted yielded positive results, or a combination of both.

"Makes sense. So, what would you propose?"

"Teach them the reality of life—that living has costs. Show them how to be responsible at an early age. As children get older, it becomes harder to mold them."

"Man, go on and have that conversation with your sister. If she can't handle it, then too bad. She's an adult now."

"Yeah, that's the problem. Layla knows she's an adult." Hakeem sighed. First, he would meditate on his approach to not come across as authoritative. Rosalyn was already doing a good job of being a dictator. The worst thing he could do was sound like their mother.

"You got that, Hakeem. Truth is truth, no matter who it comes from."

Truth dissipated illusions woven by lies and deception. People could choose either to deal with the truth or a lie, but there was no in-between because both yield consequences.

"How is your business going?" Hakeem asked.

"It's going....still building my client base. I'm teaching part-time at my father's church."

"About time," Hakeem laughed.

"Yeah, well. I've ran away from it long enough. But the church is my father's vision. Computer consulting is mine."

"I'm still trying to figure out my destiny. I've started seeing a therapist."

"What! When?"

"About a week ago."

"Are things really that bad at the job?"

"Something is always going on. My reasons for seeing a therapist have to do with some other things." He had disclosed much to Ian, including the abuse but not everything. Some things he doubted he'd ever tell. "She gave me advice similar to yours—about me changing my expectations."

"Uh-huh. Your therapist is a female?"

"Is that all you got from what I just said?"

"Is she pretty?"—Ian laughingly asked.

"In an older, sophisticated way."

"How old you think?"

"Mid to late forties maybe."

"Okay. I know Georgia has no shortage of fine Black women. You can't miss em'."

Hakeem made the same observations once relocated to Atlanta. The city teemed with beautiful, educated Black women and he did not possess the courage to step up. He had to get his mind right.

"You right. Thinkin' about coming here and marrying one of them?"

"Not now. Gotta cultivate the business before I make any more major decisions. What did you think about the therapist's advice?"

"She's right. I have to make some changes, which I'm working on."

"It took me a minute myself, and I'm still improving some areas in my life. What made you decide to go see a therapist though?"

"You know me. I don't have patience for too much and it's affecting me."

"Are you alright, man?"

"If I'm not, I will be."

Ian didn't need to know about the thoughts that lurked in the darkest depths of his mind.

"You have to do what's best for you, especially if it will help."

A buzzing sound resonated in Ian's background.

"Hold on, Hakeem. Someone is at the door."

There was a burst of excitement in the background—muffled chatter and quick footsteps making contact with hardwood floors.

"Hey, Hakeem"—Ian returned to the phone—"Let me hit you back. Connie is here."

Hakeem looked at the clock on the nightstand. It was getting close to bedtime—the wrong time to try talking to Layla. He planned to call her later in the week.

≈≈≈≈≈≈≈

The phone rang as Hakeem retrieved the cup of coffee from the drive-thru attendant. Social calls at 6:45 A.M. were not the times when he displayed the most agreeable personality traits. Nevertheless, Joseph Lewis expected a call.

"Hello!" Joseph greeted on the second ring in a strong and vibrant tone.

"Hello," Hakeem dully repeated, not feeling like talking. Let Joseph steer the conversation while the caffeine took effect. Hakeem pictured him sitting at the kitchen table with the phone pressed against an ear and a free arm folded across his chest.

"Are you on your way to work?"

"I am."

For the past six years since Evelyn died, they spoke every other morning. Joseph asked every morning whether he was on the way to work. Hakeem figured that by now, Joseph would have grown accustomed to the weekly routine and stop asking the same questions. Kaleidoscope was merely a job and casual conversations concerning the place were irritating. Sometimes, Hakeem's irritation slipped when Joseph probed into his work life. In those instances, he wrestled with responding rudely concerning the matter. Joseph had no idea how much he hated Kaleidoscope.

At seventy-nine, Joseph was alert and in good physical shape, having retired a year earlier. Retirement had been an adjustment, having a work history that traced back to the days of field labor—picking cotton and rolling hay. Although they differed with regards to their respective careers, Joseph's work ethic imprinted on Hakeem. Joseph enjoyed serving in the military, and his medals and honorable mentions evidenced his esteem. Hakeem had received awards for job performance with fading pride. Furthermore, Hakeem performed well because the clients suffered otherwise. A job well done was at the very least, owed to Kaleidoscope.

"How's the traffic this morning?"

"It's the same as it always is," Hakeem answered curtly. He did not want to elaborate on the traffic any further and maneuvered the conversation onto a different path. "What do you have planned for today?"

"Ooohhh, I've got a couple of things around the house that need fixin'. The faucet on the bathroom sink is dripping, so I'm gonna fix that. And I gotta repair the door on the shed."

"And what are you going to do afterward?"

"Run across town. Got to get my shirts from the cleaners and pick up some food for the dogs."

Hakeem was glad that Joseph kept busy. It gave him confidence that he fared positively. In the beginning, he was uncertain whether Joseph would survive Evelyn's death. They had been married for over half of a person's lifetime. Nearly sixty years of marriage further intertwined the lives of the partners involved.

"Have you spoken to your mother?"

"Yes. I talked to her on Wednesday." Hakeem mentioned nothing of his exchange with Rosalyn. What was the point of sowing discord? He certainly did not want to upset his grandfather. Joseph was even-tempered and aimed to maintain peace in the family. Reiterating her statements would only undermine everything Joseph strived to establish.

"Good, good, good." Having raised Hakeem from birth, Joseph was aware of the enmity between his daughter and grandson. "When are you planning to come this way again?"

"I'm not sure."

"It's been a while since you last visited."

Hakeem shamed in silence. He didn't appreciate the reminder of his infrequent sojourns. He wished for financial stability that would allow for more visits to see Joseph. As it was, he could not afford to make regular trips to North Carolina. Besides, he disliked the hometown anyway. Spending more than three days in Clinton City was unbearable. The city lacked the metropolitan feel of bustling activity and features of various entertainment venues, which he preferred. And, although he had not explored all of Atlanta's offerings, he wanted the options at his disposal.

What Hakeem referred to as his first home contained too many unpleasant memories. Vivid scenes of abuse played out in his mind and stirred up memories of himself as a disturbed child. The house had absorbed the essences of all who had lived within its walls. The objects within its interior were silent witnesses of everything that transpired. Moving away from home granted Hakeem the ability to seal away everything he wanted to forget.

After moving into the first apartment, Hakeem discovered the power to control the environment within. He could isolate himself from people and the world. In his abode, he found refuge and security. Nevertheless, Joseph deserved to see him more often. Thus, it was Hakeem who needed to make an effort to appease his grandfather.

"I'll see if I can make it up there the month after next." It was not a definite promise but an attempt to reassure Joseph. Hakeem strived to make promises he knew with certainty could be kept. He didn't like being disappointed and believed that other people were entitled to similar treatment.

"Just let me know."

"Have you heard from Gary?"

"I've not talked to him since last week. He told me that his car broke down."

"I see." As a child, he considered Gary to be one his favorite uncles.

Gary knew to call Joseph when he needed money. He was the only child of Joseph and Evelyn, who lived in Clinton City. It disturbed Hakeem that Gary did not communicate regularly with Joseph. When Gary was in financial straits, he remembered Joseph, showing up with a song and dance. Joseph constantly enabled his dependency, believing that Gary was incapable of caring for himself. If he didn't take action, Gary might waste away.

Hakeem wondered how Gary would survive if something happened to Joseph, knowing he was unprepared to assume the role of the family's benefactor.

"Have you talked to him?" Joseph asked.

"Not recently. Gary told me he was going to drive down here awhile back. That's the last I heard from him."

"Hey!"—Joseph interrupted the brief silence—"Do you remember when grandma and I took you to Busch Gardens, and the Scooby-Doo actor scared you?"

Hakeem didn't care to reminisce then, seeing the roof of Kaleidoscope's office building peeking above the treetops upon turning into the industrial park. Just being in proximity of the company jumpstarted his anxiety. The clock on the dash displayed 7:20 A.M. He could spare Joseph ten minutes more. Memories were precious gems that the elderly preserved. Who was he to deny him?

"I remember." The memory suddenly brought a smile to his lips. He loved Scooby-Doo and the Gang. The cartoon episodes never got old. He could sit through a marathon of Scooby-Doo episodes without getting bored.

"You almost knocked me and your grandma down." Joseph released a hearty laugh.

Hakeem chuckled. Indeed, he had put on a performance in front of the Scooby-Doo impersonator. He was six years old then, and the Scooby-Doo costume vaguely resembled the animated character in the cartoon. The mask was significantly oversized in respect to the rest of the baggy costume too. Joseph became a living tree that day as he fought to escape by climbing onto his back.

"That was so long ago." *Twenty-eight years to be exact.*

"Yep, time has gone by so fast," Joseph sighed. "I haven't been to an amusement park since Mama past."

Sometimes Joseph referred to Evelyn as "Mama". It must have been a customary habit of older generations. Hakeem did not know

71

any younger married couples where a spouse used a parental title as an expression of endearment towards the other.

"Y'all have an amusement park down there, don't you?"

"There's one. Some friends and I went three years ago." He left out the part about the excursion being on Halloween. His grandparents did not celebrate holidays. To make mention of it would solicit Joseph's rebuke and spark a debate for him to aggressively defend.

"Maybe we can go when I come down again."

"Yeah, maybe."

Whenever Joseph visited, he usually brought several siblings and in-laws, making for a family trip. Some of the family stayed in Hakeem's apartment while the rest roomed at a nearby hotel. With multiple family members, plans changed to accommodate everyone.

"Made it to work yet?"

"I'm in the parking lot, bout to go in."

7:31 A.M displayed on the dash. "I'll talk to you later, daddy."

"Okay. Thanks for calling….as always."

"You're welcome."

Why wasn't I more engaging with Dad? Hakeem chastised himself. Knowing Joseph was healthy and in good spirits gave him some solace. It was one less thing to worry about in the midst of many problems. But when speaking to Joseph, oftentimes, he forced himself to interact. He considered the matter and concluded that his own misery and secrets kept him at a distance. Joseph would be disappointed if he knew what was going on in his world.

≈≈≈≈≈≈≈

Hakeem stared at Misty's email, which enclosed a screenshot of the error message: Page is currently unavailable, please contact the systems administrator.

So what the system didn't work! He wanted to scream. Now he had to contact IT to troubleshoot the error. If they were unable to resolve the error through email, then he would have to coordinate a web-conference to discuss the end-user experience. Kaleidoscope did not pay enough.

Fifty-thousand dollars? He could easily make sixty or sixty-five doing the same job elsewhere. He needed to invest more time into job searching and make an exit.

Leafing through his planner for the current week, Hakeem saw the memo written to himself. A research paper was due in two weeks. The task of compiling information on organizational behavior had not yet begun. Kaleidoscope's management could take a couple of classes on the subject. The underhanded methods they used to manage employees were atrocious. They were fortunate that no one had gone berserk and wrecked the place.

Managers create and influence the culture in which workplace behaviors thrive. It's not just about policies and procedures that drive the organization towards achieving its goals. It's about the employees who are the key components of every outcome that an organization realizes. In the absence of the collective performance of employees, the organization failed to accomplish established goals. Kaleidoscope's work environment was oppressive—a cotton-picking field with plantation owners and Black overseers in specific divisions.

And while Hakeem fought against the tide, many of his coworkers were distraught and beaten into submission. Management observed everything—breaks and lunches, conversations and interactions, and work habits because they believed that somehow, the employees could complete the work faster. If it meant standing over an employee's shoulder to intimidate them into doing the work, some managers dared. But Hakeem wasn't the one to be tried. Several times Bill came to his cube and observed him in silence. When Hakeem realized Bill was in the cube, he promptly locked the computer and exited the space. Inwardly, he begged Bill to try him. He was nobody's slave and no one would treat him as such to obtain a paycheck.

It seemed nobody cared about the declining employee morale because dollar signs mattered. However, absenteeism and voluntary turnover flagged a rising problem. Attrition came with costs as employers spent more in recruiting and new-hire training to replenish a recurring loss of human capital. Rare and specialized knowledge, skills, and abilities were even harder to replace. Executives of for-profit companies were unconcerned since they continued to reap the benefits.

SMOKE AND MIRRORS

SMOKE AND MIRRORS

Your feet are on the ground and your legs are moving, yet,
you have no idea where you're going.

akeem logged into the university's website and accessed its electronic library. He searched for publications on organizational behavior, employee development, and leadership. Locating an article on leadership and employee behavior, he began skimming the contents until interrupted.

"Hakeem. Hi."

He turned to face Rowena. She was pretty in a ditzy way. Hazel eyes peeked through a tumble of frizzy blonde-tinted, shoulder-length hair. The effect necessitated brushing strands of hair out of her face. He thought the entire exercise bothersome. *Just pin the hair back with a clip or something!*

The tips of purple-feather earrings dangled below the ends of her hair. Her attire was just as aberrant—an ill-fitted purple sweater-blouse over black leggings, and pink suede platform heels. The image distracted from the snake that she was. But weren't many species of snakes multicolored?

"Hello." *What does she want?*

"Are you going to be here for the rest of the day?"

"Yeah, I think so."

"Okay, cause I'm gonna' leave shortly. I have an emergency."

"I got you," he said, hoping a quick response would hasten her departure from the cubicle.

74

Noticing that Rowena did not leave immediately, Hakeem turned around and caught her looking at his computer screen. Instantly annoyed, he turned the monitor off and gave her a challenging stare. His lips tightened with impatience, knowing Rowena was trying to rile him. "Is there anything that I need to keep a look out for?" The question was her cue to leave.

"Oh no. Heh"—she flashed a smile—"Just wanted to make sure that someone would be here to cover me."

"Cool. No problem." *Liar!* There were other members on the team. She could have asked anyone. Then again…no one wanted to help her because she was untrustworthy. "Hope everything works out."

Rowena's eyes were still scanning the cube. It took all of Hakeem's strength not to curse and force her out. "Thank you," she said as the silence became awkward.

"You're welcome." His thoughts were already returning to the assignment as she backed out of the cube. Rowena was an unpleasant distraction.

Hakeem noted key points in the articles intended for use in the paper. There was a seven-page, five-reference minimum requirement according to the rubric. The subject matter would be integrated with real-world experience from working at Kaleidoscope. The insight gained from observing the direct impact of leadership on the workplace was too invaluable to disregard. He didn't have to mention the company by name to apply the experience.

"Hakeem."

"Yes." He responded to Bill without taking his eyes from the computer. *What do these people want?* He typed a few more notes for the paper.

"Did Rowena speak to you?"

"She did. Told me that she was leaving early."

The nearing sound of footsteps and rustling clothes indicated that Bill had entered the cube.

"Well, I just want to make sure that everything is covered on the team."

"Is there a problem?" Hakeem watched him take a seat in the vacant chair. *Great! He wants to talk.*

"No. No problem. I'm really just touching base. Rowena seems to think that you weren't interested in what she had to say."

I wasn't. So what? "What do you mean?"

"Well"—Bill ran a hand through his hair—"Rowena said that you didn't look at her while she was talking."

I could care less what she said! "I turned from my computer long enough to see what she wanted. So, I did look at her." He was getting angry. "But to be clear, I can multitask and carry on a conversation. We all do it! Maybe that's foreign to her." He put on his poker face and let Bill continue.

"Rowena also said that she hesitates to ask you for help because you're always doing homework."

"If I'm 'always' doing my homework as she claims, how is it that I do more than most people on the team? You have quantified my contributions!" He was about to explode. "Have you received any complaints from clients regarding my work? Do I have outstanding items?"

"Uh, no. But it might help if you showed more willingness to assist your teammates. You said that you wanted to promote." Bill had to interject the last statement.

Hakeem wanted to punch him in the face. *Does he not see the coworkers frequenting my cube throughout the day because they need help?*

"I'm always helping the team." It was the same argument he presented when Bill denied adjusting his performance rating. No! Like all the managers, Bill wanted to sponge as much as possible from him while pigeon-holding.

"Do you help Rowena?"

"When she asks. But Rowena is quite capable of doing her own work. She's been a project manager longer than I have."

"Maybe she doesn't feel that you're friendly towards her."

What in the world are we discussing here? Does Rowena need a friend?

Bill's perception was accurate about him, however. He was barely cordial when interacting with Rowena because she was sneaky—always telling on coworkers. If she stopped arguing with her boyfriend throughout the day, she could work more efficiently. Hakeem did not mention her phone conversations. What would have been the point? To intensify an existing conflict? Maybe Bill knew already.

"Okay, so what would you like me to do?" Hakeem was not going to keep debating with Bill. It was time to find another job and see Kaleidoscope in the rearview mirror.

"Just try socializing with her more." Bill ran his fingers through his hair again.

Yeah, whatever. Get out of my cube! "Understood, Bill." *You've never truly supported me.*

Hakeem turned to the computer for the third time. He needed to finish typing his notes. A chime resonated through the speaker. Down in the right corner of the screen flashed an email notification. He opened the email from IT. They were unable to troubleshoot without speaking with the customer. A web-conference was necessary. Now he had to coordinate a meeting that was conducive to the schedules of both the client and IT. That is what Kaleidoscope underpaid him to do. He eagerly awaited the day to turn in his resignation.

≈≈≈≈≈≈

Alex strolled into the cubicle unannounced and perched on the edge of the left corner of the desk. "Are you going to lunch or what?"

"It's not time for lunch." Hakeem maintained concentration on modifying his resume.

"It is for me, and I need to go to the mall."

"For?"

"To get a gift for Rick."

"Not two months have passed and we're buying gifts?"

"Rick's birthday is this weekend."

"I bet it is," Hakeem mocked. "What do you plan to get him?"

"I don't know. That's why I want you to come with me."

"And…how would I know what Rick likes? I've never met him."

He didn't like that Alex was jumping through hoops for Rick so early in the game. Alex was two years his senior—far from being a newbie to the dating scene and should know better.

"You wouldn't. I just need to borrow your tastes."

Hakeem raised an eyebrow and stared at Alex, knowing he was using him. He could decline and not go to the mall, create an excuse.

"Are you coming with me to the mall or not?"

"Yeah." Hakeem locked the computer. No one needed to see his resume on the screen. That was one of the problems in the office— nobody knew how to mind their darned business. When he left Kaleidoscope, it was going to be a surprise.

"When we get back, I'm gonna send you my resume."

"For what?"

"To find me another job."

"Child, you're not leaving here," Hakeem smirked.

Alex loved Kaleidoscope. As much as he complained, Alex raved.

Hakeem saw Damien Spraggs strutting towards them in a tailored black suit as they headed for the elevators. Damien's smooth-shaven face was impassive as usual. Damien was the behind-closed-doors confrontational type. Staff complaints concerning his autocratic management style surprised employees who didn't work in the training department.

"You should push me into him so I can elbow-jab his face," Hakeem whispered to Alex. Every time he thought about Damien's deceptions, he became infuriated.

"And get fired, honey? You're on your own." Alex didn't care for Damien either. But his ability to play office politics conveyed otherwise. "Leave that man alone. He ain't worth it."

≈≈≈≈≈≈≈

Lenox Mall teemed with shoppers. Its location in the heart of Buckhead, was surrounded with office buildings, hotels, and privately-owned and chain businesses that contributed to the influx of customers. Alex led the way into Mekhi's and Hakeem braced himself. The expansive department was a therapeutic intervention. He rarely exited

Mekhi's without making a purchase, faring marginally better in the other stores. Lenox's retail offerings ranged from "necessary" to luxury. There was something for everyone, including those who aspired only to sightsee.

"What was the last cologne you bought?" Alex asked as they headed to the men's department.

"I can't remember." Hakeem was approaching a compromising situation. He cherished cologne. Bottles of fragrance occupied shelves in his bedroom. There were a few newly released colognes that he had yet to sample. If he dared to smell any now, he was uncertain of his ability to leave the store empty-handed.

"Uh-huh. You're about to help me find one….I think."

Summer clearance signage festooned the men's department. An additional thirty-percent off the sale price tempted Hakeem to partake in the offerings. Dress ties in multi-colored paisley, geometric, and solid prints were arranged on polished wooden tables. He loved ties too, but seldom wore the accessory. They were just good to have.

Alex briefly eyed the displays before moving on to sport shirts.

"See anything?" Hakeem asked.

Alex sighed, "Not yet." He ran a hand along a rounder of shirts as a child would a row of iron bars.

"Think practical then. Is there something Rick needs? Has he mentioned something that he wants?"

"Hmmm…let me think."

Okay.…what we're not going to do is walk aimlessly around the store. Some stores did not have positive perceptions of Black people who roamed without purchasing. Mekhi's sales associates were unobtrusive but maintained watchful eyes like correctional officers in a prison.

Alex continued to search the displays of apparel. His body language conveyed that nothing caught his eye.

"Since you're still looking at clothes, what color does Rick like?"

"Yellow, I think."

You think? A person's favorite color is a fundamental piece of information that people should exchange in the initial stages of an intimate relationship. You should be learning each other outside of the bedroom! Then again, dating in the gay community seemed abnormal compared to heterosexual relationships. In his opinion, if two people were comfortable having sex, they should be as equally agreeable to self-disclose. He became annoyed at the thought.

Yellow ranked high in Hakeem's preference of colors. He made a circular turn, scanning the vicinity, hoping to see flashes of yellow standing out amid the sea of dyed fabrics.

"So, ya'll just lay up all day, huh?" he whispered as Alex walked near.

"What are you talkin' about?"

"About you and Rick."

"He travels a lot for work. We…make up for the time lost between visits." Alex giggled.

Hakeem knew what that meant. "Time is not lost because of physical distance, Alex. What all do you know about this person?"

"Ugh! Child, we're learning each other."

"Is that right? You're uncertain about his favorite color."

"Knowing a person's favorite color isn't important."

"Really? And how do you figure when you intend to buy a gift for someone?"

"Honey, only you focus on the details."

"Yeah, because that's where the story is uniquely defined. One of the things Henry told me about himself when we met was that he liked blue. Whenever I bought clothes for him, they were in his favorite colors." Gift-giving becomes more meaningful when the gift-giver understands the person whom the gift is intended."

Alex flipped the price tag attached to the top shirt on a stack of yellow polos—$59.99. "Here we go. Clothes are important to you."

"You're missing the point," Hakeem challenged, slightly exasperated. "It's knowing specific details about your partner that adds dimensions to the relationship."

"Since you're a relationship expert, we're going to find you a husband too."

Rick is your husband now? "Please don't." He criticized Alex's choices in men because they were doggish. "If I need one, I can find my own." He realized how ridiculous he sounded uttering the last statement. He possessed no intention of marrying any man. That was an act of going too far in the wrong direction.

"Good luck," Alex said walking towards the fragrance counter.

Some people believed they were relationship experts after having entered an intimate union. However, if a person continually made the same mistakes, it evidenced a persisting mindset driving specific behaviors. The occurrence in itself, contradicted whatever self-belief the individual possessed of being a subject matter expert. Hakeem did not have to be a relationship expert to know that growth between two committed people depended on the parties learning about each other. Perhaps observing the relationships of his parents and grandparents played an important role in shaping his outlook concerning the dynamics between two people.

≈≈≈≈≈≈≈

"What are you doin', boi?" Khalil asked.

"Doing homework," Hakeem answered dryly. He heard the *clinking* sound of silverware through the speakerphone as Khalil loaded the dishwasher. Khalil liberally utilized the dishwasher in every apartment he rented.

"Are you sure that's all you're doin'?" Khalil asked in a mocking tone.

"What else would I be doing?" He knew what Khalil was getting at.

"I don't know. You tell me." Khalil's voice oozed with sarcasm.

"You know my schedule. I do the same thing every day. It ain't changed."

"Uh-huh. That's what you say. I don't know what you be doin' over there."

Hakeem had a short fuse for Khalil's taunts. "Look here! There's no one over here or has been over here."

In his heart, Hakeem longed for a meaningful relationship. Jesting about his love life made him testy. He envied Khalil for his ability to attract people. Like Alex, dating came easy to Khalil, albeit the acquaintances were commercials. Conversations with Khalil featured tales of short-term relations for a couple of weeks or months until he stopped mentioning the men altogether.

Hakeem was familiar with the dating cycle—a factor that inhibited his desire to be outgoing and less tolerant of men. The newness of a relationship invariably hiked the excitement of people aspiring for love and intimacy, sometimes eclipsing every rational thought. Everything nonessential lessened in priority until someone fell from cloud nine. He hadn't seen Alex outside of work for nearly four weeks. Alex would call eventually once Rick departed. Disappointingly, Khalil similarly behaved.

"Mm-hmm. Whatever you say, chile."

Hakeem shook his head. Khalil Thomas was a trip from way back. Whenever Hakeem perceived Khalil veering into his lane, he nipped him. He found it difficult to silently withstand attacks on his character, even if the person disclaimed the act ill-intended. Growing up, people said harsh things and he was powerless to do anything about their criticisms. They hardened him. As an adult, he could defend himself from anyone who attempted harm. It made no sense to be spiteful, if the act was not meant to be taken seriously. At least when he reprehended someone, he did not hide behind a harmless-appearing façade.

"Anyway…what are you doing today?" Hakeem asked, smoothing the edginess from his tone. He wanted to glaze over his mild eruption. Khalil had been his road-dog since Earl put him out over a dispute that pertained to his role as a father. He would always remember Khalil's friendship and generosity.

Saturday afternoon had replaced the morning without eating breakfast or lunch. Fueled by sixteen ounces of coffee, Hakeem pressed through a five-page paper that was due on Sunday.

Hakeem hoped Khalil wanted to hang in the city. He wanted to get out with a companion rather than brave Atlanta alone, as was the usual routine. But Khalil could be fickle and the trait didn't mesh with his own rigidness.

There were times when they frequented clubs into the wee hours of the morning, slept until midday, awakened, and met up for round two. Those were some good old days. Hakeem smiled fondly. Those activities no longer interested him. There was too much at stake now. He settled back into being an introvert—preferring the indoors, occupied with activities that stimulated his analytical mind. Video-games and comic books were still favorite pastimes.

"I'm hungry," Khalil replied.

He was hungry too. "Let's gets something to eat."

"Where, child?"

"Some place that has ribs. I have to look online, though." The thought of char-grilled, smoky-flavored ribs, lightly glazed, made Hakeem's stomach growl.

"Aiight. I haven't had ribs in a while. What time are you tryna' go?"

"Around three o'clock." He needed a two-hour window because all the time would be exhausted getting dressed—changing between sets of clothes.

"Well, I need a shower."

"I do too. I'll be over as soon as I get dressed."

"Cool."

Hakeem ended the call, went into the master bathroom and stood in front of the mirror. Black and gray stubble covered the sides of his face and chin. *Why am I graying so fast? Is Kaleidoscope doing this to me?* He wanted to get out of there. That job was going to be the end of him. He turned on the electric edger and shaved all of the hair except the mustache and goatee, lining the outer edges. He looked at his upper body, naturally toned—a gift of Earl's genetics. Calisthenics kept him fit at one hundred and sixty-five pounds, five-feet-eight inches tall. A shirt gave the illusion of a flat stomach that if exposed, dispelled the deception. The swell in his pectoral muscles helped offset the small pouch in the lower abdomen.

A six-pack could be achieved if he bothered to deny bakery goods. Fat chance. Perhaps his workout regimen should be increased, he mused. Maybe it would help improve his appeal. He did not want a bulky body though. It changed a person's gait, as the thighs rubbed together. Friction between body parts and fabric degraded threading in the material. He examined a pair of joggers after wearing them twice and saw minuscule balls of fiber along the inner seam and seat—the result produced from walking. Bulking meant the purchase of a new wardrobe—an endeavor he found uninspiring.

Checking for the current time, Hakeem looked at the alarm clock on the nightstand from the bathroom doorway. 1:30 P.M. Not a lot of time. He needed to leave by 2:45 P.M.

≈≈≈≈≈≈≈

The thermometer read eighty degrees on the car touch panel and the clock, 3:00 P.M. Hakeem had spent twenty minutes finding something to wear, settling on a striped, purple V-neck t-shirt with black cargo shorts and gray, black and purple hi-top sneakers. He was meticulous in organizing his appearance, possessing a knack for fashion and it made him feel good. It was also an effective disguise. Nobody knew how inadequate he felt.

Traffic was intense on the weekends. Windows down, R&B music pumping, Hakeem merged onto the express lane to bypass the slowing traffic on Interstate-85. From the highway, structures of department stores, gas stations, and eateries were visible where construction and landscaping had cleared away trees. The real estate market had tapped into goldmines in the neighboring cities of Duluth, Norcross and Lawrenceville for commercial, industrial, and residential development. The return on investment was significantly promising in those cities, given the exorbitant property value within Atlanta's metropolitan area. Residential homes ranged from the mid $300,000's to over a million in the Downtown and Midtown Districts. The price tag for commercial leasing was steep, justifying some businesses' decisions to uproot and move outside Metro Atlanta.

Alas, as businesses relocated outside Atlanta's parameter, rural communities were negatively impacted as the economic value decreased. Assessing the dilemma from the perspective of private ownership, the withdrawal of big business gave mom-and-pop shops the breaks they needed for successful entrepreneurship. A drive along Martin Luther King Jr. Drive from the Westside of Atlanta eastward into the city unveiled independently-owned barbershops, beauty and nail salons, clothing, novelty and nostalgic stores, carwashes, and eateries specializing in Soul Food, Jamaican, Chinese, African, American, and Italian cuisine that were common in the rural community. Independently, they could support themselves and possibly employ a few workers at low wages. However, their combined income was insufficient to contest particular franchises and chain department stores that sold a variety of goods and services in larger quantities at significantly low prices, thus, undercutting neighborhood businesses.

Strong and steady competition eventually drove smaller businesses to close shop, leaving behind abandoned architectures of collapsing roofs, boarded or broken windows, and dilapidated walls. Larger corporations were not exempt in this regard. When a company entered a community, it displaced living and nonliving obstacles to transplant its business. Once the company withdrew, it left behind a physical reminder of its temporary presence. It was the homeless, addicts and animals that benefitted then, who were able to take refuge within the abandoned edifices until the industrial cycle renewed. As industrialization resurged, market value spiked and gentrification ensued. The once affordable neighborhood transitioned into an affluent community, forcing the working class and low-income to relocate elsewhere.

Hakeem lived 23-miles from Kaleidoscope and farther from Khalil. The rent for a one-bedroom apartment in the inner city was at least one and half times that of an apartment in Lawrenceville and other cities on the outskirts. Generally, the farther someone lived from the metropolitan area, the cheaper the cost of living. That assumption held its validity until businesses started to spring up in a low economic locale.

Proximity reduction of businesses placed additional demands upon the denizens, which at one time, they conveniently serviced. People had to travel farther to obtain goods and services that were previously accessible four blocks away. If bereft of personal means to commute, public transportation bridged the gap between home, business, and employment to a limited degree. The public transportation system as it existed, throughout Atlanta and its surrounding metro counties: Dekalb, Clayton, Cobb, Fulton, and Gwinnett could hardly be described as integrated.

For decades, tracing to the early 1960s, public officials and voters within the counties—advocates for the extension of the MARTA transit system into the sprawling provinces and the opponents of the initiative contended. On the surface, the central issue pertained to obtaining funding necessary to undergird MARTA's development. The initial bill proposed an increase in property tax—a recommendation that was rejected by those in opposition to absorbing the expense. The bill was re-proposed several years later, suggesting an allocation of sales tax to finance MARTA. The new proposal won favor only from the City of Atlanta, Fulton, and Dekalb. Behind the wall of non-supporters pervaded a disinclination to equip Blacks with a resource for transportation into predominantly white suburban neighborhoods. Racists loathed the idea of Blacks possibly living among them. Many of their descendants would carry forth such abhorrence into present day.

Hakeem turned into the gated community, the signage: Alistair Vineyards posted at the corner of the driveway. Tri-colored three-storey buildings stood beyond the gates, the foundations constructed of brick, the second and third levels, brown and beige stone. The brilliance of the multicolored stones indicated relatively recent development. He appraised the complex as being no more than a year old. Unlike himself, Khalil favored living close to the city and possessed the financial capacity to exercise his preference.

But even if financially capable, the property's location offered a last resort among poorer alternatives. The local news reported crimes in the area, especially near the historical university within the neighborhood. Hakeem wanted no parts of it—fearful that someone might jump the gates and vandalize or steal his car. He could not sustain the additional expense.

He entered 3-7-3 on the gate panel's dial pad and tapped the Call button.

"Hullo," the voice sounded over the intercom.

"Open the gate." A high-pitch buzzing sound resonated from the speaker on the dial pad. He drove forward as the gate opened, slowing to a stop at the guardrail. It remained inert until the entry gates stood completely ajar.

Hakeem pulled into the open carport parallel to Khalil's Silver BMW sedan. Hostas and azaleas outlined the foundation of the apartment building and marigolds clustered the outer ring of the flower beds. The shades of color complemented the trees planted across the lawns. The overall effect evidenced the landscapers' talents. *Probably Hispanics*, he speculated. Wherever landscaping transpired, he found the majority of the workers to be of Spanish descent. And people felt that Mexicans should return to their home country? Why, when many were earning their keep, not to mention filling occupations that citizens of the United States passed up or refused to fill. How many U.S.-citizens were willing to drive around with landscaping tools looking for work? Wherever a need exists, there is an opportunity for service.

Khalil lived on the second floor. Inside the breezeway, the paint held a vibrant luster and the stone floors shown mostly white, free of compacted dirt. He answered the door on the second knock fully dressed and turned away, moisturizing his arms with lotion. Hakeem knew that if Khalil came to his apartment, he would likely still be putting clothes together.

Hakeem flipped the deadbolt and entered the living-room. The scent of candied fruit filled the area as candles burned on the coffee- and end-tables. Khalil loved pictures and the walls of the apartment illustrated his passion. Above the loveseat hung an oil painting depicting a bar where the motionless figures of people of African descent danced to an unknown groove. Bold reds, yellows, orange, blues, purples, whites, and blacks enlivened the canvas. Sensuality radiated from the gyration of the women's hips and the men's caressing hands upon their bodies. Black music—rhythm and blues created that kind of vibe. Hakeem spent many nights in the bars and clubs buzzed from the allure of alcohol, seeing its effects take over the dance floor as partners paired up and grinded themselves into ecstasy. There was a time when he engaged similarly, the breath of a dance partner against his face and neck. In those moments, nothing else mattered because someone desired him, if only for the duration of a song.

Wresting himself from the reverie, Hakeem peeped through the blinds. Few cars populated the parking lot.

"Are you ready to go, child?" Khalil asked from the other side of the room.

"Yeah. Who's driving?"

"I am. You drive too slow."

Good! He seldom had the luxury to be a passenger. "I drive skillfully....I'm not going to tear my car up."

"You're not gonna tear your car up cause you drive like an ol' woman." Khalil said, collecting his keys and wallet from the kitchen counter.

"If you say so. I drive in accordance with the law."

As they prepared to leave, Khalil looked at him from head to toe. He stood half an inch taller than Khalil and weighed 20-pounds more.

"Someone's wearing a new outfit," Khalil observed.

Hakeem shrugged. "I've worn this before."

"When?"

"To work."

"Yeah, well. I've neva seen it. I think I need to stop ova your apartment and do a little shopping in dat closet of yours."

"Child, please. You can't wear any of my clothes." He gave Khalil an incredulous look.

"Why not? You ain't wearing dem." Khalil was dead on.

Hakeem didn't like anyone wearing his clothes, friends or family. Body odors and shapes were not the same. Variances in shape further deteriorated the original contour of the clothing. When he donned clothing, he expected the fit and smell to remain consistent to character. New clothes were not usually worn immediately after purchase. Sometimes a year passed before he got the urge to assemble, preferring to reserve the better pieces for special occasions, such as a date. Unfortunately, the infrequency of dates only lengthened the archival period for unused purchases.

"Why don't we go to the mall, and I can help you find a bargain."

"I'm not buying any new clothes right now. I'm on a budget!"

"Your BMW does not say 'budget. You should've gone to a buy-here-pay-here lot if that was the case."

"I'm not gonna be seen in a hoopty."

"You could've bought a nice used car."

"But I didn't want a used car."

"Apparently. But I KNOW what a budget is."

"Budget my tail. Your walk-in closets can be turned into a department store"—Khalil paused—"What restaurant we going to?"

"Flame House Grille on Piedmont."

"Hmmm….that's new, isn't it?

"Yep."

"Those ribs better be good," Khalil said, walking out the door.

WRONG TURNS AND DETOURS

There are paths that we've taken, knowing that they led in the wrong direction, and yet, we advanced despite the warning signs.

"Keep focused!" Hakeem snapped. It amazed him how Khalil managed to see everything while driving. A well-built man jogged down the street with his shirt removed, and he caught Khalil staring.

Khalil glanced sideways, his left eyebrow arched. "I got this….stay in ya lane."

"Keep the car on the road," Hakeem insisted. He was not particularly concerned with Khalil's driving skills, familiar with his ability to whip a car on the road. Rather, he was accustomed to having a measure of control and fearful that any situation could change in an instant.

Hakeem considered the fact that they seldom hung out unlike in the past. Khalil relocated to Atlanta, established a new network of friends and spent the majority of time hanging with them. He didn't fit in with the group, so Khalil did not invite him along to partake in recreational activities. While the subject never arose, Hakeem suspected he was a sore thumb among Khalil and his friends. And just like Alex, Khalil rotated him when other friends were unavailable. Thus, Hakeem exploited their friendship as much as possible.

When a person observes and analyzes human behavior, it is easier to recognize distinctive patterns.

"So let me tell you what Tory told me," Khalil blurted all of a sudden.

"Uh-huh."

"He met some dude online and they were supposed to blaze."

"Still meeting those thugs, huh?" Hakeem knew better than to deal with thugs. Mess around and meet the wrong one, a person could get robbed and killed. He had heard horrible stories.

"Child….why did he agree to meet the dude at an abandoned house?"

"Did Tory know the house was abandoned?"

"I don't think so. Tory said the dude told him the electricity was off because he didn't pay the bill."

"And what happened?"

"He said that when he walked up the driveway, the dude told him to come around the back of the house."

"And he did?"

"Yep. Walked around that house and got knocked. Then the dude stole his weed!"

"What? Get outta here!" Hakeem erupted into laughter.

"Yez, honey!"

"So, where is Tory now?"

"Said he's gonna lay low for a bit."

Tory got knocked several years ago in a similar situation. That time, two thugs ambushed him. They stole his cellphone, weed, and car. A neighbor hearing the commotion, asked Tory why was he in the abandoned house. Tory explained that he was meeting friends, prompting the neighbor to call the police. Tory filed a police report and the police found his car a few days later. The criminals flattened the tires and smashed the frontend, possibly by ramming the car into an obstruction.

People made mistakes. But when they repeated the same mistakes, sometimes those errors in judgment evolved into habits. Thoughts drive behavior and at some point, an individual must acknowledge the repercussions of his or her choices in recurring circumstances. Hakeem was still licking his wounds from the past.

≈≈≈≈≈≈≈

It took patience and skill to navigate Piedmont Avenue to find reasonable parking on a Saturday afternoon. Cars parked bumper-to-bumper, crammed the main and side streets while patrons frequented the restaurants, bars, and the park nearby. Events, festivals, exhibits, and concerts were popular at Piedmont Park, lasting throughout the weekend. Hakeem enjoyed the Annual Dogwood Festival most of all. Painters, sculptors, musicians and other artisans came from near and far to sell their wares. They were uniquely talented, and their prices conveyed the worth of their laconic self-appraisals.

Khalil spotted a parking space on a side street between 11th and 12th. Flame House Grille stood on the next block.

As they approached the brick building, Hakeem heard music resonating through the open door on the restaurant's deck. Patrons stood outside the entrance and along the sidewalk.

"A little packed don't you think?" Khalil observed.

"It's a Saturday. What you expect?" He followed Khalil into the restaurant.

The hostess, wearing a tailored white short-sleeve button-down shirt and black trousers, rested a hip on the side of the host station. "Hello!" she exclaimed with sparkling, clear emerald-green eyes. "How many are in your party?"

"Two," Khalil replied.

"Do you prefer a booth or high-rise table?" she asked.

"A booth, please," Hakeem interjected. He wanted no one sitting behind him, preferring privacy and limited visibility.

"There is a thirty-five-minute wait on booths."

"That's fine," he said.

The hostess reached behind the station and retrieved a pager with dim red lights, and then handed it to Khalil since he was the closest.

"She's cute"—Arms folded, he slowly turned clockwise, referring to the surroundings. A smile widened across his face, revealing straight white teeth. "There's some eye candy here, too." He raised his eyebrows twice in quick succession to convey the meaning.

Hakeem shook his head, hoping no one overhead. He understood the implication, following Khalil's gaze around the restaurant. Khalil had no shame.

"How's class comin'?" he inquired.

"It's coming along. I was finishing up a paper when I called earlier."

"When will you be done?"

"With the class or the degree?"

"The degree."

"2017. Almost a year and a half." Completion time had averaged two years but it was going to be close to three years when he finished the educational journey. Motivation continued to decline as he slowly neared burnout. The will had to be mustered to complete the paper turned in just two weeks ago.

"Is this the last one?"

"Not sure. I wouldn't mind getting a PhD from Georgia Tech." He heard about the university's acclaimed academic programs. Obtaining a doctoral degree from Georgia Tech would be a greater achievement.

"oOo! That's a good choice. You'll be makin' the big bucks." Khalil chuckled.

"That's my goal."

Khalil's lips parted to respond when the lights on the pager began blinking rapidly. He took it to the station and showed the hostess. She retrieved the pager and tucked two menus under her arm.

"This way," she instructed.

Hakeem followed on Khalil's heels. Patrons looked briefly as they passed. Flame House Grille serviced a mixed clientele. Whenever there was a mutual interest, a diverse people could put aside their differences.

The hostess seated them in the farthest right-corner of the restaurant. *Perfect!* Hakeem took the wall seat and perused the cocktail menu once settled. A picture of a large, chilled goblet containing blue liqueur with the description: Blue Hawaiian, filled the second page.

Hakeem had a weakness for the mixture of rum, Blue Curacao, pineapple juice, and coconut with a shot of Hennessey—a tempting tropical beverage. By the time he returned to Khalil's apartment, the alcohol would be absorbed into his blood. But then, the DUI case was still pending. He made a promise to God to never drink and operate a motor vehicle again. Too bad that such conscientiousness was ignored a year ago.

≈≈≈≈≈≈≈

Proud of achieving a second master's degree, Hakeem presumed acceleration to the top of the career ladder with nothing in the way. He planned to use both master's degrees to land a job making at least $65,000 a year—a $15,000 jump from the standing salary. A student with a 4.0 GPA could not fail. However, he soon discovered that overconfidence combined with a carefree attitude can sometimes cause a person to trip hard.

Two months following graduation, former friend, Rayvon invited Hakeem to a birthday party. He accepted, justifying his attendance as well earned. What was the problem with partying occasionally? Hakeem was confident in self-perceived control and believed that the party could possibly help make new friends and widen his social network.

The party was a bring-your-own-bottle affair. Guests who arrived together mingled within their own familiar circles. Newcomers were eyed thoroughly, but unless someone knew them, greetings were not exchanged. The exaggerated personalities and cattiness that always seemed to be present at such parties constantly challenged Hakeem's personality. Despite the desire to be part of an enlivened social circle, assimilation was difficult. This duality factored into the consumption of increasing quantities of alcohol to resolve the mental conflict.

Twenty minutes into the party, Hakeem began consuming alcohol. His nerves demanded calming. Rayvon and other companions entered the house where Hakeem followed. In the middle of the living room, they surrounded the birthday host, each person holding a shot glass.

Hakeem participated in the rounds of Tequila shots, the eventual drive home far removed from his mind. He could have opted not to drink, making an early departure the probable outcome. The idea lacked appeal because it meant returning home to solitude.

After several impactful shots, Hakeem inspected the food table pushed against the wall adjacent to the living room. The appetizers were unfit for his consumption. A sheet of foil partially covered a tray of party wings. The skin on the chicken had a yellowish-gray cast, causing him to question the cook's preparation methods. A competent cook himself, the coloring of the wings was unappetizing. He watched guests eating the wings and was still unconvinced. *Let them take the risk.* Another tray contained picked over red-skinned potatoes. Celery and carrots were scattered in a third tray and he frowned in disgust. The overall presentation of the food was horrible. He decided to grab something to eat on the way home.

Rayvon shared that the club was the next stop after the party. He was a party animal who enjoyed prolonging nights of fun-filled adventures—an enthusiasm that failed to project onto Hakeem that night. Hakeem felt lethargic from having consumed a considerable amount of alcohol and decided that going to the club would be overkill. Thus, the band split upon reaching Downtown Atlanta where Rayvon's group exited onto 10th Street.

The night air was faintly cool. Hakeem lowered the windows halfway and cranked up the music driving home. A van traveled one car's length ahead while he coasted. Almost five seconds later, red, white and blue lights began flashing in the rearview mirror. Hakeem knew in that moment that a patrol car tailgated him. He merged onto the shoulder lane, stopped the car, and waited for the officer to approach. Nervousness rippled through his body, sensing imminent trouble. He removed the vehicle registration and insurance papers from the glove compartment just in case, unaware of the reason for being pulled over.

The officer approached the driver side window, aiming a flashlight into Hakeem's face. Shaken with rambling thoughts, he waited for the cop to provide an explanation. The cop explained that he clocked him driving twenty-five miles over the speed limit. Hakeem attempted to swallow but fright had drained the saliva from his mouth. He furnished his driver's license at the officer's request.

After reviewing the information, the cop returned and requested Hakeem to exit the car and walk to the trunk. Likely informed by the smell of liquor on Hakeem's breath, the officer peered into his eyes again, concluding impairment and solicited him to perform field sobriety tests.

Hakeem failed. Raging thoughts and nervousness distracted him from listening to the officer's instructions. Instead of turning around after completing the specified number of steps and before returning to the starting point, he walked forward then backward. Hakeem believed that he successfully passed the field test because he remained standing. However, the officer promptly stated that he did not follow instructions and would be detained for a breathalyzer test.

It did not pay to be ignorant of the law. In hindsight, Hakeem could have refused participation in the breathalyzer exam, but at a cost. A refusal granted an officer the authority to impose a twelve-month administrative suspension on his license. If driving while illegally intoxicated, the driver's license may still be confiscated and suspended, given indications of impairment. An attorney is then able to request an administrative hearing with the officer to reinstate driving privileges (with limitations if the charges must go to trial). Moreover, in the case of a refusal and relating circumstances, an officer is not obligated to comply, especially when detaining someone who appears intoxicated, is legally justified. The situation then becomes a matter of legal contest.

For Hakeem, a suspended license was unthinkable. Personal transportation was necessary for commuting to work and fulfilling other obligations. He thought of excuses that could potentially convince the officer to let him drive home. Every scheme failed. The officer transported Hakeem to the police station in handcuffs and subjected him to the breathalyzer test.

Hakeem sat on an uncomfortably cold steel bench watching as the officer prepped the device. Hakeem blew and twice registered over the legal BAC limit .08. There was no going home as the officer explained and escorted him to booking where another officer captured his mugshot. Hakeem wondered if he dared wear the outfit anymore because it appeared in the picture. Considering everything that happened that night, he managed to have enough concern for his attire. He spent the next seven hours in jail until permitted bail.

A smaller area on the front side of the detainment center enclosed the women who were arrested during the course of the night. They numbered less than the men. Hakeem saw an attractive Black woman dressed as if she had been to the club earlier that evening. She did not look the type to be arrested. But appearances do not necessarily mean anything or tell a complete story about anyone.

Cells lined the walls along the outer parameter of the detainment center. Each cell contained a bench behind which stood a tiled partition. A man entered the cell closest to Hakeem and walked behind the partition to use the bathroom. *No privacy.* He heard the man relieving himself and determined right then that he had to get out! Nothing else occupied his mind more than liberation from jail.

Around 5 A.M. Sunday morning, an officer instructed the men to line up and read aloud the bond amount for each detainee. The officer then gave each inmate a paper slip with contact information for bondsmen. Hakeem randomly selected a listed bondsman and called the toll-free number. He subsequently paid five-hundred and sixty dollars for his own liberation.

Everything seemed to lag Sunday afternoon. The first person who Hakeem called following release was Ka'ron to ask for a ride home. Ka'ron lived in proximity to the bondsman's office. On the fourth attempt, he left Ka'ron a voicemail, briefly narrating the events of the previous night and morning. For three weeks, Ka'ron remained unavailable. When Ka'ron finally called, Hakeem deleted his phone number. He only wanted to see how long Ka'ron intended to avoid him. Three weeks was too long and too late. *Caring people come to the aid of others in need.*

Aid arrived from an unexpected source. Pedro, a friend-associate hybrid and a wildcard in terms of dependability, drove Hakeem home from the bondsman's office. Nearly five hours passed when the towing company confirmed record of his car. Hakeem had to present proof of registration and pay one hundred and seventy-four dollars for the car to be released from impoundment.

Excluding the driver's license, Hakeem recovered all of his belongings. Having to collect each personal item confiscated felt like he was putting himself together again. Once alone in the car, Hakeem cried. He had been stupid, too cocky, and it had cost dearly.

Returning home, he called Sharon detailing the arrest. She recommended hiring an attorney given the seriousness of DUI charges. In her opinion, the possibility of contesting or lessening the impact of a pending DUI conviction warranted retaining an attorney. Heeding the advice, he searched online for a reputable attorney in Atlanta and contacted a highly respected firm. The owner of the particular firm answered the phone and asked him to summarize the incident, ultimately extending an invitation to his office for further legal counsel.

Hakeem erroneously assumed that in hiring an attorney, the case would conclude in a few months. The attorney forewarned him of the lengthy processes in DUI cases and subsequent trials. In the interim and as part of the rehabilitation process, the attorney recommended one-hundred hours of community service, which Hakeem volunteered at an animal shelter. He had a fondness for dogs and cats, and the task of attending to the animals seemed easy enough. The challenge existed in coordinating community service hours around his work scheduled.

Hakeem compared his life to the animals, saddened by their condition. Like the animals, he had endured abandonment and abuse. He despised people that took advantage of the defenseless—a feeling that fostered his wolfish attitude as an adult. And, even though his attentiveness to the animals objectified rehabilitation, the work was both fulfilling and humbling.

The attorney also instructed Hakeem to attend a meeting for surviving victims of drunk driving. The session commenced with videos of victims of drunk driving. One victim in particular, was born the same year as himself. The victim did not live to celebrate his thirtieth birthday because of a drunk driver. Fortunately, Hakeem had not been involved in an accident. Yet, the fact did not release him from responsibility. He could have severely injured or killed himself and/or someone else.

Members of the victims' families who addressed the attendees were angry and heartbroken. Even though years had passed for some of the surviving family members and friends, they still mourned as if the tragedies were recent. Guilt settled in Hakeem's stomach. He wondered whether their pain would ever subside and realized that if he hurt someone because of misjudgment, he would be unable to live with himself. There is no apology in the world that is capable of restoring the breath of life to a person.

A suspended license landed Hakeem in a mandatory three-day driver's risk reduction course. In those three days, he decided to cease partying altogether. When he partied, he drank alcohol. If he could not party without drinking, then it was necessary to retire from both activities.

Invites to parties decreased as Hakeem continually declined with excuses. Rayvon did not know about the arrest for being a blabbermouth and his associates were not entitled to knowing anything about the situation. Hakeem preferred that only a few people knew of his healing wounds.

A substance-abuse counselor evaluated Hakeem for alcoholism and drug dependency, as the assessments were crucial to the attorney's building case file. The counselor was a Caucasian man, who gave surprising feedback during the examination. In reviewing Hakeem's educational achievements, the counselor commented that he should be self-employed. The counselor identified potential, which Hakeem had overlooked within himself. *Even a stranger might see potential in someone else.* For the first time, Hakeem questioned whether he invested too much time into Kaleidoscope.

No one can choose the consequences of their actions. Hakeem shelled out three-hundred and fifty dollars to participate in the risk reduction course. He tallied the cost of bailing himself out of jail, the towing company, attorney retainer fees, the group sessions, and the driver's reduction course. The attorney's fees alone amounted to $5,000, not including the fine for driving under the influence. In total, he spent in excess of $7,500, which was as much as he had accumulated in his savings account. While trekking the road of redemption, Hakeem also saw the journey as a setback. The monies spent could have been invested into the acquisition of a new home or something worthwhile. *Poor decisions yield negative consequences.*

≈≈≈≈≈≈≈

Hakeem looked at the cocktail menu again. The ordeal of enduring the pending DUI case gave him pause. *The time and money invested in redeeming myself should be a deterrent to drinking and driving.*

The State of Georgia permitted operation of passenger vehicles for drivers 21 years of age or older with a BAC of 0.8 or less. Hakeem conjectured that a single cocktail would trigger a low BAC, absorb into the bloodstream and completely metabolize by the time he went home. But there was the struggle with limiting consumption to one drink. Hakeem enjoyed sticky-sweet mixtures of fruit juices and liquor. Unless he fell asleep, the first drink served as the appetizer for more consumption.

On numerous occasions, Hakeem drove home inebriated without encountering the police. Successful avoidance reinforced a deviant habit of drinking and driving. However, time and money held significant meaning in his world. When those liberties were negatively affected, he viewed the events as inconveniences. There was no positive return-on-investment for the time and money spent to extricate one's self from a costly mistake. In reflection, Hakeem acknowledged the necessity of learning the lesson that only trial could teach. It was a pivotal moment that lingered in his mind and he pledged to never forget. Everything that held importance—self-perception, finances, freedom, criminal record, and career were jeopardized.

Through maturity, an individual potentially learns that their mentality and behavior must evolve with age. Maturity as an aspect of personal growth can also impart wisdom. Hakeem was deficient in the area, failing to break away from the self-destructive behaviors of young adulthood. Misjudgment forced him to look into the mirror and question his future. A DUI conviction stunted a person's career potential in certain industries. More importantly, a criminal conviction on a Black man's record was possible career-suicide in many contexts. The best hope for a Black man is for a criminal charge to be reduced or dismissed. Even if Khalil drove to and from the restaurant, Hakeem intended to go home later. Good sense advised avoidance of a chance encounter with the police and going through the shameful experience again. The penalty for a second DUI within five years of a prior incident doubled. *Consequences accompany every decision—most unforeseen, and ignorance does not release an individual from responsibility.*

"Child, are you gonna stare at the menu all night?" Khalil's raised eyebrow.

"I'm gonna pass."

"You can have a drink, Hakeem."

"No, I cannot. The case isn't over."

"Suit yourself. I'm gonna have me a cocktail." Khalil reached for the drink menu.

Hakeem surveyed the restaurant, examining the inverted, multicolored and cone-shaped ceiling lamps hanging from the wooden beams above. A groovy tune resonated through the sound system. He reflected on telling Khalil about his arrest, and how he would not drink and drive anymore. Khalil tried to convince him that one drink was acceptable despite knowing of the ordeal. Khalil's suggestion disturbed him and he considered a reprimand.

Some friends are incapable of providing sound advice, and Hakeem saw that Khalil possibly deserved to be classified as such. Khalil wasn't arrested for violating the law. What influenced him to believe that an arrest was something to be taken lightly? Hakeem's account of the event should have dissuaded Khalil from mentioning the absurdity. *Good friends—those who deeply care for each other, exchange counsel that reduce margins for personal error.* Few people understood the true meaning of friendship and Hakeem decided against giving Khalil a crash course on the matter.

It was crucial to the DUI case that Hakeem remain steadfast in his resolve. A second DUI within a five-year period resulted in the culprit's mug shot being circulated in the city newspaper—publicly accessible on the internet, up to three years driver's license suspension, and as many as 1,000 hours of community service.

Hakeem could not afford to make the same mistake twice, and was proud to demonstrate sensibility and restraint. However, an obscure future framed within his mind. How was the case going to impact that which had yet to happen?

A male waiter approached the table. He stood an inch taller than both of them, physically toned in the way of a gymnast. Thick eyebrows hooded brown eyes and a thin goatee framed his mouth.

Hakeem thought the waiter's features Hispanic in nature, noting Khalil staring him down.

"Good evening! My name is Miguel and I'll be your waiter tonight."

Miguel's name had Spanish origins. Hakeem possessed a knack for identifying ethnic origins in people. Moving around and living among people of diverse ethnic backgrounds increased his perception regarding ancestral ties.

"Can I get you, gentlemen something to drink?"

"I'll have the blueberry lemonade….virgin." Hakeem answered.

"And I want a peach margarita on the rocks," Khalil added while trying to lock eyes with Miguel.

"Any appetizers?" Miguel tried not to blush.

"The sampler"—Hakeem replied, seeing what the sampler included: fried catfish nuggets and shrimp, potato skins, and grilled corn on the cob. The combination was too delightful to pass up. "You gonna get something?" he asked Khalil.

Khalil declined with a nod and looked at his cellphone.

"I'll put your orders in." Miguel said, backing away from the table.

"Mmm, Mmm, Mmm, honey." Khalil drawled once Miguel disappeared. "He might be my new husband."

"You were embarrassing him."

"How?"

"By blatantly staring him down. You don't know how to be discreet."

"Gurl! Don't nobody play Miss Innocent like you."

"You mean nobody gets around like you." Hakeem retorted. Unlike Khalil, he respected boundaries when dealing with people.

If Khalil understood boundaries, Hakeem couldn't remember a moment in their friendship where such knowledge was demonstrated. An individual with common sense accepted that certain behaviors were situationally-inappropriate. There was no overt indication of Miguel being homosexual, which didn't necessarily validate heterosexuality. Some gay and bisexual men were adept at being discreet. Only their bed partner knew of their taboo preferences.

Hakeem didn't see the point of trying to engage Miguel, even if there was an intimation that he messed around. Miguel was too accessible and who knew how many gay men hit on him throughout the day? How many numbers would he take home? How many would he turn down? Concerning the dynamics of dating, it was not just about a person's conduct in the presence of their partner. An equal amount of attention needed to be directed to how they represented themselves when not in their partner's company. Hakeem knew the pattern of gay men, having met a man who worked as a bartender. The bartender was a server indeed. Hakeem caught him in the corner of the bar on more than one club night, entangled with another man, whispering in the shroud of music and darkness. The bartender's flirtations signaled drama and Hakeem wanted no involvement.

"I'm not ashamed of what I do." Khalil defended, still focused on his phone.

"I can see that. Who are you texting?"

"Omar"—Khalil looked up briefly—"Talkin' about wantin' to see me tonight."

"Is that right?"

"I'm not sure just yet."

"You're sure alright. You'll be at Omar's house tonight." *Why are we playing these games?*

"How you know what I'm gonna do, honey?"

"Because you're predictable. You keep saying you're done with Omar but continue accepting his calls and going to his house."

Resistance was as foreign to Khalil as speaking Spanish. Whenever Omar called, Khalil went running despite knowing that he was promiscuous. Hakeem saw Omar as a risk on two legs and had advised Khalil to take precautions. Promiscuous gay men were red flags to Hakeem and he had evaded his share.

"I just have needs," Khalil said in a lower voice.

"If that's what you want to ca–" Hakeem didn't finish the statement, seeing Miguel approaching their table.

"Are you ready to order?" Miguel asked after placing the drinks and appetizers on the table.

"We are"—Hakeem answered for the two of them—"Khalil" he called, breaking his concentration. "He's ready to take our orders."

"Oh!" Khalil placed the phone face down on the table.

Hakeem sipped the blueberry lemonade, listening. Without gin and vodka, the lemonade lacked a spiky edge.

"What time is Omar expecting you over?" he asked Khalil after Miguel walked away.

"I was thinkin' about goin' over there when we finish here."

"Sooo, no movies?"

"Child, hush. We can always reschedule."

Ain't this bout a blip! I'm being stood up! It was what their friendship had become—a rotation of conveniences. Khalil wanted to run into the arms of Omar. The plans that he made with his best-friend apparently didn't matter.

Hakeem tried not to be resentful but irritation took over. Sulking replaced his appetite. He did not think their friendship was going to survive. No relationship was worth maintaining if only one party benefited from the association. Before the arrest, Hakeem might have drank a cocktail to calm his mood, but drinking alcohol was off limits now. There were more effective remedies free of self-destructive elements, for the immediate situation.

A FOREST HIDDEN BY TREES

A FOREST HIDDEN BY TREES

Some things can be in our line of sight for so long that over time, we cease to see or...intentionally ignore them.

Hakeem would never forget when Khalil vanished on his birthday weekend, months following the DUI arrest.

In the weeks leading up to Atlanta's Gay Pride, Khalil said he was going to skip the annual event and not get caught up in the hoopla.

Hakeem broached the subject about hanging out—going to dinner and the movies. Khalil was open to the suggestion, and thus, Hakeem coordinated plans. However, on his birthday, Khalil was unresponsive to phone calls and text messages. Khalil called three days later, claiming he had been sick from what started as a hangover. Hakeem thought to put distance in their friendship then, but his friendships were already few.

≈≈≈≈≈≈

The DUI charge hovered ominously over Hakeem since the case was still open, progressing towards the two-year mark. Making more mistakes would worsen his position. It was stressful enough worrying about what the final judgment would be. The last he heard from the attorney was that the next court date had been postponed. Hakeem did not want to accept the idea of going to jail, having agonized during the hours of detainment. Returning to jail deposited a nauseating lump in his abdomen, causing a flareup of anxiety.

105

Hakeem tried to think of someone to call on the way home from Khalil's. He owed Rosalyn at least one. Not that he had anything important to say, just as long as she was alright.

"Hello," Rosalyn answered monotonically.

"Did you call that place to setup payment arrangements?"

"Who this?"

"It's Hakeem." Already, his patience began to fade. *Why can't she recognize my voice?*

"Oh. Yeah, I called. Spoke with some lady and she gave me an extension."

"Good."

"Yeah. I'm sittin' here waiting for your sister to come home."

"Who? Layla?" He heard the aggravation in her voice. It wouldn't be long now. Soon he would be annoyed with her and prepared to derail her when she did. There were other things on his mind.

"Yep."

"What happened?"

"She hasn't been here in a couple of days. When she gets in, I'm gonna' tell her that she can stay where she's been stayin'."

"I see...when was the last time she came home?" He tried to remain unconcerned, anticipating that changing the subject was not going to prevent an argument with Rosalyn. When she was irritated, disagreements were inevitable unless he ended the conversation.

"Last Saturday."

Almost a week. "Has Layla called?"

"She called to check on me two days ago."

"Okay. Did you two resolve the issue with her paying rent?"

"Yeah. But now it seems like she's using my apartment as a storage place."

Wasn't the original issue about Layla paying the right amount of rent? Now she's talking about Layla not being there all the time! That was another reason he couldn't tolerate Rosalyn—she was impossible to satisfy. No wonder Layla frequently stayed away from home—living with Rosalyn was insufferable. There was little value in interjecting an opinion because Rosalyn had the right to set the rules for living in her apartment. Doing so however, put her at a disadvantage whenever in need of help. Oftentimes, none of the children wanted to come to her aid.

It is audacious for parents to expect their children to offer care subsequent to their mistreatments. For anyone who leaned on the Scripture, **"honor your father and mother..."** (Exodus 20:12; Ephesians 6:2), the Bible also advises parents not to **"provoke their children to anger"** (Ephesians 6:4; Colossians 3:21). Rosalyn used to say, "I brought you into this world and I can take you out."

Hakeem disagreed. God made it all possible, and the laws of the land can exact punishment for varying types of abuse. Regardless of what parents may believe, they don't get free tickets to mistreat or abuse children. Child abuse and neglect cause lifelong hurt, pain, suffering, anxiety, depression, and resentment. It is perhaps humanly impossible for children not to harbor long-term resentment towards the parents and guardians who abused or neglected them at some point in life.

When parents sit in nursing homes without so much as an annual visit from their children, they should ask themselves if cognitively possible, "What did I do to deserve abandonment?" Abused children may be unable to elude psychological damage, but they can physically escape their perpetrators when the opportunity arises. Some never look back when they get the chance to break free. Irony exists in life's tendency to make the oppressively strong, weak and dependent. Oppressors are mortal despite whatever they believed. The cycle of life and the passage of time shifts and balances power.

"Of course, it seems like Layla isn't there. But she is paying rent, which was your goal."

"Right. Layla is paying rent. It's just time for her to get her own place. All of you are grown now. It's time for you all to take care of yourselves."

Hakeem agreed that Layla needed to find an apartment, primarily for her benefit. Rosalyn needed to live alone to marinate in misery. He noticed over the years that misfortune always seemed to befall Rosalyn and believed it was the consequence of her treatment of the children. There was little need to be critical since she made her own life complicated.

"Hopefully, Layla will get her own place."

"Maybe you should talk to her."

"I probably will." *But it won't be for your benefit.* He turned onto the street to his apartment. "Look, Ma, I'm almost home. I'll talk with you later." After dealing with Khalil, he was emotionally drained.

"Alright. Call me later."

Once settled, he was going to contact Layla. They needed to talk.

≈≈≈≈≈≈≈

"How was work today?" Gail asked. She wore a coral jacket over a light-blue, cowl-necked dress along with tangerine stilettos. The upward twist of braids granted her a youthful sophistication.

Hakeem stared at the painting of a singer in a form-fitted white gown standing in front of an audience and a pianist in a black tuxedo at her side. He heard Gail's question but wanted to think before responding.

"I was just there."

"What do you mean?"

"Like going through the motions….just working while mentally somewhere else."

"More problems on the job?"

"Yes."

"Do you want to talk about it?"

"They're watching everything now….every move we make. There's this coworker who keeps running back and telling my supervisor that I do homework at my desk."

Gail rolled her eyes dramatically and quickly regained composure, as if realizing what she had done.

"How do you know that the coworker told your supervisor?"

"Because he brought it to me."

"Are you doing homework at your desk?"

"Yes. I do it between work." Hakeem flexed his shoulders. "I meet all of my deadlines, so I don't see it as a problem."

"Did you discuss all of this with your supervisor?"

"I did."

"What happened?"

"In essence, he wants me to help the team more."

"How do you feel about his feedback?"

"He irritated me. Believe me, I already help the team and everyone else. My supervisor knows this."

"Why does everyone rely on you for help?"

"I think it's because I avail myself to learning and articulate what I learn. It was one of the reasons why I was previously selected to be a training assistant."

"But you are no longer a training assistant, right?"

"Right."

"Does your company not have a training department?"

"They do. It's just that management tries to exploit every valuable resource."

Gail chuckled. "Sounds like good ol' Corporate America alright."

"They are turning that place into a cotton-picking field.... monitoring how long employees are away from their cubicles....I'm going to choke one of them if they keep watching me." He pictured his hands encircling Bill's throat, thumbs forcing his larynx to collapse.

Gail's eyebrows rose as she stared into his eyes. "Are you taking the medication?"

"I am, but not consistently."

"Are you having complications with the medication?"

"No. I just don't believe in medication. I mean....I don't want to become dependent on it."

"Understandable. However, I prescribed the medication specifically for your panic attacks and sleep. Both are intended to help you manage your anxiety."

"I'm sleeping a little better and I don't feel the chest pains when I take the medicine."

"Glad to hear that. Can you try taking the medication more often"—she maintained eye contact with him—"until you're able to manage your anxiety and anger better?"

Hakeem smirked, wishing for an alternative. "I'll try," he agreed reluctantly.

"Let's talk about your anger. Earlier you mentioned that you're 'going to choke someone at work.' Is it just your job that makes you angry?"

"Not really."

"Do you want to talk about it?"

He shrugged. "I don't mind. It's life in general."

It was a vague response.

"Okay....life. How is your relationship with your family?" She pushed away from the desk and settled further into the chair, arms folded on her lap.

"Whew! Where do I start?" He licked his lips. Discussing his family wasn't a light conversation.

"You may begin with your childhood or any point where you feel most comfortable."

"Well, my grandparents raised me. My mother lives in Philadelphia and my father lives in Minneapolis."

"Do you have a good relationship with your grandparents?"

"I do....for the most part. They've supported me my entire life."

"What about your mother?"

"Our relationship has never been great. Not what I'd call high quality."

"Why is that?"

"She just wasn't capable."

"Is that why your grandparents raised you?"

"Partly. My mother and I have rarely got along because of the way she treated me."

"Do you want to elaborate?"

"Things worsened when I moved to live with her in Philadelphia. I had believed that things would be better."

Hakeem proceeded to tell Gail about the domestic abuse Rosalyn endured and the abuse that he suffered under her guardianship. He told her about Rosalyn calling him derogatory names, insulting his sexuality. He mentioned feeling satisfaction when Rosalyn sent him to live with Earl.

There were no tears in recanting the past. Hakeem had stopped crying about Rosalyn years ago. Any tears shed in the present flowed from self-pity.

"How do you feel about your mother now?"

"This might sound really bad coming from me....but I force myself to tolerate my mother. I can go weeks without talking to her." He had few kind words for Rosalyn. To preserve the little respect that remained, he tried to suppress most thoughts regarding her. Oftentimes in private, he cursed Rosalyn for the pain and suffering she caused.

Gail maintained an expressionless face.

What am I expecting to see, a tearful Gail?

"Do you get angry when you think about your mother?"

"Most of the time." Hakeem withheld the secret tirades in which he vocalized anger towards Rosalyn.

"Do you believe yourself capable of forgiving her?"

"I thought I had, and yet, she still makes me angry. So...perhaps I haven't." He looked at Gail questioningly. Maybe she had an explanation.

"What would it take for you to forgive your mother?"

"For her to own up to what she did to me."

"Have you tried to have that conversation with her?"

"Indirectly. We were arguing over my siblings. She was talking about how irresponsible they are. But she and their father are to blame."

"What did your mother say?"

"Oh, she doesn't take responsibility for anything she's done. It's exhausting talking to her. She's always claiming to be a victim."

"You mentioned that your mother was a victim of abuse. Do you think it played a role in her relationship with you?"

"I haven't given it much thought."

"Sometimes the abused subject others to maltreatment. Their actions aren't justified, but there is a link between childhood experiences and adult behavior." Gail made several notations in the folder. "How is the relationship with your father?"

"Not good. It's almost the same as the relationship with my mother. Sometimes I don't know who is worse."

"Why do you feel that way?" Gail betrayed nothing of her thoughts.

"He's a liar and a manipulator. He even denied me as his son."

"How do you know that?"

"Which part?"

"That your father denied you."

"He told me to my face that he believed my father was another man. I also overheard him saying the same thing to one of my sibling's mother over the phone, right after my stepmother left him."

"How did you feel when your father said those words?"

"I felt betrayed...felt lower than the ground...like I was nothing." Hakeem gritted his teeth. He wanted to fight, to destroy something. Almost everyone who was supposed to care, had trampled him instead.

"How do you feel now, talking about your father?"

She resumed taking notes, her pen moved back and forth on the paper.

It was a sign to continue.

"Irritated somewhat." Hakeem guessed that his facial expression matched his stony attitude.

"Do you want to continue discussing him?"

"I don't mind." He didn't talk about Earl much to anyone. Talking to her was the best alternative.

"Can I conclude that you've lived with your father?"

"Yes. For a couple of years."

"What was it like living with him?"

"Stressful. I tell you,"—his voice elevated—"my father is like my mother....dominating and controlling! If you didn't do things his way, he'd slander your name. I do okay without him being in my life."

"Your pain is understandable. Most people desire a strong bond with their parents and you were denied the experience. For as long as the time that you describe, it's not something that's easy to overcome."

"Yeah," Hakeem croaked. His throat constricted from frustration. Although it was the past, thinking about Rosalyn and Earl made him want to fly into a rage. Many times, he wanted to curse them and hurt their feelings too.

"Did your parents go to college?"

"My mother did."

"What about your father?"

"College, no. And I've wondered whether he completed high school. He never talked about it."

"I know I've commended you before. You have achieved a great deal at your age, possibly more than either of your parents whether you believe it or not, and you haven't reached your full potential yet. What do you think?"

Gail had a way of restoring hope and he found a spark of optimism. "You're right. I have accomplished more than they have."

"Take pride in that, Hakeem. You're on a good road." She smiled reassuringly. "But I still want you to continue to work on controlling your anger."

She wrote a few additional notes in his folder. "Tell me something. Do you go to church?"

"Not on a regular basis." He reflected on the last time he went to church. "Actually, I haven't been to church in several years."

"Any particular reason?"

"I just haven't felt motivated to go." It wasn't the complete truth. There were other reasons for his absences. He just wasn't comfortable divulging those motives.

"Do you like church?"

"Definitely. I'm a member of one on the Southside of Atlanta."

"Would it be too difficult for you to start attending again?"

"Not at all. I don't do much of anything on Sundays."

"It doesn't have to be the same church. I just believe you'll find some solace there as well." She glowed warmly.

"I accept your advice." He would be a fool not to. Nothing Gail said was unreasonable. He needed to get better and break out of the darkness. Attending church was an activity that had become less of a priority. The comfort of staying at home had taken control.

≈≈≈≈≈≈≈

Contention riddled the mother-daughter relationship between Evelyn and Rosalyn much like the persisting disharmony between Rosalyn and Hakeem. The strife between parent and child was a familial curse that transferred to the succeeding generation. Rosalyn did not exhibit qualities, which Evelyn believed were befitting of a daughter. Hakeem displayed none of the mannerisms Rosalyn deemed appropriate for a male child. Consequently, both child and grandchild resented their parent's misdeeds.

A senior in high school, Rosalyn conceived with Earl—a married man who lived less than a mile from her parents. Fearing exposure of the scandal within the neighborhood and their religious congregation, Evelyn took the initiative to inform both Earl's wife and clergy of Rosalyn's sexual indiscretion. Information traveled quickly in a town with a population of eighty-four hundred people, and Evelyn dreaded the idea of being the center of gossip.

Earl knew with certainty that Rosalyn was pregnant because he suffered from *couvade syndrome*, and told her about the symptoms. Fearful, she tried to conceal the pregnancy for as long as deceptively possible. When Evelyn realized that Rosalyn was pregnant, she could do nothing other than inform Earl's wife.

No one foresaw Earl's reaction. After Evelyn apprised his wife, he shot two bullets into the roof of her house as a warning. Luckily, Joseph and Evelyn were out of town. Rosalyn was not as fortunate. The clergy excommunicated her for being unmarried and pregnant. Meanwhile, Earl faded into the shadows, withholding involvement and never attempted to cultivate a relationship with Hakeem.

Rosalyn was psychologically and financially unprepared to raise a baby. Her new predicament worsened the already unstable relationship with Evelyn. Rosalyn told Hakeem that after he was born, Evelyn struck her with a belt while she held him. In response, Rosalyn placed him in the crib, turned and punched Evelyn in the face. After the physical altercation, Joseph and Evelyn threw Rosalyn out of the house, and she took Hakeem along. Not too long afterwards, a family friend told them that Rosalyn was struggling to care for Baby Hakeem. With Joseph leading in the decision, Rosalyn agreed to allow her parents to raise their grandson.

Few lucrative career opportunities existed in Clinton City for African-Americans during the eighties. Thus, Rosalyn moved to Philadelphia with relatives to obtain a sustainable job. Throughout the years, she maintained communication with her parents for access to Hakeem. However, the passage of time failed to improve upon her relationship with Evelyn. Joseph oftentimes, served as mediator with Hakeem being the connection between all parties.

The longer Rosalyn and Hakeem remained separated, the more they became estranged. A combination of living in the ghettos of Philly and relationships with no-good men hardened Rosalyn. She was very critical in her opinions about Hakeem when visiting Clinton City. While she didn't know about his abuse, she perceived signs of effeminate characteristics in him at seven years old and became angry. Rosalyn verbalized none of her suspicions to Joseph and Evelyn. Instead, she confronted Hakeem while they were away at a religious service.

Rosalyn hated the way Hakeem walked—head held high, shoulders straight, and the switch in his hips according to her observations. She made him walk back and forth repeatedly in her parent's kitchen, trying to correct his gait all the while yelling threats. He might have cried from the intimidation were it not for thinking how he wanted her to leave. The Monday morning that she was scheduled to depart for Philly could not arrive fast enough.

A full-sized Hakeem might have slapped Rosalyn or said something profane. The playback was as vivid as the day the incident occurred. His worst experiences burned fiercely among countless memories. He believed that hateful parents did not deserve children because they cultivated seeds of malice in their offspring. For Hakeem, that darkness dwelled a lifetime.

For thirty years, Rosalyn stayed separated from the faith. And, for thirty years until Evelyn's death, mother and daughter bickered, never reconciling completely. Rosalyn said that Evelyn told her in later years that she never loved her. The disclosure wasn't improbable, as Evelyn told Hakeem before he moved to Philly that Uncle Daryle was her favorite child. Evelyn further stated that she would only acknowledge the grandchildren that Daryle sired. She was forced to swallow her spitefulness as Daryle's sexual orientation confirmed he would remain unmarried and childless until his death.

Rosalyn re-dedicated her life to the faith without Evelyn to witness. Considering all that transpired between them, Hakeem wondered whether the event contained the potential to demolish three and a half decades of bitterness. Sediments of animosity rested deep within each of the women's hearts, persisting despite their proclaimed devotion to the light of faith. They were also reflections of his grim disposition.

≈≈≈≈≈≈≈

Hakeem simmered silently about the fact that he made 0.076 percent of Horizon's $45 million service portfolio. Kaleidoscope robbed its employees to fund the executives' seven-figure salaries. *Who cares that the top-execs were decision-makers?!* They were not the innovators. The lowly, underpaid employees within the firm conceptualized and developed everything of which the company benefitted. Reading periodic financial reports and presenting performance reviews did not require exceptional skill. The analysts had already done the hardest part of the job—compiling, organizing, analyzing and articulating the data. Who knew better than Hakeem? He performed the same tasks for management. *No!* He needed to resume job hunting and get far from Kaleidoscope before he awakened in a cell with padded walls.

The sound of wind chimes resonated from the smartphone lying on the desk. Hakeem had set the tone for notification alerts. Layla's thumbnail picture from her social media profile floated across the display screen. It took her two weeks to respond to his online message. He anticipated that she would delay as habit when something serious was amiss. Layla might challenge Rosalyn but not her older brother.

"What's up?" she texted.

Hakeem did not sugarcoat his reply, "What's going on with you and mom?"

"What do you mean?"

"About you not coming home. I heard that you haven't been home in a few days."

"I was just home two days ago."

Rather than tell Layla that Rosalyn planned to put her out, Hakeem pursued another route. "Have you considered getting an apartment?"

"Not until recently. I just got a job with the airlines."

Good! "Doing what?"

"Flight-attendant."

He could see Layla composing another text in the message window.

"Why did you ask me about getting an apartment?" She returned to his previous question.

"I think it would put you in a better position. That way, you can come and go as you please."

"You've spoken to mom?"

"Yeah, I have."

"What did she say?"

"I'm not going to tell you what was said." He knew that recanting the conversation would exacerbate the situation. "But I believe it best that you find a place for yourself. Then you can live by your rules."

"Are you serious?"

"Yes, I am. You know how mom is. Yet, you continue to challenge her, in her apartment. It doesn't make sense!"

"You were always mom's favorite."

"You're so far off base. If only you knew how wrong you are." *This isn't about me.*

"Mom always speaks highly of you."

Of course she does, now! Hakeem decided to indulge Layla's deflection. He'd shut her up then. "Let's get one thing clear. I was never mom's favorite. Katrina, Tyrell and you were….the love children of mom and your father"—he paused momentarily, then continued typing—"Mom speaks of me the way she does because I defied her predictions. You must've forgotten all the rotten things mom used to say to me…all the things she did."

"I don't remember what she said," Layla texted.

"It doesn't matter." Layla probably didn't remember. She was too young to be concerned with such matters. "The advice I've given you is for your benefit. Not mine."

"Well, I didn't ask for it."

"And that doesn't matter either. If Rosalyn puts you out, you have no other place besides your father's house to go. That's for certain."

Layla stopped typing. He wondered whether she had abandoned the conversation or was thinking of another response. But he intended to close the conversation.

"So that you know, I defended you. Then I contacted you to motivate you into taking initiative in your life. You have yet to build anything for yourself. If you continue to depend on mom, you will end up with nothing because she doesn't have anything to give you."

Nothing. No activity on the screen. Then finally, Layla began typing again.

"Alright. You right, big brother."

He didn't know whether Layla was being empathetic or sarcastic. She was quite capable of emoting both. Perhaps it was best to let the matter settle for now. At least he planted the seed that needed to be sowed. Layla's future decisions would confirm whether the seed rooted into her branching maturity as an adult.

Tough love, Hakeem resolved. He had no idea of the type of emotional support her boyfriend provided. As far as he was concerned, the majority of Layla's associations were incapable of motivating her to be greater than present circumstances. He would not give Rosalyn the satisfaction of seeing her children struggle as she had.

≈≈≈≈≈≈≈

"Hey, you!"

Hakeem swiveled his chair in the direction of the feminine voice.

Josefina stood inside the entrance of the cube, hands resting on her hips. "Where you been hidin'?"

"I've been here. You know they're watchin' us now."

"Ugh! I know it. The same thing is goin' on over on my side."

Josefina stationed herself in the empty chair and scooted close. "Your friend has been keepin' up mess."

"Who?"

"Nora."

"What has she done?" Hakeem had not told anyone that he was no longer friends with Nora. In fact, they were little more than associates now. Even Alex had advised to be wary of Nora because she had burned several employees. Other coworkers had also warned to use caution..

Hakeem defended Nora and made excuses until witnessing her in action. Nora actively blocked employees from the possibility of promotion when they applied for internal jobs and didn't hesitate to give bad references. Hakeem was aware that some of her subordinates were low performers. However, Nora was deficient in the area of personnel development. As a supervisor, she shared the responsibility of ensuring that employees performed successfully. When their performance exceeded expectations, she received recognition and incentives. It seemed only equitable that she bear part of the blame when the employees' performance fell short of the target.

Nora reported everything to management. And, it wasn't her right to blow the whistle on misconduct that bothered Hakeem. Instead, it was her inconsistency in the practice when members of management were culprits of unethical and inappropriate situations. She exhibited double standards and sometimes, a bully mentality, and Hakeem scorned her behavior. In his opinion, people who sought to harm others without provocation were malicious. Even when provoked, there were honorable methods to exacting retribution.

"You know Myra has back issues, right?"

"I heard her mention it. Just not the full details."

"Well, your friend"—Josefina clinched her teeth on the last word—"has been trying to get Myra fired because of her excessive absences. Nora knows very well that Myra's problem is legit. So, when Myra returns to work, Nora denies her schedule changes and piles on extra tasks. It's like she's trying to force Myra to quit!"

Hakeem frowned, shaking his head in disgust. He trained Myra in a new hire class four years ago. She had developed into a competent employee. But even if Myra was a poor performer, she didn't deserve mistreatment. He felt sorry for her and himself. Only the employees who benefitted exponentially or had nowhere else to go, remained loyal to the company.

"I've got to get outta here, Josefina!"

"Baby, me too. But your day is coming. Just hold on." Josefina scanned the walkway outside the cubicle, checking for eavesdroppers. "Did you see the doctor yet?"

"I did."

"How do you feel?"

"A little better than before. Oh! I've decided to start going back to church."

Beautiful straight teeth flashed through her red lips. "I wasn't aware that you stopped going. You coulda came to mine!"

Going to church with Josefina might have been a pleasant experience. However, church was a personal experience to him. He had reasons for his hiatus.

"Still....I'm glad you're returning." She gave him a light rub on the shoulders.

"Have you made any yellow rice and beans?"

"Not recently. This weekend...maybe."

"Please remember to bring me some if you do." He loved yellow rice and beans.

There was a Spanish restaurant in Philly that served yellow rice and beans—two blocks up the street from the apartment building where he once lived. The allowances from Joseph were used to buy roasted chicken breasts along with yellow rice and beans. Rich brown bean gravy heaped in the middle of the rice bed spilled down the sides. It was a delectable meal indeed. *If a person dared, they too, can find a pleasant memory or two, buried beneath the rubble of the painful ones.*

≈≈≈≈≈≈≈

Parents are the first and most important contacts in a child's world. By role and function, parents greatly and significantly impact a child's psychological development. Moreover, parent-child relationships are schematic in that a child first learns how to develop relationships with others (i.e., siblings, peers, etc.) based on the quality of interaction with their parents.

When parents reject or abandon their child, they are indirectly communicating that something is wrong with the child. The child picks up on this behavior and quality of interaction, and if it is never corrected, the child matures believing that something is wrong with themselves and thus, low self-esteem and other psychological abnormalities develop. It is for this reason that low self-esteem is common among victims of child abuse, abandonment, and products of dysfunctional homes.

Low self-esteem will ultimately and negatively impact most self-perceptions the child will possess about themselves throughout the various stages of life. Low self-esteem will play a major role in the child's decisions relating to career, friends, intimate partners, and offspring (generational transference).

An attentive parent/guardian consoles the child when the latter makes mistakes or the odds stack against them. When the outside world rejects or ostracizes the child, the parent/guardian offsets those negative experiences with substantive displays of love and encouragement, such as:

- *"You're good enough."*
- *"You're special."*
- *"You'll do better next time."*
- *And most importantly, "I love you."*

The mature and attentive parent/guardian will also take ownership of their own problems and challenges instead of blaming the child for their mistakes. They will not make negative statements or project onto the child that their existence is an inconvenience or mistake. Consider the following negatively-impacting statements.

- *"I should have never married your father/mother."*
- *"Having you was a mistake."*

- *Or as Earl said regarding Hakeem: "Your mother got pregnant by another man."*
- *Rosalyn's statement: "Arnold and I planned to have your brothers and sisters."*

The last four statements are not only hurtful but will cultivate bitterness and resentment within the child.

PREVAILING WINDS AND BROKEN WEATHERVANES

As a weathervane shows the direction of the wind, so does a person's senses alert to brewing trouble. But many of us have abandoned our instincts, allowing them to fall into disrepair.

Hakeem sat on the sofa in front of the television. On the news, a reporter covered the protest for a Black male teenager—a former member of a local gang, who was shot multiple times by the police. The camera panned two blocks of densely populated people standing outside the courthouse, awaiting the verdict of the officers involved.

The shooting followed a 911 emergency call reporting a street fight that erupted near a grocery store. Police officers arrived onto the scene, finding the teenager lingering after many bystanders had dispersed. A cop ordered the teen to surrender but the teen attempted to flee, and another officer opened fire. Sadly, the teen died as paramedics attempted to stabilize him.

"Not guilty," the defense attorney read the verdict of the grand jury aloud from the steps of the courthouse. The protestors' angry voices exploded into raw outrage. If the protestors could have laid hands on the attorney, they would have ripped him to shreds. But both the policemen and National Guard were patrolling the rally, prepared for a riot—equipped with face and body shields and batons.

Law enforcements' attendance proved not in vain. Five minutes later, the verdict fully absorbed in the onlookers' minds, sounds of shattering glass joined with their angry chants. Looting and environmental destruction renewed, fires igniting through the windows of parked cars.

The newswoman tried her best to keep up with the surrounding chaos. She fought a losing battle. Between the rushing people and angry voices, she lost ground. A woman, seeing the reporter unable to advance through the moving crowd, pushed forward and grabbed the microphone, screaming injustice.

In the days leading up to the night's protest, the news recorded a Black man wheeling a 55-inch flat-screen television away from an electronic store. A gas station was torched and burned to the ground. Theft, vandalism, and environmental destruction were incapable of resolving the issue of injustice in the United States' legal system. The activities undermined the economy within the area, causing job losses. Someone's relative or friend lost a stream of income—their place of employment reduced to rubble and ashes. What if the company opted to forego rebuilding and relocated business elsewhere? The people impacted, either became permanently unemployed or had to travel farther for work when their jobs used to be three blocks away, or a short commute on the bus line. For every action, there are ripples of reactions and effects. Causing additional strife did not improve upon nearly four centuries of systematic oppression in African-American communities across the nation.

Hakeem criticized the African-American community for its ineffective double standards. Many within the community cried out injustice while failing to take cohesive stances against Black-on-Black crime. Although the teenager was killed by the officer, the situation began with a crime of violence. In another city, a Black teenager was shot by a cop while fleeing the scene of an armed robbery in an African-American neighborhood. In both cases, crime preceded the outcome. Yet, crime was not a factor in every homicidal situation involving police brutality.

A youth was killed after a cop perceived his toy gun as a threat. A teenager was murdered after a resident in the same neighborhood within which the victim lived, profiled, grappled, and ultimately shot him to death. An officer shot a young adult in the back following a commotion at a train station. Supposedly, the cop 'mistook' his firearm for a taser-gun. Two policemen held a man to the ground and one of the officers found it necessary to shoot the victim in the chest, even though they had already restrained the victim.

The African-American community evaluated each instance of police brutality as a demonstration of racism and discrimination when the justice system permitted acquittals for the white perpetrators. The excessive force exhibited by law enforcers in 2016 is reminiscent of the brutality exercised by police officers in the 1960s and beyond. Given the judicial partiality displayed towards whites, there is no guarantee that even if a Black person obeyed the law, they have a greater chance of survival.

The scenarios described illustrated two major issues within the African-American community: an unwillingness to collaborate to address crime within Black neighborhoods, and a limited understanding of judicial systems and politics. Many Black people did not spend enough time learning about the law and its intricacies. Perhaps if more African-Americans displayed as much fervor for familiarizing themselves with laws as they did with acquiring knowledge about the most frivolous aspects of this world, they'd become astute at maneuvering through its loopholes. Unless a practitioner of the law, a large number of African-Americans acquired understanding through participation in legal proceedings. Other than knowing that drinking and driving was unsafe, Hakeem understood very little pertaining to the legal ramifications of the act. But in the court of law, ignorance could not shield him from the consequences of his misdeeds.

When Black people were condemned for their transgressions, some quickly compared their actions to whites. But how did finger-pointing and denying accountability eradicate the repercussions of wrongdoing? It did not. Someone was victimized or harmed by a crime, and there should be penalties in such instances. The law when justly interpreted served as a deterrent against misconduct. Therefore, a crime should be judged illegal regardless of the suspect's race. Unfortunately, the judicial system in the U.S. failed to consistently ensure that justice was equitably served in these contexts.

Supreme White America did not consistently forget or forgive the crimes that African-Americans committed. Once a Black man's name went into the criminal justice system, there it remained—a haunting and impeding reminder of mistakes paid. But a Caucasian could enter a public facility, kill multiple people and children, and leave the courthouse with barely a misdemeanor conviction or be deemed clinically insane. The legal system and sympathizers of the suspect often allowed biases to cloud their evaluations of the evidence, or dismissed the evidence as credible, or determined that the offense was due to mental instability. A white criminal could still experience preferential treatment in obtaining employment over a Black person who had no criminal background. A Black person could kill or harm an individual, be labeled "dangerous", and be lucky to make it to a jail cell alive. Then the legal system came along, locked the Black man or woman behind bars and threw away the key.

One of a Black ex-con's greatest aspirations is self-employment unless he or she is content with struggling to obtain a mundane job that paid average wages. The Black ex-con's criminal background was a dead weight that trailed their arduous climb up the socioeconomic ladder. It is this inequitable treatment demonstrated towards Black people that perpetuates their dismal view of America. Considering the challenges that Blacks face, it is best that they avoid entanglements with the negative side of the law as Hakeem learned.

The African-American condition is discouraging without flames of optimism. An objective assessment of the Black man's plight reveals that self-employment and entrepreneurship could potentially create the advantages that the African-American community desperately needs. These communities could certainly benefit from circulating financial resources within its interiors for socio-economic development and sustainability. Through social cohesion, African-Americans possess the capacity to build their own schools, libraries, hospitals, recreational facilities, shopping centers and restaurants as they did in the 1920s (see Black Wall Street). Jews, Italians, Hispanics, and Asians are quite efficient in the practice.

Collectively, African-Americans must do their part in reforming the justice system and fighting crime. If African-Americans courageously addressed crime in their neighborhoods and households, the efforts could potentially remedy a segment of a much larger systemic problem in society and thus, minimize the number of Black youths and men entering the prison systems. Male figures should be in the households standing shoulder-to-shoulder with the mothers of their children and in the community, prepping their successors. They cannot serve as pillars of their community behind bars. Socio-environmental change must begin from within and be propelled by members sharing mutual goals.

As it stands, the advantages that African-Americans possess to turn the tide of racial injustice are the very weapons they toss aside. The African-American increased in wisdom when they acknowledge who held the majority of political power in the United States and functioned cohesively to execute effective strategies to thwart systems of oppression. Voter participation is inconsistent during mid-term and presidential elections in the Black communities. Consequently, African-Americans often miss their chance to infiltrate the White House and legislation with significant representation, namely, politicians and lawmakers— those of whom were willing to rally for the Black community. Thus, Blacks become vulnerable to the occupation of white supremacists in seats of political power.

White supremacy has persisted for nearly four-hundred years because its foundation remains. Oppression remains because its' architects understand systems and have implanted their successors in every generation with the knowledge necessary to maintain operations. The socio-economic progress that minorities in the United States reap in the present, results from years of partnership and collaboration between Blacks and Whites fighting against prejudice and discrimination.

Somewhere along the way, vigilance diminished in the offspring of the freedom fighters. Perhaps the liberties birthed out of the Civil Rights Movement and the removal of racial barriers in certain contexts rendered many minorities naïve—believing that the battle had been permanently and irreversibly won. Such naivety has only served to weaken the Black peoples' comprehension regarding systematic oppression and capacity to establish an impenetrable opposition. Is it an accurate statement that

African-Americans prove a greater adversary of injustice when they have nothing to lose?

From atop the walls of socio-economic division, sympathizers see contention and disorganization within African-American communities. How else does one explain the outright disrespect and violence that Black people display towards another? Debates that pit light-skinned and dark-skinned people against each other—why should the shade of a person's skin matter when the outside world already judges an African-American on such basis? It seems almost commonplace to kill someone for an expensive pair of brand name shoes. But these situations are casually or dismissively discussed without formulating solutions to the problems. Where the cost of merchandise acquisition is a constant issue, Black people could simply boycott celebrities profiting exponentially from their consumption and do not reinvest in the community.

Sympathizers also observe that some African-Americans are too arrogant and ignorant to obtain and retain an accurate account of Black history. Unquestionably, white supremacists and those who exercised privilege know Black history and oppression, using the ignorance of African-Americans for subterfuge. As long as Black men and women chase after the bone on a string and are distracted by shallow promises, they will be constantly undermined and dominated by white supremacy. Think not? Whenever the Black people forsook their right to vote, they gave oppression a stronger foothold. As long as the African-American prioritized superficial pursuits over substantial goals and the opportunity to improve their mind, they left themselves vulnerable to ignorance. Anytime an African-American betrayed their brethren for selfish gain, their actions hindered communitywide progress. Every time a Black person harmed their brethren, the occurrence was an affront to the Black community and the outside world ridiculed them for their actions.

≈≈≈≈≈≈≈

Hakeem stretched the full length of the sofa, pulling the draped royal blue throw across his body. The medicine would take effect soon. Closing his in expectation, he drifted into the past.

Shortly after turning nineteen, he entered the criminal justice system, pockets filled with arrogance and ignorance. Distant from his mind was the idea of life being better than working two jobs—a waiter at a restaurant and a sales associate at a wholesale retail store in Minneapolis.

One particular weekend, Fred—a coworker from the restaurant came into the store. At the register, Fred asked for a "discount" on three articles of clothing. Reports of theft were already circulating the store, but Hakeem gave little attention to the matter. He had stolen nothing, so there was no reason to be concerned.

Examining each piece of merchandise, Hakeem rung up the $29.99 jacket and subtotaled the sale, intending to bag two shirts free of charge. He was preparing to complete the sale when a man appeared at his side, questioning the pending transaction. Hakeem stuttered, at which point, the man collected the merchandise from the counter and told him to follow to the back of the store. The security that accompanied the plainclothesman led Fred in another direction.

In a small room furnished with a wooden table and four chairs, the plainclothesman introduced himself as an investigator. Coincidently, he was in the store that day for another incident. Hakeem disliked the man. The investigator was aggressive and made numerous presumptions. When the investigator permitted him to speak, he tried to bully a confession. Hakeem denied any wrongdoing and claimed the subtotal button was keyed by mistake. The investigator argued that the store's surveillance camera indicated otherwise. He considered the investigator's response and decided that a thorough review of the camera was impossible given the short amount of time that transpired and refused to comply further.

The investigator left the sparsely furnished room and returned with a policeman to continue the investigation. It was apparent that a conversation had transpired outside. According to the investigator, Fred confessed to being offered the merchandise free of charge.

Although unsure whether the investigator's claim was a tactic to compel a confession, Hakeem believed it probable that Fred snitched in fear. But it was too late and didn't matter anyway, he had thought.

He should have ignored Fred. He wished he had scanned all of the merchandise and made him pay. The wrong decision compromised his job, and he stood the chance of being prosecuted. He was aware of the store's theft policy, but never foresaw an instance where he would be penalized by those rules.

The store manager entered the room near the end of the interrogation. Hakeem also disliked the boxed-cut blonde haired woman, Cathy. For a manager, she was standoffish and interacted with employees only when tasks warranted dictation. Cathy and the investigator engaged in a private conversation in the corner of the room while he waited. When they finished, she confirmed his termination and because the incident involved theft, she requested his picture for the loss prevention unit. Using a Polaroid camera, she took the photo, placed it in a manila folder and exited the room.

The policeman handed Hakeem a citation for the theft attempt. Misdemeanor of the First Offense, the citation read. The total value of the merchandise equated to sixty dollars—an amount that did not meet the criteria for grand theft but was enough to create legal problems. Having no outstanding warrant or pre-existing record, the officer did not make an arrest. Hakeem was escorted from the premises and advised never to return as employees watched from a distance.

Embarrassment took root, and for a week, Hakeem kept the incident secret from Earl. With their relationship already spiraling downward, his termination and scheduled court appearance for the theft incident increased the tension between them. Determinedly defiant, he continued to enter Earl's house after curfew. Earl, in response, held fast to threats of sending him back to Philadelphia. But Hakeem undermined Earl's warnings by moving out, revealing his whereabouts only to siblings—Malcolm and Michelle.

Just a month before Hakeem ran away, Faizon introduced him to Keith. From the moment Faizon and Keith met at the club, they were intertwined. Keith needed a roommate, and Faizon, aware of the tentions between Hakeem and Earl, recommended him as a potential candidate. Keith accepted the proposed arrangement and Hakeem seized the opportunity to take refuge while awaiting arraignment.

The peace afforded was short-lived.

On the day of the first hearing, Hakeem crossed paths with Earl in the courthouse. Earl was enraged because his plans to send him back to Philly had been thwarted. Resorting to intimidation, Earl coerced Hakeem into returning home by attacking him in the corridor with a painful neck jab. Once home, Michelle helped Hakeem escape again as soon as Earl left the house. All of his children had tired of the threats he issued to control them.

Within a week, the pain from the assault vanished.

A month later, Hakeem returned to the courthouse for the second hearing. Earl was unable to attend for lacking knowledge regarding details from the proceedings of the initial arraignment. Hakeem intentionally excluded him from being involved. As he would not risk being forced to return home a second time.

He subsequently pled guilty to the judge in the absence of a public defender and an attorney. Deficient of adequate financial support, it was impossible to procure the latter alternative. Besides, Hakeem figured that by virtue of admitting to the crime, the judge would show compassion for having a previously clean record. He also hoped to leave the courthouse by noon and get back to living on his terms. It was this delusion in part, that factored in the unexpected outcome.

The judge sentenced Hakeem to thirty days in jail, suspending fifteen in response to his admission of guilt. A bailiff promptly placed him in a detainment cell for preparation to be transported to the city jail for booking. There was no going home that day, much to Hakeem's disappointment. Presumption of how events would unfold during the hearing had erased all ideas of a possible unfavorable ruling by the judge.

Privacy was a luxury in jail. Correctional officers instructed Hakeem along with the new inmates to remove and surrender their clothes and personal items. They directed all inmates to bathe in an open shower room and don orange uniforms. Hakeem recalled having to pass his bowels in a doorless stall during the early hours of the first morning spent in jail. He was grateful that few men were awake to notice, which would have intensified his embarrassment.

The meals served in jail for breakfast, lunch, and dinner were horrible—processed meats, bland starches and vegetables. Hakeem would never forget the slimy, tasteless grits that seemed to glow on the food tray. The translucent ground corn kernels seemed to have absorbed the light in the room. Confined with men whose breath and bodies stank, heightened the unpleasantness of the undesirable environment. He disliked being told what to do and unable to escape rigid authority. Jail stripped him of his autonomy and humanity. Rare was there a time when he did not think of everything he should have done to stay out of jail.

Hakeem initially wanted to keep the jail incident secret. He resisted contacting Earl, anticipating that he would try to force him into returning home. Joseph and Evelyn would be alarmed and ask questions that he wanted to avoid. The less they knew, the less he felt compelled to disclose. As reality set in, pride gave way, and he made a collect call to Earl's house. Malcolm and Michelle then informed their father of his imprisonment.

On Day Three, the city jail transferred Hakeem to a remote correctional facility for misdemeanor-class convicts completing the duration of their sentences. The transition rescued him from a leering cellmate, who he caught watching him on numerous occasions since arrival. If the man tried to do anything, Hakeem had resolved to do something terrible. Once victimized in jail, an individual was subjected to a submissive role indefinitely. He had been victimized too much as a defenseless child. If someone attacked him, he determined they would pay with their life if necessary. Fortunately, no one tested his limits.

The remote facility's recreational features attempted to distract from its rehabilitative purposes. There was a common room with one television and a gaming area that all inmates agreeably shared. The bathroom and shower were compartmentalized without doors. And yet, the accommodations failed to put Hakeem at ease, as confinement and minimal privacy were still a reality.

Unlike the city jail, the sleeping area was divided into rooms—each containing two bunkbeds. Hakeem was assigned to a bunkroom with three men. The inmates had committed minor misdemeanors—serving sentences of 30 days to 6 months.

Of the three roommates, two were Caucasian—one of whom was close to Hakeem's age. The young man had a DUI conviction involving a collision. Although they interacted brotherly, Hakeem's thoughts kept straying to his release date. No matter the cordiality and recreation, he could not escape the feeling of being a caged animal and prayed daily for a miraculous release. Time passed slowly with him counting the passage of each day. Oh, how he confessed to God about learning his lesson, promising to demonstrate sound judgment in the future. He wished frequently for the hands of time to be reversed to the moment when Fred asked for the discount. He would have told Fred to pay for all the merchandise. When the wish failed to materialize, he tried to sleep the hours away.

Several days had passed when Hakeem learned from Malcolm that Earl wanted to wire money but needed to know his location. Hakeem distrusted Earl's intentions, fearing another hostile encounter. Thus, he declined to provide any information—foregoing the offer of assistance, considering that the fifteen-day sentence would be soon fulfilled.

A correctional officer collected Hakeem from the recreation room on the morning of the fifteenth day. He was escorted to the front desk to collect his belongings secured in plastic bags. Excitement surged as the chains that temporarily denied freedom fell away from his bound wings. Fifteen days of confinement convinced him that honesty and integrity offered benefits he took for granted. Only stupidity caused a person to make the same mistake twice.

Back at Keith's house again, Hakeem noticed changes. While in jail, someone had rummaged through his belongings. Several shirts and sweaters had strangely disappeared. Hakeem wanted to confront Keith but had been inconsistent with paying his share of the rent. Keith's actions reminded him how some people take advantage of others when the odds are against them. Losing the retail job reduced his income significantly. Being incarcerated further worsened his financial situation.

The one possible source of streaming income that remained was the restaurant. Hakeem returned and immediately discovered that he had been terminated for missing work. After a conversation with the general manager and shift supervisor about being incarcerated, he was rehired. They valued his work ethic and gave him another chance.

Life has a way of recompensating for hardships endured.

Faizon stopped visiting after discovering that Keith was still intimate with his ex-boyfriend, Clyde. Keith had tried to keep his duplicity undercover, but Clyde refused to be a secret lover. One day, Clyde entered the house through a porch window while Keith and Faizon relaxed in the bedroom. When Keith realized that Clyde was inside, a brawl erupted. It was the first time Hakeem witnessed the destruction of an entire room at the hands of two gay men. Televisions, stereos, and picture frames flew through the air, and furniture broke as bodies smashed into the structures.

Once Faizon and Clyde faded from Keith's world, he began to make subtle passes at Hakeem. Hakeem rejected Keith's interests out of respect for Faizon and himself. Keith sought sex partners possibly out of loneliness, but Hakeem refused to be one in the number. He quickly made a habit of locking the bedroom door when going to sleep, apprehensive of awakening in the night and finding Keith lurking in the dark.

Keith's quality of life steadily deteriorated. He started missing work and was eventually terminated. Hakeem wondered if his tattered love life was responsible. The furniture rental company began visiting the house weekly, seeking payment from Keith for loaned merchandise—what remained of it from his battle with Clyde. One afternoon, Hakeem exited the house to go grocery shopping when a repo-man from the rental company stepped onto the porch. The repo man presented Keith's rental agreement, stating that he had come to collect the rental furniture. Keith was two months behind in payments. Until Keith paid the debt, the furniture was technically stolen property.

Hakeem wanted to avoid another encounter with the legal system. Under no circumstances was he willing to go to jail again, especially for something theft-related. The penalty would be worse for a second and similar offense. Fearful of the negative consequences for refusal, he permitted the repo-man to enter the house and reclaim all of the rental furniture.

When Keith came home, Hakeem admitted that he allowed the repo man to collect the rentals. He braced himself for a brawl, but it never happened. Keith's confrontation with Clyde and Faizon's departure had broken him. Keith's income stopped flowing and eventually, the landlord evicted them. Rather than accept defeat and subject himself to Earl's authority again, Hakeem exploited a past acquaintance with Brian Alessi who was notorious for his rounds within local gay circles.

Black and Italian with a preppy demeanor, Brian's good looks distracted most people from his less than charming qualities. He was a pathological liar and Hakeem had called it quits long before their acquaintance became serious. They had enough respect for each other to maintain cordial communication.

Hakeem called Brian from a payphone in a Metro Transit station and asked whether he needed a roommate. Mud-stained snow that caked his boots thawed onto the ground while awaiting a favorable answer. It just so happened that during the time he was in jail, Brian evicted his roommate, making available a spare bedroom to rent. A safety net always seemed to break Hakeem's fall just in time.

For two years, Hakeem rented with Brian. And by the end of the first year, he saw signs of their harmonious roommate agreement unraveling. Brian's door revolved with guests, several being of questionable character—thugs and trade boys. Hakeem kept to his room most of the time when they visited. He struggled with creating façades of liking people for whom he held minor regard. Sometimes, he overheard Brian discussing his antisocial behaviors with the visitors. The sounds of their deceitful laughs drifted through the air vents from the living room. *Let them talk!* He said to himself when overhearing the conversations. He looked forward to the day of finally becoming somebody. But at nearly twenty-one years old, he had no idea when that would happen.

Hakeem still reached three impactful milestones in the middle of his twenty-first year. He enrolled at Metropolitan State University, confessed his life to Jesus Christ, and was baptized in the Holy Spirit. His love for singing was motivation for joining the church choir.

Joseph and Evelyn were offended by his decision to attend church. While their religion did not respect church traditions, it was not enough to stop Hakeem from embracing a different faith. He had reasons for defecting. Many of the practices upheld by their religious circle were rash and illogical, and he consistently resisted their brainwashing.

Hakeem might have walked a straight and narrow path if he disassociated from homosexuality. Instead, he tucked his habits into a box, believing that its closed lid would keep the gay tendencies under control. The road of homosexuality twisted, abruptly ended, inverted, and double-backed—a path he failed to permanently abandon. It was the outcome of an individual choosing not to be honest with the inner self and dealing directly with the situation.

THE HEAVENS HAVE EYES

THE HEAVENS HAVE EYES

The things we strive to hide from those around us, God knows and remembers all that transpires.

*I*n the late fall of year 2000, Hakeem met Calvin Williams—a sophomore majoring in finance at Metropolitan State and established an instant rapport. According to Calvin, he was single and sought a serious relationship. Hakeem yearned for companionship and Calvin's availability suggested the potential for more to develop between them. Hakeem basked in his attentions. However, Calvin's true character soon emerged. Like Brian, Calvin was promiscuous, differing only in the transparency of their intentions. When Brian intended to sleep around, he informed his partners beforehand. Calvin in contrast, maintained a façade of benevolence while plotting deception. He tried to keep Hakeem in the dark about his licentiousness, but carelessness betrayed him nonetheless.

They had planned to go to the movies one particular evening. Calvin asked Hakeem to use his cellphone to make a call and shortly thereafter, stated there was an emergency and left. Whether Calvin was cognizant of the fact or not, both the number and passcode to his pager stayed in the call history. With plans changed abruptly, Hakeem flipped open the cellphone to call Faizon for small talk and saw the information. It was at that point he began reflecting on Calvin's anxious and detached behavior, considering it odd. Hakeem also acknowledged minute changes in the quality of their relationship.

Hakeem was perceptive—an ability that developed from enduring abuse and anticipating pending trouble. When he was objective, his perceptions were acute. His intuition went haywire laying across the bed. Finally, curiosity took over and he dialed the number to Calvin's pager, figuring the excess of numbers included the passcode. He gained access to the voicemail, finding multiple messages from a dude named, Tevaris. The newest message detailed arrangements for the same night Calvin stood him up. Hakeem listened to the voicemails repeatedly, wrote down Tevaris' phone number and called him.

Tevaris answered the phone and Hakeem asked for Calvin. Tevaris tried to derail the request by asking Hakeem to identify himself. Brazenly, Hakeem told Tevaris to tell Calvin to call him back and hung up the phone.

As much as Hakeem hoped for an immediate callback, Calvin called later that night. His delay was Hakeem's ammunition to end the month and a half long association. Hakeem took no chances in the gay lifestyle. In his opinion, a dishonest man was a risk and incapable of commitment. Still, he became depressed over Calvin and the idea of starting over with someone new. Getting to know a person beyond amity demanded time, interest, and effort. Gay life was cold and hard. Who in their right mind believed that it was a good life?

Depression weighed heavily on Hakeem, adversely affecting his work ethic until he was terminated for excessive lateness. He had been responsible for opening the restaurant and overseeing morning operations. Shortly after being rehired, he promoted to shift-supervisor. But he allowed a heavy heart to interfere with his paycheck. There were many days that he wanted to stay in bed. Depression from disappointment eventually won.

Unemployed and without a stream of steady income, Hakeem began to experience the effects of having a criminal record. A person's past mistakes tend to haunt their present and future. The reality warranted greater awareness in people who believed they were laws unto themselves. Even when a person refuses to hold him or herself accountable, laws in the spirit and natural realms will eventually impede progress.

There was no one in Hakeem's circle of associations who had a firm understanding of the law. His friends had liquor, clubs, and men on their brains. He was ignorant concerning diversion programs available to young adults who were first-time offenders, and expungement proceedings to seal convictions. He progressed through the years, hopscotching job requisitions. He discarded applications that requested specific details pertaining to the circumstances of his conviction and consciously withheld the information on many others. For Hakeem doubted that if the potential employer had access to all of the information, they would consider him for employment. He was a Black man with a criminal record and many times, such combinations strengthened an employer's resolve to reject the applicant.

Labor-oriented, factory and environmental occupations typically hired candidates with prior criminal convictions because a segment of the population bypassed the opportunities. Fulfillment of the job responsibilities demanded physical engagement. Hakeem hated manual labor and roles with immutable job responsibilities. They restricted autonomy and creativity, boring him quickly with the restraints the jobs created. He worked one day at a factory on an assembly line, attaching rubber hoses onto the backs of coffeemakers. The repetitive work lulled him into a doze. He almost met the floor were it not for Malcolm catching him teetering backwards.

Hakeem wanted to do something creative but believed it was too late to see his dreams materialize. He was too old to be a singer or a fashion designer—having not invested time in developing those areas. Thus, he pursued entry- and intermediate-level job opportunities. In the quest to obtain employment, he found that certain legislative and law enforcement professions were off-limits because of his conviction. A person with an open criminal record could not obtain employment in the fields given the expectation of an incumbent to lead by example. Because his charge encompassed breach of dishonesty and theft, no financial institution was willing to extend a job offer. Their bylaws prohibited employment to job-seekers with criminal convictions related to trust and theft. Hakeem found it difficult to land jobs that paid above ten dollars per hour. The jobs he secured with wages remotely close to the objective were retail and customer service jobs. Eventual employment at Kaleidoscope would begin at that level.

Earl was the one person who could have schooled Hakeem on what he needed to know. Earl knew the streets and possessed some cognizance of the law through experience as a teen and serving in the army. The possibility of being enlightened by Earl might have benefitted Hakeem. But their feuds prevented stable bonding. Furthermore, Hakeem's recalcitrant nature and an overarching goal to prove to Earl that he could survive independently clouded his judgment. Therefore, Hakeem learned through trial and error.

Five years later, an HR manager at a credit-card company, advised Hakeem to consider expungement. The company's policy prohibited extension of a job offer until his conviction was sealed. The manager was courteous to give counsel regarding the undertaking of the process. Hakeem heeded the advice and filed a petition in the court where the sentencing occurred seven years earlier. After a sixty-day review period and fee, the court determined that he met the criteria for expungement.

Much to Hakeem's chagrin, expungement did not exonerate him entirely. A recruiter for a national bank in Atlanta stated that a lapse of ten years since the conviction was necessary for hire. Only eight years had passed. The phantom of discouragement resurfaced as Hakeem worked second shift at a print shop and third shift stocking at a retail store. The combined work schedules barely permitted six hours of sleep. He soon began to suffer from elevated stress and back pain.

Hakeem's ten-year class reunion passed without attendance. Ashamed of his accomplishments, he skipped the event to avoid giving former peers vague answers regarding activities post-high school. He certainly wanted to miss being put in a position where he had to glaze over his conviction, which in part, contributed to a slow-moving career. When Kaleidoscope Technologies made an offer of employment, a bit of hope resurged. However, Hakeem was twenty-seven years old with no long-term goals, having continued to move forward into an undefined future.

In a moment of reflection, Hakeem analyzed the events of the day he was fired from the store. It mystified him that the investigator did not target other employees. He had not violated any policy before the incident. The store however, offered monetary rewards to tipsters of theft. Someone may have accused him of a previous occurrence. Even if it were the case, he still exhibited poor judgment that triggered a chain of consequences he was unprepared to sustain. "The harvest is always bigger than the seed," as the adage goes. If given a choice between doing right or wrong, it was best to choose right.

≈≈≈≈≈≈≈

November ushered in festive holidays for family, love, and cheer. During the winter months, Hakeem tried to be cheerful, as the times made him most aware of being alone. Even with family and friends, he felt estranged and that feeling stirred up the motivation to go to church as Gail suggested.

Hakeem entered through the double doors opening into the narthex of the Baptist Church. Some coworkers had mentioned the church before, and he remembered the name. Reading positive online reviews further convinced him that the church was worth a firsthand experience.

"Good morning, Brother," greeted a graying older man standing on the left side of the door, wearing a purple shirt and black pants. A woman dressed in the same color combination stood on the right side, smiling warmly with a welcoming nod.

Hakeem nodded in silence, and then wondered if the woman saw him reciprocate the courteous gesture. He was self-conscious about some of his characteristics—having a habit for giving people nonverbal responses. It was unsurprising that some people perceived him as aloof. Their perceptions were partially accurate. Insecurity, shame, and fear of rejection—each psychological trait attributed to Hakeem's manner of interacting with people. Outsiders were ignorant of the factors underlying the behaviors. They did not know that years of abuse and rejection had made him feel inferior, inadequate, and empty.

From the standpoint of intentional hostility and negativity in certain contexts, a person's thoughts or the collective of a group are irrelevant, so long as their opinions are harmless. This sentiment is certainly applicable to situations where the scrutinized individual has complete control over themselves and their environment. Positive advice and encouragement contain restorative properties to uplift someone rather than tear them down. However, the time in which victims of abuse develop self-confidence is variable. The process is internal as it is external—involving the modification of self-concepts through feedback and interaction within the victim's environment. For example, counseling sessions with a therapist can help a patient improve his or her self-esteem and life management. Destructive criticism and the effects of negative environments can send a victim downward-spiraling into despair and low self-esteem.

Hakeem wanted to turn around and speak to the doorkeeper. But thinking it might be awkward because he missed the first opportunity, he made a mental note to make a better effort to speak in the future. Besides, people were still entering the church.

Gospel music played softly through the sound system—small white speakers installed in the corners of the ceiling. An usher stopped Hakeem at the door to the sanctuary and offered a brochure containing the church news bulletin, ministry listings, and service times. Hakeem tucked the booklet between the pages of his Bible. People were already seated in the pews forming a semi arc from the west to east wall. The early birds.

Hakeem looked at his watch. 9:40 A.M. Service began at ten. He spotted a seat in the middle of the third to last row towards the back of the pews, off-centered to the pulpit's left. He preferred not to be disturbed by the cross traffic of people moving through the narrow walkways between rows. Sitting in the middle reduced the chances that he might have to move to permit someone passage during service.

9:47 A.M. displayed on the watch when Hakeem looked it a second time. A man and woman walked to the front of the stage holding microphones and turned to face the audience. "Bless the Lord," exalted the man dressed in a tailored black suit, white shirt, and gold tie.

"Glory to your name, Father," the woman followed. A single strand of pearls hung between the collar of her black skirt suit just above a white blouse.

With their eyes closed and free arms raised to the heavens above, they prayed for the church.

Hakeem remained seated while other attendees stood. He leaned forward with head bowed and clasped hands, listening intently as the intercessors took turns praying. They gave thanks to God for being able to live another day, food, shelter, good health, healing, stability, protection from harm, and the animals. They prayed for the sick and the poor and those in need of encouragement. They asked God to forgive the sins of the people. Hakeem absorbed their words into his spirit—what they came in askance and acknowledged. He was amazed at what he took for granted in prayer—something as simple as the air he breathed.

As the intercessors continued to pray, the atmosphere stirred. There was something especially powerful and convicting in the female intercessor's voice. A refreshing calmness filled the sanctuary. The presence of the Holy Spirit was there. Hakeem heard soft affirmations as the prayer continued. He remained silent, focused intently on the intercessors' words, not wanting to miss anything.

Music began to entwine with the exaltation of Jesus Christ. As if on cue, the praise team and choir assembled on the stage behind the pulpit. The song of praise and worship intensified as the intercessors concluded prayer. Hakeem was familiar with the song and joined the congregation in singing. There were not a few times being a soloist came to mind for people to hear him sing. Then they would see his talents too.

The pastor's sermon postulated that confession of sin is a step in restoring one's relationship with God. *How ironic,* Hakeem thought. He always acknowledged homosexuality as a sin, constantly praying for forgiveness. His prayers contained promises to never venture back down the road from which he traveled. But at some point, he reneged. It was a habit that influenced the decision to stop attending church. He disliked breaking promises, and more importantly, it was uncomfortable standing in the presence of God while living a lie. Hakeem believed that if he could just see the other side again—life without the shadow of the past, then it would be easier to move forward.

During the sermon, he realized that self-management of sin was the wrong approach. Confession of sin extended beyond mere acknowledgement of the admittance of wrongdoing or guilt. Since repentance embodies confession in humility and the expression of remorse, it contradicts willful sin. Moreover, the sinner must pray for deliverance and allow the Holy Spirit to take control. Hakeem believed he was in control of himself and seldom prayed for deliverance. How could he repent when in his heart existed an uncertainty about leaving homosexuality behind? It was impossible. Doubt is a cognitive force that has influenced the decisions of many people not to move forward. Submission and faith are actions of the Spirit, which remove all doubt.

≈≈≈≈≈≈≈

"Hello," Rosalyn answered the phone.

"How are you?" Hakeem asked.

"I'm alright. Sittin' here watchin' tv."

Hakeem disliked the droning in her voice. It manifested whenever she was irritated—a precursor to drama. It would not be long now. He predicted that she would say something annoying. But he would at least try to apply Gail's advice, and resist the effects of Rosalyn's brooding.

"What are you watching?" he asked, trying to make light conversation. Moments of small talk were far too infrequent between them.

"The news. These Philadelphians are some of the dumbest people I've ever seen."

He clinched his teeth. "Okay…well, ignorance is everywhere, not just in Philly. Have you heard from Layla?" He deftly redirected the conversation to curtail further negativity from eroding his cordiality.

"Layla moved out this week"—Rosalyn paused, distracted by the television—"Just as well, cause I was gonna' tell her that she can stay where she's been staying."

A smile widened Hakeem's lips. Layla must have taken his advice for which he was glad. He believed that people like Rosalyn and Earl needed to live alone, without the company of their children.

"I see." Telling Rosalyn about his conversation with Layla a month earlier was unnecessary. Most likely, she was irritated that Layla was no longer under her control. Hakeem knew his mother well—remembering the years as a teenager when they disagreed. Sometimes, Rosalyn put him out of the apartment to sit in the hallway until nighttime. Now, no one could dictate his comings and goings. If paying rent for an apartment equated to freedom, then so be it. "Where did she move?"

"Newark, so she could be close to the airport."

"That's good news, isn't it?"

"Yeah. I just hope she'll able to keep the job."

"Is there some reason she wouldn't?"

"No. I'm just saying Layla needs to grow up."

"And…perhaps this is a sign that she is maturing." *It was time to change the subject again.* Rosalyn was becoming annoying.

"Have you spoken to Tyrell?"

"Yes. And he ain't doing much of anything."

You didn't teach them how to be responsible. What did you expect? "Is Tyrell working?" Hakeem was slipping into flip-mode.

"I don't know what Tyrell does. But I know one thing. If he doesn't figure something out, he's going to be nothing just like his father."

Hakeem had enough. He refused to tolerate a second more—listening to Rosalyn bad-mouth his siblings as if she had everything figured out at their age. She could not say much about Katrina. Katrina was successful and married. Both were accomplishments that Rosalyn never achieved.

"How do you know that? Tyrell is only 22 years old!"

"I'm saying based on what he's doing now."

"Okay. You and Arnold didn't teach the kids how to be responsible. Did you forget that until I moved with Earl, you had me doing all of the household chores while they tore up the apartment?"

"I don't remember that. And what is your point?"

"Of course, you wouldn't remember because you were getting high in your bedroom! But it goes like this. If you don't teach a child when they are young, don't expect them to know any better when they get older. You don't know how Tyrell will turn out. He could be more successful than any of us!"

"Well, it doesn't look good for Tyrell or Layla."

145

"Then pray for them. Encourage them. I think there's something wrong with how you refer to your children."

"What do you mean by that?"

"No mother in her right mind would say the things you've said about any of us. And you wonder why your children don't want to be around you?"

"I've done the best I could for all of you."

"You really believe that? Calling me 'faggot' when I was little is 'doing the best you could do,' huh?"

"I don't remember that."

"Oh, it doesn't matter. I remember what you said and haven't forgotten it. Just like you remember everything mama and daddy said to you."

"Well, I was abused."

"And I wasn't?"

Rosalyn had disclosed that she was abused as a young girl. Abuse at the hands of Evelyn was apparent, given their relationship throughout the years. There was no intervention.

Rosalyn was unaware that Gary told Hakeem about the first-cousin that molested her. It was the same cousin, who many years later, gave her the pornographic magazines she kept in her bedroom. The revelation further defined her psychological issues and on that basis alone, Hakeem was receptive to the abuse she endured as a youth. Nevertheless, he refused to accept any form of mistreatment or disrespect from her. Moreover, he was unwilling to verbally acknowledge her issues until she admitted the wrongdoing that pertained to him.

Parents like Rosalyn had children when they were mentally unstable and immature. They transferred into parenthood unrepaired psychological damage originating from unresolved issues that plagued them throughout their lifetime. This psychological damage is what corrupts the relationship quality between parent and child.

Hakeem vowed not to subject his children to the same suffering. The only way to prevent that future from happening was to seek healing and develop a stronger relationship with God.

Certainly, Rosalyn had legitimate grievances, and so did Evelyn.

146

But neither mother was mature enough to prevent negative childhood experiences from transferring to their offspring. The children of both generations of women suffered at their hands and the cycle advanced to the succeeding generation. The cycle must be broken or else, Hakeem and his siblings would author the next. No one, young or old, family or friend, deserves to be subjected to the emotional instability of another individual. Rosalyn needed to learn how to conquer her demons just like Hakeem. If she was unable to self-manage, then professional help was necessary.

Hakeem was angry with Rosalyn. But at the same time, he remembered the advice about forgiveness from Gail and the pastor. He needed to forgive Rosalyn. It was the only way to free himself from bitterness of the past.

Silence passed on the phone. "Hello?" he asked, expecting a response or acknowledgement.

"There's a lot that I don't remember."

But you can remember everything that happened to you? Her response was unacceptable. "I'm gonna' talk to you later." He ended the call before she could respond, deciding to deal with her another day.

The constricting chest pain returned. Shoulders hunched, Hakeem laboriously removed the bottle of anxiety pills from his backpack and untwisted the cap. He popped a pill and chased it with water, which provided no relief as he swallowed. He was certain that his chest cavity had squashed the esophagus.

≈≈≈≈≈≈≈

"Yo! Hakeem, you got a sec?" Tariq peered into the cube. The partition hid the rest of his body.

Hakeem turned away from the computer and looked at him. "Yeah, I got a minute."

"Cool, cool." Tariq held a black folder.

"What's goin' on?"

"You got a master's degree, right?" he asked, sitting down.

"Yeah." *Why is he asking me this?* Hakeem eyed Tariq's crisp royal blue, black, and white plaid shirt. It reminded him of an orange, green, blue, and white version hanging in his own closet.

"Did you ever have to do a business plan?"

"Once when I was an undergrad." Hakeem dreaded the project as it required time and effort. He received a B for the assignment. "Why? You gettin' ready to start a business?"

"Somethin' like dat. I'm tryin' to reach some goals for me and the fam. These chips ain't cuttin' it."

It was logical to believe that greater seniority equated to higher salaries. Tariq and Anaya had worked at Kaleidoscope much longer than Hakeem. But apparently, their combined incomes barely covered the household because Kaleidoscope pimped its employees.

Hakeem and Tariq had discussed the challenges of supporting a family with limited financial resources. Life was already hard for a self-sustaining single person—the reason that Hakeem wanted money overflowing in bank accounts before he started a family.

Tariq opened the folder and Hakeem saw the rubric secured in its pocket. *Ugh! He's going to ask me for help.* He wanted no parts of it. Developing a business plan was time-consuming.

"What did you have to do?" Tariq's expression was serious.

Ask me about anything except a business plan. "A significant part of a business plan is the research." Hakeem wanted to see if a high-level explanation would suffice.

Tariq raised a busy eyebrow and twisted his lips—incredulity was evident on his face. "Research on what?"

"What your potential competitors are doing in the industry—where you intend to conduct business. That information will inform you how to differentiate your products and services."

"I gotcha."

"You also need to include a cost analysis—the financials necessary for startup and to maintain operations. For long-term success, you must incorporate sales and marketing strategies to generate streams of revenue, and thus, profit." *That was enough information for now,* he assumed. He didn't want to overwhelm or discourage Tariq.

"How did you learn all this?"

"Initially, I had a textbook to guide me. But there's a lot of information on the internet, which can help you develop a business plan."

Hakeem glanced at Delores walking past the cube leafing through a stack of papers. He did not respect her and she disliked him. Delores was the type of supervisor who believed that their title demanded respect. He upheld the opinion that respect was earned, not forced. People who utilized their positions of authority to bully others did not impress or intimidate him. They only motivated him to resist. Delores could not handle this aspect of his character.

Delores was deceitful as management came at Kaleidoscope. She once recommended an employee for termination and accidentally carbon-copied the subordinate on the email sent to HR. When the employee questioned her about the email, she advised to disregard the correspondence. The next day, Delores called the employee and instructed him not to report to work. Almost everyone had a run-in with her condescending, flip-mouthed demeanor. It was a wonder that none of Delores' employees had slung her to the floor yet.

Not a trace of enthusiasm appeared on Tariq's face. "Good enough," he said, rising from the chair. "I'll holla at you if I need more info."

"Cool," Hakeem said, turning to the computer. He did not doubt that Tariq would seek help again in the near future and hoped to be more patient.

≈≈≈≈≈≈≈

Hakeem tapped a foot impatiently, waiting in the solicitor's office. The attorney, Wendy Fitzpatrick sat nearby, texting on her phone. They had been waiting an hour for the clerk to confirm that the video footage from the night of the arrest was ready to review. Hakeem was both curious and apprehensive to see what the police officer's dashcam recorded.

A heavyset Black woman exited from the door leading to the back office. "Ms. Fitzpatrick?"

"Yes? Is the video ready?" Wendy asked.

It took a year for the Atlanta Police Department to recover the video. Hakeem had hoped that it was lost in the flowing chaos of processing. The less evidence there was to prosecute increased the odds of the judge dismissing the case.

"Come on back. It's ready." the clerk said, beckoning with a hand.

Hakeem couldn't help noticing that the heel on the woman's shoe leaned in the opposite direction of the toe. The narrow stem struggled to support her weight. *What was the point? Invest in a durable pump.*

Wendy grabbed her tote bag from the floor, securing it on one shoulder.

Hakeem followed.

The clerk escorted them to a room that resembled a living area. "The disc is in the DVD-player," she said before exiting the room and closing the door.

Along the farthest wall stood a floor model television with two office chairs positioned in front. Hakeem thought the model outdated in 2015, as flat screens were the going trend. Perhaps the solicitor office staff did not see a need to modernize every piece of equipment.

Wendy sat in the chair closest to the adjacent wall. "It took the office long enough," she said while retrieving the remote from atop the television.

Hakeem settled in the vacant chair. "What was the delay with recovering the video?"

"That's how the APD operates. They take a long time processing paperwork. It's rather frustrating."

The camera footage started at the point where the officer first began to tailgate. Hakeem cringed hearing his own voice trembling on the recording. Dignity abandoned him on the night of the arrest.

"Why did you walk backward?" Wendy asked in disbelief of his performance of the field sobriety test.

"I don't know..." Hakeem was astounded by his behavior on camera. "There was so much going through my mind. I just didn't hear him correctly."

"I understand" —Wendy paused the video and looked at him— "But if this goes to trial, the jury may use this evidence against you."

Hakeem's bowels liquefied. If the jury found him guilty, he could go to jail and lose everything.

"The hardest part of this case is making the evidence go away. Did you know that you could have refused to take the breathalyzer test?"

"Not until the officer read me my rights. I wanted to keep my license."

"But he took it anyway." Wendy underscored the obvious.

Hakeem had hoped that compliance would strike compassion in the officer, but those efforts failed.

"If it ever happens again, which I hope it does not"—she looked him directly in the eyes—"know that an attorney may be able to preserve some of your driving privileges."

Hakeem realized that the situation was a precarious one. Wendy was correct. After he retained the law firm, they worked quickly to obtain limited driving privileges.

"Our best hope is to suppress some or all of the evidence against you before this case goes to trial."

OPEN GRAVES AND UNSPOKEN EULOGIES

There were thoughts in my mind and feelings in my heart that I wanted to bury, to put behind me. But I held onto the pain they caused me. I could've benefited from the release.

"How is your week going, Hakeem?" Gail asked.

She looked the part for a CIA agent in a black pants suit and white-collared blouse. A lily-shaped brooch bordered with pearls, pinned on the left lapel of the blazer and pearl-finished buttons were the garment's only adornments. Hair styled in a severe bun, enhanced a painted face. Silver and pearl drop-earrings sway when her head moved.

"This week has been better." He attributed newfound feelings to church fellowship, although desiring a better job or leaving Kaleidoscope had not changed.

"Sleep still improving?" Gail peered over silver thin-framed glasses while writing in the folder.

"Here and there…. I get restless when there's a lot on my mind."

"What's troubling you?"

"Everything." The last conversation with Rosalyn still blazed in his memory. "My mind goes from one thing to another, and then I can't sleep."

"That's one of the reasons why you need to take the meds for anxiety"—she gave him a meaningful look—"to stabilize your thoughts."

Hakeem said nothing, understanding the purpose of the medication. He just didn't want to develop a dependency.

"Last time we talked about your parents."

He nodded. "Right."

"Have you spoken to your mother?"

"Yes, I have. Two weeks ago."

"How was the communication?"

"Horrible." He narrated the dialogue with Rosalyn and his disapproval.

Gail took notes. "The conversation with your mother, is that part of what's troubling you?"

"Yes. I thought I could get past my issues with her. But I need more time."

"That's understandable. This journey towards healing is really about you and not your mother."

"Do you have a support system—other family members or friends that you feel comfortable talking to, who encourage you?"

"That's hard to say." Hakeem thought of Khalil and Alex. They were friends. But they didn't think and see the world the same. Ian lived in Newark—eliminating him as a friend that one could run next door in case of an emergency. As far as siblings were concerned, they lived their own lives. He wasn't among their priorities and they weren't necessarily his.

"Why is that?"

"There are things that I don't talk about with everyone. What some of my friends know, my family doesn't know. There are things about me that no one knows, and I'd be ashamed to tell anyone."

"That makes sense. So let me ask this—in case of an emergency, who would you call?"

"My grandfather."

"Have you and your grandfather always been close?"

"Yes."

"So, is it safe to say that he is the most stable support system you have?"

"Yes, I think so."

"I detect a bit of uncertainty in your response. Why is that?"

"While my grandparents have supported me throughout the years… we aren't unified in the area of faith."

Gail observed Hakeem, saying nothing. She leaned back from the desk with the folder in her lap, a pen in hand poised to write.

He continued. "My grandfather and grandmother—when she was alive are part of a religious organization that teaches that the world as we know it, is going to end. Members of the faith are discouraged from getting caught up in the system."

"The system?" Confusion flashed across Gail's face.

"The system refers to governmental and worldly associations. Voting, envisioning long-term dreams and aspirations, and continued education are all considered futile because none of it will matter in the end."

"Indulge me for a second. What's wrong with voting?"

"Their religion teaches that voting exemplifies an individual's involvement with the world and serving man. They liken voting to idolatry."

"So these followers…they don't see the connection between voting, legislation, and politics?"

"From what I know, they overlook it. As long as I've known my grandparents, they've never questioned their faith."

"Your grandparents, your grandfather rather, still believes in these ideologies?"

"Yes."

"How do you feel about that?"

"Begrudged, I guess."

"Why?"

"In my opinion, my grandparents' religion hindered them from exercising common sense on some matters."

"Have you ever had disagreements with your grandparents about their religion?"

"Oh, yes"—Hakeem nodded—"several times and once, my grandmother hung up on me."

"Why did your grandmother hang up?"

"She didn't like that I said their organization had no right to throw someone out of the faith because of a mistake without giving the person a chance to repent." No one knew that his response was a silent jab at Evelyn for what happened to Rosalyn.

"That's harsh."

"Well, the congregation did the same thing to my mother for being unwedded and pregnant by a married man."

He elaborated on the events that followed Rosalyn's pregnancy.

If Gail's eyes were corks, they would have popped out of the sockets.

"There are definitely some generational issues in your family history."

"You have no idea. I could write a book."

"Hmmm...perhaps you should." she encouraged. "Each of our lives is a story in and of itself. Tell me...how did your grandparents react to you starting grad school?"

"They initially tried to discourage me for the reason that I mentioned—that the world is going to end."

"How long have your grandparents been saying that?"

"I've been hearing that the world is going to end since I was a little boy. So, as long as I've known them."

"That's a long time."

"Yeah, and I got tired of waiting. The decision to go to grad school was my choice. I wanted them to support me in something that I was doing on my own."

"I understand. And despite their lack of support, you enrolled anyway?"

"Yes."

"How did your grandparents respond?"

"They accepted it I imagine. I mean...I can't recall a moment where they actually said they agreed with my decision."

"Were your grandparents happy when you graduated?"

"My grandmother passed away six months after I started."

He imagined that Evelyn would have been proud.

"Forgive me. What about your grandfather?"

"He was happy—told everyone in the family. And, he tried to find me jobs within my field back home."

"Do you believe your grandfather's attempts to help you find jobs were his way of showing support?"

"That didn't cross my mind."

"Would you say that your demonstration of willful independence forced your grandparents to accept that you were making your own decisions?"

"Definitely."

"And as they saw you making progress over time, and the world was still intact, they became optimistic about your academic pursuits?"

"Oh, yeah." *Where is she going with these questions?*

"Your grandparent's lack of support didn't have much effect on the eventual outcome, did it? I mean, you went on to school anyway, and obtained two master's degrees."

"That's right. Those were my decisions to make."

Something came together for him at that moment. He was naturally defiant. Typically, whatever he decided, action followed—his method of operation. The questions and afterthoughts of those who opposed were inconsequential.

"I think I see where you're going."

"Tell me what's on your mind."

"Regardless of what my grandparents said, I determined my own course and proved them wrong."

"Exactly."

Once again, Gail guided Hakeem to see another dimension of his situation. Stubbornness enabled him to challenge his grandparents' misgivings. Achievement repelled their dissuasion. Through introspection, a realization emerged—that the majority of his resentment arose from a desire for Joseph and Evelyn to admit they were wrong. The concession would have esteemed Hakeem, but was also superfluous because his actions disapproved their beliefs. What better method was there to prove someone wrong than through accomplishment? Was it necessary to state the obvious? Joseph at least, deserved some slack. Hakeem realized that now.

"Would you have appreciated your grandparents showing more support at the beginning instead of the end?"

"Yes...I guess so. I wouldn't have felt like I was doing it all alone."

"Have you always felt alone?"

"For as much as I can remember...yes."

"Have you had this conversation with your grandparents or your grandfather?"

"I really didn't want to have that discussion with either of them. They already wanted me to move back. That's one of the reasons my grandfather was trying to help me find jobs."

Joseph and Evelyn also wished for him to move home because they were transitioning into old age. His presence would have benefitted them. But he couldn't oblige his grandparents. In his mind, Clinton City was an agonizing and stifling place.

"And you didn't want to return there?"

"No. Not unless I had to."

"Is there a reason you didn't want to return home?"

Sure there is an explanation. "Yes." He disclosed nothing further.

"Do you want to talk about it?"

"Not right now." The majority of the backstory was too depressing and exhausting to narrate. Maybe he would talk about it during the next session. They had talked longer than usual anyway, approaching an hour and thirty minutes. He was probably the last client of the day.

"Would you be offended if I ask you something personal, Hakeem?"

What does she want to ask me? "No, I wouldn't," he answered after a moment of silence. Curiosity had taken control.

"Are you dating?"

"No, I'm not."

"Is there any particular reason why?"

"It's a challenge."

"In what way?"

"Well...I've been involved with men." He searched her face for a change in expression. *What's she going to think now? That she knew I was gay all along?*

"Okay. And what challenges have you encountered dating men?"

No change in her face, not even an eyeblink. No discernible judgment.

"Inconsistency...and a lot of emphasis on sex." He could not forget the countless times that communication went dead after a day or week, or the famous question, "what you tryin' to get into," entered the conversation when talking to bisexual and gay men.

"I know several gay men, and I've heard all of that before. There's a lot of sex and sensuality revolving around their encounters. If you put it in context with men being visual creatures, it's unsurprising."

"Yeah, and I'm tired of it. I just stay to myself now." Nobody was checking for him and he wasn't constantly checking for anyone either.

"Do you think you'll ever find the right guy?"

"I'm a romantic and have entertained the idea. There were times when I dreamed of being in a relationship with a guy. But the dream never evolved into a long-term desire…like to the point where I'm in my fifties and sixties dating a man."

"Is there a reason why?" Gail placed the folder on the desk and crossed her legs so that the bulk of her weight shifted to the right hip. For the first time, she looked completely casual in the chair.

She might think I'm harsh when I say this. "I'm not going to take care of a man in my old age. Wrinkled men aren't attractive to me. I also refuse to combine assets with another man. None of it makes sense to me. I mean, taking care of a woman and children is logical. But a grown man? No."

Hakeem heard horror stories of gay couples who had joint accounts where one partner dipped into shared financial reserves to cater to another man. He would sooner put a man six feet under before letting them misuse the money he worked hard to accumulate. No. A man needed to work and take care of himself. Just like Joseph. Just like Earl. "Besides, there's the risk of sexually-transmitted diseases. I will not have it."

"Have you been in a relationship with a man?"

"Yes, once."

"How did that turn out?"

"In the beginning, things were good. Towards the end, I was glad to be done with it."

"What happened?"

"It just didn't work…we were different. And at some point, I just wanted to be away from him and out of the relationship."

"Did you love him?"

"I think my emotions were along the lines of infatuation."

"Have you ever been in love?"

Hakeem paused and considered the question for a moment. "No. There were some guys that I really liked. But most of them were bad for me. It helped that I…wasn't comfortable enough for love to develop."

"What do you mean?"

"My relationship with God…" Hakeem looked at the pastel painting of an ambiguous figure standing on a hill, facing a sun rising above the distant horizon, hanging on the wall. The painting had been there since the first therapy session, but he hadn't appreciated its beauty until now. A yellow sun shone forth on the background of a cloudy blue sky. "I grew up believing that homosexuality was wrong."

"Do you still hold these beliefs?"

"Yes, I do. Nothing in my experience has convinced me otherwise. It's a promiscuous, superficial, and risky lifestyle in my opinion."

"If you don't mind me asking, why have you continued to deal with men?"

"Honestly, I haven't had the courage to permanently put it behind me. I have been inactive for three and two years at a time."

"So, why do you revert?"

"I get lonely and it's familiar territory."

"That's understandable. But you eventually tire of these men, is that correct?"

"That's an accurate assessment."

"What do you do then?"

"Find a way to leave."

"How?"

"Re-prioritize what's important to me—my work, studies, or goals."

"How did they respond?"

"One guy was hurt, but he was bisexual. He had no shortage of pursuers. There were dudes on his waiting list when I met him. I'm certain someone stepped in after I left. Another guy brushed me off after I suggested being friends. I might've handled it differently, if I didn't feel that our continued acquaintance was contingent upon sex."

Gail sat in silence, processing their dialogue. "Do you consider yourself gay or bisexual?" She asked finally.

Hakeem evaluated the question before answering. Even some of his gay associates had asked him the same question. "Gay, I guess. I haven't had sex with a woman before." But he was attracted to women.

"Let me ask this then…if you don't mind."

"Go ahead."

"Have you tried dating a female?"

"Not since I was a teenager."

"Are you interested in dating females?"

"I've thought about it." The idea circulated with greater frequency in his mind after turning thirty. He knew of men over forty—many of whom were single, hopeless, or burned out from trying to establish long-term relationships with other males. They became either intimately reclusive, settled into the cycle of hooking up, or sacrificed their standards to be with anyone. None of those scenarios interested him.

"There's a reason I've asked you these questions," Gail said as she leaned forward. "I see a pattern in your life, which…is counterproductive. Some of your actions conflict with your beliefs. This unresolved conflict within yourself is a catalyst of the cycles that you are experiencing. Does that make sense?"

"It does." Hakeem understood the implications of her evaluation. He believed that homosexuality was wrong but continued to engage. He was inconsistent—rotating his beliefs and emotions in this regard. The habit was unproductive for a homosexual or heterosexual lifestyle. Eventually, he must make an unwavering decision to move forward and cultivate a healthy relationship of stable companionship and intimacy with someone.

Gail made one last entry before closing the folder. "Look"— compassion shined in her eyes—"I think you have some important decisions to make because your future is bright with possibilities. My purpose is to help you see those opportunities and find a path that will lead to the greatest positive outcome."

"I appreciate that." He felt assured and liberated.

"Did you know that women go through many of the same things with men as men do with each other?"

Hakeem knew the statement to be true. He heard complaints from women about the men in their lives—the struggle as single mothers. He witnessed what Rosalyn went through living with Arnold and understood what women had gone through dealing with Earl. Irresponsibility, lying, and cheating—Hakeem also went through it with men.

"The main difference"—Gail paused momentarily to retrieve a burnt-orange purse from beneath the desk—"between men and women, is that we are nurturers, which makes us naturally accommodating, tolerant even. With two men, you get much of the same innate characteristics that repel each other."

"I can see that," Hakeem concurred. Gail's assertion was logical. As a man, he understood the implications. "A man's world," was an understatement pertaining to the homosexual association involving two men. His own personality and characteristics were jarring. He was drawn to strong-willed, independent men like himself. But once acquainted, their strong personalities clashed. The men asserted themselves and he avouched himself. A man could be replaced in situations of irreconcilable differences—a philosophy that he understood and practiced. Apparently, many men did too for various reasons, which accelerated relationship turnover.

A BLUEPRINT FOR UTOPIA

You can envision yourself living the most fulfilling life, and life will deal you a hand of uncertainty. There's nothing but strategic planning and navigation from that point forward.

akeem sat in his old bedroom looking through class work and report cards from grade school, which had been stuffed between books read as a child. Oxidation had faded the ink and turned the papers yellow. There were fewer A's than B's, many C's, and a couple of D's. The teachers had written comments on the back of the report cards, stating that he was disruptive and failed to pay attention in class. He suffered when it came to following directions and completing class work on time, and it compromised his potential to excel academically.

Teachers earlier on in Hakeem's academia feared he was a special-needs student and believed that he could benefit from learning in an environment structured for students like himself. Classroom observation revealed that he paid little attention to instruction and was a distraction to other students unless the curriculum permitted art and creativity. It was during these instances that his artistic talents fully displayed, which were consequences of possessing a vivid and unlimited imagination. However, teachers deemed Hakeem's imagination abnormal for his age and grade level. At the age of seven, he wrote about a family bonded by marriage and separated by death for a creative writing assignment. His skills in reading were advanced because Joseph and Evelyn encouraged reading at an early age. "Hakeem can be an exceptional student, if he

162

applied himself," the teacher wrote. The evaluation was a consensus amongst all of his teachers.

Hakeem decided to take a trip to Clinton City before Thanksgiving. There was no purpose in visiting during the holidays because half of the family's religious affiliations prohibited celebration. He planned to endure the holidays alone in Atlanta where he could sulk in private, being dissatisfied with personal life. His family was not what he envisioned a family should be—too divided and dispersed. Thus, the holidays were the most depressing times of the year. No one needed to see him at his lowest or emotionally deteriorating.

Hakeem respected Joseph more than Evelyn who was entrusted with his daily care. As the lead-income generator, Joseph worked long hours between two jobs. He rose early in the morning and came home in the evening. On the weekends, Joseph took Hakeem fishing. Their outdoor adventures were the most joyous of times they shared together.

It was through observing Joseph that Hakeem first learned the importance of a man working to make money. Joseph always worked, and along with Evelyn, instituted the earn-reward system that shaped Hakeem's expectations regarding compensation and advancement in employment.

Evelyn was an entrepreneur of sorts, often working from home with Hakeem under her watch. But their relationship was far from what he considered pleasant. Hakeem was uncertain whether the mistreatment was a consequence of the estrangement between her and Rosalyn, or resentment for having to raise a grandchild. Sometimes in route to her clients, he awakened to Evelyn slapping him across the face for falling asleep. She drew blood more often than not. When he dozed during worship services, she dug her round-tipped nails into the back of his elbows to wake him. Many times, the skin was broken from the pressure she applied.

Evelyn was the one who came to Hakeem's elementary school and informed his teachers regarding their religious affiliations. She instructed the teachers to remove him from the class whenever there were birthday and holiday parties in the classroom. Classmates laughed and teased him, causing much alienation. Few childhood friends were had for being isolated and discouraged from establishing associations with peers outside the family's religion. Children within the faith were approved associations.

Hakeem could not remember when he first exhibited behavioral problems, although acknowledging they were present in kindergarten. He stole what he wanted from stores and other people. When Evelyn learned of his thievery——finding toys and miscellaneous objects hidden in his bedroom, she whooped and tortured him. She bit his fingers until the impressions of her teeth broke the skin. Oftentimes, Hakeem wanted to slap her face. For days, his fingers were swollen and stiff. One time, she even went so far as to inform his first-grade class to be watchful of his tendency to steal.

Hakeem's behavior progressively worsened. Dared by two female classmates, he pulled down his pants and mooned half of the class while returning from recess. When Evelyn received the disciplinary referral in the mail, she beat him naked with such intensity that the belt buckle flew from her hand, striking him in the eye. His eye swelled and she kept him home from school until the swelling subsided. But upon returning to school, Hakeem's teacher noted the fading bruises and notified Social Services. Evelyn blamed Hakeem for their discovery. Social Services would have taken him into protective custody had Joseph not intervened. The ensuing investigation only made Evelyn more shrewd in her methods of administering discipline.

The principal considered expelling Hakeem for the mooning incident. Fortunately, the teacher, school counselor, and Evelyn agreed upon him repeating the first grade. Hakeem was subsequently transferred to a Special Education class, given a review of his academic and behavioral history. He was diagnosed with Attention-Deficit/ Hyperactivity Disorder, prescribed medication and subjected to clinical counseling for behavioral management. The psychiatrist warned Evelyn that the side-effects of the medication included stunting of growth, but she dismissed the warning as long as Hakeem's behavior could be controlled.

After completing first grade on the second round, Hakeem transitioned back to the main classroom environment. The medication proved effective in helping him focus in school and at home. But it wasn't a cure-all, as Hakeem's potential for misconduct persisted. As long as he took the medicine, it suppressed the impulsive behaviors. His mischievous-self—a chained prisoner, watched from the darkest corner of his mind, waiting for an opportunity to escape. He enjoyed being the center of attention and causing disruptions—making animal sounds in the classroom to shock teachers and make students laugh.

When the medication lapsed, Hakeem's impulses and mischief influenced his behavior. Evelyn meted harsher punishments as recourses. She recruited her eldest son, Daryle, to aid in implementing discipline. Together, they threatened Hakeem that if he said anything to Joseph about their cruelty, they would worsen the punishments. Joseph's long work hours prevented him from assuming a more direct and protective role in Hakeem's guardianship. Thus, Hakeem silently endured with few days passing when he didn't wish for misfortune to befall his abusers.

Daryle's personal motives exacerbated Hakeem's situation. It was difficult enough to stay out of trouble without having to deal with the negative emotions that developed from abuse. Daryle preferred Hakeem to be undressed when administering whoopings. Daryle would look over his nakedness and caress his backside before commencing. There was never a time when Daryle whooped him fully dressed or missed an opportunity to be the disciplinarian.

Evelyn had bought a tabby cat and charged Hakeem with its care. In a burst of curiosity, he toppled the cat into a pot of cooling ashes taken from the basement stove. Reflexively, the cat jumped out of the pot with singed whiskers, showing no other signs of harm. Evelyn noticed the cat's missing whiskers and questioned him. He fabricated that the cat had fallen into the ashes. She did not believe his story and beat him. Then she told Daryle what happened to the cat. Daryle promised to administer a whooping and waited two weeks for a chance to fondle and strike.

Rosalyn had known about Daryle's sexual tendencies since childhood—the justification for her dislike of him. To hear Rosalyn tell the story, she had seen Daryle molesting children in the neighborhood. However, no one in the family or neighborhood reported his inappropriate behavior. Rosalyn expressed her belief that an uncle—Cousin Byron's father, who allegedly abused several family members, had also also molested Daryle. If the accounts were accurate, then the sexual perversion had transcended multiple generations and victimized numerous children within the family. No one spoke or did anything about the abuse. The power of secrecy has few bounds.

In hindsight, Hakeem could have risked telling someone about what happened in his grandparents' home much sooner. He exhibited many of the psychological and physiological characteristics (i.e., bedwetting, mood swings, misconduct, etc.) of an abused child. He could have told school administration when family members refused to believe him. But threats of retaliation from Evelyn and Daryle were effective in discouraging sounding of the alarm. The duo exhibited a slave-master mentality of extreme intimidation and domination, which is inappropriate for rearing children.

Coercion is an abuser's closest ally, and usually, children cannot see through the smokescreen. Perpetrators—bullies, violent abusers or child-molesters draw strength from imposing fear through intimidation and isolation. Perpetrators exploit their victim's weaknesses until they destroy the latter's sense of self-worth. The victim, in turn, develops a false belief that they deserve whatever happens to them.

Nearly every place Hakeem went, he misbehaved. A school disciplinary referral was mailed home at least once per month. Eventually, it became necessary for teachers to document his behavior in progress reports. These occurrences would cause anyone to doubt a problematic person's character because oftentimes, the observer makes decisions based upon overt behavior (what they see) and not the precursors (causal factors of the behavior).

Nobody knew about the times Hakeem, at 8 and 9 years old, applied Evelyn's makeup to his face when left home alone. These events would transpire after she called him stupid or an embarrassment, angrily voicing her shame to be with him in public.

Makeup—an artificial enhancement, is mankind's tool to create beautiful illusions. Hakeem understood that much from being in the presence of women. Such understanding in combination with artistic skills—a significant contrast to his behavioral problems, freed his imagination and self-expression. When he applied the makeup—eye shadow, rouge and red lipstick, he became someone else. He would stare at himself in Evelyn's vanity mirror and feel beautiful because of the colored paints until drifting into sadness. The makeup hid the hurt and ugliness inside. There was no one to make his dejection abate. Everyone was oblivious to his darkness. They were too busy living their lives while he endeavored to make sense of his own chaotic world.

Once, Evelyn almost caught Hakeem tampering with her makeup upon returning home unexpectedly. He hurried to remove the makeup, hearing gravel shift in the driveway as her car rolled to a stop. Most of the evidence from his activities had been disposed of, except for a wet paper ball stained with rouge. Frantic, he threw the wet ball into the basement not knowing where it landed after flushing half a roll of toilet tissue used to clean the mess.

One day, Evelyn discovered the tissue ball along with the red stain it created on a table while Hakeem was at school. She collected him from school and beat him. He learned that the tissue ball had damaged some of her work. Why did he throw the ball down the stairs instead of flushing it in the toilet? Was it guilt that dampened his ability to think coherently? Twenty-six years later, some of Hakeem's past still mystified him. Maybe he ceased caring about what he did so many years ago.

Hakeem continued to experiment with makeup sporadically as a teenager. There was the babysitter, Pam, who was much aware of the quality of life within Rosalyn's household. Pam had witnessed her verbally abusing Hakeem. Pam would let him sit at her vanity table and assist in applying makeup to his face. They would laugh and watch TV together like long-time friends.

Reflecting on the events, Hakeem believed that Pam pitied him. The desire for friendship and acceptance blinded him from seeing the harm in her level of support.

Pam's pandering to Hakeem's fascination with makeup reinforced his identification with women instead of men. This behavior is exhibited in accommodating women who are unable to help confused males embrace their biological identity. Intolerant women like Rosalyn, who stood on the extreme side of the continuum, pushed males with effeminate tendencies in the wrong direction. Moreover, the absence of positive male role models in the lives of confused male youths who struggled with defining their self-identity, factored into the possibility of the latter becoming effeminate or gay. The positive impact potential of strong male role models on young boys justifies the need for fathers wherever possible, to be actively involved in their sons' development. Men who abandoned their families and communities don't have the right to criticize effeminate or gay men.

Hakeem's final masquerade in full makeup happened as a dare from Arnold's daughter, Felicia. It was Felicia's outburst of excitement that alerted Rosalyn and Arnold to his antics as they talked in another room of the apartment. When Rosalyn and Arnold saw Hakeem's painted face, they began to call him derogatory names in front of his siblings. Rosalyn even threatened to throw him outside for the neighborhood to ridicule. They reduced him to tears and embarrassment. Felicia cried because she was shaken by their cruelty. The surging pain and sorrow in Hakeem's heart caused him to grow colder towards Rosalyn. She could have died and he would not have shed a single tear. Why should he cry for her? She had done nothing to warrant his mourning.

During the remainder of grade school, Hakeem received weekly counseling from a therapist. In the third grade, he was institutionalized for threatening to commit suicide during a group counseling session with other children who were mentally disturbed. Hakeem had not expected the therapist to take him seriously. His threat was voiced in part, to attract attention in the midst of a commotion that broke out between three children displaying emotional episodes during the session.

Joseph and Evelyn unexpectedly visited the school later in the week. Through the school's intercom, the secretary summoned Hakeem to the main office where they waited in unreadable silence. He tried to remember whether he did something wrong, but had been good that week.

Joseph and Evelyn maintained silence as they settled into the car. Puzzled by their unusual behavior, Hakeem looked across the backseat and saw the suitcase laying there. He asked where they were going, prompting Evelyn to disclose knowledge of his outburst in the group counseling session. The therapist had recommended institutionalization, fearing that he was mentally unstable. Joseph spoke few words while driving, understanding very little of what occurred in the counseling sessions unless Evelyn shared the information.

As in Special Education classes and group therapy, the psychiatric hospital specialized in creating structured environments for children with psychological disorders and dysfunctional behavior. Like Hakeem, many of the children were stable until agitated. The hospital staff was proficient at controlling patients when they behaved erratically. From room confinement to curtailing recreational activities, the orderlies enforced stability without menace.

Hakeem behaved satisfactorily during residency. His sleeping quarters—comprised of a one-mattress bed, white tiled floors, a narrow and reinforced glass window, and coat closet were strangely comforting. All of the children attended class during the day in the same manner as a traditional school, and he demonstrated the ability to concentrate without disrupting the classroom. Friendships developed without having to disclose religious affiliations. The brief period that Hakeem spent at the psychiatric hospital afforded peace.

Short-lived as it was, the hospital released Hakeem after thirty days of clinical supervision. He returned home to an unchanged atmosphere and Evelyn's abuse. Some bad habits, such as lying and stealing gradually resurfaced, but taking Evelyn's perfume in the fifth-grade was the final straw.

Hakeem intended to give the perfume to a white girl he admired. Suzie had bright green eyes and orange-red tresses held in place with a headband. He stored the perfume in his locker until midmorning to present it to her. Suzie stated that the fragrance smelled old and made a big to-do about it to other classmates. After homeroom period, Hakeem returned to his locker where she came poking around. Irritated, he sprayed the perfume in her face. It was payback for embarrassing him in front of everyone.

Suzie reported the incident to the school nurse. The principal confiscated the perfume and contacted Evelyn. Evelyn beat Hakeem for stealing and causing another disruption in school, but he no longer cared. A nonchalant disposition dulled the pain she inflicted.

Rosalyn had brought Baby Layla along on her last visit to Clinton City. Hakeem, 11, was motivated by Layla's birth to tell Evelyn that he wanted to live with Rosalyn. It was a satisfying blow because Evelyn revealed that Daryle would always be her favorite child. She also declared that no other grandchildren would be acknowledged except those sired by Daryle. Whether Evelyn admitted the fact or not, she could not deny lineage. Furthermore, sharing guardianship of Hakeem was a demonstration of her acceptance of Rosalyn's child.

Interestingly, and too late, something changed in Evelyn in the days leading up to Hakeem's move to Philadelphia. She became amiable towards him. Was it guilt or regret that changed her demeanor? It was certainly possible. Joseph was shocked upon hearing that he wanted to leave. Both grandparents tried to discourage him from moving, stating that Rosalyn's living situation was unsuitable. As Hakeem would soon learn, their assessment was valid. But his decision was final. He wanted to escape Evelyn's clutches and Rosalyn was the means to achieving the goal.

≈≈≈≈≈≈≈

Hakeem entered the living room and sat on the sofa. On the coffee table lay a stack of photo albums. He usually skimmed the pictures when visiting. Many were of himself as a child, but he saw abuse in every picture. To people who didn't know him, there was only a little boy with big brown eyes and a timid smile. But Hakeem knew what existed beyond the illusion, remembering the welts and bruises from beatings on his child body. Few fond memories carried forward from childhood as the bad times far outnumbered the good.

The big brown eyes of youth made Hakeem sure of one thing. If blessed with children, only he and the mother could provide direct care until confident they could defend themselves. His children would know that no matter the situation, they could tell him anything, especially if someone hurt them. No adult had the right to touch them inappropriately. He secretly vowed to deal directly with the person who dared harm his children. The pain of the past was too devastating to be forgotten and too debilitating to carry forward as a burden.

As Hakeem prepared to place a photo album atop the stack, a picture fell from between its pages onto the floor. Flipping it over, he saw that it was a photo from his college graduation. He smiled. The first college degree was indeed an accomplishment.

Joseph and Evelyn were unaware that the university had placed Hakeem on academic probation, and that he risked expulsion. While they boasted to family and friends that their grandson was pursuing a bachelor's degree, he was either job-searching or partying when the opportunity presented.

Hakeem transferred into college the same academic habits he possessed in high school. He was an undisciplined student, entering with a 2.7-grade point average that dropped to 1.64 after the first four semesters. The university's academic policy included a freshman-forgiveness provision that allowed students to retake a limited number of failed courses in pursuit of higher letter-grades. Higher grades earned, replaced the lower ones recorded on the transcript.

By the time Hakeem received notification of academic probation, he had already invested two years completing general coursework while accumulating nearly $15,000 in student loan debt. He learned aimlessly without declaring a major. Fearing embarrassment amongst family, he decided to turn the situation around by taking advantage of the freshman-forgiveness policy, re-enrolling in the four classes previously failed. He sought tutors for accounting, calculus, finance, and economics. At the end of the fifth semester and each subsequent term, he averaged a 3.8 GPA. A's and B's replaced the initial D's and F's received, enabling consistent placement on the Dean's List until graduation. Gradually, his overall GPA increased to 2.95. Hakeem proved to himself the capability to accomplish the seemingly impossible. *Unproductive behavior is not always an indicator of mental aptitude or intelligence.*

Hakeem ran an index finger across the glossy surface of the photo that captured him standing next to Rhonda. Rhonda was the only friend who witnessed the receipt of his bachelor's degree. She was the first woman in his adult years who displayed an authentic affection for him.

"She was a pretty girl." Joseph stood in the middle of the living room doorway, looking down. He saw the picture of Rhonda in Hakeem's hand. "Your grandmother and I thought you were gonna' marry her."

To be in his early eighties, Joseph was in better physical condition than Earl who was junior by nearly two decades. When Evelyn was alive, she ensured that Joseph maintained a healthy diet and visited the doctor regularly. Joseph consumed beer primarily and wine occasionally but was not a smoker or drug-user.

Joseph and Rosalyn had in common the same syrupy skin tone. It showed smoothly through thinning gray hair. The slight stoop in Joseph's shoulders made him appear shorter than Hakeem remembered. Or, had he not paid attention to Joseph's gradual physiological regression throughout the years? He realized that preoccupation with his own maturity overshadowed the fact that Joseph had aged significantly. The passage of time had affected them both.

Joseph verbalized what Hakeem thought some time ago. Rhonda was model slender, long-legged, and toffee-complexioned. Hakeem liked petite, shapely women. Rhonda was natural as any woman could be and tomboyish. She maintained a sleek wrap of black hair. Whenever she wore stilettos, the effect was analogous to a sundae topped with whipped cream and a cherry. Rhonda was responsible—paid all of her bills, maintained good credit and a clean house. And although she had a quick temper, she was respectful until someone became disrespectful. A wife type that even a blind man could see her potential.

Several times, Rhonda came through for Hakeem. The cable company was going to disconnect his service, but she paid the bill. Although he refunded the money, there was no question that she had him. Then there was the time when he had a nasty hangover from the club. He almost left the apartment heading for work wearing only underclothes. He left work an hour later, unable to drive all the way home for nearly blacking out on the highway. Rhonda lived midway and allowed him to crash at her house. She bought food and watched over him until he recovered.

Rhonda was also a single mother, who did everything for her daughter. It was this trait above all qualities, which conveyed to Hakeem that she would have made a trophy wife. His ideal spouse was someone who not only adored him but loved their children too. If anything happened to him, he would not have to worry about their safety.

They went to church together on several occasions. Rhonda along with her daughter, walked together at his side. A stranger might have thought they were family. When females—those Hakeem knew from choir and college, approached in church, Rhonda became irritated. While she did not make a scene, her facial expressions communicated inner emotions. In those moments, he knew she wanted him and could have married her.

Hakeem gave Joseph a half smile. He could not marry Rhonda at a time when he was living a double-life. Being confused and marrying her would have made matters worse. Not marrying her was to both of their benefit. He never told Rhonda about his sexuality, fearing that it would permanently damage their friendship. And generally, he did not tell females about his sexuality, anticipating the day he would change and do a three-sixty. The fewer people who knew about his sexual orientation, the fewer criticisms and explanations to endure. How often did one hear about a reformed gay man? Did most people believe that such an occurrence was possible?

"Do you still talk to her? What was her name?" Joseph pressed. His gaze drifted to the floor, trying to recall her name.

"Rhonda."

"Yeah, Rhonda. That's her name!"

"I still talk to her....not as much as I used to though."

Rhonda was upset when he moved to Atlanta. On the day he left, they met at a gas station where she dropped off his coat. He heard the trembling in her voice as she spoke, which made him feel guilty. As he drove away, he saw Rhonda from the rearview mirror and thought her face crumbled. It broke his heart that he was no good for her, or to himself.

173

The memories brought tears to Hakeem's eyes. He focused on the window on the far side of the room, blinking rapidly. He didn't want Joseph to see his watery eyes. *God, why is my life such a mess?* No sooner did he ask, God gave answered. *Choices.* He had made some costly decisions with a troublesome past trailing behind.

"You're getting older, Hakeem. Have you thought about getting married? Having children?" Joseph's face turned serious.

Joseph reminded Hakeem of Evelyn. She asked the same question shortly after he graduated from college. At the time, he claimed that both pursuing a career and establishing himself before settling down were his main goals. She dismissed the excuse, stating that he could build a future with a wife. The longer he waited—she further stated, the more selfish he would become. To an extent, Evelyn was right. He became obsessed with the luxuries of freedom so much that nothing else mattered.

"I have and I'm working on it." He was just getting started.

"So, you've met a young lady?"

"Not really. Just talking." He would rather speak on another subject lest he lie.

"I'd like to see some great-grandchildren before I'm gone. I was in my late twenties and in the military when your Uncle Daryle was born."

Hakeem disliked Joseph referring to his own death. He feared that when Joseph died, there would be no one left from which to draw emotional support. "I know, Dad. You've told me." He said, clearing his throat.

"Are you alright?" Joseph peered closely at his face. "You don't sound right?"

"I'm fine, Dad." Hakeem lied. He was barely okay, being depressed from grieving about past mistakes. But he did not want Joseph overly concerned with him. Joseph would worry and did not need the additional stress. His hands were already full caring for two adults—Rosalyn and Gary.

"Okay. I have to run to town. You going with me?"

"No. I'm gonna' stay here." Depleted was Hakeem's energy to be around people and socialize. When Joseph went to town, he also drove around visiting relatives. Today was not the day.

"Okay. Make sure you lock up if you leave the house."

Hakeem exited the living room en route to his bedroom, passing the door that led to the basement. As a boy, he had nightmares about the basement. In every dream, the same vampire waited at the bottom of the staircase. It was a strange phenomenon because he was not allowed to watch violent or horrific television programs and movies, which were restricted in the household. He would tell Joseph to close the door to the basement when going to bed at night. He thought that closing the door would prevent the vampire from coming up the stairs while he slept.

As an adult, Hakeem still did not understand what the dreams meant. However, he knew that nightmares were the mind's way of processing painful and traumatic experiences. Perhaps a hypnotherapist could uncover the truth. He had read psychological studies in which hypnotherapy was used to retrieve suppressed memories.

There were gaps in Hakeem's memory that inhibited his ability to recall when the abuse first began. How could he remember abuse at 6 years of age, but nothing prior where behavioral problems also existed? If he underwent hypnotherapy, what would the therapist find? He did not think he had the stomach to find out. What point would it make anyway? The abuse at the hands of Evelyn, Daryle, Byron, Rosalyn, and Earl would always taint his past. Byron, Daryle, and Evelyn were dead now. The past could not change the present or future. And since Hakeem was on the road to healing, the past was slowly losing its hold, becoming a powerless memory.

A BOX OF BROKEN TOY SOLDIERS

If a father is broken, how is he able to teach his son to be a man of character?

*H*akeem parked on the side of the road, in front of the driveway winding up to the house where Earl once lived with his ex-wife and four children. He was a baby then, living three houses down the road with his grandparents. Earl never called or visited. *To have lived so close and yet, possessed no interest in being involved as a father.*

Subconsciously, Hakeem raised a hand mid-air, imagining Earl walking through the yard. He visualized himself playing—riding his tricycle in the yard as he had as a little boy. Earl was thirty-one years old when Rosalyn conceived. He had auto-mechanical talents and Hakeem pictured him working on his vehicles.

What would I have learned living with Earl? How to fix cars and trucks? How to confidently interact with females as a male? How to be a man? How different would it have been if he raised me instead of Joseph and Evelyn? Would I have been physically and sexually abused?

Although Hakeem would never know a past that never transpired, the realization didn't eliminate curiosity.

Rosalyn sought Earl's whereabouts through his ex-wife after learning about Hakeem being molested. As with all of Earl's ex-wives, he left them behind with bitter memories. Merely mentioning Earl's name set off a barrage of scathing remarks. When Rosalyn finally reached Earl, he questioned whether she sought child support. Rosalyn told Earl that

176

it was time for him to develop a relationship with Hakeem and needed nothing else.

In the summer of 1993, Earl drove alone from Minneapolis to Philadelphia to meet Hakeem, 12. As Hakeem learned five years later, Earl had lied to his current family—telling them that he was going on a business trip. Every detail of that day was meaningful because Hakeem was overjoyed with the idea of meeting Earl. The sun gleamed high in the sky and white blossoms on the trees along the sidewalk were in full bloom. There were few flowerbeds on the mowed lawns in the projects. Few subsidized housing programs provided for those types of outdoor aesthetics. An unvaried melody resonated through the air from the music box atop the neighborhood ice-cream truck. Street hustlers, young and old, congregated on the corner adjacent to the apartment building where he lived. Teenage boys played basketball in the gate-enclosed court as tenants populated the benches, and drug-addicts panhandled. The scenes were daily visuals that took on new meaning.

There were two payphones on the street opposite the apartment building and across from the corner store. Earl called Rosalyn from one of the phone booths after arriving on the block. Cellular phones were unheard of then. People carried beepers instead.

Earl wore a fisherman's hat, red t-shirt, black cargo shorts, and sandals. Rosalyn told Hakeem that Earl was muscular when they first met. Age and an indulgent appetite had added weight to his former athletic build. Earl's shoulders and upper-chest muscles were the only vestiges of a younger physique. When Earl smiled, Hakeem understood from whom he inherited his dimples.

Earl chauffeured them around the city, catching up on lost time. Rosalyn did most of the talking while Hakeem rode along. Was the meeting about her or him? Earl departed that evening for New York promising Hakeem that he would stop through on his trek back to Minneapolis. It was a promise that Hakeem somehow knew, would be broken. Twelve and a half years had passed. Why would Earl change drastically, and so rapidly? Uninvolved parents underestimated their children's uncanny ability to perceive their environment and make associations between them and events. Earl did not display the kind of enthusiasm, which a doting father would when meeting their child for the first time. And as sure as Hakeem predicted, Earl returned to Minneapolis without a return visit.

Despite meeting face-to-face, communication flows progressed slowly between Hakeem and Earl. Hakeem initiated most of the exchanges. It seemed that distance prevented the development of stronger emotional attachments. Three years later, and Hakeem more of a cynic, Rosalyn relayed Earl's disproval of him protecting her from Arnold. According to Rosalyn, Earl said that Arnold should have broken his arm. She could have lied—something Hakeem could not confirm unless he inquired. But what would have motivated Rosalyn—her relationship with Arnold?

Some parents sacrificed themselves and their children to salvage intimate relationships. Earl had repeatedly sacrificed relationships with his children to procure women. Why a father would utter hurtful words concerning his own son perplexed Hakeem. But Hakeem was no more regretful than the day he saved Rosalyn. He would always believe that men should refrain from hitting women. In reflection of Earl's statements, an important inference from Rosalyn's recant was made—that Earl was unbothered by women being subjected to domestic violence.

Living with Earl confirmed Hakeem's assumptions. Earl also had a track record of beating up on some of the women he entangled. Like Arnold, Earl experienced no shortage in women. He enjoyed the accommodations they afforded. This preoccupation interfered with his capacity to build healthy relationships with all of his children. His interaction with them or lack thereof, indicated a disregard for the impact of being an absentee father.

Hakeem quickly discovered that moving into Earl's household was a transference from one hell to another. He witnessed firsthand, Earl's dominatingly combative nature, working on destroying a third marriage. Earl tried to use him to monitor younger sister, Chantel and her boyfriend. When Hakeem failed to provide updates, Earl threatened to send him back to Philly as a means of intimidation. Earl stalked both of them when off from work. It was the only possible way that he could know anything about their activities, given his work schedule. It was nothing for Earl to return home unannounced. In fact, he delighted in the practice.

Earl's suspicions of Hakeem were partly a consequence of Rosalyn's lies. Thinking that Hakeem was lackadaisical in job searching, Earl became impatient—firing criticisms regarding his slow progress. They argued. During the verbal exchange, Earl spat more insults at Hakeem, claiming that Rosalyn said he had problems with men. Rosalyn's lie was stunning. Hakeem had not been willfully involved with any man. It was not enough that she drove him to escape, so she sent drama along too.

The lie was effective enough to widen the rift in an already delicate father-son relationship. Hakeem had yet made a conscious and willful decision to be involved with a man. Earl demanded his entire schedule— the beginning and end times for school and work, and anything that occurred between. Any gaps unaccounted, Earl wanted an explanation, and if Hakeem was unable to provide a plausible excuse, he responded with threats of buying him a bus ticket to Philadelphia.

The stress of living with Earl exceeded what Hakeem felt in Rosalyn's environment. While walking down the street, heading home, a man passed and circled. Once close enough, the driver lowered the passenger window and asked whether he needed a ride. Hakeem refused and unwisely told Earl about the encounter. Earl blamed him for the incident, stating that he gave the man reason to stop and solicit the ride. Every instance in which Hakeem was molested or approached by an older man must have been his fault too. It was this self-blaming behavior that eroded the self-esteem of a victim of abuse or violence. Eventually, they stopped fighting their demons and accepted defeat, as their self-esteem fully deteriorated. In many cases, the abused became living definitions of their persecutor's perceptions and criticisms.

Earl denied the existence of his own demons. In the early winter, the household fell apart. He confronted his wife, Jacqueline, concerning Chantel having a boyfriend without his approval. As Jacqueline stood accused of enabling Chantel, Chantel revealed that she saw him leaving the house of a woman who lived several blocks down the street. Earl exploded in rage and slammed Chantel onto her bed while Jacqueline struggled to separate them. Hakeem remained in the living-room, afraid to intervene. A chill coursed through him—the kind that a person felt when standing below an open air-conditioning vent, and nausea unsteadied his stomach. The sounds of angry yelling, uttering of profanity, and moving furniture as bodies collided with the structures reminded him of living with Rosalyn and Arnold. Hakeem wondered whether he would ever be able to live in an environment where there was no fighting.

Jacqueline was prepared to leave Earl that night. It wasn't the first time he physically attacked her as she defended her children. Hakeem tried to convince Jacqueline to stay. He did not want to live with Earl alone but dreaded returning to Rosalyn even more. Jacqueline had an endearing presence, whereas Earl was insufferable. She was a light in his sea of oppressive darkness. When Hakeem moved to Minneapolis, it was Jacqueline who helped him enroll for high school. Earl claimed exhaustion from work and could not help him prepare for senior year.

Further disappointment arrived at Christmas. Earl purchased a car for Hakeem and Chantel to share. Hakeem believed that the consolidated gesture was Earl's way of escaping the obligation of buying him a personal gift. However, he used money earned from a part-time job to purchase cologne that Earl asked for as a gift.

Shortly after the New Year, Jacqueline separated from Earl. One day, she came home from work, packed her clothes and sentimental items into suitcases and laundry baskets, departing forever.

Chantel soon followed her mother's footsteps. She tried alternating residence in both households until enduring Earl's rules became too difficult. In a last save effort, Earl granted total ownership of the car purchased at Christmas to Chantel. He justified that she was a female and could get pregnant. But Hakeem saw through the excuse. Earl was competing for Chantel's loyalty in the wake of Jacqueline's separation, only to see his bribes were in vain. Chantel preferred living with Jacqueline who permitted her pursuit of liberties, which Earl restricted. Meanwhile, Hakeem continued riding public transportation to school and work.

Earl treated Hakeem more like a stepchild than a biological son.

While Earl never spoke on the subject, Hakeem believed he was reluctant to provide financial support. His behavior conveyed a grudging attitude. During senior year, Earl instructed him to contact Rosalyn to see if she was willing to contribute financially. Self-employed, Earl grossed in excess, an estimated $3,000 per week, which was more than she made at any point in her career. He knew she was living on a fixed income from disability. Thus, Earl advised Hakeem to use the money earned from his part-time job to pay senior dues. Fortunately, Joseph and Evelyn continued to provide a financial cushion.

Work motivated Hakeem. He understood that a job generated his own money—just not enough of it. His grandparents had raised him on an earn-reward system. Rewards were contingent upon satisfactory grades, behavior, and the completion of chores. Earl held similar expectations, excluding consistent disbursement of compensation. Earl should have contributed more financially. Providing a place to stay was the least he could do. Joseph and Evelyn had fulfilled every obligation. Earl should have followed their example.

Aside from achieving senior status, the final school year ignited minor enthusiasm in Hakeem. He pursued academia with the same degree of nonchalance as exhibited in preceding grades. He was an average high school student with a passive view regarding achievement. The one difference was an increased hunger for the freedom that graduation would surely bring.

A newcomer without a longstanding social network in high school, Hakeem was a relatively unpopular senior. The notoriety he gained among peers resulted from vocal talents in music class. Singing enabled him to accumulate a small measure of respect amongst juniors and seniors.

A shrewder application of his talents might have attracted more female admirers. He observed that most of them enjoyed the vocal capabilities of a competent male singer. But he was neither aggressive nor self-confident. Hakeem feared approaching girls only to be rejected. On a deeper level existed the belief that he lacked the attributes necessary to satisfy a female. Consequently, he avoided making the first move. If a female expressed interest, then he was in the clear. If she outright overlooked him, then it negated the chance of embarrassment and having to re-evaluate self-perceived inadequacies.

Hakeem met Avery, a junior student in drama class. The teacher paired them together for a class assignment, setting their friendship in motion. Hakeem suspected that Avery was at least bisexual. Sometimes, he caught Avery staring from across the classroom like a bird watching its' prey. It was unusual for a male to stare at another in such a manner. Hakeem wondered what thoughts lurked behind those large dark-brown eyes.

After hanging out at the mall a few times, Avery confirmed his suspicions. Hakeem was intently inspecting a stack of folded sweaters in the department store while Avery scoped their surroundings. He missed when Avery wondered away. Avery shopped but with comparatively less enthusiasm and frequency. After deciding to buy a navy blue and gray wool sweater reduced from $89.50 to $29.99, he observed Avery standing across from the display, eyeing another man.

The guy who piqued Avery's curiosity, approached and asked if he had seen a gold belt. Avery's eyes sparkled with amusement. Hakeem silently considered the question odd because the clothing store did not sell specialty merchandise for men. From storefront to backend were displays of apparel in neutral tones. A few shades of red, blue, and green colored fabrics spattered the landscape. In the center of the men's section was a belt stand and each ordinary belt was made of leather. He owned a metal belt designed with dollar signs. Rosalyn had bought the belt from a store that sold urban hip-hop clothing. That kind of belt could not be found in the average retail clothing store. No, the man was in search of something else.

Avery didn't give Hakeem time to verbalize his rationale. He whispered that the guy "messed around," and volunteered to assist in the search for the gold belt. Avery left him standing in the aisle and explored the store with the stranger.

Hakeem purchased the wool sweater along with a red plaid shirt and exited the store to wait for Avery, not interested in participating in the pointless search. When Avery exited the store with the guy in tow, it was apparent that they had exchanged more than belt-related dialogue. Avery introduced the stranger as Faizon and for a while, they dated.

As the third wheel in the friendship, Faizon inducted Avery and Hakeem into frequenting gay bars within the city. Before Faizon, neither had heard of after-hour spots or needed fake IDs. Faizon was senior in age to Hakeem and Avery by two and three years, respectively. Fake IDs were unnecessary for Faizon because he knew the bouncers at the clubs, and by association, Hakeem and Avery had unrestricted access.

Having found a new recreational outlet, Hakeem was excited when Earl's business trips extended. With Earl gone, leaving the house without permission and returning with no one being the wiser was possible. Hakeem knew Earl disapproved of going to bars and clubs, so asking for permission was futile. Gradually, he became more comfortable getting around Earl's rules.

Frequenting the gay clubs and bars lifted the veil between fantasy and real-life in the gay community. What people overheard in conversations or saw on television differed from the in-your-face dramatics. Some gay and bisexual men and women drifted through the establishments dressed exaggeratedly or out of character. Some had maintained the masquerade for so long that it was a wonder whether they remembered their authenticity.

Faizon inducted Hakeem and Avery into his social network of gay friends and associates—young men, some of whom exhibited feminine characteristics beyond what mainstream society deemed appropriate. They behaved more like females than males, having adopted feminine mannerisms in the absence of genuine masculinity. Hakeem could identify with the group to an extent, as he and Avery had sometimes referred to each other as "sisters". But Hakeem maintained social distance from some of those associates because they were distractingly catty and superficial.

Homosexuality as a subculture blurred the line between genders by fostering environments where individuals behaved as they perceived themselves, instead of reminding them of their biogenetic compositions. But how much blame were they responsible for owning? Several of the associates had been ostracized, forced into being homeless, and

183

disowned by their families. In the end, many gay people found comfort and support amongst those with similar origins and experiences. The associates had formed a brother-sisterhood. An unfortunate consequence of those bonds was an embrace of counter-productive, self-destructive behaviors. Grimmer still is the reality that the wounded and abandoned lead each other in the dark.

Avery continued entertaining Faizon for a time, and Hakeem eventually met an admirer. Hakeem had switched to a part-time serving job to earn additional money and met Juan, 38, soon after. Juan lived within five miles of the restaurant and was a regular customer, having a friend who worked as a cook in the establishment. It was later disclosed that Juan had dined in the restaurant and observed him waiting on customers over the course of several weeks. When he decided to express interest, his friend arranged the introduction. Curious, Hakeem accepted the invitation and started seeing Juan regularly between work and school, reveling in the newness of their acquaintance.

Hakeem did not understand it then, but the twenty-year age difference was a silent wedge in their association, which limited commonality. Juan was a confident gay man, whereas he was floating in limbo. However, he took advantage of the companionship and emotional support Juan provided. Juan was a solution for loneliness. Juan loved music and was mesmerized by his ability to articulate emotion in his favorite songs. If there was anything that Hakeem felt, it was pain and sorrow. He dreamed of love and romance. Juan, reclining on a sofa, would listen in silence while he crooned.

So enamored was Juan that he introduced Hakeem to his mother, hinting at a possible growing attachment. But Hakeem was emotionally fickle. Despite Juan's amiable demeanor, sneaking around was discomforting. His grandparents could never know that he was dating a man. Earl was certainly out of the question. The thought had played out in Hakeem's mind—the embarrassment from seeing the expressions of disgust and outrage on their faces. The scene convinced him that it was best to keep Juan in the dark and maintain their surreptitious engagements.

≈≈≈≈≈≈

Reflecting on my senior year, and on Juan, I realize that I'd been living a double-life for much longer than consciously acknowledged. At school, I projected a semblance of heterosexuality, which fed my misjudgments. There was a girl in my chemistry class, who had engaged three male students and me in a sexually-charged conversation. I overcompensated by drawing graphic images of a female in sexual displays on the back of her notebook paper. Why I would commit an incriminating act, I can think of no other reason than that I was trying to fit in. I tried to convince myself that there was nothing wrong with me. All these years I have been confused—living a lie within myself.

Embarrassed, the female student reported me to the teacher without indicating the other boys' involvement. The teacher dismissed me from class and sent me to the principal's office. The principal imposed a five-day, out-of-school suspension rather than expulsion, as there was no prior history of misbehavior. She saw the lewd images that I had sketched and scolded me for the graphic details. Sometimes when I recalled her mixed expression of disbelief and amazement, I almost laughed. That's my dark humor, which changes to embarrassment as I continue to reflect on the matter. I wouldn't dream of doing what I did then, now. I was fortunate.

If not for Malcolm, my eldest brother by ten months, moving from Clinton City to live with us, Earl would have sent me packing. Malcolm was low-key, chill, and personable. His personality was the semblance of a river's bed—cool and rocky at the same time. He knew how to maneuver around our father, having lived with him intermittently throughout the years. Malcolm knew Earl from birth, and between them existed a stronger bond, much like Chantel. I never expressed to Malcolm how grateful I was for his presence in the house. He was a buffer to the misery that Earl emitted, and more conveniently, distracted away from my own extracurricular activities.

≈≈≈≈≈≈

Trysting with Juan didn't prevent Hakeem from going to the prom. As a senior, he believed it his right to attend, knowing that Juan had been a senior once. But whether Juan attended his own prom was irrelevant. Hakeem would not allow their associations to interfere with his own decision to attend. He had dreamed of going since the first day of high school and wanted to experience the fanfare of donning a tuxedo and escorting a pretty girl. Formal events mesmerized him, as they were magical, creating representations of style and grandeur.

Much to Hakeem's chagrin, circumstances also constructed memories that he would rather forget. The girl he took to prom wasn't the first choice. There was another senior named Jalesa who captured his attention. She was smart and beautiful. Hakeem debated asking her to the prom until abandoning the idea altogether. All of the senior guys fell over themselves just to speak to Jalesa. They appeared to have more to offer a girl like her.

On the night of the prom, Hakeem stepped into the hallway outside the hotel ballroom. His companion had caused a two-hour delay by helping a friend shop for a gown. He salvaged the remainder of the night observing everything that transpired.

Jalesa stood in the hallway in a red strapless gown with gold accents, preparing to take pictures. Golden pins held up tresses of black hair that dangled down the length of her slender neck. Beautiful was insufficient to describe Jalesa that night. She was breathtaking.

After graduation, Hakeem confessed to Jalesa that he had wanted to take her to prom. She was surprised by both his interest and hesitancy. Shockingly, Jalesa stated that had he offered to be her escort, she would have accepted the invitation. She came to the formal alone. No one asked her to the prom. Hakeem felt embarrassment and regret.

≈≈≈≈≈≈≈

How might my life have turned out, if I had taken Jalesa to the prom? Would I have successfully ended the time I spent living as a closet homosexual? In a crack of the farthest corner of my thoughts, I knew that my dealings with Juan were going to be temporary. Juan claimed he wanted to evolve our acquaintance into a relationship, but I was unsure of moving in that direction. In part, I feared that Earl would eventually learn of my secret.

His suspicions never waned, which seemed to increase surrounding my ambiguous behavior. Unlike Malcolm, I didn't bring females to the house or make mention of going on dates with them. I also made vague references concerning my small network of friends and Earl didn't know much about them. Juan living on the opposite side of town made it difficult for Earl to track and it was my advantage. Even still, game recognized game. Earl was a master player, whereas I was a novice. One was wise not to underestimate a married man who was an expert at hiding his extramarital affairs.

I ultimately decided to sever ties with Juan, but it wasn't the pressure of living with Earl that primarily drove me to that decision. Juan had seen Malcolm once when he dropped me off in front of my house. He remarked on having a sexual encounter with my brother. His comment was disrespectful, and I told him as much. Furthermore, Malcolm wasn't bisexual or gay, and no matter how involved I was in homosexuality, I disliked the idea of my siblings being gay. I was inexperienced in dating and relationships but possessed no misunderstanding regarding respect and fidelity. When a person's eyes starts to wander, the heart soon follows. I knew the effects of infidelity through the eyes of Rosalyn and Jacqueline. Their relationships weren't the kind that I was willing to maintain.

Troubling matters further, Juan knew of my ordeal living with Earl, and did little to alleviate my fears. Not once did he extend an invitation for me to live with him. There were times when I was unwilling to sexually engage, and Juan would threaten that he could "find" someone else. Not once did I think him incapable of executing his threats, which gave me pause. On the other hand, I had dealt with people who threatened me before, and yet, I did what I wanted. Juan would not be an exception. Nonexistent was my patience for ultimatums as a means to control me. All of my life, people used coercion to keep me under their thumbs. It became apparent that Juan couldn't provide for me in the most extreme circumstances. I saw no other purpose for him. I decided, let Juan find another young male to manipulate. Better them than me! It was just a matter of time when I would be done with Earl too.

≈≈≈≈≈≈≈

Life during the summer post-graduation for Hakeem was analogous to a boy in a toy store. He could not fathom anything sensible except fun and money. He acquired the notion that working two jobs equated to more liberties and exercised those beliefs. After graduation, Hakeem believed he was old enough to make independent decisions. Earl would have none it, stating that he was "maintaining a Christian household." He expected his children to be in the house no later than 1 A.M.

Because many club activities kicked into full gear at 12 A.M., it was difficult for Hakeem to adhere to Earl's rules. The curfew was a major problem. He knew that Earl was 'entertaining' women—a habit that did not reflect the values he attempted to instill in his sons.

As eldest, Earl entrusted Malcolm with driving his vehicles. Malcolm willfully complied because of the proximity of his recreational activities. He had little use for the cars besides commuting to work. The majority of his friends lived around the block, so he often walked. Hakeem's friends, however, were dispersed. Access required transportation. Thus, Malcolm and Hakeem forged an agreement that allowed Hakeem to drop him off wherever he needed to be. Hakeem then had full access to the car. When curfew approached, he was supposed to pick up Malcolm, and they would ride home together. The plan didn't always run the entire course. Sometimes, Malcolm returned home earlier than Hakeem preferred. And because of Hakeem's reluctance to adjust to the impromptu changes, he often encountered Earl's wrath when returning home after 2 A.M. "Pack your (expletive) and get ready to go back to Philly," Earl raged. Although fearful of returning to Philly, Hakeem delayed packing anything. By mid-day, Malcolm had diffused Earl's threats, and saved him.

Time finally granted Earl an opportunity to assess the characteristics of Hakeem's friends. One evening, Avery arrived at the house to pick Hakeem up. They were going to the mall and meet with other associates. Earl must have watched Avery's mannerisms and tucked the observations away to interrogate Hakeem later. That's how Earl was—anyone whom his children affiliated and he disliked, he would observe in silence and inquire after they departed. It was a hot seat that he constantly forced the children to occupy and another source of contention between him and them.

Malcolm knew Avery, having become acquainted through Hakeem on a previous occasion. Seeing that Malcolm knew Avery, Earl attempted to siphon information from him. But Malcolm never expressed or behaved in any manner that conveyed an awareness of the lifestyle Hakeem and his friends lived. Thus, it was unsurprising that he had nothing to offer Earl in the way of information, not that he even cared. Malcolm was not the type of person who pried into the affairs and secret dealings of people.

When Hakeem returned home, Earl set in—asking whether Avery was gay. Hakeem denied knowledge of Avery's sexual preferences, further angering Earl. It was an intentional lie. To reveal Avery meant exposing himself. If it ever happened, Hakeem decided that such disclosure would be on his terms, not someone else's. Besides, Avery's sexual orientation was none of Earl's business.

The same year marked Hakeem's nineteenth birthday and awareness of the fact only fueled willful, defiant behavior. It was this cocksure attitude that factored into the trouble he soon found with the law. Arrogance gradually brings a person to heel, and he certainly met the ground. Despite the knowledge at his disposal, Hakeem underestimated the potential for shortsighted decisions to lead to his undoing.

Communication between Hakeem and Earl remained severed for two and a half years, following release from jail. Somewhere during their period of irreconcilable differences, Earl entered into a lengthy and nettlesome relationship with Felisha who was a drug-addict.

At Earl's request, Hakeem (now 21 years of age) moved into his apartment after room-mating with Brian. Earl claimed to be proud of his rehabilitative efforts—working full-time and attending college after incarceration. As Hakeem discovered, Earl still possessed manipulative ways. Earl offered a place to stay in exchange for paying the utility bills. Hakeem had forgotten that dealing with Earl was just as problematic as its worth.

It became immediately apparent to Hakeem upon returning to Earl's household that there had been a shift in priorities, and a descent in quality of life. Felisha disappeared periodically for crack binges, and Earl accommodated her addiction. Earl purchased Felisha a car for which she expressed gratitude by loaning it for crack. Hakeem continued commuting to work and school via public transportation, perceiving Earl's indifference as another slight. Earl made excuses for Felisha's drug use—stating that he was "helping her out." Hakeem perceived their relationship as accommodatingly enabling—Earl supporting Felisha's drug use and Felisha providing Earl with companionship.

Earl tried to assign Hakeem the duty of watchman once Joseph and Evelyn purchased him a car. When Earl was away on business, he wanted Hakeem to provide updates regarding eFelisha's whereabouts. His instructions were to deny her entry into the apartment when she disappeared. Hakeem disliked Felisha, so enforcing Earl's directive without apprehension came easy. However, he quickly learned of Earl's double-talk.

Felisha knew Earl's schedule and would call when she was ready to return home, to which he obliged. Hakeem ignored her knocks at the door and it caused contention. Felisha returned to wherever she came and called the house phone, making threats and insults. Hakeem cussed her out and when Earl learned about the arguments, he constantly sided with Felisha. Eventually, Hakeem learned that Earl was bad-mouthing him to Felisha and some of the family members. Earl's sister, Wilma disrespectfully and falsely accused him of trying to bring Earl down. Hakeem cursed her to lake of eternal fire. Wilma's knowledge about him could have only come from Earl. Aside from siblings, Hakeem had limited social ties with Earl's side of the family and blamed Earl for Wilma's knowledge concerning him. Independently, she did not possess any insight regarding his past. Interestingly, Earl minimized how much insight the family had regarding his contributions to Felisha's drug addiction.

It was a blessing in disguise when Faizon introduced Khalil and Hakeem, as the feud between father and son reached its climax. One morning, Hakeem was preparing for work as Earl berated him for not paying the phone bill. During the verbal exchange, Earl stated that none of the children met his expectations. Hakeem retorted that he had yet to meet his children's expectations. Earl flew into a rage and told him to get out. By 12 A.M. the same night, Hakeem had moved into Khalil's apartment. A month later, he moved into his own apartment and never looked back. The moveout only agitated Earl.

Hakeem had befriended Nick while living with Brian, and for a couple of years, their friendship flourished. But Earl disliked Nick. He came home from work one day and saw Nick sitting on the living room couch while Hakeem dressed for a black party in the bedroom. As habit, Earl later questioned Nick's sexual preferences, which Hakeem feigned ignorance.

After Hakeem moved out, Earl told Joseph and Evelyn about catching him in the bed with Nick. Like Rosalyn, Earl lied—retaliating as a parting gift to Hakeem. Evelyn then called Hakeem with Joseph in the background, demanding that the car they purchased and were paying the note, be parked immediately. They planned to drive to Minneapolis and repossess. Hakeem told Jacqueline about what Earl had done. She contacted his grandparents and defended him from Earl's lies, and restored their confidence.

Whether it was consequences of his past or lifestyle habits, Earl's health failed, leaving him physically impaired. Even in a reduced state, he was selfish and manipulative. He tried to gain sympathy from his children through reminders of his financial sacrifices. In Hakeem's opinion, loving parents made selfless sacrifices. Nonetheless, he pitied seeing Earl—a once proud man who now, was dependent upon a walker and unable to clean up his own urine. Was Earl's predicament a direct consequence of how he lived and treated people? While Hakeem believed that God would never give a definitive answer concerning the matter, he entertained the irony. As Earl's children surpassed him, he was localized, forced to watch them mature while having minimal influence in their lives.

Hakeem avoided Earl for nearly four years. During the last attempt to communicate, Earl put him off for a woman. Earl called a week later, but Hakeem sent the call to voicemail. Eventually, they ceased trying to contact each other.

Hakeem refused to allow Earl to manipulate him. Now reduced to a state of dependence, Earl wanted his children around. But Hakeem did not want to deal with him. Why should he settle for a ghost of Earl's former self? In a sense, Earl robbed him of the years in which he was most virile. Earl could have taught him more then.

Hakeem analyzed Earl's motivations for mistreating him, as he push-started the car's ignition and drove away. Perhaps, he might have fared better if they never met. All he gained was resentment. His heart pulled unceasingly for something out of reach. When would the pain subside? Did Earl's mistreatment result from doubts of him being a biological son? Or, did Earl mistreat him because of his potential to be a greater man than he was? The only thing Earl had going for himself was money. Without money, he was nothing because he bypassed the role of being a caring father.

≈≈≈≈≈≈≈

For the life of me, I just couldn't rid myself of the resentment I had for my father. I could see that he was suffering and I found no satisfaction in the fact. The day that I saw him supporting himself with a walker, I cried. I knew that I needed to forgive him. My faith demanded it. But I hadn't reached the point of forgiving Earl just yet because I was holding onto the past. I had locked Earl in the cell where all the other people in my life had betrayed me were held captive.

There were times when I was angry at God for the gnawing pain that ate my insides. You know, like an allergy that itches inside your body, and you can't scratch. It makes you feel like you want to claw your skin off to reach it. Then when you take medication to soothe the irritation, it dissipates. That's what letting go did. I had to find a way to permanently release my anger. As it was, I didn't feel it as much when I suppressed my thoughts. I also believed that living far away from my problems was an effective remedy. Gail had accurately interpreted my motives. It was when I saw or read about depictions of abuse, or endured events such as Mother's and Father's Day that my anger resurged with a vengeance. Truly, I was envious of every person that I perceived had a healthy relationship with their mother and father. Why couldn't I have a family like theirs?

I had deceived myself. Suppressing and escaping problems didn't free a person permanently. At some point, the dynamics of life cornered the person. The individual had no choice but to face their past. Depending upon how the person handled their problems, they either experienced restoration in mental health or deterioration thereof. If the latter outcome occurred, typically it manifested in destructive behaviors in which the individual encountered trouble within their environment, employment, and in their interpersonal relationships. My life is a testament of these scenarios. I have been irascible for many years, and it wasn't until I sought therapy that I began to understand myself. I was angry at my parents for not being who I thought they should have been. I was just as disgusted with my life.

BEAUTY AND THE BEAST – MAN'S DUALITY

As much as there are appealing aspects of a man, there are frightening and destructive aspects of his nature.

*G*ail's contrast of hetero- and homosexual relationships echoed in Hakeem's mind while stretching across the bed. Nonexistent were the benefits of dealing with different men and repeating the same cycle for sixteen years. It was time unwisely spent in self-destruction. Hakeem was as single as the first day he consented to same-sex relations. Having evaluated the circumstances and years of repetition, he was convinced of homosexuality's terminality. A person can experience an event and not comprehend the phenomenon immediately. However, subsequent observations and interactions can generate waves of clarity.

Men are by nature, seeing and feeling creatures—acting based upon what they visualize. Supplementing these traits are the male characteristics of machismo, dominance, assertiveness, stubbornness, and selfishness. As such, a couple comprised of two men with similar sets of personality traits are bound to encounter conflict. The stronger the personalities, greater is the potential for friction. One would be lucky to find the house frame intact once these two collided because long-term harmony is uncommon in intimate male pairings.

As it happened, some gay people modeled heterosexual relationships from multiple aspects. Within these same-sex couples, partners assumed dominant and submissive, or masculine and feminine roles. The more extreme representations underwent transformations—modifying their behavior and outer appearances to reflect the opposite gender. Natural relationships in Hakeem's opinion did not require such adjustments for progression because biology defined gender-specific roles and characteristics, removing debate concerning a person's place in the relationship. Ideally, men exhibit aggressive masculine behaviors as counterbalances to the nurturing femininity of women.

Among the majority of relationship-seeking gay men, their unfulfilled hope is to secure monogamous relationships. However, life-long commitment in same-sex couples is exceedingly rare, because physical attraction and sex are the essential ingredients for catapulting male partnerships forward. There's an adage, "nothing lasts forever." The adage befitted the lifecycle of homosexuality and its aesthetic attributes. Youth, vitality, and sex appeal stimulate the eyes but degrades with respect to the steady progression of age. It stands to reason why older gay men encounter greater difficulty securing relationships beyond "hook-ups" within their age bracket. Older men are considered less desirable than younger males in the gay community, which increased the likelihood of being alone and decreased chances for stable companionship or marriage.

To compete with younger generations in an era of superficiality, some men in their mid-thirties and older, strived to preserve their youth and allure by frequenting fitness centers to develop hard-defined physiques and observing rigid diets. Unfortunately, such practices are insufficient for capturing the heart of a promiscuous man. A typical promiscuous gay or bisexual man will establish a pseudo-relationship with a man while pursuing other men who appeared better packaged in some form or another. This behavior sustains the perpetual revolving door that gay and bisexual men experience whether they desire a fling or a long-term relationship. Sensuality and sexuality ruled in the gay and bisexual world so much that it overshadowed everything worthwhile.

Society and culture are guilty of commercializing the most appealing virile gay men and disguising the ugly truth of gay life. The least showcased were the depraved communications that took place on gay online dating sites. Most conversations between men transpired with inquiries about body specs and the more private details. Scantily clad and nude pictures further roused their interests. Compared to a gay online dating site, a strip club had more decency. Conservative gay and bisexual men finished last. According to some advocates of the gay lifestyle, love overflowed in abundance. No, many homosexual and bisexual men dated or 'hooked up' discriminately.

In men, sexual interaction is predominately physical. What men visualized served as a basis for sexual stimulation and any emotional aspects were subsequential. Few men entered into a romantic or intimate relationship without physical attraction as a decisive factor. For those who would debate this assertion, consider what it takes for a man to achieve an erection and climax, and go from there. The idea is no less plausible in the context of gay and bisexual men.

When men entered into a relationship on the basis of any factor besides physical attraction and sex, they were either driven by: 1) a desire to accomplish a specific purpose—companionship, love and/or extend their legacy through offspring; or 2) desperation (fearful of living out the rest of their lives, after spending many years alone or in short-term relationships) and sometimes, settled for anyone. In the context of gay men, adoption is an alternative for those who remain homosexual, but desire children. For several reasons, the idea of two men raising a child made Hakeem uncomfortable. Moreover, he believed adoption unnecessary since being a man himself, was capable of siring offspring who would continue his bloodline. Still, man's psychological nature and biological factors hindered longevity in gay relationships. Believing otherwise is self-delusional.

Hakeem remembered Ali from Minneapolis, an acquaintance of several years. Ali divulged being romantically involved with a man who had the same sexual 'preferences' as himself. There are limitations to what two men or women can do in a sexual capacity without modifications. The relationship between Ali and his boyfriend expanded to allow participation from a third male to accommodate the couple. For a while, Ali boasted about being in the perfect relationship. According to him, the "arrangement" was fulfilling. Then Ali discovered that his boyfriend was secretly and regularly entertaining their mutual lover.

Ali confronted his boyfriend concerning the infidelity and they split. Frankly, Ali's boyfriend was unwilling to dismiss their companion.

A few men had propositioned Hakeem with opportunities for open relationships, but he declined their proposals. He believed that if an intimate relationship required a third member, then the initial two partners should go separate ways. The more he resisted mainstream homosexuality, the longer he stayed in singlehood.

Hakeem, 29, met Lionel, a mail carrier through online dating. Lionel claimed to be "talking" to someone else, but the relationship was "on the rocks". After some deliberation and conversation with Alex who advocated pursuit, Hakeem continued communicating with Lionel. Interaction during the first month of the acquaintance seemed promising. Movies, dinner, parks, and sports events, their companionship flowed smoothly until Lionel began pressing for intimate relations. Hakeem knew that Lionel was still conversing with Guy #1. Whenever Guy #1 called, Lionel walked beyond earshot to continue the phone conversation. But when Lionel received calls from family and friends, his conversations were less secretive. Hakeem quickly realized he was Guy #2 and delayed intimacy.

Hakeem refused to be intimate with anyone knowing they were sexually active with someone else. He could not prove that Lionel was intimately involved with Guy #1, but intuition alerted the obvious. When a person's communication and behavioral habits change, trust your instincts! You are imbued with instincts and intuition for a reason. Waiting for tangible proof is not always advisable. Sometimes, waiting too long can be too late.

Hakeem was characteristically observant. Since their acquaintance, Friday evenings and Saturdays were the designated hangout days. On a particular Saturday, Lionel said that he was exhausted from work and heading home to sleep. But Lionel didn't go home because their conversation began and ended in his car. At some point, Lionel turned off the ignition and continued to sit in the vehicle instead of entering his apartment. Occasionally, Hakeem heard the sound of people talking in the outside background. Lionel promised to call back after taking a nap but did not call anymore that day.

Hakeem slept restlessly and was tempted to drive to Midtown. He wanted to verify whether Lionel was home. Intuition said that Lionel was elsewhere. But checking on Lionel's whereabouts was pointless because wherever he went, Hakeem had no control. Sunday morning arrived and there still was no call from Lionel. Hakeem went to church and left his cellphone in the car. After service, he saw Lionel's missed call and the flashing voicemail indicator on the phone display. In the voicemail, Lionel disclosed leaving his cellphone in a restaurant. It was 11 A.M. on a Sunday morning! Few dine-in restaurants opened earlier than 11 A.M. on Sundays in Midtown, which Lionel preferred to frequent. The facts narrowed the range of possibilities. Lionel's actions raised the question of when his cellphone was misplaced.

Most likely, Lionel left the cellphone at the restaurant the previous night, having gone out with Guy #1. The event coincided with the timeframe he claimed to be resting. In truth, he had made other plans. Lionel delayed calling Hakeem because Guy #1 would ask questions. It was logical to use resting as an alibi to eliminate questions for being out of character.

Emotional, Hakeem called Lionel after listening to the voicemail and confronted him about his lies. An argument ensued and Hakeem ended their associations. Looming in the back of his mind was the memory of Lionel telling him that sex was required for them to be in a relationship. Reflecting on their association enabled Hakeem to realize his place as Guy #2.

Hakeem tried to salvage the acquaintance during a moment of weakness, but Lionel refused for two reasons. First, Lionel stated that no one had ever initiated a break-up with him. Secondly, he confessed that he could not be the type of dude that Hakeem needed—there was someone better out there. Lionel was focusing on Guy #1. The more compliant among two options had won the bid. Hakeem considered his own stupidity for listening to Alex's advice. Blameless as Alex was, Hakeem knew himself capable of making wiser decisions.

Heterosexual relationships were not devoid of drama, but as Gail positioned the dynamic the opposite sex, women are mutable and accommodating compared to men. Their traits are biologically and psychologically inherent. A woman's emotions are complementary and compensatory to a man, and vice versa. Hakeem's emotional disposition was more suited for a woman. Although he had scarcely chipped the surface of intimacy with a female, he understood the potential offerings associated with being romantically involved with a woman. He witnessed moments of affectionate interaction between Joseph and Evelyn. They were a model for his ideal relationship. In sixteen years, none of Hakeem's romantic or intimate dealings were comparable. Quality, long-term gay male relationships are virtually nonexistent or rare.

Hakeem's need for emotional support remained unfulfilled. Abuse and rejection factored into a constant seeking of emotional connections to fill the void in his life. The men who told Hakeem that they cared for him, were the same ones caught slipping and entertaining other men. Intuition and observation were his silent alarms. As far as he was concerned, when perceiving that a man was entertaining someone else, they were. The only thing that changed in the dating game was the players. It was unnecessary to seek proof of infidelity because when a person searched for evidence, they were looking for reasons to stay in the relationship. Without fail, time proved his suspicions valid. Better that he exited intact than expose himself to a lingering problem.

Homosexuality in the men's arena is especially risky from the perspective of intercourse. People place too much confidence in the use of condoms despite knowing that the preventative measure is not 100 percent safe. Due to human error in the utility of condoms and aggressiveness of sexual activity, "condoms are about 82 percent effective" (Planned Parenthood, 2017). The rising number of cases in which gay men were either diagnosed with a sexually-transmitted disease, HIV or AIDS, suggested that gay men weren't thorough in implementing safety precautions before engaging in sexual activity. The *Centers for Disease Control and Prevention (CDC)* reported "gay, bisexual and other men who have sex with men account for 83 percent of primary and secondary syphilis cases where the sex of a sex partner was known in the United States" ("Sexually Transmitted Diseases," 2016). "From 2005 to 2014, HIV diagnosis decreased in the United States by 19 percent overall, but increased 6 percent among all gay and bisexual men, driven by increases among African-American and Hispanic/Latino gay and bisexual men" ("HIV Among Gay," 2016). In Atlanta alone, the CDC reports that "1 in 51 Georgians will be diagnosed with HIV in their lifetime" ("HIV in the United States," 2016).

Daryle advised Hakeem two years before his death, to "always protect" himself. Hakeem, 25, accepted the unsolicited advice. He had not been open with Daryle regarding his sexuality, given all that had happened in the past. Their overt commonality was moving away from home and establishing private lives inaccessible to other family members.

Hakeem chose not to ask Daryle about the meaning of his counsel, as there was little need. Daryle was sick, and both Joseph and Evelyn possessed some knowledge concerning his diagnosis, but seldom spoke openly regarding the matter. In all of Hakeem's experience with his grandparents, Daryle's conditions was one of few topics where they demonstrated an unwillingness to be forthcoming with information. Despite their secrecy, Hakeem maintained suspicions, having seen pictures of how Daryle looked towards the end. It was not an outcome he envisioned for himself. Daryle was a wraith of his former self— five-foot-eleven, curly black hair, thick eyebrows, caramel complexion and model physique. He had the type of looks that could make women trip over their heels. Apparently the men did too, and their affections came with costs.

Daryle's cryptic advice indirectly signaled the elephant in the room that some gay people tried to ignore and avoid discussion—the *Human Immunodeficiency Virus (HIV)* and *Acquired Immunodeficiency Syndrome (AIDS)*. They disliked hearing the explicit connection made between homosexuality and sexually-transmitted diseases, namely, HIV and AIDS. It wasn't difficult to comprehend. The subject of HIV and AIDS attracted criticism and its' diagnosis was stigmatizing. Is homosexuality worth limiting one's life to taking additional safety precautions, medication, and subjection to filtered dating? Medical treatment was a problem in itself for various reasons.

Hakeem (26) remembered an associate who was HIV-positive. For a while, the young guy endured discomforting side effects as a result of the prescribed medications—including yellowing of the eyes, stomach cramps, and diarrhea. He would listen on as the guy shared experiences of having to switch medications. It was further discouraging when considering an individual who had to deal with HIV, in addition to other health-related issues. A(n) prolonged and/or improper use of some modern HIV-prevention/regulation medications can damage liver or kidneys. How many people lived for the day without expectations of living through the next ten, twenty, or thirty years? Disbelieving that homosexuality was worth the potential complications still wasn't enough to permanently separate some people from the lifestyle.

Hakeem had a close call with an attorney, Alonzo who withheld his HIV+ status. Hakeem estimated that in the gay community, there were three degrees of separation amid the social networks. Between Hakeem and Alonzo was Marvin, a mutual associate who briefly dated Alonzo. Marvin typically referred to Alonzo in third-person, and had only provided Hakeem with a general description of his mystery lover. When the acquaintance began to turn serious, Marvin's best friend divulged that Alonzo was HIV+. Marvin confronted Alonzo to validate the accusation. Alonzo initially denied the claim and eventually confessed. His excuse for concealing the truth was, "the good guys always get away." Hakeem remembered the entire story.

When Hakeem met Alonzo a year later through an online dating site, he didn't make the immediate connection. They maintained steady contact for a couple of months until an argument triggered his recollection. They argued about whether celebrities should be role models—an idea that Alonzo opposed. While Hakeem formulated a theoretical basis for his viewpoint, Alonzo told him that presumptive statements shouldn't be made without factual evidence. Given Alonzo's legal background and Hakeem's education in psychology, they stood at opposite ends of the argument. Hakeem understood legal professionals were adept at proving and disproving factual information, whereas psychologists often considered the role of cognition in behavior—a covert and dynamic phenomenon. Neither backed down in their opinions, and

Alonzo's aggressiveness peeved Hakeem. He was dissatisfied with how the debate ended.

Hakeem called Marvin, simmering over the matter. He pointedly asked Marvin for the name of the attorney he had been involved. He remembered Marvin saying that after distancing himself from Alonzo, Alonzo started appearing outside his apartment demanding conversation. Marvin divulged Alonzo's name, and Hakeem stumbled while listening. Not once did Alonzo mention his status while expressing romantic interests.

Alonzo called a week after their argument. When Hakeem confronted Alonzo, he denied being HIV+. The most insulting aspect of interacting with Alonzo was his expression of romantic interest, knowing he was infected. No wonder Alonzo derided presumptive statements! As long as he could conceal the truth, everything else was irrelevant!

Despite Alonzo's denial, Hakeem knew he was lying. Marvin did not have a logical reason to fabricate the story because his brother died of complications with AIDS. By all external appearances, Alonzo displayed symptoms of being HIV+. He took medication regularly without explanation, had a persistent dry cough, sunken eyes, and hollow cheeks that made his face gaunt. Alonzo's fair skin was splotchy and oddly flabby as in a case of rapid weight loss. As an undergrad, Hakeem studied HIV and AIDS. He had read about the *wasting syndrome*, which some people living with HIV experienced. Sexually-transmitted diseases were discussed in the field of psychology because they are phenomena that practitioners encounter in patients ailing from the afflictions.

A platonic friendship might have been possible had Alonzo been truthful and respectful. Hakeem experienced a shortage of authentic friendships. As the debate climaxed, Alonzo called Hakeem crazy and said that he needed professional help. Alonzo was correct to an extent. Hakeem needed help, just not based on his insinuations. A sensible person declined a ride from a suspicious driver. An HIV test or the results thereof, might have officially resolved the matter, but Hakeem trusted Marvin's disclosure and lacked the desire to contest further.

The insults exchanged during the arguments ultimately destroyed any admiration for Alonzo that he possessed.

People who thought as Alonzo, are obligated to inform those of whom they intended to engage intimately. Withholding such information is selfish and undermines the fostering of positive relationships. Potential partners are entitled to knowing whether they are at risk of contracting sexually-transmitted diseases. In retrospect, Hakeem considered his association with Alonzo as another warning of risking HIV infection. It was a reminder of the importance of HIV-testing. Thus, he submitted to testing because of past involvement with men. The tests confirmed that he was HIV-Negative. However, even in sexual activity that did not involve intercourse, proceeding with caution is still imperative. A man of small interest once told Hakeem, 19, that in addition to practicing safe-sex, it is vital to think of all men as being HIV-Positive. The advice in applied practice proved self-preserving. Cognizant that the stakes were high, Hakeem relied increasingly on pornography to satisfy his sexual urges.

Pornography was another problem because of its addictive properties, which Hakeem capitulated. He viewed straight and gay films with equal enthusiasm, which quickly became habitual. Where companionship and constant emotional support were lacking, sexual gratification filled the void and also served as a stress-reliever. For men who engaged in sexual activity with conscious restraint, masturbation on an individual or partnered basis was typically the preference. Unfortunately, some found it wearisome to secure relationships with any noteworthy commitment as a result of their restrictions. Pornography served as a compensatory mechanism for them too.

Hakeem preferred single gay and bisexual men who held onto their masculinity. He avoided married men, given his respect for the sanctity of holy union and females. Moreover, his preference was influenced not only by exposure to the sexual curiosities of older males, but also a realization that the more masculine were discreet in their dealings with other men. The experiences were the same. Secrecy limited evolution in same-sex relationships, as the partners hid their involvement from family, friends, and the world.

Hakeem struggled to accept the duality of bisexual men. He was often told by the willfully uncommitted that if they wanted a relationship, they would be with women. The danger in entertaining bisexual men is their regular rotation of both sexes. Sexual activities and safety precautions varied between partners, increasing the probability of contracting sexually-transmitted diseases. Hakeem believed that if two people were intimate, they should be exclusive to each other. Unsuccessfully, he constantly tried holding onto men who wanted uncommitted arrangements. Gradually, he began to understand what bisexual men had implied all along. He desired companionship comparable to a heterosexual relationship, which they were unwilling to provide and thus, the associations were short-lived. Hakeem did not believe that sex had to be the focal point of a relationship, and this belief steadily pushed him to the sidelines as more willing participants entered the game without stipulations to satisfy men that he preferred.

It is easy for two mutually-interested men to be intimate because the risks aren't as numerous compared to interludes between members of the opposite sex. The possibility of conception and/or contracting sexually-transmitted diseases causes conscientious consenting members of the opposite sex to pause. Women, especially the career-focused and self-sufficient, tended to exercise their knowledge of risk in sexual activity more readily than men primarily to prevent pregnancy. In contrast, gay and bisexual men primarily need to worry about contracting and spreading sexually-transmitted diseases. Whenever a non-committed man achieved his 'objective', he moved on without emotional and physical ties. Child-support and conception are not the concerns of gay and bisexual men, which could potentially increase their inhibitions for 'hooking up'. Distinguishing male from female behavior and the motivations thereof, are in part, essential to understanding the prevalence of homosexuality and bisexuality.

≈≈≈≈≈≈

There are three important takeaways from the situations involving Marvin and Alonzo, and Hakeem and Alonzo. First, it is necessary to evaluate the true character of so-called friends and associates. No person who cares for you and has your best interest at heart would intentionally withhold a secret that is detrimental to your life, such as when Marvin's best friend failed to reveal that Alonzo was HIV+ before hooking them up. Secondly, ask questions when your intuition fires up and pay attention to warning signs. Inquiry can save your life! Finally, know the HIV status of whoever you decide to be intimately involved and inquire about the contraction of any other sexually-transmitted diseases. Any person who is offended by such inquiry signals a red flag. Stop!!! Concern for your personal health gives you the right to ask. I thank God for His protection for He knows that I did not always proceed with caution.

This chapter does not aim to vilify people living with HIV or have died from complications related to the disease. With that being stated, all human beings are obligated to ensure the safety of others regardless of personal experiences.

TRAVELING STRANGERS WALKIN' AND TALKIN' LIKE ME

Life experience makes us homogenous despite our selfish pride, attitudes of indifference, and demonstrations of superiority.

Accustomed to the challenges of homosexuality, many gay men succumbed to the inevitable. Like Ali, they compromised fundamental relationship values and standards to avoid being alone. It was difficult to secure emotional stability regardless of whether a gay man accepted the reality. When a male couple achieved relationship status for several years, they became a model for every homosexual who aspired to obtain a same-sex relationship of their own. But when the relationship bombed, their hopes deflated.

Hakeem's ideal relationship required consistency and exclusivity. His friends and associates were not as demanding. They sacrificed peace and happiness. Men had cheated on Alex countless times and he accepted their apologies. They went missing-in-action for several weeks, always returning with an unverifiable excuse—"my mom was sick." Hakeem heard those lame excuses too. They were lies. An online dating account with a status of: "Active within the last week" or "Active 48 hours ago," and unexpected sightings at the local club put dating in the proper perspective. As communication lapsed, associations of any quality decreased in priority.

Alex took the men back with open arms. Khalil received them on his terms. Hakeem either responded with silence or aggressively demanded the men to lose his number. He wanted respect. If a man was disrespectful and inconsiderate, then Hakeem parted ways. Had he been willing to trek similar paths as Alex or Khalil, it would have meant losing his self-identity and subjection to misery. Or the consequence could have been much more serious, involving violence or worse given the encounters. Hakeem would always remember Santino.

It was December, and Hakeem 21 years old. He and two friends went to a bar on the Westside of Minneapolis that particular night. The bar was an old, dimly lit establishment. Most of the furnishings were made of wood that matched the linoleum walls. The patrons were a mixture of African-American, Caucasian, and Hispanic. Cloying cigarette smoke intermingled with marijuana, creating a thin fog throughout the area. The jukebox played 80's pop music.

Hakeem and companions walked past the bar and ascended the stairs on its right side. The landing widened out and extended into a 13x12 room. Along the right wall stood floor speakers where hip-hop music blared. A DJ bopped in the middle behind a turntable. Hakeem watched one of his two friends, Calvin, enter into another room off to the left of the main. He followed behind, finding four parallel pool tables spaced 3 feet apart.

In the corner by the pool table closest to the window, Horace, the second companion perched on a stool, texting on his cellphone. Calvin was the pool-player of the trio and while examining one of three pool sticks leaning against the wall, another dude entered, surveying the room. Calvin eyed the newcomer who gave a quick nod.

Calvin's gray fitted hoodie displayed sculpted biceps and triceps that drew attention, but his bug-like eyes and wide-set mouth were distracting. The newcomer was outfitted in a black three-quarter-length leather coat, red sweatshirt, and baggy light-blue jeans over wheat-colored construction boots. Short tapered curly hair glistened from melting snowflakes that accumulated outside the bar.

Whenever Calvin saw an attractive man, he initiated an introduction. But his prowess failed him that night. After a short conversation with the newcomer, Calvin approached Hakeem who perched on a stool next to Horace. The vantage point permitted observation of the entire room.

Calvin whispered that the man in the three-quarter length leather coat was interested. Hakeem agreed to talk to the stranger, and Calvin delivered the message.

The man approached and introduced himself as Santino. Santino was rugged as a street thug with a thin scar that ran the length of his left cheek. His eyes glittered like golden amber and seldom blinked. They beheld a quiet danger and for a moment, Hakeem glimpsed himself.

In the week following the acquaintance, Santino casually informed Hakeem that he snorted cocaine. During the same week, Brian told Hakeem that he knew Santino. He advised to be wary because Santino was crazy. Heeding Brian's advice, Hakeem began to distance himself from Santino. Unfortunately, he was not quick enough.

In the early hours of New Year's Day, after Santino introduced Hakeem to his Uncle Terry who drove them home from the club, a scuffle ensued. Santino was sloppy drunk and belligerent, having embarrassed Hakeem by slouching and staggering around the bar. Hakeem pointedly chastised Santino for his drunkenness. Resentful, Santino became hostile towards him once inside Terry's jeep. He grabbed Hakeem from behind as if to pull him backwards through the front passenger seat. Hakeem's position hindered his ability to free himself from Santino's grasp. Terry yelled at Santino, ordering him to release Hakeem and proceeded to berate him for his behavior. In a surge of outrage, Santino jumped out of the moving jeep and ran into the brewing blizzard, screaming like a wild animal in the night. Snow flurries had begun to fall again. Terry and Hakeem were unable to recover Santino as visibility decreased.

The next day, Santino called Hakeem from a payphone, informing that he fell asleep outside of a gas station. During the night, he lost his mother's cellphone, explaining the reason for calling from the payphone. Hakeem looked at the phone receiver in disbelief. The craziness that Brian had warned him about had emerged. Santino ended the call saying that he was going home.

Hakeem did not hear from Santino for two weeks. The next time they saw each other, Santino unexpectedly appeared on his doorstep. He had not called beforehand to give notification of an intended visit.

Hakeem was vacuuming the living-room and saw Santino standing on the porch, silently staring with unblinking hazel eyes through the screen door. He had stopped through on the way to a bar and further disclosed that he had been in jail for assaulting a relative.

The Spring Semester enabled Hakeem to put more distance between Santino. Four classes and a full-time job gave little breathing room. Santino tried to hold onto their fraying association, calling occasionally. He gradually caught onto Hakeem's casual indifference and revealed his possessiveness. Santino told Hakeem that he didn't have to let him go if he didn't want to. The implied threat caused Hakeem to be concerned for his safety. He considered the possibility of fatally harming Santino in self-defense. Hakeem was determined that abuse would remain in his rearview mirror. A man stupid enough to try to hurt him was one that would go quickly to his grave. Santino had showcased a mean streak, but had no idea of the lengths Hakeem would take for self-protection.

There was a frightening dark side to Hakeem. In the interest of self-preservation, he would defend by any necessary means. Imprisonment was a probable outcome and problem. But in review of all the evidence of acting in self-defense, the court might rule in his favor. The question was, how long would he have to spend in jail until judgment arrived? There were too many factors to anticipate. There had to be a safer way to rid himself of Santino.

Hakeem was baptized the year before meeting Santino. His sister, Vanessa, had taken him to church with her. He was re-introduced to the power of prayer and the spiritual protection and covering from danger it provided. Those memories carried forward. Thus, he prayed for protection and the permanent removal of Santino from his life. It was better for God to handle the situation than Hakeem bloody his own hands in an act of self-defense. God answered. Santino stopped calling and there were no more unannounced pop-up visits.

Whatever happened to Santino is a mystery. A few years passed, and Hakeem thought he saw someone who strongly resembled Santino from a distance. He was not curious enough to confirm, believing it best to let a rabid dog sleep. He had beseeched God to intervene, and God obliged his request.

Hakeem conceptualized a relationship in the context of romanticism and intimacy, as one that subsisted of a minimum of six months. The interval permitted commitment and life integration to cultivate, or at the very least, unveil potential. Although self-disclosure and compromise are ongoing behaviors in a relationship's course, the practice is critical during the early stages of acquaintance. Six months allows prospective partners to discover and adjust to unique personality traits, habits, interests, and values. If the superficial aspects of an acquaintance distracted a person, it partially explained their delayed reactions. For example, physical attractiveness and sex don't guarantee the long-term survival of a relationship. These characteristics are the basis for physical gratification. Honesty, loyalty, companionship, and consistency in comparison to physical attractiveness and sex, stabilize a relationship's foundation. In the totality of sixteen years, Hakeem had secured only one relationship, which lasted fifteen months. Encounters before and after were associations undeserving of laudation. Most of his acquaintances had a 30-day shelf-life. He was habitually decisive in male encounters and so were the men.

When Hakeem, 27, met Henry through a gay online dating site, their acquaintance rapidly evolved. Henry sought a long-term relationship, and after unremitting failure on Atlanta's dating scene, Hakeem seized the chance to go steady. Henry provided consistent companionship, and Hakeem reveled in what it afforded. Within five months, Hakeem and Henry moved into an apartment together. The transition liberated him from the agonizing roommate situation with Brian, which intensified as Henry visited frequently.

Brian had moved to Atlanta three years before Hakeem. He was Hakeem's means of relocating to an unfamiliar city without friends and relatives. However, the metropolitan gay life failed to improve upon Brian's character. In fact, he worsened as the culture's brash sensuality hardened him. To Hakeem, Brian became a distraction.

Whenever an attractive man was visible, in the parking lot of their apartment complex or on the television, Brian obnoxiously and audibly expressed admiration. Then he brazenly summoned Hakeem's attention. Hakeem perceived his shenanigans as attempts to sabotage the moments he shared with Henry. Brian lacked deference for men in his own dating life. Hakeem had to remind him periodically to respect Henry who quickly grew weary of the interruptions. Henry was frank in verbalizing his contempt for Brian and discord soon unfolded between them.

Living with Henry laid bare an untrodden journey, which routed through rocky terrain midway. An individual discovers more about themselves and their partner when living conjointly. Henry was intrusive—displaying little regard for Hakeem's belongings. Dating and relationships should not negate a person's right to privacy. Henry was also insecure—disapproving of Hakeem's late-night hangouts, even though well acquainted with Alex and Robert. Hakeem didn't care and defied Henry's urgings to come home early on those occasions. Henry ineffectively retaliated with several days of silent treatment. Unremorseful, Hakeem showed no indication of concern. He disobeyed Earl and refused to comply with the unreasonable mandates of anyone else.

Of the men Hakeem dealt, Henry was no exception to possessing an overwhelming desire for sexual gratification. For Henry, companionship was insufficient, which made them incompatible. Halfway through the relationship, Hakeem withdrew from intimacy altogether. It was this oppositional mentality that illuminated flaws in his own thinking. Hakeem was in love with the idea of being in a relationship but wanted few obligations beyond companionship and exclusivity. He thought it possible to manage sex in a monogamous relationship and felt guilt instead.

Despite Hakeem's decisions, there was no point where he believed that his homosexual pursuits were acceptable in God's eyes. The challenge lay in emancipation from living in the oddly comforting and familiar. If only he could have a relationship with a man that was free of sexual demands. Reality flagged the idea as impossible. Thus, he stopped singing in the choir and utterly refrained from going to church. What was the purpose of going to church if one consciously decided to live sinfully, refusing to bring their sin under subjection? Through introspection Hakeem saw himself living a life of contradictions.

Resentful of Henry, Hakeem crippled their relationship by

withdrawing affections. Henry adjusted by secretly entertaining other males on his days off while Hakeem worked. Sometimes the signs were subtle—the disappearance of double portions of food, inclusive of items Henry did not consume. Henry claimed that friends had visited without advanced notice. Those same friends were gone before Hakeem came home.

Hakeem never caught Henry in a sexual act but finding the door dead-bolted from the inside suggested that something was happening with guests. He was forced to wait until Henry permitted entry into the apartment where he shared in paying the bills.

On three separate occasions, Hakeem entered their apartment and found three different males seated on the couch. One of the guests was Henry's ex-lover, Wayne. According to Henry, Wayne relocated out of state for a job several months prior to meeting him online. Henry never revealed the name of his ex-lover. However, Hakeem deduced the connection, identifying the ex-lover as Wayne upon introduction. Wayne eventually lost his job, forcing a return to Atlanta.

Henry invited Wayne to the apartment without Hakeem's permission. Had Hakeem cared, he might have felt threatened by Wayne's return and opposed. Yet, he had never been jealous of another lover. He had grown accustomed to the promiscuous nature of gay men and was of the opinion that a man can be replaced.

Hakeem did not want to salvage the unraveling relationship with Henry. If Wayne's presence could distract Henry from the distance he wedged, it was for the better. Hakeem was certain that Henry still had feelings for Wayne. Before their relationship began its rapid descent, Henry complained about the types of men Wayne entertained, following his return to Atlanta. Hakeem listened in silence. Only an emotionally-attached person would have shown the amount of concern Henry displayed for Wayne. But Hakeem endured until he gained the confidence to try and make it on his own. He learned how to exploit every opportunity afforded him.

A visit from Joseph and Evelyn, three months before their apartment lease ended, gave Hakeem (27) resolve to separate from Henry. They were genuinely cordial to Henry. Evelyn, however, perceived the undercurrent of friction.

On the last night of their visit, Evelyn saw Hakeem sitting on the living-room sofa and asked, "Are you happy here?" She took position on the loveseat adjacent to the couch where he reclined, watching television. Her gaze circled the entire room, and then settled upon him.

"I'm fine." He shrugged. His portrayal of nonchalance was intended to disarm Evelyn of her suspicions.

Evelyn's eyes did not waver.

Deep down, Hakeem knew the reason she asked the question.

Hakeem never told Evelyn about his sexual orientation or the nature of the relationship with Henry and had no intentions of revealing that Henry was his boyfriend. The idea was embarrassing. But he believed she knew without stating the obvious. After all, Evelyn was nearly two and a half times his age and had witnessed Daryle live out a similar pattern. And like Daryle, he did not have a girlfriend. Over the years, Evelyn directly and indirectly met several of Daryle's lovers. Joseph once even rescued Daryle from a domestic violence situation.

"You know I can tell when something is going on with you." Evelyn's statement weighed heavily with concern. "I raised you, remember?"

"I know," Hakeem laughed halfheartedly, confirming nothing. Those were some troubling years too, he thought.

"You don't have to tell me. But I know when you're unhappy. And...I know that you don't want to come home." She gave him a meaningful look.

Hakeem still said nothing. He gave a half smile and nod. Although constantly astounded by Evelyn's compassion, given all that he endured in her care, returning home was out of the question.

The conversation imprinted in Hakeem's mind, nonetheless. He was unhappy and had secretly wanted to be done with Henry for some time. Uncertainty of his capacity to self-sustain discouraged him from making the decision. The cost of living in Atlanta was higher than Minneapolis. Living alone was expensive but possible with adjustments.

When the property manager sent the lease renewal letter, Hakeem suggested moving into separate apartments. Henry interpreted the suggestion as a breakup and Hakeem concurred. Their separation meant a chance for freedom and he embraced it, aware of the potential costs. Never again would he live with a man.

Henry stole articles of Hakeem's clothing and electronics. Hakeem inventoried missing belongings upon settling into a new apartment. Constant shopping made it difficult to constantly monitor everything he accumulated. Still, there was no reason for Henry to violate his belongings because he was financially secure even more so. Hakeem reckoned that Henry sought to repay him for their split as he had done with silent treatment in the past. The conclusion removed any compunction that Hakeem may have felt for leaving him.

Hakeem was transparent to Alex and Robert about his relationship with Henry. Nevertheless, they questioned his motivations for the separation. Alex asserted that a year invested was worth trying to make a relationship work, regardless of possible infidelities. Robert took a stance of neutrality, having spent almost double the number of years in the gay lifestyle as Hakeem. The glamour of it all had faded long ago. More interesting was the fact that dating for Robert slowed to a trickle once he reached the mid-forties. In his opinion, Hakeem and Alex were children playing in the mud.

As much as Hakeem hoped for full support from Alex and Robert, his decision was final. Freedom and self-preservation were invaluable. He held onto his belief that homosexual relationships were unworthy of sacrifice in one hand, and a desire for the fringe benefits of the lifestyle in the other. Hakeem's mistakes were repetitious because he habitually walked away while looking back, wondering if the circumstances would be different on the next go-round.

Single anew, Hakeem resumed use of pornography for sexual gratification, rationalizing that pornography was harmless compared to homosexuality. There was no risk of contracting sexually-transmitted diseases or emotional rollercoasters. It was a distorted view.

Pornography and homosexuality are capable of subverting an individual's psychological, physiological, and spiritual growth. Naturally, pornography is indecent and perverted—purposing to stimulate eroticism. Pornographic images and interactions assist in the construction of sexual thoughts and fantasies, which the viewer establishes mental links with physiological responses and outcomes.

In *pornography addiction,* there is a direct connection between a person's increasing desire to achieve sexual fulfillment through viewership and their dependency upon pornographic materials. The stronger the addiction, greater is the person's sexual dysfunction. A porn addict is usually unable to sustain conventional methods of sexual interaction with their partners, which gradually creates marital problems. Porn addicts appraise pornographic mediums as stimulating sources of sexual fulfillment instead of their spouses or partners, whereas the latter party may perceive pornography as problematic to the relationship. Even controlled use of pornography has the potential to disrupt intimacy within relationships. Unless both partners share a mutual interest in pornography, porn addiction is divisive. Pornography is an addict's ever-enticing mistress and sometimes, full-time lover.

Pornography can alter a person's perceptions and attitudes regarding sex. As with drug addictions, porn addicts search for more potent means to achieve sexual gratification once they reached a plateau. Porn addicts reach plateaus in the sexual context when erotic stimuli fail to generate the same degree of climatic effect, or pleasure as produced during previous instances. An example of this phenomenon is when a specific pornographic medium no longer stimulates sexual arousal, or to a level of intensity comparable to occurrences in previous exposures. In extreme cases, a porn addict's insatiable appetites led them into trouble of varying proportions as they engaged in chancy sexual activities.

From a biblical perspective, pornography along with every form of sexual immorality is prohibited in God's kingdom (1 Corinthians 6:9-11; Ephesians 5:3; Galatians 5:19-21). A man and woman were to unionize under God's ordained covenant. Sexual unions outside of God's prescription are considered unholy and immoral. Pornography nourished lustful thoughts and desires of the heart. *Lust* as defined by Merriam-Webster (2017) "is an intense longing, craving, or unbridled desire." Lust and porn addiction can be psychologically complementary because of the mental feedback loop that the constructs created.

Hakeem became a porn addict, and it gradually took on the role as his virtual and pseudo-spouse. Regardless of the temporary gratification that pornography afforded, it nurtured the hurt and pain, loneliness and emptiness that raged within. On the flipside, as with homosexuality, pornography widened the rift that was Hakeem's separation from God. The very nature of sin is to hinder a sinner from pursuing a relationship and closer connection with the Heavenly Father. As Adam and Eve hid from God in the Garden of Eden, after eating from the "tree of good and evil" (Genesis 3:6-10), convicted sinners similarly tried to hide their sins. Hakeem refused to go to church after engaging in sexual activity. There were also moments when he did not possess the courage to pray for forgiveness, guilty of his choices. He knew enough of God's Word to be ashamed of using pornography, and yet, continued viewership.

≈≈≈≈≈≈≈

Platonic friendships could've sufficed as support systems, were they capable of solving for my warping emptiness. Ian, Robert, Alex or Khalil couldn't fulfill me. Even if one of my friends expressed interest in me, I would have rejected them. Most people don't cross the line between friendship and intimacy. Friendships have limitations unless re-classified as friends-with-benefits. Friends-with-Benefits situations set the stage for problems because as intimacy flounders, they reform into awkward friendships. I preferred to keep my friendships within established parameters.

In the context of homosexuality, friends-with-benefits accelerated the ever-present revolving door of men that entered and departed a man's life. I suspect that within the span of a lifetime, gay and bisexual men average more partners than heterosexual men. Acquaintances, associations, and relationships were just that numerous and fleeting. There's no anchor in homosexuality or sexual immorality. It's not a life that I wish for anyone.

I realize that I was no better than most of the men I criticized. How many of the men had abandoned hope and conformed to the thing they hated most? How many of them had been molested or exposed to sex at early ages, but were unable to escape the living nightmare? I knew of an older gentleman who had an inappropriate relationship with a female teacher when he was in high school. Eighteen years later, after a divorce, he was

216

seduced by a gay man. Khalil had told me that an older cousin molested him. This experience was a commonality Khalil and I shared. Another associate confided in me that the pastor of his church pursued him at the age of fifteen. It is evident that something is wrong with this world when adults see youths as objects of their sexual fantasies.

I was fortunate because there were gay and bisexual men who hadn't been as lucky after their traumatic experiences and sexual indiscretions. Some were diagnosed with HIV or AIDs, or succumbed to anxiety and depression, or committed suicide. I believe that God's grace and my stubbornness is what saved me. The grace part, I didn't do anything to earn or deserve it because I was contrary. My determination and rebellious nature fueled my resistance and mobility even when I was in situations, which I shouldn't have been involved.

I remember every man with whom I was intimate. I'm not proud of this confession. But I dare this transparency so that you may understand my former disposition. I would have drained the very essence of those men if it were possible. I was empty, and each one of them provided temporary relief from an internal deadness that I couldn't purge. Perhaps for the men, I fulfilled the same purpose. They saw me as someone who for the most part, demonstrated the best intentions as it pertained to dating them. I didn't juggle multiple men, preferring monogamy above alternatives. And when the acquaintance ended, I recovered and went in search of another. The men replaced me and I returned the favor.

There was something else that I discovered during my introspections. A sexual spirit shrouded me. It explained why I was sensitive to sensuality initiated by men and women. That spirit had attached itself to my life from the time I was molested—exposed to sexuality at an age in which I couldn't understand most of my feelings. I was unable to control my emotions. While the molestation was no fault of my own, I was ignorant. I grew older believing that many of my actions were somehow, tolerable, even excusable. But how could any of it be deemed positive? Intimacy with different men, addiction to pornography, and alcohol aren't healthy or productive behaviors. They are potentially life-long problems if a person doesn't seek psychological or spiritual help. The glamorization of gay life deceives many into thinking it can offer something fulfilling and sustainable.

Ra-Ra M. J.

My head was barely above the water, and I was still thirsty. My condition was indicative of searching for contentment in people and things that were unable to satisfy and complete me. The lifestyle I lived was unholy in the eyes of the Father. Nothing can convince me otherwise.

THE SAME, WE WERE NEVER MEANT TO REMAIN

"He who walks with wise men will be wise, But the companion of fools will be destroyed" (Proverbs 13:20).

"I went home before Thanksgiving."

"Really?" Gail straightened the creases in her skirt as she shifted in the chair. "How did it go?"

"Okay, I guess." Hakeem silently admired the color-coordinated ensemble she wore.

Gail sat outfitted in a cream cowl-necked sweater, apricot wool skirt, and tanned leather boots. Black tresses spilled over the pins holding up her hair. The style was best because of the sweater's high collar.

"You sound doubtful. Do you want to talk about it?"

Hakeem did not care either way. "I don't remember if I told you, but my grandfather and some of the family do not celebrate Thanksgiving. So, the holidays are usually boring." He fell silent. The holidays were in truth, depressing. He would feel better when the New Year came around.

Oftentimes, Hakeem rolled solo. When discontentment overshadowed positive thinking, he preferred being alone to sulk—wondering why he lacked a better quality of life. His disposition only opened the door for all the bad memories to flood, allowing bitterness to fester in the darkness.

"How long did you stay?" Gail pulled his folder from the desk.

"Three days."

"That's a short trip."

"Yeah. I didn't want to stay any longer than I intended. I went home before the holidays began to get back early. I just wanted to be by myself."

Gail nodded. Perhaps she understood his reasons.

"Did you at least enjoy yourself while you were there?"

"A little. My grandfather is doing well. So, I'm glad about that."

"Was he happy to see you?"

"He was. It's different seeing him alone…my grandmother was always there."

For a short while, after Evelyn died, Hakeem feared Joseph was going to emotionally deteriorate. His grandparents spent most of their lifetime together. Many married couples were less fortunate to accomplish such a feat. Nowadays, it seemed that more marriages terminated in divorce or transitioned to a state of separation after a few years.

"Are you going back to visit soon?"

"A part of me wants to visit again. But a bigger part wants to stay away."

"You know, something has been on my mind"—Gail smoothed a fold in the skirt and crossed her legs—"I'd like to go back to a discussion from one of our previous sessions. First, do you mind?"

"Yeah, go ahead." He trusted her enough to discuss whatever she contemplated.

"Have you been distancing yourself from your origins? Is this why you ultimately moved to Atlanta?"

"Partly, yes. I was tired of Minneapolis. Atlanta represented autonomous change for me…and freedom from the source of some of my resentment." He resented Earl for the misery that he felt.

"So, Atlanta was your means of escape? The farther the distance, the more you could try to forget?"

"Yeah, I will agree with that. Out of sight, out of mind." he clarified. Every place he lived was an escape route—to get away from someone or something. He didn't want to deal with anything that wasn't of his choosing.

"That makes sense." Gail re-established eye contact after jotting additional notes. "What will it take for you to stop feeling that you must escape everything?"

Now, that is the question. He hadn't thought much about not having to run. Escaping had become habit. He didn't feel closely connected to some family members, which made it easy to distance himself. Of course, he wished everyone in the family well, but something was broken, missing inside of him. The bonds that existed should have been stronger. *Is it my expectations?*

"I don't know. I mean…I need to think about that."

"Take your time. There's no rush. But I did ask that question for you to consider in the course of you planning a future."

Hakeem considered her perspective. His future was in the next hour, tomorrow, next week, a month from now. He understood the necessity of making wiser decisions. Circumstances could change instantly for better or worse. But at the moment, he could not escape Kaleidoscope—needing the job for no other reason than income. No one else could pay his bills or provide financial support. Joseph was too old to be responsible for another grown man.

"I guess my expectations…maybe. I don't like being mistreated by people or taken advantage of."

"In those scenarios, there's nothing wrong with putting distance between yourself and people who mean you harm. And I don't recommend that you subject yourself to anymore abuse." Gail removed her glasses, laying the frames atop the desk. "You've been through enough. However, in less extreme situations, there are times when we might be unable to escape or do so quickly…such as in the case of a job. That kind of scenario requires strategic thinking."

"I gotcha." He realized that he did not possess the power to change family or people. Although on the road to making improvements, he struggled occasionally with accepting the fact.

"Are you okay?" She inquired when he didn't respond. "You got silent on me. Do you disagree?"

"No. I don't disagree with anything you said. I'm just trying to see how I'm going to get through all of this."

She leaned forward with the folder nesting in her lap. "That's why I'm here to help you. We're only in the fourth month of therapy."

"That's all? Seems like I've been coming here longer."

"You're growing. Changing. That's a reason."

"Am I? Really?" He invested little time reflecting on his progress.

"Yes, you are," she affirmed. "You're more spirited now than when our therapy sessions began."

Hakeem savored the appraisal, reassured that progress was being made although much ground remained to cover. Darkness lingered at the fringes of the light. As long as he remained close to its center, he felt invigorated and optimistic. But those feelings fluctuated. When he entertained painful memories and encountered challenges, he ventured towards the darkness. Anger came easily as an intake of breath. Hakeem was certain that a significant portion of the growth Gail perceived was attributed to his renewed faith. Only the Spirit of God possesses that kind of staying power.

≈≈≈≈≈≈≈

The silver clock on the desk flashed 6:00 P.M. The final project assignment was due. Hakeem clicked the OK button in the document-uploader window and awaited confirmation that his paper was accepted. Three minutes later, the screen refreshed, showing that the document had converted to an attachment with a submission timestamp. He knew without a doubt that the professor was going to give him an A for the course. He sat in silence as the adrenaline rush subsided.

The desk lamp and the illuminated computer monitor provided the only source of light in the room. Now that winter break had begun, Hakeem was uncertain about how to pass the time outside of working. Kaleidoscope and academia nearly consumed his time. Both Alex and Khalil were busy with their families and boyfriends.

Meanwhile, Hakeem marinated in gloom, contemplating whether to go to Josefina's house for Christmas dinner. She had invited him to celebrate with her family. He was hesitant because of knowing few of her relatives and feared feeling like an outcast around the rest of the family.

A car alarm sounded outside, and Hakeem opened a slit in the blinds to see if his car was causing the disturbance. The headlights on the car were dark. But the headlights on the truck parked two spaces over, flashed steadily. No one had approached the vehicle. Surely the owner was inside an apartment or nearby. After two minutes, the pickup suddenly chirped in quick succession. Whoever owned it disabled the alarm remotely.

Hakeem continued to scope the complex from the living room window. Several of the residents had turned on Christmas lights, replacing the natural light of the day. Red, yellow, blue, green, and white radiated in the spreading darkness. Some tenants had even opened their curtains to showcase elaborately decorated trees. He thought about adopting the practice to feel festive, having never decorated any of the apartments he lived. It was time for a change.

≈≈≈≈≈≈≈

Hakeem grinned while scrolling through the photos that Layla posted on social media. She had flown to Paris with her boyfriend for Christmas. Knowing Rosalyn, she had an opinion about Layla making the international trip. He expected to hear scathing remarks on the next call.

"I hope you're not going to play that game the entire time you're here," Josefina interrupted, holding a ladle.

"Nah, I'm not." He chuckled, looking up at her from the couch.

Josefina's family populated the living room and dining area. Although she introduced him to the family, he remained inconspicuous, speaking only when addressed. He was adapting to their personalities through observation. Besides Josefina, his phone served as a familiar presence.

"Uh-huh. The rice is almost done." She placed a free hand on a hip. Exhaustion shadowed her face. "You play spades?"

"I haven't played in over a year." He couldn't wait until her rice was on his plate.

"Are you any good?"

"I'm okay."

Hakeem was not in the mood for card games. One time, he cussed Alex for reneging while playing as his partner during a game of spades. He hated losing if the outcome could be avoided.

"Is that ladle for the beans?" he asked, noticing a spot of reddish-brown sauce on its tip.

Josefina laughed. She made a mean pot of Charro Beans. "Why, yes, it is!" She turned to watch her mother carry a platter of sliced ham towards the dining room. "We're going to assemble in the dining area in a minute."

Hakeem noticed the buffet-style layout that Josefina arranged upon arrival. Turkey, macaroni and cheese, dressing, potato and macaroni salad, turnip greens, green beans, barbecued ribs, and fried chicken and fish comprised the menu. The red velvet and pound cake that he made, sat on the dessert table. He baked the desserts with extra care. Love in cooking made all the difference.

All things considered, Hakeem was grateful for Josefina's invitation. This time, he didn't want to spend the holiday alone and hoped that one day his family could assemble in one place, at one time, and enjoy the holidays like her family.

≈≈≈≈≈≈≈

Hakeem entered the apartment from Watch Night Service. It was 1:23 A.M., January 1st, 2016. An entire new year spanned ahead, filled with possibilities. The time had come to activate New Year resolutions.

While placing his Bible on the dining room table, the cellphone rang. Hakeem withdrew the phone from his black leather motorcycle jacket and looked at the caller ID. Michael was calling. He pondered answering the phone.

Michael was relatively decent. He just tended to be unidirectional in the way that he perceived the world and the matters that pertained to him. They were similar in that Michael wanted people to treat him with the utmost respect but sometimes, differed in his capacity to reciprocate the expectation. When someone made a mistake, Michael called their attention to the fact. He didn't appreciate when people returned the favor.

Michael was thirty-nine, smoked marijuana, and drank heavily. When inebriated, he became flirtatious and raunchy. Emboldened in the past, he expressed interests. Hakeem turned him down, believing anything beyond a platonic friendship signaled disaster. Michael's inconsistency did not go unnoticed, and Hakeem often wondered whether he was intellectually-challenged when debating moral principles.

"Happy New Year!" Michael's baritone voice boomed over the speakerphone.

"Same to you."

"How you been?"

"I've been good...doing me."

Michael laughed. "I thought you always did."

"What are you doing up?"

"Drinkin'."

"At this hour?"

"Yeah. What are you doing up?" The huskiness was perceptible in Michael's voice.

"Just got in from church."

"Oh, okay. How was it?"

"Really good. How come you didn't go?"

"I was at my boy's house."

The details were unnecessary. When Michael said, "my boy's house," it meant someone he kept company.

"Okay." Hakeem replied easily, wanting to avoid provoking self-disclosure.

"Why you say it like that?"

"Say it like what?"

"Like you don't care."

"I just said, 'okay.' Didn't mean anything by it."

"Cool."

Michael was drunk. He questioned nearly every statement when under the influence of the bottle.

"You in for the rest of the night?"

"Of course I am. Where else would I go?"

"I don't know. I never hear you talkin' bout goin' on a date or nothin'."

"You know I don't hang out late anymore, since the arrest."

"Yeah, yeah, yeah. Forgot about that."

"As for dating…there won't be any of that for a while."

"Why not?"

"I've decided to make some changes…do some things differently."

"Oh! Like what?"

"Like no longer dealing with men."

"Wait….what! You mean….like going straight?"

"Yes."

"How you come up with that?"

"It's been on my mind for a while now. But we haven't talked in a minute. So you wouldn't have known."

"That's a big jump. People don't make sudden changes like that!" Michael's stupidity was surfacing.

Hakeem's irritation surged as a consequence. The pastor had just preached on the subject that when people made life-changing decisions, sometimes, associates within their social circles attempted to discourage them.

"People like who? Yourself?"

"I'm just sayin' in general."

"You must know something I don't."

"So who are you trying to convince?" Michael continued.

Woe, woe, woe! "Who the hell are you talking to?" he snapped. One thing for certain, when he made a decision, all rebuttals were irrelevant.

"I'm talking to you!" Michael challenged.

Hakeem held his ground. "Look here! You know no more than what I've told you. I've spent the majority of the past four years alone, meeting people and reaching dead ends."

"I gotcha, Hakeem. I'm just sayin' it seems all of a sudden."

He was angry. "What do you mean, Michael? We don't even talk on a regular basis. This is the first time you've called me in months!" *Why did it even matter?*

Michael fell silent. A closed mouth suited him.

Hakeem categorized him with the other men of his past. When he made it clear that he held no inclinations for being intimate, Michael stopped calling regularly. He tried to steer their acquaintance into a friendship, suggesting recreational activities, but Michael expressed disinterest through unavailability. Weeks passed before Michael responded to calls and messages. It took Hakeem a while to see that their association would not evolve into a stable friendship.

"Why does it bother you that I have decided to go straight?"

"Like I said…it seems all of sudden."

Yeah, we're not getting anywhere with this. "It's not inconceivable. If you had listened from the beginning, then you would've understood that this lifestyle has never worked for me. I was never satisfied with it. This transition is easy."

They had discussed their challenges in dating men and the fear of living the rest of their days alone. Both of them re-entered the dating cycle, understanding the potential outcome. The main difference was that Michael desired a long-term relationship inclusive of marriage.

Hakeem could not envision living the remainder of his life entangled with a man, and decidedly refused to marry one. The notion contradicted the Bible. In Hakeem's mind, same-sex marriage was a step too far. For such a marriage to be possible, he would have to walk away from God. Hakeem lacked the capacity to love anyone to the extent of renouncing his faith. The realization was a cause for wondering whether he truly loved any man.

"You know what? I'm sorry…my fault." Michael's speech slurred. "I wish you the best. And I hope that everything works out for you."

"Thanks." There was nothing else to add. Hakeem realized the mistake in sharing his resolve. Some decisions, plans even, should be kept secret.

"Hey, man…I'm gonna' call it a night," Michael said abruptly.

"Okay. Goodnight."

Michael ended the call.

Hakeem mulled over his question. *So I'm straight,* he thought while changing into bedclothes. He might as well proclaim it because there was no turning back this time. Michael's personal feelings were irrelevant. It was necessary to believe in himself. The opinions of other people don't always matter in every contextual situation. A person's definition of another becomes effective when the individual who is scrutinized, does nothing to define themselves through exemplification and character. Know thyself!

The last male encounter was a year ago. After two weeks of communication, Neal invited Hakeem to his apartment. There, he acceded to Neal's advances. Like tar—dark and viscous, guilt clung to his spirit afterwards. An industrial strength cleaner could not remove the taint.

Hakeem tried to steer their association into a friendship. And as with Michael, Neal surprisingly brushed him off with excuses of unavailability. Contact dwindled and again, Hakeem was alone and rebounding. The question arose then, how many more times would he make the same mistake? The game hadn't changed, nor would it ever. He expected a break within a persistent pattern where he was the repeating element.

Hakeem put an X next to Michael's name on his list of associations and acquaintances. Michael no longer had a purpose in his life. In reviewing his history with Michael, Hakeem did not see any benefit to maintaining communication. He needed to stop seeking friendship and companionship in people who were counterproductive to his life.

Thinking constructively, it was crucial that he learn to share the most valuable ideas only with the like-minded. Stagnant and complacent minds reject change, as that which they perceive as constant and familiar creates zones of comfort and stability. Few gay men believed in the possibility of conquering homosexuality. The success of those who sought a heterosexual life was contingent upon the modification of social networks and physical environments.

Nick was Hakeem's role model for referencing the actions necessary for personal change and one of the few people he knew, who abandoned homosexuality. Nick was eight years older, but the difference in age didn't hinder their friendship.

Nick's family were members of the same religious organization that Joseph and Evelyn affiliated. And like Hakeem, Nick had broken fellowship. However, this commonality wasn't the nexus of their bond. It was Nick who encouraged Hakeem to enroll for college, having served as a student advisor at the university. He was pleasantly outgoing and agreeable—characteristics that positively affected Hakeem.

Nick also endured the uncertainty of dealing with men while walking on the median strip of sexuality. But he grew weary of the emotional ups-and-downs much sooner than Hakeem anticipated. During the last in-depth conversation they would ever have, Nick simply stated, "I am done with it all."

In the final year of their intimate arrangements, Nick learned that Ericson was in a long-term relationship. Suspicious of his lover's infidelity, Justin stalked Ericson one evening, discovering where Nick lived. Justin later confronted Nick following a fight with Ericson. Justin had considered killing him over Ericson. The plan was to wait near Nick's house until he emerged and stab him to death. Justin had a change of heart upon learning that Nick knew nothing about him or the relationship.

Like Hakeem, Nick didn't take chances with warnings and ceased involvement with Ericson. But he became distraught because of Ericson's deceit. Tears flowed from bitterness and disappointment. Nick had developed an emotional attachment to Ericson. It wasn't long after the separation when Nick announced his decision to resume dating females.

Hakeem didn't discourage Nick, having sympathized and concluded gay relationships were short-term. Their friendship dissolved as smoothly as it formed. One day, Nick stopped calling and returning Hakeem's phone calls.

Nick remained true to his goal and eventually married a woman. As far as Hakeem knew, Nick never looked back. He briefly mourned the end of their friendship, understanding the logic in Nick's decision. If the time came, he would make the same choice if necessary.

Twelve years later, he did.

≈≈≈≈≈≈

Brian eventually befriended Ericson through a dating hotline, enabling Hakeem the chance to get a glimpse into the character of the person who Nick once dated. Ericson was just as conniving and depraved as Brian. Their friendship made sense.

Brian revealed that Ericson had an open-relationship with Justin despite the latter's stake in the matter. Justin remained attached and also entertained men outside the relationship, including Brian. They deserved each other.

Whether it was vindictiveness or desire that motivated Justin to pursue other men, Hakeem could only imagine. But what became increasingly clear was that most gay relationships evolved into polyamorous couplings because such partnerships were significantly limited—psychologically and physiologically, as compared to heterosexual unions.

Hakeem went to bed thinking about the conversation with Michael. Uncertain about what changes awaited, he prayed.

Who possesses foresight into the future? God. God is the main reason Hakeem prayed to receive strength and courage for the journey ahead. This action is a demonstration of faith. It was through prayer that Hakeem communicated readiness for deliverance and an expectancy of God to lead the way through unknown terrain.

God answers when a sinner sincerely calls upon Him, as He knows the heart's intent (Jeremiah 17:10). When God intervenes, He proceeds in His way, and it is the sinner who must abide. Therefore, a gay person who seeks deliverance, must also possess a heartfelt desire to change. They cannot linger in their past or hold onto specific aspects, which are contrary to deliverance. Furthermore, spiritual change requires constant submission to God's Will, the path of Jesus, and the Holy Spirit. Much like an addict, the person overcomes an addiction when they are ready to relinquish the source. There was no point during Christ's time on earth where He <u>forced</u> people to abandon their sin. He has always permitted our free-will in choosing whether to do good or evil.

≈≈≈≈≈≈≈

On a new path of deliverance, Hakeem stopped viewing pornography and disposed of all films with homosexual elements in the apartment. He actively monitored television programs and where there were emphases on homosexuality and eroticism, discontinued viewership. Wherever weakness exists, an adjustment is critical. An addict who endeavors to become clean does not remain in or return to a trap house.

Addiction and temptation operate in tandem. Initial steps towards mastery require acknowledgment of one's weakness in respect to a vice. Self-denial and underestimation of an addiction increases one's susceptibility. Temptation arrives personally and conveniently packaged.

Hakeem's core weaknesses were the desire for affection and companionship. Although abuse and rejection were precursors of his disposition, the methods used for rectification were inadequate for the task. Men and pornography temporarily solved for Hakeem's psychological deficiencies. He needed mental and spiritual healing, which therapy and church provided.

Hakeem believed that in continuing on the destructive path, he would spend the remainder of life alone or experience something worse. Why did being alone have to be his reality when women who were able to provide companionship and emotional support, exist in abundance? Surely a woman might find him suitable. Only God possesses the power to work miracles of that magnitude—to place one of His children in Hakeem's life and care. With hope renewed came rededication of life to God and a joining of membership to the Baptist Church.

≈≈≈≈≈≈≈

Khalil's response was marginally positive, lacking the enthusiasm of an elated supporter. Hakeem initially contemplated mentioning the transition, remembering Michael's reaction. However, confidence in their friendship overrode his reservations. It was a decision that set the course for the unexpected.

Hakeem quickly realized that he was the only one changing. Contact with Khalil continued regularly with subtle changes in the quality of dialogue occurring in the three months that followed. Hakeem practiced refraining from asking about his dating life. When Khalil voluntarily discussed recent escapades, he listened in silence.

The friends-with-benefits arrangement that Khalil and Omar shared eventually capsized. He discovered that Omar was entertaining other men while traveling for business. Hakeem gave Khalil consolatory advice where possible. Completely depleted was his own confidence in gay dating. He reminded Khalil that Omar had been dishonest since the beginning—believing it worth underscoring the facts.

By the fifth month, communication dwindled to once per month. The last Hakeem knew, Khalil had met someone new, who lived out of town. He refrained from asking questions about the new suitor. Hakeem also began to find Khalil's conversations distracting and trivial, much the same as conversations of partying and drinking. Like liquor's biting flavor upon the tongue of a recovering alcoholic, those activities became remotely familiar and strange to an individual who sought to separate themselves from destructive habits.

During the same month, they played phone tag, neither making direct contact with the other. A week later, Hakeem called Khalil again only to reach voicemail and never received a call-back. It was his last attempt at contact.

The growing distance was for the best. Hakeem saw the signs of a degrading friendship earlier on when Khalil moved to Atlanta. Atlanta's gay underworld thrilled Khalil while he seethed in it. Khalil swore not to get caught up, and yet, was captivated by the city's glamour.

As Hakeem found sturdier ground on his journey, the path steeped and narrowed. Further advancement required one less traveling companion. The choices he made eliminated the capacity to maintain their friendship.

Sometimes the trajectory of growth and change parallels a lonely road. At different junctures in life the road widens to allow for traveling companions. Goals and life-altering decisions determine whether the company is short- or long-term. It is the traveler's inability to adapt to changes in bandwidth that causes them to proceed at a slower pace or derail entirely. Ideally, life should reflect progression, not stagnation or regression. When stagnation or regression occurs, it necessitates cognitive restructuring and behavioral changes.

An individual will encounter many people throughout their lifetime and meet few of long-standing quality. Decade-long friendships as characteristic of Hakeem and Khalil were indeed challenging to replace. Even so, two truths exist in this world—people change and nothing lasts forever.

The maintenance of most gay affiliations after reversion is exhausting because complacent homosexuals don't see anything wrong with the manner in which they live. Thus, the reason that a person in which they formed kinship, wanted to leave the gay lifestyle was beyond their understanding. Michael's sarcasm echoed what many gay and straight people presumed—that once gay, always gay. If someone 'switched' sides, they were projected to return eventually. Bisexuals were dubious because they unpredictably alternated between their sexual orientations. Because many gay people lack a wholehearted desire to conquer the seemingly impossible feat of overcoming homosexuality or bisexuality themselves, they don't believe anyone else capable, going far to criticize and discourage those who fight against the tide.

Cresting the tidal wave, a person struggling to stay afloat, saw the possibility of their former life swept away while the distant shore beheld mystery and unfamiliarity. It is plausible to suggest that within some of these individuals, a cognizance develops of having to abdicate the familiar—behaviors and associations. Such awareness then activates depression and anxiety upon realizing that they must move outside of their comfort zone and never look back. This conclusion may provide some explanation as to why a large number of gay people are reluctant to depart from their situation.

Hakeem had communicated with numerous men via online dating sites and obtained few steady connections. Few were worthy of friendship classification. He had known Alan for six years. They met officially through an invite to a charity event, which Alan extended, and their friendship blossomed. In the latter days of their association, Hakeem's disclosure of his transition was ignited by Alan's flirtatious remarks, which he felt needed to be halted. Alan's response was almost offensive, stating that the "ball was in his court," if communication was to be maintained.

According to Alan, he had former friends who became heterosexual and eventually ceased contact. He further stated that he wouldn't infringe on anyone's personal preferences. Shocked and disappointed at the shift in the conversation, Hakeem removed Alan's number from his cellphone, no longer interested in preserving their friendship. A healthy friendship requires the continuous input of two people for it to thrive.

The DUI charge solved for Hakeem's tendency to frequent bars and clubs altogether. He didn't attend either outlet without consumption of alcoholic beverages. A change in habits efficiently and sequentially impacted his network of gay associations. Without an interest in drinking and partying, the phone calls and text messages for nightlife excursions slowed to a trickle.

Abstaining from pornography eliminated Hakeem's dependency upon sexually-explicit multimedia to fill the void of loneliness and as a means for sexual gratification. In hopes to reconcile life to God, he understood the necessity of making an effort to cleanse himself. **"For this is the will of God, your sanctification: that you should abstain from sexual immorality; that each of you should know how to possess his own vessel in sanctification and honor, not in passion of lust, like the Gentiles who do not know God" (1 Thessalonians 4:3-5; NKJV).**

Mature believers of the Word of God didn't attend church with the expectation that they could remain the same in sin, if they desired to increase their faith in Christ Jesus. It was this realization that primarily affected Hakeem's willingness to attend church. The Bible advises of God's requirements for the Christian walk and the repercussions for engagement in sexual immorality (1 Cor. 6:9-10, 18; Ephesians 5:5; Galatians 5:19-21; Rev. 21:8). The important question is how much does a relationship with God the Father, His Son Jesus Christ, and the Holy Spirit mean to the individual who seeks deliverance? God is a loving God, who forgives through repentance. But a believer in Christ must confess their sin.

Hakeem's decision to actively monitor viewership of television programs directs attention to psychological phenomenon concerning the effects of society and the environment on cognition. He respected the research of Psychologist Albert Bandura who posited in his social cognitive theory that "children learn through observation and modeling."

People of all ages learn through observation and modeling. Our adoption of fashion trends and various forms of behavior were driven by television personalities, celebrities, and social media. Television programs, films, and music influenced information-processing and consequential to constant exposure, people subconsciously replicated what they saw on the screen. The past two decades contrasted with prior years, reflects a significant change in censorship where the constraints on profanity, sexuality, nudity, and violence have now decreased. As a result, people now trade morality and traditional values for immorality or the inappropriate. It is no coincidence that more than ever, people are open with their sexuality and debauchery. Neither men nor women, gay or straight, young or old can keep their clothes on, and society conveys that these behaviors are acceptable.

Unquestionably, it was necessary for Hakeem to be intentional in thinking and behavior for the sake of personal and spiritual growth. If former friends and associates were unsupportive of his transformation, then it behooved him that they fade into the past. Resentment was temporary as he gradually adjusted to the absence of Alex, Khalil, and Michael. He would not allow anyone to cause him to backtrack through foolish counsel. Sixteen years of being gay and reckless with nothing positive to show for the time and energy invested had been fruitless. He spent nearly half of his lifetime making the same mistakes, and none of the past could be changed or recovered. Thirty-five, single and miserable was an unpleasant disposition. Hakeem wanted peace, marriage and more importantly, a happier life. It was only possible through faith in God to do what no human could accomplish.

God took on a new meaning for Hakeem through recommitment, as the Baptist Church taught not only about His forgiveness, but also His capacity to perform miracles. God is the source Who possesses the power to deliver from seemingly impossible situations. For people with troubling pasts that are similar to Hakeem, God is the ultimate answer to their life-long problems. God worked through Gail to encourage Hakeem, which influenced redirection of focus heavenward. Through the power of the Holy Spirit, he found the strength to turn away from homosexuality and self-destructive habits. Hakeem also believed it possible to serve in a greater capacity because his soul had been reconciled.

What other people think or verbalize when an individual decides to walk with God is irrelevant. The surrounding world seems short of compassion. Otherwise, prejudice, discrimination, and hate would be scarce. When a person cannot gain support from people, they should seek God and place all cares on Him.

Believing that God is capable of conquering personal issues is the component for propelling forward. God is the sustainer of our faith! Everything that contributes to the advancement of His kingdom and the return of Jesus Christ, He permits passage and materialization. What does this assertion mean as it pertains to human behavior?

The New Testament provides the narrative of Jesus Christ establishing His ministry on earth. Jesus was rejected by the people— descendants of the nation of Israel whom He was sent to save. Where the Jews rejected Christ, the Gentiles whom can be referred to as non-Jews or the world, received the Son of God. Through miraculous works, deliverance and testimony, it is found that everything, good and bad, collectively contributes to the Will of God. The casting out of demons (Mark 1:39, 7:24-30; Luke 11:14), healing of the sick (Matthew 9:1-8, 27-29; Luke 6:17-19), resurrecting the dead (Matthew 9:18-26; John 11:38-44), and Christ's own resurrection confirmed Him as the Son of the Living God. After Christ's ascension, His disciples continued the work that He began. The Scripture tells of Saul, who became Paul, and his conversion to Christ's discipleship. Paul testified and glorified God everywhere he went, converting unbelievers to Christianity.

≈≈≈≈≈≈≈

In some of my interactions with people, I've heard the question, if God is real, then why does He allow bad things to happen to people?

Here's one answer. If God restricted or intervened in every action that humankind performed, the question would be pointless, as freedom of choice would be nonexistent. Our thoughts and behavior would be robotic with minimal autonomy. The feelings, desires, and pleasures that we experience today, wouldn't contain sentimental values. How many of us have sought God <u>when</u> we decided to get married or involved in a relationship, applied for a job, purchased a car or home, relocated to another state or, on a serious note, sinned or committed a crime? It is not a practice that we've made habitual because God granted us the ability to employ freewill. Oftentimes, when we bear good fruits from self-governed decisions, we rejoice, and even take credit for the results. However, in harvesting the rotten fruits of our actions, we shake our fists angrily at the heavens above.

In the context of violence and abuse, silence and denial prevail. Few people desire to engage in candid conversations focusing on rape and sexual abuse. I have found that women are likelier to discuss these subjects more voluntarily than men and it's unsurprising. Statistics report higher percentages of victimization in women and children than men. Perhaps a combination of societal expectations and ignorance discourages male input on the topics of violence and abuse. I've seen expressions of discomfort appear on the faces of men when rape or sexual abuse enters group conversations. I've heard ignorance spout from the mouths of men who have never undergone sexual abuse and wondered how they would respond if the victims were their children. If they feel anything, it should be outrage. But why must violence and abuse enter into the home before we find our voice or get involved?

Persons of every nationality, ethnicity, and religious affiliation have mistakenly asserted that violence and abuse only happen within certain socio-cultural environments. For example, I've heard some African-Americans suggest that sexual abuse only occurs in white communities. Many Caucasians insist that a large percentage of violence transpires in Black communities, and will downplay the mass school and public shootings, which transpire within their own communities. This nescience exists everywhere—one racial group vilifying another while discounting their own imperfections and sinful nature. It is an

237

ignorance that survives despite historical data and a world, which defies delusions.

How can traumatic situations be controlled without discussion and intervention? Are we waiting for God to stop the perpetrators, or change their hearts when there are tangible resources of aid at our disposal to assist those in need? God created us not only to worship and honor Him (Exodus 20:3; Deut. 5:7), but also to uplift and love each other (John 13:34-35). In our interactions with one another, we are to ensure the preservation and goodwill of all. Thus, the question mentioned earlier is modified. Why do people allow bad things to happen to people?

We witness atrocities while keeping our mouths closed, and don't get involved in movements to preserve the welfare of our neighbors. Central to many of humankind's problems are fear, hate, and a constant desire to self-gratify whether it is through exerting dominance or disobedience. People of all demographics yearn for power and wealth for personal benefit, lacking a vision to upbuild and empower entire communities. We seek thrilling experiences at the expense of ourselves and others. In our quests to be true to ourselves, we become further removed from God's Will. Christ didn't advocate selfishness or greed. We are quite capable of minimizing potential harm towards our brethren. Yet, we fail to employ this capability consistently.

Although choice is individually-relative, it creates rippling effects that impact the self and environment. Some people believe that they are laws unto themselves. However, when decisions and actions backfire, the same defiant and lawless people cry out to God for help. When the assistance comes, it is sometimes rejected (just like the Jews rejected Jesus Christ) because the help isn't packaged according to the requestor's expectations. The woman who refuses to evacuate from an abusive household to safety, jeopardizes her welfare and children if present. A victim of rape or sexual abuse who doesn't report the incident, encourages the perpetrator to repeat the vile acts. Problems will evolve into systems of oppression and despair if unmitigated.

In cases where help is received, it takes nearly as much time to repair the damage as it took for it to occur. This gradual process of transformation and reparation is a result of God working through people. His recruits are organized and prepared in the general course of human development. Every person has a purpose. As God strategically places them throughout this world, they interact and affect people and environments. God's interaction was evident in Gail counseling Hakeem who was in need of psychological repair. In the process of healing and growth, he re-established faith in God. Where God intervenes, it is for His ultimate purpose and glory, not a person.

GATEKEEPERS AND THE WORD OF TRUTH

Rely not solely on those learned persons, who preach and teach the Word of God. Know Him for yourself in accordance with the Scriptures.

akeem struggled to ignore the conversation between the two women in the lounge while relaxing on an oversized beanbag. The lounge's layout was designed to be therapeutic—featuring soft yellow lights, and blue and green reclining chairs. He was trying to regroup from the conference call with Ray and New Horizons. Again, Ray had made promises without knowledge of the potential requirements to accomplish the tasks, and Bill volunteered him to support the effort. Hakeem considered going home to inconvenience Ray and Bill. Three hundred hours of accrued vacation tempted early departure. Instead, he went to the lounge to restore his nerves.

The women—Barbara and Candace worked in the collections department. Hakeem heard Barbara recount a conversation with someone regarding the subject of homosexuality. Not only did Barbara disapprove of homosexuality, but she also declared it biblically wrong and voiced several expletives. Candace cosigned everything Barbara said and laughed at the derogatory statements. And yet, they proclaimed themselves Christians. For the record, God does not need anyone vulgarizing His Words, as they are effective without embellishment.

Barbara reminded Hakeem of Vanessa who expressed disapproval of his lifestyle fifteen years ago. During the verbal exchange, he reminded

240

Vanessa about the children she birthed out of wedlock and questioned her right to judge. She exploded on the phone and he ripped into her. He made it clear that he was not intimated and threatened that the argument could escalate to something physical. He believed that when a person threw a rock, they should prepare to catch a boulder in return. Subsequently, Hakeem went two years without speaking to Vanessa. The reunion was spurred by a wedding where she broke the tension. He accepted her efforts to make amends and re-established communication.

Vanessa was not the only sibling to express disapproval of Hakeem's sexual preferences. Their older brother, George broached the subject to Chantel. Chantel told George to discuss the issue directly with him. Apparently, George was uninterested in a confrontation. Instead, whenever George spoke to Hakeem, he made the typical offhand comment, "I'm gonna' pray for you." Like Vanessa, George had children out of wedlock. The interesting question was, how many times did he pray for himself?

Hakeem disagreed with Christians who actively condemned homosexuality and those sins they didn't commit while simultaneously downplaying or hiding their own transgressions. The act was hypocritical whether one sinned openly or in secret. He knew about the shortcomings of Barbara, Candace, Vanessa, and George. Barbara and Candace were unmarried women, known to be sexually involved with men in the workplace. Barbara also gossiped and circulated other coworkers' personal business. Whether they atoned for their faults was not the issue. Rather it was the fact that they sinned at various points in the past and present. Moreover, if they were genuine as the devout Christians they proclaimed to be, then they should have been seeking God's grace and mercy. Where does the Bible state that one sin is less deserving of His forgiveness than another? That scripture does not exist.

Out of all the sins, ***hypocritical Christians*** magnified homosexuality as the worst. "It's an abomination in the eyes of God," they proclaimed from the pulpit and the pews to the street as if homosexuality is the only sin God despised. Indeed homosexuality is biblically classified as an abomination because it opposes one of God's first commandments to mankind—**"be fruitful and multiply…"** (Genesis 1:28). Regardless of

241

the advances in science and medicine, and society's attempt to redefine the concept of gender, only a human male and female can procreate. Reproduction between man and woman is what God ordained.

For all intent and purpose of informing the unenlightened, it should be understood that homosexuality <u>is not the only abomination expressed in the Bible</u>. Proverbs 6:16-19 (NKJV) references seven abominations: **"a proud look; a lying tongue; hands that shed innocent blood, a heart that devises wicked plans; feet that are swift in running to evil; a false witness who speaks lies; and one who sows discord among brethren."** Why weren't these Scriptures referenced, in addition to the verses concerning homosexuality? Did no one lie or sow evil? Was no one prideful or arrogant? Hypocritical Christians cherry-picked the portions of the Bible that were most salient to their cause. Ignorant Christians waited until Sunday morning to be informed by their preacher, having gained no independent knowledge to supplement what they heard from the pews. It explains why typical churchgoers knew little about God's grace and mercy, which is available to everyone who believes in Jesus Christ pre- and post-resurrection.

Listening to hard-hearted Christians talk ignorantly about gay people grated Hakeem's nerves. He wanted to rage and demand that they examined themselves. A liar, a thief or murderer without repentance was subject to the same penalty that a homosexual faced, which is death according to the Bible (Romans 6:23). The ability to hide one's sin or practice it in secret does not make the individual exempt from God's judgment. They were a hypocrite regardless of whether they openly admitted the fact.

Hakeem wanted to interrupt Barbara and Candace and correct their ignorance, but the Holy Spirit compelled silence. Their discussion was not the platform for him to witness. There are times that even in possession of insight, one should be silent (Proverbs 17:27-28; Ecclesiastes 3:7). Exercising restraint, he simmered over his bitter experience in the Church.

≈≈≈≈≈≈≈

Had I been attentive, I might have seen trouble brewing. In March 2004, three weeks before Resurrection Sunday, I was awakened by a dream. In the nightmare, I stood on a slanted, elevated brick platform that stretched along the side of a courtyard surrounded by a building. Assessing the structure and its stained-glass windows, I perceived the building to be a church, although entirely different from the place of worship where I fellowshipped at the time. In fact, the structure and surrounding area reminded me of the church that was next to the elementary school I attended in Philly.

Dozens of people passed me, oblivious to my presence as they entered and exited the church and courtyard. I remained stationary and apparently, invisible. Then a strange figure in the likeness of a man materialized approximately five paces in front of me. It stood waiting, observing me for some unknown reason. The eeriest aspect of the figure was its shifting form. After a time, the figure asked me condescendingly, "So you can prophesy now?"

"I don't know," I responded hesitantly. I didn't know what to make of the question.

The figure laughed, and at that moment, I saw the reddish glow in its' eyes. I knew then that the devil had spoken to me. I forced myself to awaken, finding the crewneck collar and armpits of my t-shirt drenched in sweat. The Gift of Prophecy was not a spiritual gift that I believed I possessed. I had visited a church once where a visiting pastor confirmed that the Gift of Discernment dwelled within me. The pastor was correct, even though he had never met me before. I could discern things that other people were unable to, often baffling them because they saw nothing beyond the natural.

After choir rehearsal in the week that followed, the minister of music, Tyrone Miller requested a meeting with me. I agreed to meet him after Wednesday Night Bible Study of the following week. On the day of the meeting, I became anxious and left work early. Part of me imagined that the meeting was to rehearse for another solo in preparation of Resurrection Sunday. During the Christmas service of the previous year, three female choir members and I led a medley. The schedules for rehearsal had been arranged similarly. Yet, my hopes were overshadowed with the foreboding of something grim.

Bible Study had ended by the time that I arrived at the church. I made my way to the stage where Tyrone was shutting down the keyboard. His musicians were packing their equipment in preparation to depart.

"What's goin' on, Tyrone?" I asked from the bottom of the stage.

He turned to me and I glimpsed the shiftiness in his eyes. "Hey, man! How you doin'?"

"I'm good. Just got off work."

I ascended the stairs onto the stage, and he signaled me to follow into the musician's room in the right corner of the platform. Inside, he gestured to close the door. When I turned around, he was standing across the room. I sensed uneasiness emanating from him. Something was wrong. A brief silence passed between us before he spoke.

"One of the things that we are concerned about…"—Tyrone began and paused, consciously structuring his statement—"is whether our members in ministry are living a Christian lifestyle. And that means whether they are heterosexual, homosexual, or bisexual."

"Okay…" I managed, nervously licking my chapped lips. Alarm crept into the pit of my stomach. "So… you're asking me if I'm straight?" I perceived was his probe. It was a straightforward question and I was no fool. No one inquired about a person's sexual orientation unless they sought an answer. It seemed that Tyrone wanted me to ask the question, and thus, relieve him of its burden.

"Yeah…yeah, man. That's what I'm asking." he responded quickly.

"Well, I am." It was a lie that I risked willingly.

"Great, man. But, I'm gonna' have to ask you to step down from the choir at this time, and not attend any rehearsals. I have people that I must answer to."

Tyrone's statement stoned me. I dazed for a moment because I couldn't believe what he said. *Step down from the choir. Don't attend any of the rehearsals.* He communicated the directive like a medical professional counseling a patient with a contagious disease. His admonition was inappropriate in the absence of proof or a witness. I had been moderately conservative in my dealings with men. There were no public displays of affection or broadcasts of my excursions.

When I became active in the ministry, I immediately discontinued bar-hopping. I also severed communication with questionable associations. As far as sex was concerned, I had little difficulty refraining from intimacy with other men, given problematic encounters. I understood that ministry demanded a striving for holiness in both declaration and application. The fact posed the question, how could Tyrone ask me to step down? Furthermore, why couldn't I attend any of the rehearsals?

I didn't refute Tyrone's insinuations, although he denied me a thorough explanation. The guilt of my past defeated me. Maybe I was unworthy to serve in the church in a spiritual capacity.

I descended the stage's steps on leaden-heavy legs. The walk through the aisle leading outside was arduous. I saw familiar faces, remnants of the night's Bible study that vanished like apparitions in passing. Dysphoria inhibited my ability to speak. I thought that if I spoke, the people would not recognize me. I felt spaced and disconnected, and stricken with disbelief. Fortunately, no one said anything to me. I wondered if my face looked like someone smeared fresh excrement on it.

Not a spark of light illuminated my soul as I walked to my Pontiac Sunfire. Sitting inside, I unfolded the visor to look at my face in the mirror, expecting to see someone else, something different. What the hell was I looking for? I ransacked my brain trying to think of something that I might have done to contribute to the situation. I found nothing but still continued to grapple with my racing thoughts. I needed to call someone. I needed to do something. The person I thought I was, I no longer believed. My world began to unravel.

Taking out my cellphone, I dialed a close friend—Vincent. He was a gospel singer and musician in the city. Besides Ian, Vincent was the only friend who was firmly rooted in faith and spirituality.

I waited for Vincent to answer much longer than I normally do for anyone. He did not answer as I hoped. Concluding that he was still in church, I left a voicemail, anticipating his call upon hearing the news.

My dysphoria persisted throughout the entire journey home. The forty-minute drive seemingly stretched for hours. I could not get there fast enough. I just wanted to lay down as habit when depressed. Balled up in fetal position away from people and distractions comforted me as I tried to make sense of my troubles.

I entered my fifteenth-floor apartment and headed to the bedroom. After stripping down to my underclothes, I got into bed. Nausea churned in the pit of my stomach, creating an urge to simultaneously vomit and use the bathroom. The black and blue comforter could not warm the chill that washed over my body. Goosebumps covered my skin. I was amazed that my heart continued to beat despite the deadness spreading inside me.

I awakened to the sound of the cellphone ringing, unable to recall when I fell asleep. Seeing Vincent's cellphone number on the display, I scrambled to open its flip.

"Hello," I answered.

"Hakeem?" Vincent asked.

"Yeah."

"I just got your message. What happened?"

"They removed me from the choir," I replied short of providing the details relayed in the voicemail.

"They, who?"

"Tyrone did."

"Oh, hell no! You've got to be kidding. For what?"

I sighed, low on energy to analyze the account of events. Nevertheless, I began the story from the point where Tyrone requested a meeting after Bible Study.

Shock mixed with anger tinted Vincent's voice.

"Look here, Hakeem. Tyrone is wrong. And I assume the 'people he must answer to' refers to the pastor," he said passionately. "Who the hell are they to sit you down and have no legitimate basis for it?"

I remained silent and listened to Vincent vent. I should have been raging like him.

Vincent continued. "Listen. Don't let this get you down. It's a trick of the enemy."

"...."

"Are you there?"

"I'm here," I whispered from underneath the comforter. The phone rested on my cheek while a pillow cushioned the other side of my face.

"Find yourself another church. If you don't, this will make you bitter. The church is for the sick. How else can anyone be healed? No one is perfect! You hear me?"

"Yeah. I hear you." I felt a miniscule spark of hope.

Vincent was the best person to talk to about the situation.

"Look, I'm just getting in from church. I'll check on you tomorrow. Pray about it, Hakeem. Don't let this keep you down."

"Okay." I still wanted to be alone to think. I appreciated that he was doing his best to be encouraging and uplifting.

"Talk to you later." Vincent hung up.

The next morning, I awakened to fresh memories of the events from the previous night. My dysphoria transformed into anger. It was raw and deadly, and I wanted to do something terrible to Tyrone and the pastor. The feeling intensified so much that I forgot to breathe. *Who in hell was he to do this to me? Tyrone didn't know who he was messing with! Someone had hurt me again.* This time it was the church. I was tired of people doing things to me and getting away with it. Despite Vincent's advice, I couldn't douse the anger and bitterness. In my heart dwelled malice for Tyrone and the pastor, where it lingered for half a decade.

Gradually, I reined my destructive thoughts. I possessed no desire to do jail time for anyone, especially for doing something rash and stupid. Not again. Life behind bars was not an option for me. The restrictions and confinement would be my death sentence. I had contemplated suicide if I took drastic measure for revenge. Doing so would put an end to the pain of dealing with rejection, disappointment, and betrayal. And then, I realized that my thoughts were just as foolhardy as the mission, which I considered executing.

If I did something devastating or committed suicide, Joseph in particular, would be disappointed and distressed. Wreaking havoc created rippling effects that affected more people than the perpetrator intended or anticipated. I could not live with that kind of guilt nor leave such devastation behind. Therefore, once again I accepted defeat.

247

I decided that Tyrone and the pastor were unworthy of the pain I would cause my grandparents and myself, and even their families. My persecutors were unworthy of the consequences I would endure by committing a harmful act.

I resolved to move on with a positive outlook somehow. If I harmed myself or someone else, then my oppressors and the enemy won. In the midst of the maelstrom of turmoil, a light beaconed. I was in school, pursuing a bachelor's degree. No one in my immediate family had obtained a four-year college degree. I had something to live for. My success would be a trophy for which my grandparents could boast.

No matter what happens, try to find some aspect of goodness and hold onto that bit of light until it eclipses every dark thing.

In the weeks that followed, I heard from Tiffany, a college peer and former choir member. She updated me on a couple of events that transpired post-departure from the choir. A tenor was also asked to step down from the choir. Several choir members trashed-talked me, stating that they suspected my sexual preferences. They were the same members who smiled in my face while I attended. Yet, none of those women dared to express their prejudices to my face. Speculations and gossip exchanged in the shadows had exposed their true nature.

Still, I was no fool as to the stimulus of the members' suspicions. I sat in the alto section of the choir instead of the tenors. I could have sat with the sopranos, but it would have been overkill. I displayed my talents alongside a lyric soprano during the Christmas medley, receiving an overall positive reception. Evelyn herself, was a lyric soprano. Perhaps my talent originated from her. The alto section provided the vocal flexibility that I needed.

In the Black Church, it was exceedingly rare for adult males to sing alto or soprano in the natural octaves without stigmatization. If a Black man sang in the registers categorized as female, the church automatically assumed that "sugar" was in his tank. However, the same critics listened to male Pop and R&B artists with comparable vocal ranges. Apparently, no one was aware of the countertenor in the classical genre of music. Tyrone never asked me to sing lead again despite knowing about my vocal range when I first joined the choir.

Vincent's advice was invaluable. I toured several churches before settling at an Apostolic Church and joining the choir there. The members welcomed me like a long-lost brother. However, my backstory remained secret. No one needed to know the particulars of my faith journey. I was uninterested in becoming a target of their opinions, which would only stir the coals that smoldered within my mind. Anger lurked just beyond the veil separating my conscious thoughts. I nursed my emotions carefully.

I eventually learned that news of the sit-downs in my old church spread to other churches. The Black church community was relatively average in size with overlapping social networks. One local pastor took to his pulpit and insinuated the actions of my former pastor. Like Vincent, this local pastor stated that the Church was God's temple and was a healing place for the sick. He asked the congregation, who was anyone to put the afflicted out of God's church? I reveled in a brief moment of satisfaction, hearing of the pastor's sermon. It refreshed my confidence knowing that at least one church leader understood the purpose of God's house.

My emotional disposition assumed a semblance of normalcy. Nevertheless, I continued thinking about how it all happened. The most traumatic things in life are hard to forget. *Had someone double-crossed me? If so, who? What did they say about me and for what reason?* I rarely made enemies, at least to my knowledge. It could have been someone from my past, who knew me directly or through association.

The more I brooded over the incident I remembered seeing the face of an ex-lover in the Sunday service crowd while sitting in the choir stand, weeks preceding my meeting with Tyrone.

My associations with James ended roughly for the reason that he was intimately involved with another man. James tried to explain, but I refused to accept his excuses. I wanted him out of my life! He could be catty—a characteristic that I observed. He was not above calling the church and outing me. I could have obtained proof one of two ways: 1) question James, which I was unwilling to do; 2) or ask Tyrone directly. Carrying out the latter option was unthinkable because I risked exposure. A guilty party questioned the source of an accusation and in all honesty, I lied to Tyrone to protect myself.

The damage was done and irreversible. Suddenly I remembered the red-eyed figure from my dream. I had unconsciously witnessed my departure from the church. But despite the foreshadow, I lacked the proper insight and wisdom regarding how the event would transpire.

IN WHOSE EYES WERE THEY PERFECT?

"Brethren, if a man is overtaken in any trespass, you who are spiritual restore such a one in gentleness, considering yourself lest you also be tempted" (Galatians 6:1).

*I*f the church is supposed to be the meeting place for Christian teaching and healing, why are hard-hearted Christians turning the lost away? It is possible that some Christians founded their practices on 1 Corinthians 5:1-13 where Apostle Paul addresses the Church at Corinth concerning the sexual immorality of one of its members. The case references a member who was acting against the teachings of the church, and Paul advised the church to disassociate themselves from the sinner. However, 2 Corinthians 2:1-12 displays Paul's humility in causing grief within the Church of Corinth. Paul admits his **"affliction and anguish"** (2 Cor. 2:4) in the composition of the first letter (1 Corinthians 5) and counsels the church to extend **"forgiveness and comfort"** (2 Cor. 2:7) to the offender. Apostle Paul realized the potential outcome of harsh judgment—that its weight could utterly crush a person.

Matthew 18:15-17 prescribes conduct for handling the sins of brethren. This passage instructs Christians to first address their brethren in private regarding sins committed against them (v. 15). If the accused refuses to make amends or repent, then the accuser is to seek **"one or two witnesses"** (v. 16) and finally, bring the issue to the church (v. 17) if it remains unsettled. In Matthew 18:21-35, Jesus and Peter discuss forgiveness. Here, Jesus states there is no limit to the number of times that a brother should forgive another. As our Heavenly Father forgives us for our transgressions, we must also be willing to forgive others.

The doctrinal approach expressed in 1 Corinthians is inadequate for proselytizing unbelievers outside of the church because they have yet to come to know God as a mature Christian and thus, establish a spiritual relationship. As Jesus demonstrated, Christians who strive to be more like Him, should teach and correct with love and patience (2 Timothy 2:24-25). If unbelievers resisted initially, who is to say that they won't seek God later on? Plant the seed of God's Word in love and the power of the Holy Spirit shall make provisions for ongoing nourishment. Oh, how the power of the Most High is effective in humbling the spirit of man.

The Christian endeavor is not to irritate and hurt people through arrogance and pride. They are supposed to spread the Word of God, in addition to healing and restoring. Did they forget that God has tolerated them for their transgressions? How long did it take for Christians with histories similar to Vanessa, George, Barbara, and Candace to walk the path of the righteous? A month, several months, one year, five years, or sixteen years like Hakeem? God is patient because the Bible declares His stance against sin—all sin (Romans 6:23). There is no purgatory between heaven and hell to accommodate sinners. There is no sacrifice aside from the blood that Jesus shed, which is sufficient to remove sin (Hebrews 10:3-4). All unrepentant sinners and unbelievers will receive eternal death on judgment day.

Many hard-hearted and ignorant Christians were quick to reference the Old Testament—namely, Leviticus 20:13 (men sleeping with men), forgetting that Jesus died for the sins of all mankind. The story of Sodom and Gomorrah and God's destruction thereof is a common recollection of His judgment of homosexuality. But Christians overlook some of the more interesting aspects of the account—Abraham. The most remarkable element of Sodom and Gomorrah's narrative as it pertains to this discourse is Abraham's compassion despite knowing God's view of sin and disobedience. Before the destruction of Sodom and Gomorrah, Abraham interceded on the cities' behalf, asking God to **"spare the righteous"** (Genesis 18:23-33).

Abraham's nephew, Lot, and Lot's family resided in Sodom. It can be suggested that Abraham was referring to his relatives while conversing with God. This proposal is debatable considering that Abraham attempted negotiations with God in verses 23-33. The narrative details a gradual decrease in the number of the "righteous," who Abraham suggested potentially lived within the city. Abraham's approximation indicates his limited knowledge while his actions evidenced the condition of his heart. Each time, God stated that He would spare the city if such numbers existed.

God knew about all that transpired in the cities from the very beginning. Sodom and Gomorrah were ultimately destroyed because its denizens were completely consumed by **"ungodliness"** (2 Peter 2:6), **greed** (Ezekiel 16:49), sexual immorality, and blatant disrespect for God's manifested presence—the two angels in the form of men, who were guests in Lot's household (Genesis 19:1-29). Most of Lot's household perished along with the cities, except for him and his two daughters.

Despite Israel's disobedience, Moses interceded on their behalf (Exodus 32:30-33). 1 Samuel 12 narrates Samuel's intercession (v. 23-24) for Israel after Saul is appointed king. Israel had rebelled against God as they were historically accustomed. King Solomon intercedes for Israel, praying to God for His forgiveness should the nation stop sinning and turn back to Him (1 Kings 8:33-53). But most important of all is Jesus Christ, the Supreme Intercessor—He who trumps every prophet, apostle and disciple that ever lived. Jesus died for the sins of the world (Hebrews 9:26-28), and He is the one that Christians should strive to imitate. The palpability of Christians hastening to witness the destruction of others not entirely unlike their former selves suggests hardened-hearts and hypocrisy.

Why aren't "mature" Christians demonstrating more love and compassion in their efforts to up-build God's kingdom? There are two possible theories: 1) some are in need of more training and development regarding how to advance the ministry of Jesus Christ; or 2) they simply believe they are doing God a favor in stopping sinners at the gate. Removing persons of influence from positions of authority may be necessary in the case of a false teacher or prophet who contradicts or twists the Word of God in the church. In the Book of Revelations, John addresses the Church at Pergamos (2:12) regarding its tolerance of false prophets and teachers who encouraged idolatry and sexual immorality (2:14-16). Blasphemy undermines God's ordinances and precepts that the church strives to uphold. Yet, in service to God, not one of us will sit in the seat of judgment on the appointed day. We must walk with spiritual authority in humility.

There is a segment of Christians who believe that ranking members of the clergy—particularly those proclaimed as apostles and prophets, are permitted to harshly criticize sinners. They revel in the possibility of pending doom and destruction. However, Jesus rebukes the disciples, John and James for their desire to **"call down the fires of heaven"** (Luke 9:54) on a Samaritan Village after the locals refused to receive Him (Luke 9:53). Jesus declares, **"You do not know what manner of spirit you are of, For the Son of Man did not come to destroy men's lives but to save them"** (Luke 9:55-56; NKJV). Matthew 18:6 narrates Jesus' view against those who would hinder others from entering God's kingdom. In this verse, He states that **"it would be better for the one who causes another to stumble to hang a millstone around his neck and drown."**

Within the hierarchy of God's kingdom, Jesus reigns as Supreme Intercessor and Prophet. Clergy members are supposed to defer to Him like John the Baptist and demonstrate humility (John 1:15, 19-28). In verse 23, John recites Isaiah in his reply to the Jews, **"I am, 'The voice of one crying in the wilderness: Make straight the way of the Lord'"** (NKJV). John is conveying that he is a messenger whose assignment is to draw people to Christ and nothing more. Hakeem had walked out of churches where pastors used vulgar vernacular in preaching against homosexuality while the congregation laughed and snickered at the sermons. These behaviors are not of God. Hakeem could deal with sermons which focused on homosexuality and any other sin where the Spirit of God was present because the Spirit bridled the tongue. Every person who attended church is a sinner with an affliction regardless of what they believed themselves because according to Scripture, no one is perfect. **"For there is not a just man on earth who does good and does not sin"** (Ecclesiastes 7:20), except Jesus Christ. Clergy title and tenure, affluence, and works do not make a person exempt (Matthew 19:30, 20:1-16).

Notwithstanding the circumstances, God expects sinners to evolve in Christ. People who possess a desire to know Christ, should not avoid the fellowship of His assembly because of ignorance. Ignorance is everywhere—on the job, in the grocery store, schools, and every other place where people frequent. Hosea 4:6 informs us **"people perish for lack of knowledge"**—an admonishment, which is relevant to our lives today. Had Hakeem possessed the foresight of being arrested after leaving the house party, he would have made different choices. Ignorance regarding the consequences of drinking and driving did not excuse him from the legal ramifications. Refusing to take precautions and ignoring warning signs when engaging in sexual activity did not negate the possibility of impregnation or contraction of sexually-transmitted diseases. Actions cause reactions and incur consequences beyond the scope of human control.

Sometimes, searching for a suitable church is analogous to trying to merge onto an interstate. It seems that every driver wants to deny you entrance until finally, one driver makes room for you to merge. The analogy enables us to see that there are good people in the world just as God's angels walk among us. The church is imperfect because it is filled with flawed people. And unfortunately, even those who believe they possess the most positive of intentions allow themselves to be tools for evil. The only place where perfection exists is in the Kingdom of Heaven. If a person perceives a particular church as offensive, the best recommendation is to find another place of worship where the Holy Spirit is growing its' ministries and reflecting God's vision in the process.

Technology makes information conveniently accessible. You can utilize the internet to find churches within your city and state. If you find the first church unsuitable, visit the next church on the list. More importantly, pray in earnest that God leads you to where you are supposed to be. Every person on this earth has a purpose. You will be amazed at His revelations—how He communicates through signs and people. Vincent was the lighthouse that shown in Hakeem's tunnel of darkness and discouraged him from leaving the church forever. Broken and distraught, Hakeem would have pursued the road that led to complete self-destruction.

It is imprudent to affiliate with religious institutions that advocate complacency in sin. This doctrine is a direct contradiction of God. While God loves everyone, He expects His children to reciprocate His love. **"For if you love Me, you will keep My commandments"** (John 14:15). These commandments carried forth into the New Testament and were fulfilled through the death and resurrection of Christ Jesus. It is His blood that extends grace to the world.

Personal testimony and transparency aided in the revelation of God as demonstrated throughout the ministry of the Apostles (see the Book of Acts). It is testimony that provides unbelievers with points of reference regarding the manifestation of God in the witness's life. Affirmation grants strength and reassures the sinner that they too, can conquer the struggles within their life. When Christians are transparent, their capacity to exude superiority in faith is reduced. In the absence of superiority is humility, which is necessary for the advancement of God's work and promise (Matthew 18:3-4). Hypocritical Christians strive to keep their transgressions secret because in the eyes of a sinner, the main differentiator was their relationship with God. Sin—both past, present, and future leveled the playing field. No one can harshly criticize without being denounced in return.

If it were intended for Christians to traverse the world saying and doing whatever they pleased, Jesus wouldn't have commanded the disciples to await the descending of the Holy Spirit for instruction in Jerusalem (Luke 24:49). Their firsthand witness of the miracles and wonders He performed would have been sufficient to advance the ministry of God's kingdom. Arrogant and prideful Christians believe that they are working miracles on behalf of themselves. For if they were concerned that their actions caused lasting hurt and confusion, and drove people away from the church, they would abandon their practice of personal biased, self-motivated preaching and teaching.

Only the enemy operated through confusion and sought to **"steal, kill, and destroy"** (John 10:10), undermining the advancement of God's kingdom. Jesus declared that a **"house divided against itself cannot stand"** (Mark 3:25). Therefore, if Christians are operating in the flesh—behaving in a manner comparable to the evil one, how can they correctly profess that they are fulfilling God's plan? **"Though I speak with the tongues of men and of angels, but have not love, I have become sounding brass or clanging symbol"** (1 Corinthians 13:1; NKJV). Christians cannot destroy and heal people at the same time. It is self-deception and unequivocally, a lie.

Apostle Paul informs the Church at Corinth that although in possession of the gifts of prophecy and faith, without love he was incomplete (1 Corinthians 13:2). He further emphasized that among faith and hope, **"love is the greatest"** (1 Corinthians 13:13). Consider Paul's witness from the standpoint of life application. Love in action mends and restores. It endures and is capable of compelling devotion. Love in interpersonal relationships upholds honor and integrity. When people demonstrate genuine love towards one another, they endeavor to preserve the well-being of each other. They do not delight in the pain and suffering of the afflicted. Instead, they encourage and comfort the disconsolate. Love resists darkness and oppression.

≈≈≈≈≈≈≈

Hakeem's eyes narrowed as he refocused on Barbara. He had a problem with Christians like her, who in their self-righteous toting of the Bible, played a significant role in driving people away from, rather than drawing them into the church. While some people dislike Christians, there are others who only despise arrogant and hypocritical Christians. Arrogant Christians are annoying birds that should make a practice of being silent if they were unable to demonstrate love and compassion to minimize the spread of ignorance and hate. Evil was already successful at creating chaos.

People like Hakeem and Rosalyn were nearly destroyed or left the church permanently because the so-called mature in faith were devoid of restorative judgment and encouragement. Not once were they given a chance for restoration. Considering Rosalyn's case, she was pregnant with him and unmarried. Perhaps if she aborted him, the act would have exemplified her repentance because she was able to relieve herself of the sinful evidence conceived. Hopefully, you note my sarcasm here.

Given the unlikelihood of silence ever occurring, seekers of God's kingdom—sinners and unbelievers alike, who desire to establish a relationship or renew their faith in Jesus Christ, should not be discouraged. As a recommendation to not forsake a relationship with God, seekers should tour churches until feeling compelled to commit to a long-term affiliation with a particular ministry. The Holy Spirit compels the called into action, and God sends messengers to assist in steering the flock. Understand that concerning the observance and teaching of core Biblical principles, churches are dissimilar in terms of vision and operation—realities driven by denomination. Hakeem observed this fact early on in his travels notwithstanding a hope for it to be otherwise. By virtue that people differ with regard to spiritual knowledge and maturity, it stands to reason that churches are different. As people grow spiritually, their spiritual needs evolve, but not at the same pace.

True unbelievers rejected and bypassed the church because they were unable to withstand the convicting presence of the Holy Spirit. Jesus Christ walked the earth among His kin and was rejected constantly by those who witnessed His miraculous works. Christ's transmogrification of water to wine, healing the sick and diseased, and raising the dead did not sway the unbelievers, even keepers of the Law. Jesus and later the disciples' response to rejection was **"shaking the dust from their robes and feet"** (Matthew 10:14; Luke 9:5; Mark 6:11; Acts 13:50-51; Acts 18:5-6). They continued to spread the Word elsewhere. Therefore, it is unnecessary to insult or threaten the sinful and unlearned. A hardened heart changes only through the power of the Holy Spirit. Without the Holy Spirit, mankind has no power or authority over sin.

If a person's heart and mind never change and remain unrepentant, then they are damned. This is true for the homosexual, liar, fornicator, murderer, and thief. As it is critical for them to understand that they cannot remain the same in sin forever. **"But you have not so learned Christ, if indeed you have heard Him and have been taught by Him, as the truth is in Jesus: 'that you put off, concerning your former conduct, the old man which grows corrupt according to the deceitful lusts and be renewed in the spirit of your mind, and that you put on the new man which was created according to God, in true righteousness and holiness'"** (Ephesians 4:20-24; NKJV).

An optimal approach to converting unbelievers into sustainable Christians is teaching with love. In Galatians 6:1-2, Paul wrote: **"Brethren, if a man is overtaken in any trespass, you who are spiritual restore such a one in a spirit of gentleness, considering yourself lest you also be tempted; Bear one another's burdens, and so fulfill the law of Christ"** (NKJV). 2 Timothy 4:2 supports Paul's advocacy for teaching with gentleness by stating, **"Preach the Word; Be ready in and out of season; Convince, rebuke, exhort, with all longsuffering and teaching"** (NKJV).

Hakeem understood the life of a struggling Christian, unable to master the demons alone. He knew the discomfort of guilt and shame, which made him feel unworthy of going to church. Hard-hearted Christians didn't demonstrate compassion in dealing with homosexuals, and the gay community perceived their deficiency. Unless cowered, no one tolerates insults or disrespect, and on those grounds, it wasn't a matter of being resistant to the Word of God, it is human nature. It was enough to endure ostracism in the world at large, not to mention being an outcast in one's family. Then a sinner was expected to enter the church where they encountered the same prejudices they faced in the outside world. Why must the abused come into the church and still be mistreated? It is too much to bear, and an unreasonable expectation. Some people were time-bombs on the final countdown, waiting to detonate.

The Spiritual Gifts of Discernment and Wisdom are crucial to understanding the root of sin in the sinner's life. Abuse, molestation, rape, and addictions weren't experiences that people readily divulged. Even in the privacy of Hakeem's therapy with Gail, he felt uncomfortable disclosing his past. People are usually embarrassed about the unsavory elements of their background. But unless they confront their affliction, thorough healing is impossible. If the church is God's hospital for the sick, then the Christians advancing His ministry are spiritual physicians. Christians must endeavor to discern the basis of a sinner's affliction and then apply the Word of God to lead the sinner towards deliverance. If unable to penetrate the farthest corners of a sinner's mind, the best course of action is to pray earnestly, and teach and preach with love, granting the Holy Spirit space to heal the broken and distraught.

A fundamental principle in counseling and therapy is building trust. Counselors and therapists alike overcome patient resistance upon gaining the trust of their clients by attending the latter party's needs. Matthew 14:13-21 narrates the **"compassion that Jesus Christ bestowed upon the sick and He healed them, rather than turn them away"** (NKJV). Jesus met the people's needs, feeding as well as teaching them. If Christians boldly profess to be like Christ, then their actions should exemplify their proclamations. As Jesus commissioned His disciples, **"Go therefore and make disciples of all the nations, baptizing them in the name of the Father and of the Son and of the Holy Spirit, teaching them to observe all things that I have commanded you"** (Matthew 28:19-20; NKJV). It seems an impossible feat when some church members rejected the sick and turned them away. How could the sinner ever be saved? The answer is a rather simple one. If God can't use the Christians who turn sinners away, He will call upon others to fulfill His work. God counters one-dimensional Christians and the disobedient by operating through people like Gail and the testimonies of the delivered to advance His kingdom. In Hakeem's deliverance, he acquired a testimony to witness and proclaim. He vowed to remember all that happened to him and his triumph.

≈≈≈≈≈≈≈

The origin of homosexuality is a long debated subject. Is there merit in the belief that some people are born gay? If so, how many people were born with a predisposition to be gay? Unless someone assumed the responsibility of administering questionnaires to parents within the first five years of their children's birth, there is no sure way to approximate. Nonetheless, the Bible does establish that homosexuality is a sin, and the disobedience of Adam and Eve in the Garden of Eden set in motion, sin's entrance into the world. Unknowingly, the first man and woman subjected all of their offspring to sin. The Book of Genesis narrates that Cain kills Abel out of jealousy (Genesis 4:8)—a sinful and immoral act, which is a common occurrence in the world events of today.

Framing Earl and Rosalyn in the context of Adam and Eve, hypothetically, it can be suggested that because Hakeem was the product of an adulterous affair, he in turn, was conceived in sin. In considering this analogy, do not conclude that married couples conceive perfect offspring. However, if you want to understand why sin exists, then you must know its origins and causal factors.

Earl's absence as a father in conjunction with the dispositions of Evelyn and Rosalyn, subjected Hakeem to harmful situations, and thus, negatively affected his development. A positive male role model's consistent and interacting presence balances the effects of feminine involvement in child development. The male role model further defines a male child and helps create stability within the youth's environment.

The Book of Genesis also records early accounts of homosexuality in the cities, Sodom and Gomorrah. Sodom and Gomorrah were inhabited by Canaanites (descendants of Noah's son, Ham; Genesis 9:22, 10:19), who worshiped idols and honored paganism. It is out of idolatry and paganism that homosexuality originated. As idolaters worshiped false gods, they engaged in sexual immorality as demonstrations of patronage and celebration. Priests and priestesses in the temples of the false gods (e.g. Molech, Ashtoreth) engaged in orgies, sodomy, and sacrificed children. Over time, that which was a pagan tradition became a common practice outside of the temples. Unnatural, idolatrous sex occur in film, music, and behind closed doors as the world continues to be receptive.

One must consider that not every idolater was an official within the temples. As these practices were observed and embraced, idolaters returned to their homes and continued observance much the same as worshippers of any religious or occult doctrine. However, the immediate gratification of sexual immorality perpetuates the behavior, which cycles unchecked from household to community, gradually becoming widespread. It is not happenstance that in the adoration and indulgence of the human body and its sexual reproductive organs, a person's sensuality stimulates their sexuality. Sadly, in the course of seeking sexual gratification, some people engage in self-destructive, sinful behaviors and in the most extreme cases, victimize others in pursuit of satisfying their desires. These experiences are not what God intended for His children. In our desire to please self, we move further away from God's Will.

Children, while born naive of the world, exhibit signs of disobedience in the early stages of development, and it is the practical methods of discipline in child-rearing that steers them onto the right path. **"Train up a child in the way he should go, and when he is old, he will not depart from it"** (Proverbs 22:6; NKJV). When cohesion and stability are absent in the home, the variables that potentially cultivate the development of homosexual tendencies increase.

Unmistakably, molestation and rape negatively imprint upon children psychologically. Children do not possess the mental capacity to decipher the emotions that accompany sexual activity, especially when forced. Even adults struggle with sexuality and the psychological impacts thereof. Dysfunctional households account for some instances where children are sexually abused or raped. The psychological and physiological absence of mothers, fathers, or both, and child neglect pave the way for perpetrators to violate their children. Since Joseph worked extended hours, he was unable to mediate the strained relationship between Evelyn and Hakeem. Parents or guardians can be physically present but psychologically disconnected. Hakeem's behavioral problems worsened the situation, and Byron and Daryle took advantage. The director of a boys' choir once preyed upon him after learning that a positive male role model didn't live in the home.

Perpetrators exploit knowledge of their prey and environment to manipulate them. This is not to say that child predators don't target unified homes because they do. Some of the most calculating abusers are family members or friends who possess intimate knowledge of the targeted victim's environment. The difference is that predators encounter more challenges in attempting to win a child's confidence to execute their perversions when both parents are not only living in the home, but also actively involved. Parents must reconcile differences in their interpersonal relationships and close the gap of emotional disconnect between their children. As for individuals who desire children, informed decisions should be made regarding potential spouses. Aside from God Himself, parents and supportive social networks are a child's greatest hope for navigating through the influences of the outside world.

Finally, some attribution to the rapid spread of homosexuality and sexual immorality should be given to multimedia. Television programs, films, cartoons and video-games script gay, bisexual, and transgender roles with increased frequency. Song lyrics are laced with sexual innuendos and advocate little about abstinence, safe-sex, marriage, or morality. Content-filtering and censorship are fading into the screenwriting and film production practices of decades past. As with straight-depicted characters, gay characters are now displaying intense sexuality on the screen. Celebrity lifestyles influence norms and foster trends, which society embrace. It stands to reason that globally, viewers are becoming desensitized as sexuality and sensuality are constantly spoon-fed to them. Where healthy parenting and spirituality are deficient, children model what they see on television uninterrupted and uncorrected.

Choice is a major factor in a person's actions when he or she exercises autonomy regardless of past experiences. The sexual abuse that Hakeem endured, affected his self-confidence, sense of self-worth and sexuality. But upon growing into adulthood, he chose to sleep with men and engage in sexual immorality—actions that temporarily assuaged the pain. Sinning is no more justified than if Hakeem abused, molested or raped someone else, and used his past as justification. Unless a person is forced against their will to commit an act, their actions are driven by choice in the presence of alternatives. God understands our intent, hurt, and suffering. But He also expects obedience and is long-suffering as we strive towards demonstrating our commitment. Counseling, therapy, and support from family and the church are an individual's greatest chances for psychological and spiritual healing. As old folk have said, "you have to get right with God before the end." The Bible supports this adage (1 Cor. 6:9-10; Galatians 5:19-21; Ephesians 5:5; Hebrews 12:14; Rev. 22:15). Since no one will ever know when their end is nigh, it is advisable to step onto the path of righteousness rather than play Russian roulette. Obtain salvation through Jesus Christ and proclaim Him as Lord and Savior.

For the church to gain a foothold on battling homosexuality and assisting in deliverance, it must adopt a multidimensional view. Such adoption in no way implies that homosexuality or any other sin is permitted to settle as dust to the ground. Instead, the recommendation supplements the proposal aforementioned—suggesting that the source of a sinner's pain must be cauterized and healed. Sensitivity should be given to a person's sinful diagnosis to understand the prognosis. A doctor cannot effectively treat the patient through insensitivity and incorrect identification of the symptoms.

Some within the community and church do not boldly and consistently address issues pertaining to incest, rape, pedophilia, and molestation. Instead, the community and church condemn the resulting manifestations of the perpetrations in ignorance. For example, instead of holding a sexual predator accountable for molesting or raping a child, some clergy members and parishioners criticize the victim for subsequent demonstrations of homosexual tendencies, sexual perversions, violence, or other types of deviant behavior. When an unmarried woman is impregnated, she is condemned rather than given a chance to repent while her male counterpart's reputation often remains unmarred. Or when a person struggles with an addiction, they are criticized instead of restored. However, when an individual of high-ranking status stumbles or commits an atrocious or similar act, they are often pardoned. The community and society do not always hold public figures to the same standard as a Joe Schmoe.

Society has placed significant value on social status, which often overshadows human error. Esteemed persons are considered upstanding pillars of society and when wealth supplements their reputation, such valuations increase a hundredfold. And because social status dictates the value placed on people, double standards exist with regards to how they are treated. Similarly, within the home, abusers who are either respected family members or friends, aren't always exposed. Fear and sometimes a false sense of security has much to do with a victim's willingness or ability to report abuse or violence. To illustrate how this is possible, I ask you to internalize the following cases:

1) A teenage girl is put out of her home after telling her mother that the live-in boyfriend has been sexually abusing her. Rather than seeking professional help for the daughter or contacting the police, the mother ultimately chooses the boyfriend over daughter.

2) At a young age, a woman's mother sold her and her sisters to men. The victim now suffers from mental illness and lives out her entire life in the shadows of her home. Her children are her means to accessing the outside world.

3) A woman who endured sexual abuse as a child becomes a victim of domestic violence as an adult. She develops both a drug and sexual addiction.

4) Several teenage boys were sexually abused by a respected member of clergy within the community. When the inappropriate acts were exposed, the church and community vilified the youths instead of the abuser. A few became sexually promiscuous as the others developed drug and alcohol addictions.

5) An adolescent girl is sexually abused by her mother's boyfriend. The only reason that the situation reaches the attention of local law enforcement is because the girl contracts a sexually-transmitted disease. A nurse at the hospital where the victim received medical attention made the call to inform proper authorities.

I have sat in church and fellowshipped with survivors of abuse, more or less like myself. I have discerned a reluctance to empathize with troubled people in some seasoned Christians. Vacant are their hearts and minds of warmth, comfort, encouragement, and strength. Their silence conveys a desire for the ailing believer to cease crying for help. I have wondered whether they exhibit taciturn behavior to avoid being selectively judgmental. But the power of love would convict them for dismissing a widespread problem. There's also the reality that some people—Christians and unbelievers, maintain the opinion that home and family situations shouldn't be discussed outside of those environments. If these attitudes and behavior are deemed acceptable, then church and community should abandon every form of judgment, because there are times when people must be judged as in the case of law and socio-environmental safety. The drawback is that inaction increases a victim's exposure to harm. The people who remain silent when they possess the capacity to help, must share the blame. Inaction is an action because an individual chooses to do nothing to minimize potential danger.

When considering a perpetrator of violence and abuse, the central issue is an external projection of inappropriate behavior, which is socio-environmentally destructive. Not only has the perpetrator sinned, but they have also become a stumbling block to their victim. Resulting from the violence they induce is a sundry of psychological dysfunctions that victims endure. As far as believers are concerned, Jesus warns, **"it is better that a person ties a millstone around their neck and drown than cause His children to stumble"** (Matthew 18:6). This scripture's applicability to abuse exists within the aftereffects of the offense. Alcoholism, substance abuse, drug and sexual addictions, sexual dysfunction, anxiety and depression, and suicide are indicative of psychological damage. These abnormal behaviors are in and of themselves, stumbling blocks to victims of violence and abuse because until they heal, they will remain in darkness. God disapproves of abuse just as He does every other sinful act (1 Cor. 3:16-17; Ephesians 4:29-32; Galatians 5:19-21; Psalms 11:5). Much of the pain and hardship that we experience in this world is orchestrated by the heart of man (Matthew 15:18-20) and the quests embarked upon to gratify its desires.

WALKING THE GOOD TALK ON A LONELY ROAD

"He shall regard the prayer of the destitute, and shall not despise their prayer" (Psalm 102:17).

*H*akeem sat in the pew as Reverend Lynice and Sister Edwina rose from their seats on the front row. They entered the pulpit and faced the congregation. As Reverend Lynice raised an arm and opened worship service with an invocation prayer, parishioners stood to their feet. Hakeem followed their example and bowed his head. He was amazed at her prayers—how she knew what to pray for and spoke every word.

The prayers of both Reverend Lynice and Sister Edwina had to originate from a place of humility, and a profound love and respect for God. Hakeem had exchanged introductions with the women after attending Bible Study regularly. Their prayers contained the same potency in the small groups. For anyone who believed that women should not have leadership roles in the church, he thought they were fools. God was certainly using them, especially when church attendance showed that women outnumbered men. God will always use people who are willing to serve.

As Sister Edwina concluded intercessory worship, the praise team and choir assembled behind the pulpit. Hakeem scanned the groups and sighted one of the women on the praise team. Black waves of hair cascaded over her shoulders, partially obscuring the knee-length denim dress she wore. Canary-yellow gladiator stilettos sheathed her legs.

He continued to analyze the young woman. From his vantage, pink lipstick was the only indication of makeup. She was beautiful—igniting new curiosities. But he postponed this introspection. It was not the time for daydreaming. Besides, she could be married. The thought moved him to put on his glasses and see whether she wore a wedding ring. On the left hand, there was a ring on the middle finger. The jewelry or lack thereof, did not confirm anything though. She could be talking to someone. Continued fellowship in the church might allow him to learn more.

Five months later, Hakeem was singing in the choir. Serving in the church cemented spaces in his life that club-hopping and unproductive activities once occupied.

≈≈≈≈≈≈≈

The church offered an array of Bible-centered classes for its members. Several were demographically-segmented for singles, married couples, children, men, women, and coed. Hakeem enrolled in a men's group. There, he fellowshipped with other males and studied Scripture under the tutelage of the presiding pastor and assistant ministers. It was there that he began to develop a greater appreciation for being a man.

By all appearances, the men were heterosexual. More than half of them were married, fathers and grandfathers. They testified in the group setting—sharing personal and family struggles, wisdom, and experience. Instead of trivial, catty and oftentimes, feminine dialogue that transpired in conversations between gay males, the men discussed substantial matters concerning church, community, leadership, marriage, and home.

The phrases "girl" and "child" were out of place in the men's ministry. Gay subculture encouraged these effeminate mannerisms to flourish. In the presence of masculinity, behaving in such a manner would be odd and perhaps, uncomfortable to an individual who was accustomed to flamboyant conversation. Differences in the social climates were obvious. While the men's ministry did not cultivate male femininity, the members did not exclude those who lived alternative lifestyles from attendance.

The objective of male fellowship in church is to evolve the spirituality, consciousness, and masculinity of men from a biblical perspective. In part, it strives to compensate for the absence of fathers in childhood development, and the limited number of positive male role models in the household and community. It is not a coincidence that mentorships have emerged from the formation of these types of fellowships. Personal testimony, wisdom, and experience enabled the weak and deficient to model esteemed examples. Constructive communication and interaction modify cognitive frameworks. Hakeem benefitted from participating in the men's group because it supplemented his spiritual growth and masculinity.

Society advanced the perspective that the boundary between genders was blurred. How so when biological sex organs inarguably established an individual's role in the procreation process? In scenarios where people are born with both male and female sex organs (hermaphroditism) or are genitally underdeveloped, gender ambiguity is not incomprehensible. Here, an individual's orientation towards a particular gender is substantiated by abnormal biological representations of reproductive organs. Subsequently, they have a biological basis for aligning their psyche with a specific set of sex organs. This phenomenon is not the same as a case where an individual psychologically identifies with the opposite gender, despite having genitalia that contradicts their personal beliefs. Psychotherapy is available to treat individuals suffering from this diagnosis but does not eradicate the fact that the afflicted lives in a false reality, no matter how strong the illusion. Gender Identity Disorder and Gender Dysphoria are classified as mental disorders for the reason implied. Gender reassignments create physiological illusions to assist an individual in bridging the gap between the real and ideal self-concept. To date, not one transgender who has completed the gender reassignment process been able to conceive according to the natural laws of procreation. Whether the person realizes or not, they have limited themselves. Because in living a lie, they may never live in truth—a primordial truth of life itself, which extends well beyond a reality that is seen through the personal lens.

≈≈≈≈≈≈≈

The choir finished singing for the C service and returned to the choir room. Hakeem lingered around briefly. As usual, no one made full conversation with him. He tried initiating conversation in the past, but some members were antisocial as himself, or socialized in cliques, or discussed trivial matters. The lifestyles of the rich and famous and the scandals trailing their names were unimportant to him. Sports was another topic that he dared not enter for lack of knowledge regarding the teams and star athletes. He would sound foolish talking about something of which he knew minimal.

Furthermore, for a place such as the church, Hakeem wanted to stay within certain boundaries. It seemed that few members shared his convictions, for there were frequent conversations of a carnal nature. He avoided taking part in those conversations. Clubbing and casual sex were activities of the past, and more importantly, such discussions were inappropriate in the church unless orchestrated for the purpose of ministerial teaching and testimony. He considered things set aside for God to be holy and believed that they should not be defiled as such conversations were capable. This silent, unwavering perspective separated him from the idle chatter.

If the choir members perceived Hakeem as antisocial, his obvious unwillingness to assimilate gave them more reason to assume. He refused to play phony. He overhead whispered tidbits of gossip concerning him as he blundered some of the notes. Being a countertenor had its drawbacks when the tenor parts were too deep to reach. When the conversations became too involved, the same members took to texting on their phones and snickering. The fact that they tried to cover their screen displays made their treacherous behavior all the more evident. In retaliation, Hakeem intentionally distanced himself and began to disregard most of the members. It was the best he could do to keep from splitting a couple lips. He was not above fighting if provoked. When the deceitful behavior became too much to bear, he quietly departed the choir without intentions of returning. He dealt with backbiting choir folk years ago and refused to put up with them anymore.

The atmosphere in Bible class was unlike that of the choir. There, the members had inclusive, open discussions every study session. Hakeem could share in their dialogues without feeling intrusive, and they were welcoming. No one behaved pretentiously or rudely because the class members were spiritually mature. The Bible stories were intriguing and inspiring, and he was spirit-filled. He departed Bible Study feeling uplifted and restored, cherishing every session, eager to participate in the next. Then he would listen to gospel music, sometimes yearning to return to the choir. From the pews he sang, filled with spirit and emotion. In singing, he lived, he felt, he loved.

Sundays passed before the choir director pulled Hakeem aside following morning service and asked him to come back to the choir. Hakeem obliged, expecting to observe a change in the atmosphere. Nothing had changed, and no one inquired as to his whereabouts. He soon wanted to leave again. Some of the members held private outings, inviting only those for whom there was partiality. A female candidly expressed knowledge of the gatherings during a rehearsal. The conspirators feigned ignorance. Hakeem took their secrecy as a slight.

≈≈≈≈≈≈≈

Again, I prayed about leaving the choir. But God wanted me to uphold my commitment. How did I know His response? My best advice to you is, spend time with Him. In the course of Bible study and prayer, you enter into an awareness of Who God Is. He is consistent with Scripture, and therefore, never responds in a way that contradicts His Word. Followers of Christ are to serve the kingdom of God (Matthew 6:33) to the extent that their dedication overrides selfish desires (Luke 9:23). God showed me that my reasons for leaving the choir had less to do with His will than my own. I wanted to be liked and accepted, and when my desires went unsatisfied, I sought escape. If every person God called to service, took the nearest exit when obstacles arose or situations failed to bend to their expectations, where would the lights be in the world? The darkness may be ominous, but the light of faith burns brighter when we avail ourselves of God's service.

Even the most pious fail to realize that in refusing to surrender to God, they make themselves vulnerable to the enemy's devices. What did it matter whether the choir members included in me anything? I was on assignment to complete a work regardless of any seeming division. Christians are not excused from fellowship, ministering, or uplifting people because of personal attitudes and emotions. Just as Jesus endured the rejection of Jews and Gentiles, Christians are also expected to withstand hardship. Or do we value ourselves greater than Christ? To be more like Christ, consider what He went through—persecution until death.

There was something else God helped me to understand in our communion. In my career endeavors, I would encounter people who disliked and rejected me. In fact, I had already experienced those situations at Kaleidoscope and was forced to find ways to overcome those obstacles. If unable to manage interpersonal relationships spiritually and professionally, how could I possibly deal with people of similar character at higher levels in my career? I could not run forever. I'd be foolish to do so now. I was closer to the end of the tunnel than ever before. I endeavored to avoid slow progress and stagnation whenever possible because time is lost repeating the same cycles.

After joining the church, I asked God to help me develop patience and tolerance—two characteristics of which I'm deficient. It was wisdom that enabled me to visualize my present circumstances as tests, which I had to pass (Job 23:10). Otherwise, the doors of opportunity that I prayed to open would remain closed. Now, don't misunderstand me, concluding that I increased in patience and tolerance overnight. This certainly wasn't the case. Reconstruction of perceptions and attitudes were gradual—a transformation that was unlike the deliverance I previously underwent. Where I had to be patient or tolerant of anyone or anything that given a choice, I'd have chosen an alternative, I growled through gritted teeth. Therefore, choir wasn't the issue per se, rather part of the problem existed within me. The same types of personalities that formed the choir existed everywhere else in the world. I began to understand that God wanted to take me from the plateau where I stood, to higher altitudes in my life. The journey required surviving exposure to periods of high and low pressure.

≈≈≈≈≈≈≈

Rather than intrude on any of the choir members, Hakeem departed for home, lest someone perceive him as eavesdropping. They were the same, whereas he was changing. He started initiating conversations—small greetings and jokes. There was still nothing of deeper connection, and he accepted the choir for what it was—an opportunity to minister for God. However, this new perspective didn't douse the desire for friendship and companionship. He was alone in this context and it attributed to the occasional gloom.

Therapy with Gail helped Hakeem see that he possessed low self-esteem. Raising self-esteem and improving self-perception was crucial to successful integration with other people. He had to get over the inevitability of people talking about him. Some days he fared better than others. With Ian and Vincent as the only close friends, loneliness felt occasionally intense. But Hakeem was not going to beg anyone for friendship. Joseph would never know about his condition, for such knowledge would heighten the despair he already suffered. Sometimes, Joseph mentioned being alone when thinking of Evelyn.

Besides Gail, there was no one whom Hakeem felt comfortable enough to confide the deepest feelings. Malcolm and Michelle might have been able to offer some amount of solace, but they had children of their own. And so, to many people, Hakeem pretended everything was fine. Loneliness was another secret disguised by the meticulous demeanor he maintained.

Hakeem entered the apartment and was momentarily shocked by its silence. The sensation rippled through him every time he returned to the quiet place. The clock on the stove displayed 1:23 P.M. He changed into house clothes and prepared lunch. He warmed leftover fried chicken in the oven to crisp the breading, and heated baked beans, macaroni and cheese, and greens in the microwave. He added a tablespoon of store-bought coleslaw onto the plate. There was something delightful about the taste of baked beans and coleslaw combined. He arranged the food items on a snack table and erected it in front of the living room television. He prayed over the food—thanking God for all of His provisions before eating. This routine was part of his life.

While swallowing a forkful of food, his throat constricted. He was unable to shake the encroaching feeling. Tears streamed down his face. The loneliness crept again, laced with sadness. When would his afflictions pass? If he was able to cut the melancholy away, he would have performed the surgery.

Depression is a destructive beast. One minute a person is exuberant, and in the next, they are despondent. Depression makes a person feel utterly worthless. Excrement might have more value compared to a depressed individual's sense of self-worth. All of the painful memories, disappointments, anger, fear and guilt, meld into an emotional tar that is difficult to shed. When we wonder why people silence their feelings, here is an explanation. Within depression, there are a myriad of overwhelming destructive thoughts cycling through a person's mind. Who wants to be criticized by apathetic or ignorant people? Do you understand why depression leads some people to commit their final act—suicide?

Hakeem prayed again, asking the Holy Spirit to fill him and dispel the sorrow. Slowly the wave of depression receded and his appetite returned. He vowed to get through it just like everything else. He just had to. Should he fail, his mind would destroy him.

≈≈≈≈≈≈≈

Our prayers can be just as straightforward—asking God to grant us strength for the moment and help us get through each day. Every day that we draw breath grants us another opportunity to ask Him for restoration. Many people don't know that God responds to the simplest of requests. He is not complicated in this regard. There were times during the darkest hours of my life when I couldn't muster an appetite and tried to sleep the emptiness away. I was ignorant and lazy when it came to praying then.

Reverend Lynice taught me about prayer and the necessity of having faith. God comes to the aid of those who seek Him and believe. Such belief enables people to obtain deliverance and forgiveness through the power of the Holy Spirit. Prayer and faith are safeguards against the darkness in our minds.

I found that self-forgiveness was one of the most complex tasks to undertake. A person can be their harshest critic and I was a living example. Although delivered, I couldn't purge the thought of failing myself and God. I was ashamed of my ignorance—having engaged in unholy and idolatrous activities. I wasn't proud of my indiscretions. In fact, I wouldn't dare boast about pursuing them—the men and repetitive mistakes. All were scars that made me feel unworthy.

One morning while preparing for work, my guilt nearly crushed me. I was exhausted as usual at 5:00 A.M. Giving myself a much-needed boost, I turned on the docking station to a praise and worship song that chorused repetitiously about the awesomeness of God—the high and low reaches of His love. Unexpectedly, I started crying. The magnitude of my sorrow was comparable to mourning the death of a loved one. As my tear ducts emptied and face dried, I remembered my deliverance. While I couldn't erase my past, my faith and repentance expunged it. God's forgiveness is all that matters.

I was concerned about others talking about me when in the end, God is the only One who possesses the power to assign us to heaven or hell. I feared that my past irreversibly damaged all possibility of having a future wife. But thank God that Jesus Christ is our intercessor and God the Final Judge. He examines our hearts. I remind myself that God looks beyond my past to the person I'm becoming. I can't stress enough that in sincere confession and repentance, God forgives us. The enemy wants sinners to believe they can never escape the darkness surrounding them. The enemy is a liar! This knowledge is crucial for anyone who seeks deliverance.

Deliverance does not mean that a person forgets their past. Instead, salvation serves as a source of wisdom and humility. At the moment I believe myself more than what I am, salvation reminds me of my imperfections. Remembrance of our transgressions should prevent us from esteeming ourselves above others. The children of God are no more than what He allows. I know now that inclusive of all my flaws, I am sufficient for the work God has assigned me.

God knew that I spent many years in loneliness, as He knew Adam. In the Book of Genesis, He established that it was **"not good for man to be alone"** (Genesis 2:18). But instead of turning to God for sustenance, I made decisions that came along with consequences—setbacks and disappointments. I desired a companion, and one of the best things for me is a wife—one who will not be a stumbling block to my faith in God. This psychological restructuring and spiritual metamorphosis that I underwent was preparing me for a wife someday. I was damaged, undergoing spiritual repair. Healing and growth were critical for my brokenness, as it would be no benefit to God in sending a female to me and I was unappreciative. In such a case, I would be a stumbling block to the potential wife. In my pain, I could unintentionally hurt her.

Many like myself, made the mistake of seeking comfort in others as a means to curing our troubles. In this act of procuring comfort, we think that people possess the capability to complete us. The flaw in this perspective is that when people either die or depart from our lives, or material possessions diminish, we revert to a state of feeling incomplete, as our wholeness was contingent upon the presence of someone or something. The Living God and His Word are all that is everlasting. Aside from Him, everything in this world—people and things of materialistic value are temporary. Therefore, the children of God must understand that in seeking a spouse, it is still for the benefit of God's kingdom—bearing fruit for His ministry and spreading His Word in a dark world.

Encompassing my ruminations, trusting that at God's appointed time, a wife will come along, is a demonstration of faith. Scripture confirms that marriage is the will of God. But to know God's Will is to know His Word and believe. Reverend Lynice had explained this. Born from knowledge and belief is faith in God's incomprehensible power. When we internalize that our shortcomings are abysmal to the extent of conceiving the idea that God would never extend His forgiveness, we undermine the power of faith. This is where the enemy gains strength and can hinder our walk in the light by exploiting our weaknesses to his advantage. With this realization in mind, I decided to leave the apartment instead of succumbing to misery as in the past.

≈≈≈≈≈≈≈

Hakeem rarely frequented the malls on Sundays except for holidays. Judging from the crowd, Sunday was like any other day when masses of people partook in the shopping experience. He strolled by Biaggio's, his favorite boot store and noticed the Spring Clearance sign in the window. He could pass on buying another pair. There was barely room in the closet for the shoes owned. Yet, he resolved that in passing the store, a good sale might be missed.

"Hello! Welcome to Biaggio's." A saleswoman greeted.

"Thank you"—his eyes already scanning the shelves on the men's section.

Up close, he spotted the few pairs of boots that suited his tastes. The question was whether any of the footwear were worth buying.

"Can I help you with anything?" the saleswoman approached.

He turned and looked into a pair of friendly blue eyes. "I'm just looking," he said politely.

"Okay. Let me know if you need something." She spun away to the women's area to assist another customer.

"Will do"—he shouted, focusing on a $99 pair of Lucchese-style boots. Blue and tan leather made up the vamps and shafts sealed onto wood and rubber soles with 1 and ¾ inch heels. He visualized a matchup between the boots and apparel in his wardrobe. Putting clothes together heightened the thrill of shopping. And it helped when the bank account balance made the cost affordable, further boosting his excitement.

"Nice shoes, man," said a male voice.

What in the world! Can't I shop without being disturbed? Hakeem tenderly bit his bottom lip to silence frustration from the interruption.

"Yeah, they are. I'm thinking about gettin' them."

"Nah, I'm talking about the ones on your feet."

"Huh?" Hakeem looked at the guy standing approximately the same height. *What was he talking about?* Self-consciously, he glanced down at his boots—brown and tan pointed-toe, carrying the brand name of a company now defunct for many years. No one he knew owned a pair. Then it occurred to him that his pants gave the illusion of shoes rather than boots.

"My fault. These are boots." he corrected, slightly raising the hem to display the shaft.

"Those are hot, man," the stranger affirmed.

"Thank you"—Hakeem resumed perusing the display, consciously aware of the man standing nearby. He stayed on guard whenever a stranger entered his personal space to be able to react immediately to a threat. For someone interested in shopping, the man looked in his direction much too frequently, causing him to make a preliminary conclusion. It was not the boots that drew the man's attention. It was himself. The compliment was the pickup line, discreet as the man tried to be. Hakeem knew the game and signaled the saleswoman for assistance. When she approached, he asked for the blue and tan boots in his size only to learn that the pair on the shelf was the last.

Bummer! There was nothing else worth browsing. Turning, he headed for the shop entrance.

"I was hoping you'd tell me where you got those…boots," the stranger pressed, humorously.

"Man, I bought these over ten years ago. I can't even remember." The last statement was a lie. He was not going to allow the opportunity for further conversation to evolve. He could count on one hand the number of times someone directly hit on him in public in all of the sixteen years dealing with men. The man was nothing more than a distraction—a trick of the enemy to cause him to doubt himself. "The devil will always try to tempt you with your past," a pastor once stated. Being saved and delivered does not mean that the devil forgets. The enemy keeps a record to tempt us even when we forget. Be on the watch always.

Hakeem could have been rude on the basis of presumption. But for what purpose? To make a scene? A dramatic performance was unnecessary. He continued on to Maison de Luxe, stopping at a cookie stand en route. He was weak for chocolate-chip pecan cookies. Their buttery-sweet, chocolate crunchiness was delectable. He bought the usual buy two-get-one-free deal to eat a cookie immediately, saving the rest for later.

One thing for sure, there was no shortage of attractive Black women in Atlanta. Hakeem observed two walking towards him. Since they caught him staring, he gave them a respectful nod. Neither of the women smiled. Instead, they looked at each other. *Typical of that kind.* A famous athlete or entertainer might have motivated a different reception.

Maison de Luxe' extensive collection of intoxicating fragrances amazed Hakeem. A myriad of notes fused into exquisite bottles, the ingenuity behind their creation intriguing. He appreciated colognes and parfums. Hard-to-come-by ingredients made the premium kinds uniquely potent and variably expensive. Once upon a time, he scoffed at the idea of paying more than a hundred dollars for a bottle of cologne until smelling a sample. All of his colognes combined could not equate to the scent emanating from the vial.

He saw the consultant who always assisted him standing behind the counter of his favorite fragrance house. Having ceased arranging the displays, she turned around as he approached.

"Hakeem! It's been a while." Alicia greeted energetically.

He grinned. "Just a couple months."

"Whatever. Try like Valentine's Day." she replied, propping her elbow on the counter and leaning forward.

"Wow! Five months then."

"Yeeeaaah! So, how have you been?" Alicia shifted her weight, causing neck-length hair to swing towards her face. She swept the temple sections behind her ears, exposing lightly blushed high cheekbones.

"Busy as usual. I've just started writing." He had written only three pages.

"Really? What about?"

"Life experience."

Alicia was cool but he didn't know her well enough to tell everything. "It's still coming together."

"Look at you. Are you trying to be a motivational speaker or something?"

"I haven't even thought that far."

"That seems like the new thing. Some people write books, then enter into public speaking. I hope it works out for you, cause you and that job…" she chortled.

He grinned remembering that he told her about working in Kaleidoscope's stressful environment.

"While you're here, I want you to try this." She retrieved a bottle of fragrance from under the counter.

The gold, blue and white painted bottle looked like treasure lifted from the bottom of aqua waters surrounding a tropical island. The design was one of the house designer's gimmicks.

Alicia removed the gold cap from the spray pump and sprayed a plain white card.

Hakeem hoped the fragrance smelled as good as its decanter appeared. He wiggled with excitement, ready to be taken away by an exotic scent. His enthusiasm deflated quickly upon inhaling the revolting bouquet.

"Ugh!" he gasped, stepping back from the counter. The musk overpowered the flowery notes.

"Weird, isn't it?" she inquired.

"You're being modest." He was still uncoiling from the awful surprise.

"You know I have to try and sell the entire product line. Personally, I don't like it either."

"What's it called?"

"Overdose."

"It should be repackaged as 'Armpits.'"

"Oh my god," Alicia laughed. "Here, let me show you this one." She pulled another bottle from below the counter.

Hakeem gazed at its' purple and black design.

"Its name is 'Last Call' as in a bartender's last call for drinks at a club."

This had to be good. He was ready to be taken away. As soon as he whiffed the second fragrance card, his eyes closed dreamily. Last Call was intoxicating indeed. It was heavy, sticky, and sweet like fermented wine interlaced with incense smoke.

"Hot, right?" Alicia read his facial expressions.

"Oh, yes. Very. What's the price?"

"$300."

"I can't get it now," he said disappointed. It was the usual price for most of the house designer's fragrances. He could not manage that much at the moment. The car note had not been paid, but he still wanted to buy something. He surveyed the displays until spotting a cylinder decanter. He saw it previously advertised in the store's monthly magazine and smelled the sealed scent enclosed. Incense, pineapple, coconut, and $90 he recalled.

"Let me try that," he pointed at the ivory and bronze decanter, wanting to be sure before making the purchase.

She retrieved the test decanter and sprayed another white card.

He held the card up close and took a deep whiff. The scent was as he remembered and cost a third of the previous parfum's price. "I'll take it."

Alicia wrapped and bagged the purchase, tossing in a few cologne samples. She always hooked him up.

≈≈≈≈≈≈≈

At 6:30 P.M., the sun blazed orange-red in the evening sky. There was still enough time to savor more of the day. On my phone, I searched the internet for movie showtimes at the local theater. The majority were either excessively violent, erotic, or a combination of both—a waste of my time. A sci-fi film about an African hero who saves his country was showing in the next hour. The story of a hero—someone beyond all imagining was more my speed. I believed that somewhere along my solo excursion, I would find contentment in being alone. Only darkness dwelled in a sulky and idle mind.

That evening, I sat in the movie theater alone as other patrons enjoyed the entertainment with their family and friends. I thought of my grandparents' marriage. They were married for half a person's lifetime. Each day, Joseph tapped into a reservoir of strength to continue pressing forward with Evelyn gone. Then I thought of people similar to myself, single and yet to be married. They did their best to pull through. Just because life does not yield our most precious desires, we must still find appreciation in the opportunities that are available to us.

THE CAPTAIN OF MY SHIP

THE CAPTAIN OF MY SHIP

If I had only trusted in the Father, I wouldn't have been tossed by so many waves.

"You've been with Kaleidoscope for nearly ten years"—Cindy noted on Hakeem's resume—"Why do you want to leave?"

He disliked that standard interview question. Unless employed under a binding contract, an employee can seek employment anywhere at any time. Georgia is an at-will state. "I'm seeking career growth…an opportunity to utilize the education that I've acquired."

What a basic response. It was true though. And he criticized himself for not bothering to embellish.

Cindy had irritated him before the interview began. Upon arrival, the receptionist escorted him to the testing center in the office. There, she handed him two Scantron sheets to complete a Personality Assessment and Deductive Reasoning Test. After completing the evaluations, she notified Cindy that he was ready for the interview.

Instead of Cindy entering the testing center where he waited, she announced his name from outside the doorway. She clutched a laptop and folder to her breasts. She claimed that she was still contagious from a virus, which prevented her from shaking his hand.

So why come to work if you are "contagious"? Why not reschedule the interview? He noticed that she maintained a distance of five paces. It was foolish for a sick person who knew they had a contagious infection to come to work, interact with people, and touch work equipment. He analyzed her explanation and concluded that she was lying. Where were her tissues, hand-sanitizer, and cleaning wipes?

Cindy was Caucasian and apparently, was unaccustomed to close interactions with Black people. Her behavior, not to mention the absence of Black employees in the downtown Atlanta office confirmed Hakeem's suspicions. Caucasians who were genuinely comfortable around African-Americans, treated them as ordinary people. Caucasians who respected Black people, broke bread, fellowshipped, and joined arms with them.

Hakeem remembered the White people who came to Joseph's house after Evelyn died. They sat on his couches, used the bathroom, brought and ate food as they expressed condolences and encouraged the family. Those White people saw Black people as humanly equal. Caucasians, who perceived African-Americans as anything other than human beings like themselves, remained segregated in every possible capacity. Behavior does not lie nor does the demographics of a company's workforce.

"If hired, what strengths would you bring to Nexus, Inc?"

"My experience in training and development, and education in human resource management are both potential assets to your company. Nexus, Inc. operates in the talent acquisition and development space." He intentionally stated the fact to let Cindy know that he researched the company. "I understand the applications of psychology in workplace dynamics—how the job environment impedes and promotes behavior. I believe my knowledge is essential to consulting with clients regarding the implementation and application of methods to maximize employee performance."

Cindy's face was expressionless as a chalkboard. "Well, that brings our interview to a close. The recruiter will be in touch with you soon." She had not recorded anything from his final response.

Fool! I bet my education exceeds yours. Either Cindy was unable to comprehend his answer or did not care about what he said. Hakeem zipped his portfolio and rose from the table. As he extended a hand towards her for the customary handshake, she grabbed her laptop and folder instead.

He exited the interview room first because she remained stationary, moving only when he stepped into the hallway. Apparently, she was also unfamiliar with courtesy and formality. Again, she maintained a five-pace distance behind him. He turned to signal a goodbye, but she engaged the receptionist immediately upon approaching the desk. He heard, "no," from the conversation that ensued between the two women. Looking briefly over his shoulder, he saw tight-lipped expressions on their faces.

Well, I won't be getting this job. He exited the office thinking the outcome was all the better. He had enough of the subtle racism that took place at Kaleidoscope. There was no incentive for entering another work environment with a similar culture.

≈≈≈≈≈≈≈

Encouraged by my therapy sessions with Gail, I approached job hunting with enthusiasm. In eight months, I applied to six hundred and seventy jobs. The majority of the positions were Atlanta-based, although I expanded my interests to other states, thinking that relocation would perhaps solve my employment challenges. I applied to job requisitions in the public and private sector, inclusive of government, healthcare, psychology, human resources, learning and development, and management. My education and work experience granted me flexibility in applying to those opportunities. I was confident that with many applications in circulation, I would secure at least a few interviews. I knew that depending upon an employer's urgency to fill a vacancy, job applications filed for at least thirty days before recruiters began candidate screening and interviewing. Disappointingly, out of all the jobs applied, less than 5 percent replied with an invitation to interview or rejection to my application. I knew the politics surrounding recruitment and selection. Thus, I sent "thank-you" emails following the interviews, only to receive silence.

I admit that I possessed a shallow hope that in re-committing to God's service, He would bless me with a new job. Initially, the new job meant erasing debts and acquiring materialistic possessions. I was desperate for a financial increase, and yet, had not envisioned how I could appropriate God's blessings for His service. Given my ignorance in this regard, waiting for Divine intervention was agonizing. Anxiety and frustration rippled through me because I desperately wanted to escape Kaleidoscope. Was God ignoring me? I wondered why He was giving me silent treatment. The prayers I submitted to Him seemed unanswered, judging from my rate of success.

Gradually, I learned that my attitude was foolish. As I spent more time in God's service—reading the Bible, praying and fellowshipping, I began to see Him as a provider and sustainer. Although I never consciously established God as a personal genie, my expectations suggested otherwise. The Scripture does not portray or convey that He operates in a genie-like manner. It discusses the blessings of God and His provisions (Matthew 6:33; Romans 8:28; Phil. 4:19; 2 Cor. 9:8). Most notably, He blesses us according to His overall purpose for we deserve nothing, as Jesus Christ has already extended grace and mercy to us for our sinful nature. Yes, I obtained two master's degrees, was working towards getting a third, and qualified for career advancement. This self-awareness contributed to my belief that I deserved a new job and more money.

I have heard some Christians say, "If God doesn't do anything else, He has done enough." The expression was initially lost on me. It was during introspection that I finally understood. Since I believed that I deserved the desires of my heart, it was necessary for me to self-assess. How many times had I sought God's forgiveness for repeating the same sin? How many times had I forgiven others? How many times did I pass up the opportunity to help or uplift someone? How many times did I pass up the opportunity to do a good work versus something bad? How did I treat others? Did God preserve my life another day? Did God make provisions when I was unable to provide for myself? Did God send His angels to camp around and cover me, and lead me back to the light as Gail had done? These are the kinds of questions that we should ask ourselves before chanting, "I deserve."

It took constant prayer and strengthening of faith for me to realize that God had been working behind the scenes unceasingly. To depart from homosexuality without contracting sexually-transmitted diseases is a testimony. For me to maintain a steady job throughout an economic recession while other companies downsized by cutting jobs is a blessing indeed. There were brothers and sisters in my church, who lost their jobs and had been searching for employment for months, some even years. It is the simplest of blessings that we take for granted. If not for God's grace and mercy, I could have died. I cannot dismiss this realization when comparing my life to the lives of people I knew, not to mention the deceased.

For all of my earthly achievements, what did they mean in God's eyes? The answer is nothing. Indeed, God utilizes our unique sets of knowledge, skills, and abilities in His grand plans, but He does not deify these characteristics. Remember, Jesus twelve disciples were untrained when He recruited them. Jesus, in an informal manner, trained the disciples as they walked with Him. Following Christ's ascension to heaven, the Holy Spirit descended to equip the disciples with the gifts necessary for advancing His ministry throughout the earth. According to Romans 8:29-30, God knew us prior to our human birth and has "predestined and justified us" for His purpose—to fulfill various assignments during our lifetime. Allow me to expound upon this Scripture through the following example.

A hiring manager usually determines the candidate that he or she will hire, if not from the outset, then within the early stages of the hiring process. This phenomenon appears to be particularly prevalent in cases of internal hiring—where the hiring manager possesses some degree of familiarity with the candidate who they will eventually select. In my experience, such familiarity has varied from unprofessional or personal relationships to office politics. Depending upon the amount of caution exercised to avoid violating HR policies, it may take a while to discover that familiarity influenced the hiring manager's final decision, rather than qualification. By then, the hiring manager has officially "justified" their selection. Justification in hiring and selection must happen to comply with labor laws and avoid legal issues where discrimination in employment can be contested.

The central tenet of this example is that no matter what information is documented—true or false, pertaining to qualifications, in the mind of the hiring manager, they have "justified" their candidate. In contrast,

God does not document anything or reference check with anyone, except Jesus Christ (our Intercessor) when He makes a decision. His decisions are not limited to a person's 'qualifications', in the same sense that man evaluates and idolizes them. God overlooked Moses' deficiencies in speech when He commanded him to go to Egypt and liberate Israel from pharaoh's control (Exodus 4:10). Apostle Paul who was a persecutor of Christians (Acts 8:3), who through deliverance (Acts 9:17-20), God called to advance the ministry of Jesus Christ (Acts 9:15). Whosoever God chooses is the one that receives His favor of which we are powerless to rescind. When man qualifies, he or she imposes standards, which benefits a few and impedes the majority. God can circumvent all of the checkpoints erected by man when the time comes for His children to answer their calling. In God's plan, there is a purpose for everyone. If only people listen and receive His instruction, lesser would be their struggle, heartache, and pain. When I digested how God operates in this capacity, it became illogical for me to be angry with people and things that I was unable to control. I was then and still am, maturing in faith.

There was something else. I had a desire for greatness—not just to unleash my full potential, but to shine on everyone who mistreated and rejected me. By being great, I could demonstrate that I was somebody and reap the manifestations of my 'greatness'. Such thinking is flawed for several reasons. First, I am somebody whether rich or poor, successful or unsuccessful, educated or uneducated. My self-esteem needed improvement. Secondly, an individual can rise from the bottom to the top and still be criticized, disliked, and rejected. Remember Jesus, the Son of God made flesh? He worked miracles, healed, and resurrected people from the dead, but thousands of people still rejected Him!

Rather than a person's success fostering awe and inspiration, it sometimes does the reverse—loathing and envy. Some people will despise you because they believe you are undeserving of the blessings you received. When a person's heart and mind are closed, they are unreceptive to people and their environment. They change when they are willing, and not as a direct result of another person's actions. From a spiritual perspective, God did not intend for us to become idols to each other. He commanded that we worship and glorify only Him (Exodus 20:3-4). All that we will ever become is by the Grace of God. Any blessing that God bestows is for His glory and edification, and for us to bless others (see Matthew 20:26; 2 Cor. 9:11-12).

Because of where I was in life, I became less confident that my talents and abilities would ever find purpose. I believed that I knew the capacities in which to utilize my gifts and found that every idea and endeavor failed. As Josefina and Reverend Lynice advised, I needed to be "still and wait," and more importantly, improve upon my faith. In both areas, I was deficient. I lacked understanding regarding how to be patient or confident in the unseen—God working in the invisible. Every part of me wanted to rely on my own capabilities. I felt in control when situations flowed as I desired, and the outcomes reinforced my expectations. Expectations—the integration and manifestation of a person's beliefs, values, and desires often propels the individual to the point where they began to appraise God as a personal genie. My flawed belief system delayed me from receiving His direction.

I prayed for direction because God is God in every situation. He is my fortress and the captain of my ship. In those intimate conversations with God, I received clarity. Gone was the noise and chaotic thoughts. Within the silence, I saw where I had walked every path except those that God ordered. He also peeled back layers of myself and exposed hidden truths. The jobs I applied to at Kaleidoscope were never awarded because I did not respect the management team. The fact that I held most of the management staff in contempt would have hastened my transition to unemployment. I refused to be silent, tell lies, conspire to cause others to fail, and circulate false promises for a paycheck. My defiance presented a problem because it indicated an unwillingness to conform. I am rebellious. Thus, God asked me, "Why would I transfer you from one place of misery to another?" This inquiry makes Jeremiah 29:11 priceless. God designed me for a specific purpose, and His blessings do not accompany grief (Proverbs 10:22).

When you are in tune with God and the Holy Spirit, very little escapes your cognizance. Every management position demanded greater commitment and responsibility, which would eclipse my capacity to serve God. Several companies where I submitted applications paid more than 110-percent of my salary. However, they later downsized and continued semi-annual trends of reorganization. If any of those companies extended a job offer, I probably would have been unemployed eventually, given low seniority. I was already one paycheck from being homeless. I could not afford to lose a dime.

There is no mistaking that the value of a job is its extractable income. But God is first because He is the source of all existence, and thus, should be prioritized above everything—family, job, money, etcetera. In Matthew 16:24-25, Jesus Christ instructs believers in the walk of the faithful, stating that they must **"deny themselves, pick up the cross and follow Him daily."** James 4:15 prescribes the submissive attitude that believers should exhibit pertaining to His Will. Submit to the Will of God because when your life is a raging sea, you want Him to calm the waters. In the quelling of the storm, do not be surprised to find yourself changing. Your transformation prepares you for a greater purpose.

In sharing my insight, I attest that the transition from self-reliance to faith is often difficult. My spiritual and personal growth began as a slow-moving process because I struggled with submission. I had to stand face-to-face with reality. Brace yourself. Man can no more will himself into tomorrow than he can prevent the sun from rising in the east and setting in the west. There is nothing in our world that man possesses complete control. There is nothing that man creates that is eternal or indestructible. New life is born and old age eventually expires. Civilizations and nations rise and fall. Companies reach pinnacles in operational and financial performance, and then plateau as competition levels the playing field and sometimes, replaces the forerunner. Celebrities achieve varying degrees of fame and fortune only to fade away into memory. For all of the wealth that the rich acquire, money and possessions cannot prevent sicknesses, diseases, or deny death. They too will expire, leaving behind all of their accumulated wealth for family and friends to feud and claim.

God's Word—what we learn through the Bible, is the only thing that has withstood the passage of time. People will proclaim that man has written and re-written the Bible, deny the Scriptures' Divine nature, and ignore that God's Word and the ministry of Jesus Christ is still prevalent and relevant today—thousands of years later. Despite the persecution and execution of Christians, Jesus' ministry continues to advance all over the world. We are living in the prophecies of an Inspired Word that servants of God recorded ages ago. There is nothing or no one that can replace Jehovah, Jesus Christ, or the power of the Holy Spirit! When a person reaches this awareness and begins to believe in the Most High God, it becomes less difficult to trust in the unseen.

A person can experience cognitive dissonance when their beliefs and attitudes conflict with their surrounding environment or society at large. Consequently, they exhibit stress, anxiety, depression, or frustration as they attempt to resolve the internal conflict. The possibility that one does not possess the extent of control, which he or she believes creates dissonance within the self. It is plausible to suggest that an individual lacking in faith undergoes cognitive dissonance because faith requires submitting to God's Will (Hebrews 11:6) and obedience. Therefore, a change must occur to restore congruence within the self. The individual will either: a) draw closer to the Word of God and commit to His service; or b) devalue the Word of God by discrediting His existence to restore and solidify their original belief system.

All this time, I was in disarray—overlooking that God is concerned more with my faith and obedience than a career, and anything of material value. In fact, He does not care about jobs with the passion and enthusiasm equivalent to people. He understands that employment is a resource for providing financial stability, but from the perspective of wealth, it can be a distraction or stimulate greed. Business owners, CEOs, boards of directors, and shareholders, who are comfortable with profiting as their organizations and its' employees flounder, and practice corruption, do not honor and glorify God (1 Timothy 6:10). Practitioners of the faith, please believe that God rewards for being faithful and true. But all of it manifests in His timing. You do not have to engage in wrongdoing to taste the good fruits of life. You do not have to cheat, lie, or steal to gain an advantage. Sleeping around is unnecessary to feel whole when God is waiting for you to trust in Him.

What God envisions for our lives exceeds our greatest imaginings and does not operate within our limited scope of understanding, nor is He constrained by man's machinations. These statements are important because in the Book of Isaiah 55:8-9 it is written, **"For My thoughts are not your thoughts, neither are your ways My ways,"** says the Lord; **"For as the heavens are higher than the earth, So are My ways higher than your ways, And My thoughts than your thoughts"** (NKJV). I have meditated on the matter and come to the conclusion—framed by observation and personal experience, that there are three main explanations for getting "stuck in the rut": 1) we don't trust in God—believing in ourselves to have a better plan; 2) complacency and fear of change—endeavoring in unfamiliar territory; or 3) establishing relationships with toxic and unproductive people.

Nearly a year after my therapy sessions started, God slowly unveiled His plans for me. He awakened in me a vision for the story I now compose and of the things to come in the future. I knew the visions were from Him because none of the visualizations embodied goals that I constructed independently. I certainly did not consider writing for publication. Interestingly, creative writing is one of my natural-born talents. God had already given me the gifts I needed for success but I devalued some of my more notable abilities. As with teaching, I dismissed the idea of writing as a profitable career option for me. I also benched writing because the undertaking was intensive. The task demanded discipline and dedication, which was uncomfortable to me—sitting for hours at a time, transferring insightful and inspiring thoughts to paper. Who wanted to be engaged in those tasks? Nah, I was going to get an education and elevate high in Kaleidoscope. I achieved the education part, but guess what happened? For nine and a half years, there was no advancement in my career, not only internal to the company, but everywhere else too.

Exhausted from trying to do things my way, I accepted that God was trying to get my attention. There was no sidestepping His calling. Please understand what I am proposing, as it is perhaps one of the most important assertions in this book. As I mentioned previously, God is Alpha and Omega and as such, He knows the beginning from the end. He knows our thoughts and desires, and therefore, can and will circumvent them, especially when they deviate from His plans. When God calls a person to His service, He allows them to be a free agent for a season before compelling a response. I have heard testimonies from several people—some business owners who are now in ministry, that they knew God was calling them to service, and yet, continued running. Suddenly, circumstances arose in their life that caused them to turn full circle. You may be able to refuse God, but He will not permit you to persevere in defiance under His authority.

We are living in a time where people emulate superficial lifestyles. They associate financial wealth with positive values, interpreting all success as good. This is a trap within itself because while human beings have been created by God (Colossians 1:16), everyone is not of God (John 1:12-13). Through this lens, it is not difficult to understand why the nature of certain successes is incongruent with God's requirements. Celebrities, politicians, and other influential figures in society, who promote sexual immorality, atheism, agnosticism, hatred, evil, corruption and deceit, are contrary to the Will of God (Romans 1:28-32). I have expressed this sentiment on occasion and received the following responses, "they are just doing it to make money," or, "everyone else is doing it." Both statements are relatively valid. However, I dare say it is necessary to familiarize oneself with the Scriptures: 1 Timothy 6:10, Romans 12:1-2, and 1 John 2:15-17. The desire to acquire money and wealth should not overshadow a righteous way of living according to God's standards. For in the moment that money and wealth become the focal points of our attention and values, they become idols and sources of corruption.

I received confirmation from four people in different social circles. Not only were their insight and encouragement invaluable, but they also helped me focus. And yet, even with the vision burning bright in my mind, I still experienced a "Mary moment" of uncertainty (Luke 1:34). I did not believe myself capable of writing a lengthy and complete book. I have written creatively before, just not with a goal of authorship. Moreover, considering the narrative and content of the story, I feared criticism. God's message to me was, "The spirit I've given you is sufficient for this journey." I marinated on His response for a while until I gained understanding. The rebellious streak within me, my bold tongue and courage that never extinguished despite uncertainties and fears, encompassed within His captainship would sustain me. God can use everything we were, are, and will be for His purpose and glory.

≈≈≈≈≈≈≈

A female broke away from the crowd of church members gathered at the far end of the hall and walked in Hakeem's direction. As she neared, he saw that it was Ivory who sung on the praise team. He had overheard her name mentioned by another choir member and made a conscious note to remember it. He nodded and slowly averted his eyes as she passed on the left. He did not know whether she was one of those females who copped an attitude when a man ogled too long. Nonetheless, he made sure to take all of her in within the few seconds of passing.

Ivory glanced sideways and Hakeem thought a smile edged the corner of her lips. She was looking fine in a plain white V-neck tee, acid-wash fitted jeans, and nude stilettos. The church observed casual attire. Ivory's purse hung from her forearm, hips swaying as she glided down the hall. She did not walk like some women who were unaccustomed to wearing stilettos—wobbling ankles. She walked with authority. Every bit of her countenance shouted, "Woman!"

Hakeem decided there was no harm in trying to get to know her platonically. But he was uncertain about the best way in which to make an introduction. Confidence was something that he needed to improve to dispel his insecurities. Deliverance did not erase all of a person's imperfections. It is the process and aftereffect of God's: will superseding the individual's personal desires, healing power over their weaknesses, and rescue from problems they cannot overcome independently of Him. Deliverance does not occur without cognitive and thus, behavioral modifications.

Self-esteem is a psychological construct that fluctuates as an individual interacts with his or her environment and its effect on their self-perceptions. Positive feedback can elevate the individual's self-esteem, whereas negative feedback can corrode it. A man's security was critical to being a husband and father, and Hakeem wanted to be married someday. Forty was not too far away in his future, and he had spent too many years being involved with the wrong people. He did not want to invest as much time dealing with women. He endeavored to date with the intention of getting married and having children.

In thinking of Ivory, he considered what her opinion might be of him. What woman wanted a former-homosexual for a husband? Could a woman like her accept his past? Nothing is impossible for God, and His power is what people who seek deliverance must believe. Life experiences and God's interventions changed the hearts of men and women. God requires faith in His children. Believing otherwise is a trick of the enemy. The enemy exploits self-doubt, which causes an individual to err in judgment and return to the sinful habits of their past.

Women phenomenally endure a range of issues concerning men. The most virtuous of women expect honesty, security, and stability in men they consider husband-material. Hakeem resolved that when he met a woman whom he trusted, and shared common goals and interests, he would tell her about his past. Let her make the decision regarding whether she wanted to pursue a long-term relationship with him. It was unrealistic to be secretive and undermine the possibility of developing a relationship with dishonesty. If dishonesty is a stone within the foundation of a relationship, then it will eventually compromise its integrity and crumble the union.

A woman had the right to know. Hakeem knew that people could be deceitful and was not going to leave it up to anyone to sabotage his relationship. The degrees of separation in social networks are a concept not to be underestimated. Let the woman make the choice based upon the information given. Hakeem's situation was one that required divine intervention—for God prepares His children for each other. It is for this reason that we should seek God when deciding to marry, because the person that He routes is tailor-made for us. If He deems that we are unprepared, He may delay the arrival of the right mate.

Do not confuse self-driven desires with God's plans. Sometimes, those seeking relationships are committing to the wrong people instead of trusting God to orchestrate the union, and then expect Him to bless their choices on the backend. Seek Him first and He shall send the right mate! Our waiting period may be an opportunity for self-improvement.

Hakeem looked over his shoulder upon reaching the end of the hallway. Ivory had vanished around the corner. How would she respond? What would she say? Did she have a dude? That was the first question that he wanted to ask. He had asked men similar questions. There was no point wasting time trying to obtain the unavailable. Competing for the affections of another was not up for consideration.

≈≈≈≈≈≈≈

Hakeem walked through the double doors of the justice center at 7:50 A.M. After nearly three years of case-building, hearing delays and rescheduling, the court and his attorney were ready to settle the DUI case.

None of the courtrooms opened until 8:30 A.M. Police officers guarding the lobby area, organized those persons summoned for jury duty and general visitors into two separate lines that extended to the entrance. Hakeem spotted a woman who worked at Kaleidoscope at the back of the jury duty line. She seemed unaware of his presence. He hoped that she was going to another courtroom. No one else at the job needed to know about his legal situation.

At 8:20 A.M., the officers permitted the lines to proceed through the metal detectors and onward to the various courtrooms. Hakeem sat on a bench outside the courtroom where his hearing was scheduled. The doors were locked and Ryan had not arrived.

Ryan stated a week earlier that additional motions needed to be filed, which Wendy failed to submit. The disclosure added to Hakeem's persisting trepidation. There was no certainty in what the judgment would be, especially when a Black man was involved in a criminal case of any degree.

Hakeem wondered why Wendy failed to complete the additional

filings. The fact that she did not take action considering her experience was peculiar. A month before the trial, she began pressing him to pay his attorney fees. Had Wendy verified with the firm, she would have learned that he cured the balance during the prior year. In response, he emailed all of the electronic payment receipts received from the firm.

Wendy never exhibited an ounce of racism, but that did not mean that she was not prejudice towards Black people through subtle means. Hakeem wanted to know whether she treated her White clients the same. Or was she intimidated by the case and the surrounding evidence? She had expressed that the case should go to trial. Whatever her motivations, Ryan was not forthcoming. Hakeem was cognizant of his predicament, which caused him to stay some criticisms regarding Wendy. Had he exerted more control over drinking, the hearing and possible trial he now faced would be nonexistent.

Pensive, Hakeem passively noticed Ryan approaching. Confidence and calm was the aura that radiated from Ryan. Hakeem appreciated him more for these characteristics. The presiding judge was supposedly "fair and just". However, Wendy and Ryan also stated that the judge's execution of fairness and justice varied from trial to trial. What Hakeem needed were prayer and God's intervention.

The sound of clinking metal caused them to turn in the direction of the courtroom as the bailiff unlocked its' doors. They entered and sat at the defense counsel table. Both the solicitor general and assistant solicitor general entered the courtroom afterward and sat at the prosecution bench nearby. Only the assistant greeted and conversed with Ryan. The solicitor general removed files from her rolling briefcase, conversing only with the assistant and the stenographer who had made a quiet entrance into the courtroom.

Hakeem did not particularly care for either the solicitor or the assistant, as Wendy once confided, both had the judge's ear. Annoying him further was their constant rescheduling of the prior hearings, and Wendy's unsuccessful attempts at getting the case dismissed. The State of Georgia upholds a defendant's right to a speedy trial, but the court delayed him. It was a right, which Ryan filed a motion earlier that morning.

As Ryan explained the flow of the motions hearing, Reverend Lynice tapped Hakeem on the shoulder to inform of her arrival. Sister Edwina had also come along to lend support. Their knowledge of his court case was a result of him asking for prayer over the trial.

While everyone waited for the judge, Hakeem went into the hallway with Reverend Lynice and Edwina to pray. If the heavens could have opened that very moment as the women took turns praying, there was nothing to prevent it from happening. Hakeem felt renewed determination and returned to the courtroom, and asked Ryan to clarify the plea. He held out making such an inquiry because of a reluctance to go to trial, but a warning blared in his mind like a bullhorn.

Ryan confirmed that the plea entailed pleading guilty, probation for twelve months, and driver's license re-suspension for a duration of four months without jail time. Hakeem's two major concerns were having a criminal record and doing jail time—neither of which he desired. The only other option was to take the case to trial and risk everything.

Hakeem rose from his seat and confided in Reverend Lynice regarding the details of the plea. She listened and then asked him whether he was drunk while driving. He admitted his guilt and her response was that power is in the truth. If he had not experienced complete humility at any other point in his life, it was in that instant. God had given him what he asked for—no jail time. Everything else pertaining to the plea was inconsequential.

He had spent time searching the web for celebrities, public figures, and professionals who were arrested for DUI-related offenses, most of whom were still successful in their respective careers. Everyone makes mistakes, great and small. Just because a person makes a mistake or commits a crime, does not mean that their life ends. Every bad situation can be harvested for its embedded wisdom. Hakeem could live comfortably with the philosophy having some understanding of the long-term impacts of a pending decision.

Ryan tried to dissuade him from accepting the plea bargain. Where the plea waived jail time in consideration of rehabilitative efforts, it also resulted in a criminal conviction that was ineligible for expungement. Could he afford a criminal conviction on his record while in the midst of career advancement? This was the question that Ryan proposed and once again, Hakeem was doubtful. However, just as Ryan could not guarantee the outcome of a protracted hearing or jury trial, Hakeem was unable to see the future. Neither possessed the ability to see into tomorrow. Anything was possible.

Ryan prepped an impressive defense for Hakeem's trial. Yet, in spite of preparation, he could not produce a get-out-of-jail-free card. In fact, no attorney can make such an assurance, as a judge makes the final decision in the court of law. Ryan made this point clear the week before trial. To achieve a sure win, Ryan needed to disprove all material evidence that indicated Hakeem was intoxicated on the night of the arrest. (Imagine that! The dashcam video showed Hakeem failing the sobriety test.) The first wave of success was achievable during the hearing, if the evidence could be suppressed. The disadvantage was that once the motion hearing commenced, all favorable plea options were removed from negotiations. If Ryan failed, then the hearing would transition to a jury trial. There, Ryan could establish reasonable doubt within the minds of the jury and allow them to determine Hakeem's innocence. If he failed to convince the jury and they issued a guilty verdict, the judge could impose a harsher sentence. A jail sentence for a DUI first-offense in the state of Georgia ranged from 24 hours to 12 months—none of which Hakeem could afford to withstand.

Having evaluated the possibilities, Hakeem accepted the plea. Only God—the Alpha and Omega, can see all things from start to finish. Hakeem's quandary constructed a testing ground for his faith. He stood before the judge, shoulder to shoulder with Ryan as the prosecutor read aloud the list of related DUI charges. The judge turned her gaze to him when the prosecutor announced his decision to enter a guilty plea. Her blue eyes were fierce as an eagle. Ryan informed the judge of his rehabilitative efforts—100 hours of community service and a driver's reduction course. Considering the prosecution and defense, the judge conceded the plea bargain.

Time seemed to slow during the seconds of the judge's deliberation. Blood rushed to Hakeem's ears. His heartbeat quickened while tears streamed down his face. Ryan retrieved a tissue box from the court stenographer. Just for a moment, Hakeem thought that somehow, the judge was going to overrule the plea, but the opposite occurred. The judge's stern expression softened and he glimpsed a trace of compassion. Prayer worked, and God was truly merciful. As the case settled and closed, Hakeem felt an invisible weight lift from his soul. That night, for the first time in two and a half years, he slept peacefully, unaided by supplements. The peace that one receives from obedience to God confirms the rightness of their decisions and actions.

≈≈≈≈≈≈

I anticipate that despite justification of my choices, some would still ask, "why not go to trial?" Here is an explanation if the narrative was not illustrative enough. I believed that Ryan's chances of winning either round were terribly slim. Then risk the possibility of having jurors who may have either been a victim or knew of a victim of drunk driving, further decreased our chance for success. Ryan was a good attorney with a successful track record. But in my opinion, evidence is evidence. There were just too many clues indicative of my intoxication. Additionally, jail would have been a financial setback because I would have lost my job. Labor Laws do not require employers to hold jobs for incarcerated employees, especially for criminal offenses. Job loss would have transitioned me into being homeless unless I returned to Clinton City. This decision was the farthest from my mind. Freedom is everything to me.

For over two and a half years, and post-trial, I paid the consequences for my actions. Unquestionably, losing trial would have magnified my pre-existing afflictions. That is the problem with making bad decisions. A person is unable to choose or control the repercussions of their actions. I chose the plea because I was guilty of drinking and driving not only on the night of my arrest, but for twelve consecutive years since Joseph and Evelyn purchased my first car. Every time I drove home from the club, I was drunk. All twelve of those years, God had been merciful. He now required me to be accountable for my actions. The consequences I faced were justified. The past stood on my front doorstep and its arrival demanded payment. This self-acknowledgement motivated me to inquire of the ramifications associated with a plea bargain. Ryan's layout of the plea was definitive, enabling me to see the prosecutor's hand.

Certainly, going to trial could also be considered a test of faith because of an individual's trust in God's invisible workings. However, in knowing God the Father, there is a realization that He does not honor liars or tempt His children, especially when the stakes are high. 1 Corinthians 10:13 supports this conclusion by noting that God doesn't allow a person to be tempted beyond his or her capacity to handle situations, and **"will make way for escape"** (NKJV). Notice that at the end of the same scripture it mentions one's capacity to endure. I infer this to mean that even in situations of transgressions, God is gracious towards the person who falls short of goodness and alleviates some burdens so that they can endure all that remains. However, they are not totally cleared, as Scripture explains that whatever we sow, we shall reap (Galatians 6:7-8).

Meanwhile, the enemy watched as he had done with Adam and Eve in the Garden of Eden, Peter (Luke 22:31) and Job (Job 1)—looking for a way to destroy (John 10:10). Going to trial was the method the enemy used to sabotage me. I could pursue the trial route and most likely, be sentenced to jail indefinitely, or take God's sure path to safe ground. God knew that I did not possess the mental capacity to endure incarceration. He was bringing me forward to achieve my destiny, not sending me in the opposite direction.

For the guilty, winning a trial implies that one is innocent on the surface even though in reality, he or she may have committed a crime. There are many people in this world, who believe that a trial win equates to innocence. They give little attention to the occurrence of repeat offenders who gradually learn the ins and outs of the legal system. A crime committed is a crime committed in the eyes of the Father, regardless of man's methodology for suppressing, hiding, or removing factual information, which would either convict or exonerate a defendant. These are the activities of prosecutors and defense attorneys. The difference between a convicted DUI-offender and an intoxicated motorist is the conviction itself. It is just a matter of time and circumstance before the law catches a violator.

My undocumented inebriated contraventions implied that violators like me were either defiant, slow in learning from their mistakes, or untreated alcoholics. As is often the case with repeat offenders, being able to escape the consequences completely, encouraged repetition in deviant behavior. I had adjusted to behaving immaturely and irresponsibly and getting away with it. I confess that God pardoned me so many times before. This time, He would not allow me to escape, free of all possible repercussions as winning the trial could permit. I discerned it and had to accept it. If I had not been drinking and driving, the arrest would not have occurred.

Evelyn used to say, "Do the crime, do the time." Sometimes God suspends His protection to remind the intentionally wayward that consequences accompany their disobedience. As believers are to be obedient to His Word, they must also comply with natural laws (Romans 13:2; 1 Samuel 12:15). A true demonstration of faith is confession of one's sins and asking God in humility to move within and beyond the parameters of spiritual and natural obstacles.

Where God always knew my decision, it was my revelation. Thus, the plea branded onto my existence for the purpose of remembrance. In addition to the conviction it embodies, is a testimony of personal growth and experience. For everything positive and negative that occurs within our lives, there is a purpose. While instant visibility may be beyond us, the passage of time reveals all things. The length of time that it takes for us to comprehend what transpires in our lives depends upon whether we acquire wisdom. Sometimes a person may live most of their lifetime without developing a fraction. Stagnation, patterned self-defeating and unproductive behavior, cyclical experiences and/or constant strife characterize them.

God never intended for us to fulfill our lives through self-destruction and idleness. Yet, we make decisions that construct foundations of instability and uncertainty. The consequences of our actions eventually yield pain, suffering, or regret.

PROLOGUE

PROLOGUE

"Let all bitterness, wrath, anger, clamor, and evil speaking be put away from you, with all malice. And be kind to one another, tenderhearted, forgiving one another, even as God in Christ forgave you" (Ephesians 4:31-32).

*H*akeem stared blankly at the computer screen with clenched fists. Rosalyn had angered him again during their phone conversation. She condemned Tyrell for his faults and recreational approach to life. The rebuke was reminiscent of the criticisms he received as a teenager. Ending the call was best to avoid becoming belligerent subsequent to Rosalyn's disapproval of his siblings. The brewing animosity was toxic to his emotional stability.

Hakeem made efforts to apply the feedback received in therapy and knowledge acquired through church and Bible study. Aside from ceasing communication with Rosalyn, it was the last of noncombative alternatives available to withstand her negativity. He tried acknowledging her problems, listening in silence, and being mild-tempered. But when left unchallenged, Rosalyn raged without displaying accountability for the choices she made, which contributed to some of her problems. Hakeem believed that where he had to own his mistakes, she must do the same. Unfortunately, there were limitations surrounding his expectations.

Rosalyn suffered brain damage from domestic violence while involved with Arnold. According to Rosalyn, Arnold struck her in the head with a rod many years ago—some time before Hakeem moved

303

to Philly. MRI scans confirmed cell damage around the hippocampus, which contributed to her deteriorated memory.

For years, Hakeem denied Rosalyn's inability to remember aspects of her former self because he wanted her to take responsibility for how she treated him. Even with partial memory loss, she retained shards of character traits that existed prior to her mental diagnosis. Hakeem hated these aspects of Rosalyn, feeling that the reality of her partial amnesia denied him justice.

≈≈≈≈≈≈≈

No one can change the past, regardless of the amount of effort invested. Is this an unfortunate circumstance? Or can a person perceive this reality as an opportunity for growth? Every hurt and disappointment that we have endured is an essential part of us. Our experiences contribute to the totality of who we are as individuals. We can allow our experiences to be burdensome or exploit those same experiences for life application, to gain wisdom and become living testimonies.

Lamentably, there are people who have yet to overcome past hurts and continue to suffer in the present. The explanation is that their hurt transforms into bitterness, which stunts their psychological and spiritual growth. Concurrently, the perpetrator of the hurt either moved on in life or died as the miserable person continues through life unable to function effectively in various contexts—holding on to pain from the past.

While bitterness seems strangely comforting because of the anger it ignites within the afflicted individual, it is also self-destructive, overriding the capacity for rational thought and behavior. Seldom is the connection made between emotional disposition and behavioral output. As a common assumption is that distancing oneself from those who wronged them resolves the issue(s). It is a fallacious belief because overcoming hurt is dependent upon the condition of one's heart and mind. The victim's attitudes regarding the perpetrator and situation must change and they must desire that change. This is the process through which bitterness transitions to forgiveness.

I was proficient at disassociating myself from people but immature in managing my emotions. Either I lashed out or shutdown uncontrollably. My bitterness was a constant companion because of my inability to let go. I impart that if a person fails to forgive, any bitterness they retain will shroud them in lifelong misery.

We do not always get a front row seat to God's response to our oppressors and violators. Similarly, God does not always give others an inside view to how He deals with us. Being transparent as possible, we do not want people spectating how He deals with us regarding our transgressions. Most of us want God to deal with us in secret concerning our mistakes. We desire God's mercy while failing to consider that He can also forgive the perpetrators that harmed us.

I discerned that God forgave Evelyn and Daryle at some point before they died. In those latter years, their treatment towards me changed significantly. Fondness and respect were evident in their demeanor, and although they did not utilize words that I may have chosen, they apologized in their own way. I had to meet them where they were during those interactions.

God can mend the broken heart as well as soften the hardened one. A changed heart is unmistakable; for with it, an individual's attitude and behavior also change. Some people cannot fathom the multidimensionality of forgiveness because emotions and biases cloud their judgment. In the mind of the victimized, there is an expectancy of apology, retribution, or an overt indication of remorse from the perpetrator. But these events do not always occur, and the power of forgiveness is not exclusive to any given person. Where someone is reluctant to forgive, God picks up the tab. He is not restricted to our limited perceptions and attitudes. Only He knows the true condition of the heart (Jeremiah 17:9-10, 1 Samuel 16:7).

When a person goes before God and asks forgiveness through Jesus Christ, God examines the repenting heart. His forgiveness has conditions, for He expects confession and repentance (Mark 1:15, Luke 13:3, Acts 3:19, Romans 2:4, 2 Cor. 7:9). If God did not have requirements, people would never be driven towards spiritual growth in Him and commit to change. Free will enables people to go forth and engage in whatever manner they chose. The truly repentant reflect a personal change. Their old ways eventually fade away. This may be the only indication that God has forgiven the oppressor. Consider the story of Saul, a former persecutor of Christians, who God exalted as Apostle Paul. If you desire God to confirm whether He has forgiven someone who wronged you, do not expect an update from Him. One may never receive or witness His response in this regard. What God forgives is for Him to forgive.

The consequences of situations involving abuse, molestation or violence are often tethered to proceedings requiring legal interventions. Under these circumstances, the victimized can observe the outcomes associated with a perpetrator's violation of the law. Find comfort in knowing that God judges wicked and destructive behavior. Every person will be held accountable for his or her actions in time. Vengeance belongs to God (Romans 12:19), and He executes most strategically. Our responsibility is to continue being faithful regardless of the wrongdoing that transpires around us. The more we grow in the Spirit, the easier it becomes to prevail in the midst of adversity.

Love and forgiveness are qualities of our Lord and Savior, Jesus Christ. In response to Peter's question to Jesus regarding the number of times he should forgive sins committed against him, Jesus stated: **"I do not say to you, up to seven times, but up to seventy times seven"** (Matthew 18:21-22, NKJV). Jesus did not imply that there was a limit. Why would He, considering our faults and hopes to be forgiven.

Every derogatory word and criticism that my parents said to me was unthinkable. On many accounts, I believed them unfit for parenting because of the psychological damage they inflicted. Even after their apologies, they continued to destroy familial relationships, unwilling to take responsibility for roles they played. Yet, like every person on this earth, they are imperfect. Imperfect people have and continue to miss the mark over the course of their lifetime. Whether they admit the truth is irrelevant according to the Word of God (see Romans 3:23).

When I review the record that is my life, I must remember my shortcomings. At the moment that we dismiss our faults, we begin to esteem ourselves and condemn others. I have lied and stolen. I have fornicated. I have been envious and hateful, which I justified. And yet, there is no justification for my sinful behavior in Christ Jesus without repentance. On scriptural grounds, I am no different or better than anyone else. So, who was I that I could not forgive another person, considering my faults? If God has forgiven me, then I am capable of forgiving someone who has wronged me.

Forgiveness is not about benefitting someone else, albeit the act can repair damaged relationships. Forgiveness does not mean that a victim should remain in oppressive situations. Instead, forgiveness is liberating as it releases the suffering individual from the negative emotions associated with the stimuli. In the process of forgiveness, they become lighter of heart, mind, and spirit. Forgiveness is not interchangeable with forgetting because in remembrance, the person acquires wisdom through life application of past experiences. Remembrance stimulates humility as he or she acknowledges God's grace in effect. This exemplification of God informs those who desire a relationship with Him, that He is merciful if they just believe regardless of affliction.

Victims of abuse are encouraged to respond positively to their experiences by seeking counseling, therapy, and raising awareness. Through open dialogue, society is informed regarding the symptoms of abuse and how to effectively manage its' prognosis through intervention. In parenthood, I urge parents and guardians who are either perpetrators or victims of abuse and have poor relationships with their children to seek professional and spiritual guidance. Pursuing these interventions is critical to ending abuse and estrangement between family members. While some people are capable of conquering an abusive past through self-management, others fail. The assumption that one can suppress his or her feelings is a flawed belief because environmental conditions can trigger repressed thoughts and emotions of a damaged psyche. Suppressed thoughts and emotions can lead to any combination of destructive, antisocial, avoidant, or passive-aggressive behavior.

If an abused person escapes an abusive environment, success can create a self-perception of normality. In certain scenarios, the act of fleeing does rectify an immediate problem. However, where emotional or physical damage is sustained but psychological conflict remains unresolved, unpredictable behaviors (i.e., anger, anxiety, depression, violence, etc.) eventually manifest. How a victim of abuse reacts to stressors within their environment is typically indicative of their emotional composition. Professional help is crucial to personal growth and ensuring that children are protected. Otherwise, an abused person can perpetrate a vicious cycle in which the behavior is projected onto others within their environment. They can become living catalysts for the same traumatic events of which they were exposed. For the things we desire to witness an end, we must fulfill our respective duties to create those outcomes.

≈≈≈≈≈≈≈

I submit to you that in forgiving Rosalyn and Earl, I remain void of emotional attachment and unconditional love—characteristics of a child who adores their parents. I would be lying in stating that I overflow with affection. I believe this emotional shortfall can be attributed to unestablished and broken relational bonds. In the early stages of child development, parent-child bonding is critical to both the cultivation and quality of the dyad. Years of neglect, betrayal, and abandonment destroys a once fertile ground for loving kindness and tender care. Not all things lost can be recovered or rebuilt. Forgiveness overcomes hate and heals a bitter heart, but it does not create all dimensions of love. My love for Rosalyn and Earl contains concern for their welfare and preservation. They are in my prayers now.

My deficiency may be an indication of an abnormality in my psychological configuration. If there is any validity to my theory, then I advocate all the more for bonding between parents and children. I do not reflect fondly upon the darkness that once shrouded my heart and the dark thoughts, which swarmed my mind. I am not proud of the methods that I employed to relieve me of my pain. I have imagined a happier former life—a reality someone else can attest. God brought me through ordeals so that others can benefit from my testimony.

Better am I able to manage my emotions, although there is still an expanse of emotional territory that I must traverse. I increased in patience for Kaleidoscope as my expectations of the company changed. For over ten years, I prioritized my employer. During those ten years, I squandered time that I am unable to recover or compensate. When I exalted God to the number one spot in my life, no longer was I concerned about the politics within the company. In re-dedicating my life to faith, I began to understand that I had fallen off course. I had pursued paths, which God only intended to be short expeditions. I know this because of the fruit borne along another path that He directed me. The experience further convinced me that Kaleidoscope was just a means of support until the next elevation. While I remained employed, my purpose was to serve and to help others in need through work and interpersonal relationships.

In the year following my deliverance, I published two books. Despite my traumatic experiences, ignorance, and the consequences thereof, God used it all for His purpose and my good. Your past can be perpetually debilitating if you allow it. I discourse as an instrument of God to witness to you in your wasteland, whether its nature is psychological, socio-environmental, or socio-economical.

On the subject of racism, prejudice and corruption, there will always be problems in this world because of our desire for control and divisive nature. God is the true nexus of unity and peace in humanity, for in the heart and mind of every man dwells his own conceptualization of good. As I have mentioned earlier on in this narrative, mankind is moving farther away from God and His Son, Jesus Christ. The closer we are to Him, the more we understand our ordained purpose in this world and are able to overcome the challenges therein.

God has granted us the capacity to combat oppression and injustice. But it seems that some of the oppressed either cower in fear, become indifferent to socio-economic issues, or prioritize inconsequential endeavors instead of substantial pursuits. Every time we refuse to: acknowledge crime or injustice (regardless of our justifications), exercise our right to vote to ensure that our values are represented in legislation, or build people up instead of tearing them down, we must hold ourselves accountable for the pervasiveness of abuse, violence, and oppression. Action, inaction, and indifference all lead to outcomes. When we should be agents of wisdom and morality, we have become agents of ignorance and debauchery. Unless we are denied options, the power of choice is at our disposal. The passage of time will birth the end products of our decisions.

≈≈≈≈≈≈≈

Hakeem typed a period, concluding the sentence of the final paragraph. The discourse read:

From atop the mountain I looked down,
In the valley below, laid articles of my life
Too heavy were they to transport,
Although meaningful some of the things were,
Given to me were two choices, life or death.
And death tempted me, for in it, there was escape
But its darkness, I had already spent time in despair
Over the horizon joy and freedom shown bright
If I dared to press more, I could reach the light
Father God, you've known me when I was but a stranger to myself
I possess the strength, the will to fight
I shall carry the torch until I'm no longer able
When my fire extinguishes, reignite me
I shall make it to the top of the mountain
The next one is even greater
I shall crest it too because of Your Spirit that dwells within me
My past may trail me, but it no longer binds me
You have renewed in me hope, joy, and peace
I am courageous
I am free

BIBLICAL REFERENCES BY CHAPTER

BIBLICAL REFERENCES BY CHAPTER

A Forest Hidden By Trees

Colossians 3:21

Ephesians 6:2 – "honor your father and mother…"

Ephesians 6:4

Exodus 20:12

The Same, We Were Never Meant to Remain:

1 Corinthians 6:9-10, 18

Ephesians 5:5

Galatians 5:19-21

Genesis 1:28

John 11:38-44

Luke 11:14; 6:17-19

Mark 1:39; 7:24-30

Matthew 9:1-8, 18-26, 27-29

Proverbs 13:20 - "He who walks with wise men will be wise, But the companion of fools will be destroyed."

Revelations 21:8

1 Thessalonians 4:3-5 - "For this is the will of God, your sanctification: that you should abstain from sexual immorality; that each of you should

know how to possess his own vessel in sanctification and honor, not in passion of lust, like the Gentiles who do not know God."

Gatekeepers and the Word of Truth

Genesis 1:28 – "be fruitful and multiply…."

Proverbs 6:16-19

Proverbs 17:27-28

Romans 6:23

In Whose Eyes Were They Perfect?

Acts 13:50-51

Acts 18:5-6

Ecclesiastes 3:7

Ecclesiastes 7:20 - "For there is not a just man on earth who does good and does not sin."

Ephesians 4:20-24 - "But you have not so learned Christ, if indeed you have heard Him and have been taught by Him, as the truth is in Jesus: 'that you put off, concerning your former conduct, the old man which grows corrupt according to the deceitful lusts and be renewed in the spirit of your mind, and that you put on the new man which was created according to God, in true righteousness and holiness.'"

Exodus 32:30-33

Ezekiel 16:49 – "greed"

Galatians 6:1 - "Brethren, if a man is overtaken in any trespass, you who are spiritual restore such a one in gentleness, considering yourself lest you also be tempted."

Galatians 6:2 – "Bear one another's burdens, and so fulfill the law of Christ."

Genesis 4:8

Genesis 9:22

Genesis 10:19

Genesis 18:23-33

Genesis 19:1-29

Hebrews 9:26-28

Hebrews 10:3-4

Hosea 4:6 - "people perish for lack of knowledge."

John 1:15, 19-28

John 1:23 – "I am, 'The voice of one crying in the wilderness: Make straight the way of the Lord.'"

John 10:10 - "steal, kill and destroy."

John 14:15 – "For if you love Me, you will keep My commandments."

Leviticus – 20:10-16

Luke 9:5

Luke 9:53, 54 – "call down the fires of heaven."

Luke 9:55-56 – "You do not know what manner of spirit you are of, For the Son of Man did not come to destroy men's lives but to save them."

Luke 24:49

Mark 3:25 - "house divided against itself cannot stand."

Mark 6:11

Matthew 10:14 - "shaking of the dust from their robes and feet."

Matthew 14:13-21

Matthew 18:6 – "it would be better for the one who causes another to stumble to hang a millstone around his neck and drown."

Matthew 18:3-4, 15-17, 21-35

Matthew 19:30

Matthew 20:1-16

Matthew 28:19-20 - "Go therefore and make disciples of all the nations, baptizing them in the name of the Father and of the Son and of the Holy Spirit, teaching them to observe all things that I have commanded you."

Numbers 15:22-29

Proverbs 22:6 - "Train up a child in the way he should go, and when he is old he will not depart from it."

Revelations 2:12, 14-16

Romans 3:23

1 Corinthians 5:1-13

1 Corinthians 13:1 - "Though I speak with the tongues of men and of angels, but have not love, I have become sounding brash or clanging symbol."

1 Corinthians 13:2

1 Corinthians 13:13 – "love is the greatest"

2 Corinthians 2:4, 7

1 Kings 8:33-53

2 Peter 2:6 – "ungodliness"

1 Samuel 12:23-24

2 Timothy 2:24-25

2 Timothy 4:2 - "Preach the Word; Be ready in and out of season; Convince, rebuke, exhort, with all longsuffering and teaching."

Walking The Good Talk On A Lonely Road

Genesis 2:18 – "not good for man to be alone"

Jeremiah 17:10

Job 23 – "pure as gold"

Luke 9:23 – "deny ourselves"

Matthew 6:33 – "seek the kingdom of God"

Psalm 102:17 - "He shall regard the prayer of the destitute, and shall not despise their prayer."

The Captain of My Ship

Colossians 1:16

Exodus 4:10

Galatians 6:7-8

Hebrews 11:6

Isaiah 55:8-9 - "For My thoughts are not your thoughts, neither are your ways My ways…"

James 4:15

Jeremiah 29:11

Job 1

John 1:12-13

John 10:10

Luke 1:34

Luke 22:31

Matthew 6:33

Matthew 16:24-25 - "deny themselves, pick up the cross and follow Him daily."

Matthew 20:26

Philippians 4:19

Proverbs 10:22

Romans 1:28-32

Romans 8:28

Romans 8:29-30

Romans 12:2

Romans 13:2

1 Corinthians 10:13

2 Corinthians 9:8

2 Corinthians 9:11-12

1 John 2:15-17

1 Samuel 12:15

1 Timothy 6:10

Prologue

Acts 3:19

Ephesians 4:31-32 - "Let all bitterness, wrath, anger, clamor, and evil speaking be put away from you, with all malice. And be kind to one another, tenderhearted, forgiving one another, even as God in Christ forgave you."

Jeremiah 17:9-10

Luke 13:3

Mark 1:15

Matthew 18:21-22 - "I do not say to you, up to seven times, but up to seventy times seven."

Romans 2:4

Romans 3:23

Romans 12:19

1 Samuel 16:7

2 Corinthians 7:9

REFERENCES

REFERENCES

HIV Among Gay and Bisexual Men. (2016). Retrieved February 23, 2016 from https://www.cdc.gov/hiv/group/msm/.

HIV in the United States by Geographic Distribution. (2016). Retrieved February 23, 2017 from https://www.cdc.gov/hiv/statistics/overview/geographicdistribution.html.

Merriam-Webster. (2017). Lust. Retrieved March 4, 2017 from https://www.merriam-webster.com/dictionary/lust.

Planned Parenthood. (2017). How Effective Are Condoms? Retrieved February 23, 2017 from https://www.plannedparenthood.org/learn/birth-control/condom/how-effective-are-condoms.

Sexually Transmitted Diseases. (2016). Retrieved February 23, 2017 from https://www.cdc.gov/msmhealth/std.htm.

The U.S. Bureau of Labor Statistics. (2017). *Table A-2. Employment Status of the Civilian Population by Race, Sex, and Age.* Retrieved from https://www.bls.gov/news.release/empsit.t02.htm.

Made in United States
Orlando, FL
07 June 2024

47610309R00180